JH

Libraries, Information and Archives

This item is to be returned on or before the last date shown below

2 6 FEB 2016	0 2 OCT 2019
1 0 MAR 2016	- 9 MAR 2020
	0 3 NOV 2022
1 1 APR 2016	
	2 5 MAY 2023
2 4 AUG 2016	2 8 FEB 2024
1 9 OCT 2016	
0 2 DEC 2016	
0 9 FEB 2017	
0 1 DEC 2017	
2 7 DEC 2017	
- 7 MAY 2018	
2 6 OCT 2018	
2 8 DEC 2018	

F

BLACK WIDOW

CHRIS BROOKMYRE

BLACK WIDOW

Little, Brown

LITTLE, BROWN

First published in Great Britain in 2016 by Little, Brown

1 3 5 7 9 10 8 6 4 2

Copyright © Christopher Brookmyre 2016

The right of Christopher Brookmyre to be identified as the Author of this
Work has been asserted by him in accordance with the Copyright, Designs
and Patents Act 1988.

A CIP catalogue record for this book is available from the British Library.

Hardback ISBN 978-1-4087-0715-9
C format ISBN 978-1-4087-0714-2

Typeset in Caslon by Palimpsest Book Production Limited,
Falkirk, Stirlingshire
Printed and bound in Great Britain by Clays Ltd, St Ives plc

Papers used by Little, Brown
are from well-managed forests and
other responsible sources.

MIX

For Marisa

PART ONE

PART ONE

VOICES OFF

There was a low background hiss as the courtroom awaited the playback, the volume on the speakers jacked up so much that Parlabane was bracing himself, expecting the soundfile to be booming and distorted. Instead it was surprisingly clear, particularly at the police end. He could hear the dispatcher's fag-ravaged breathing during pauses, the rattle of a keyboard in the background.

Nobody knows where to look when they're listening to a recording. Parlabane glanced around to see how people were responding. Most were looking at the floor, the walls or any fixed point that didn't have a face on it. Others were more pruriently taking the opportunity to look at the accused.

Diana Jager had her gaze locked, staring into a future only she could see.

The jury mostly had their heads bowed, like they were in church, or as though they were afraid they'd get into trouble with the judge if they were caught paying less than maximum attention. They were filtering out distraction, concentrating only on the words booming out around the court, anxious not to miss a crucial detail.

They couldn't know it yet, but they were listening out for the wrong thing.

'I think I've just seen an accident.'

'Are you injured, madam?'

'No. But I think a car might have gone off the road.'

'Can you tell me your name, madam?'

'Yes, it's Sheena. Sheena Matheson. Missus.'

'And are you in your own vehicle now? Is it off the carriageway?'

'No. Yes. I mean, I'm out of my car. It's parked. I'm trying to see where he went.'

'Where are you, Mrs Matheson?'

3

'I'm not sure. Maybe a couple of miles west of Ordskirk. I'm on the Kingsburgh Road.'

'And can you describe what happened? Is someone injured?'

'I don't know. This car was coming around the bend towards me as I approached it. It was going way too fast. I think it was a BMW. It swerved on to my side of the road because of the curve, then swerved back again when I thought it was going to hit me. I jumped on the brakes because I got such a fright, and I looked in my rear-view. It swerved again like he was trying to get it back under control, but then it disappeared. I think it went off the road altogether.'

'The Kingsburgh Road, you said?'

'That's right.'

'I'm going to see if I can get some officers out there as soon as possible. You've parked your car, that's good. If you can wait beside it but not in it . . .'

'No, that's the thing. I can't stay here. I've a ten-year-old at home alone. She woke up with a temperature and we had run out of Calpol. I told her I'd nip out to the garage for some. I said I'd only be away half an hour. My husband's on nights.'

'Okay. Can you give me a wee bit more detail about where you are, then?'

'Sure, but I need to warn you: the battery's almost dead on this thing.'

'Tell us whatever you can. Anything you might have passed that our drivers could look out for.'

'There's a signpost right here. It says Uidh Dubh viewpoint and picnic area half a mile. The car disappeared just past the sign. I'm crossing the road now, in case I can see anything over the other side.'

'Please be careful, Mrs Matheson.'

'There are skid marks on the tarmac. I think I can see tyre tracks on the grass. It slopes away after that, and it's too dark to see down the slope.'

'No. Stay back from the edge. Our officers will look into it.'

'I can't see any lights. I'm worried it might have gone into the river.'

4

HER DAY IN COURT (I)

My trial has barely begun, and no testimony heard, but already I know that in the eyes of this court, I am an abomination.

As I gaze from the dock and take in all the faces gazing back, I think of the opinions they have formed, the hateful things they have written and said. I think of how once it stung, but my skin has grown thicker over time, and I have worse things to endure now than mere words.

They have to be respectful in their conduct within these walls: no shouting and barracking like when the van with its blacked-out windows pulled up outside the prisoners' entrance, a desperate photographer extending a hopeful arm and firing blind with a flash gun as he pressed himself perilously close against the moving steel.

One of these days the vehicle is going to run over one of those reckless idiots' feet: several tons of G4S hardware degloving the flesh from crushed and shattered bones as it rolls across his instep, all in the service of striving for, at best, a blurry low-contrast image of some scared and wretched prisoner cowering inside. It would be a valuable illustration of the risk-benefit equation *pour encourager les autres*.

To them, I am someone who ought to have been grateful for all that life apparently gifted me, not asked for more. I should have settled for what I was dealt, as it was generous enough in other people's estimation. The actions I took in pursuit of my desires, to better my lot and to extricate myself from an intolerable situation, these were unforgivable, depraved.

Society's judgement is always harsher upon a woman who has done grave deeds to get what she wants: a woman who has challenged their values, violated the accepted order of things. It's a crime against society, a transgression of unwritten rules that are far more precious than those inscribed in law.

With this thought I glance across the room, and to my surprise feel a sorority even with the woman I came to regard as my enemy: the woman who laid me low, brought my deeds to light. In our own ways we both acted for the purest of reasons. Her I respect. Everyone else is merely white noise to me now.

I do not expect anyone's sympathy. I do not seek forgiveness from people who have never been tested like I was. I may be guilty, and I may be sentenced, but I will not be condemned: not by those who cannot understand. Nobody here can judge me until they know the whole truth.

Until then, their opinions are no more than impotent angry words, and my, haven't those been in spate since this business first came to light. Just think how they were exercised by the revelation that this bitch murdered her husband.

The tone was one of boiling anger, and at the heart of it all was one single rhetorical question:

How dare she.

How dare she.

There's a thought: nobody ever asks 'How dare he?' when a man kills his wife. The coverage is coloured by sombre tones, its language muted and respectful. It's like they're reporting on a death from disease or calamitous mishap. 'It's dreadful, but it happens. Poor thing. So tragic,' it seems to say.

And like disease or disaster, the follow-up is about asking whether more could have been done. What signs were missed? What can we learn?

By contrast there's a conspicuous shortage of victim-blaming when it's a husband who lies slain.

'Why didn't he leave her? He must have known what she might be capable of. There must have been indications that she was dangerous. I'm not condoning it, but surely he was aware of her triggers. There's no excusing what she did, but it wouldn't have happened unless he did something to provoke her.'

Said nobody ever.

See, that's what chills them. They can just about handle a crime of passion, a moment of madness. But a clever, calculating woman who can plan something elaborate and deceitful is a far more galling prospect.

I glance at the reporters in the gallery, poised to take their notes. I think about what it looked like from their perspective.

They saw a woman who found love when she was beginning to think it was too late. She had given the best of herself to her career, and had come to sorely doubt whether it was worth the price she paid. But then out of nowhere she met her Mr Right, and suddenly everything seemed possible. Suddenly she got to have it all. A whirlwind romance, two ostensibly mismatched but surprisingly complementary personalities who found each other at just the right time: it was the stuff of rom-coms and chick-lit.

So much good fortune came her way, so much goodwill, and after that, so much sympathy. The rom-com turned out to be a weepy. The singleton surgeon who found love late was left heart-broken after her husband of only six months lost his life when his car shot off the road and plunged into a freezing river.

Let me tell you, once they've doled out tragedy points, you'd really better conform to their expectations, because the widow pedestal is a high one to fall from. She denied them first a happy ever after and then a poignant end to a tale of doomed romance. She desecrated their church, and so she had to face their judgement.

What else *would* they see? What else *could* they see?

Only one person looked closer, and he was my undoing. I know I'm not the first person to curse the day I heard the name Jack Parlabane, and I sincerely doubt I'll be the last. In my case I don't simply regret what he did to me. I regret what I did to him too. I know that in the eyes of this court, I am an abomination, but I am not the monster I will be painted.

I regard the police officers standing next to me. There are no cuffs on my wrists but I can still feel the cold steel like I can still feel the sting of humiliation that comes with wearing them. It clings to me every second I remain in the dock. There is a burning coal of moral opprobrium in the black pupil of every eye focused on me.

As the trial proceeds, the court will hear how a driven woman acted out of the oldest and sincerest of motives: to be with the man she was destined for. My crime and my actions will seem cold and heinous to everyone else because they can never know what I felt.

I think of all the anger and hate I have gone through since my arrest. It has taken time, but I have come to realise I must make my peace with what I have done. I need to take ownership of it. I need to forgive myself, because nobody else's forgiveness matters.

In the end, regardless of how my actions are judged, I know that this is about love.

ROLE MODELS

A handsome, loving husband and a minimum of two apple-cheeked children of your own: that's what you're supposed to want first and foremost in life, isn't it? That's the paradigm you're offered as a little girl, the playtime template that's intended to shape your aspirations for future happiness.

Sometimes the paradigm doesn't take, however. Sometimes the template is damaged. Such was the case for me, Diana Jager.

I had a doll's house when I was a child. I think it came from a relative, because it was old and wooden and hand-painted; nothing like the mass-produced moulded-plastic ones I saw in the big thick mail-order catalogue with its treasured and much-thumbed toy pages at the back. It had ivy picked out in oil on the outside, climbing the walls to the steeply pitched roof. It didn't look like any house in my neighbourhood but seemed to belong to an older, grander world, one that belonged in my parents' past rather than my own future. The front swung open on hinges, revealing three storeys of also hand-painted rooms. It didn't come with furniture, but my parents bought me a set intended for one of the aforementioned plastic affairs. It always looked wrong.

That wasn't the real problem, though. There was a scale mismatch. None of my dolls would fit inside it: they were all too big. Not that a better size compatibility would have made it ideal for playing happy families, because here's the thing: who was going to be the husband? All the dolls I owned were girls or babies, and all the dolls I ever saw in my friends' bedrooms, notably the ones that matched those modern plastic houses, were girls or babies.

This reflected the reality of my home. It was Mummy and the babies who were round the house most of the time. Daddy was out having a career, and what little girl needs a doll to represent that?

9

My doll's house was never a home. Why would I want a toy version of a home? I already had a full-size one. I didn't get the mini-figure set that went with the plastic furniture: didn't ask for it. Instead I asked for a hospital playset, so that's what my doll's house became, most of the time. Sometimes it was a school, sometimes it was a museum, but mainly it was a hospital. My playset comprised ten figurines: two of them were doctors, six of them were nurses and two of them were patients.

Both of the doctors were men. All of the nurses were women.

I tried making a little green tabard out of crepe paper to drape over one of the nurses so that she could be a doctor too: a surgeon like my father. It looked rubbish and it kept tearing and crumpling, so eventually I gave up and made the female patient the surgeon, and put both of the male doctors in beds.

I remember one day asking my mother why women couldn't be doctors too. I must have been about six. That was when she told me that she *was* a doctor.

Let me warn you now that this was not the inspirational epiphany you might be anticipating.

My parents met at university, where they were both studying medicine. Early in their final year, they decided to get married, arranging to have the ceremony a couple of weeks before graduation. Sounds quite romantic, you might think: tying the knot before striking out together on this path they had both aspired towards, the shared ambitions they had studied so hard to realise. But here's the thing: somewhere along the path of that final year, they decided that my father would pursue his medical career, and my mother would be a housewife.

She wasn't up the duff, by the way. I could at least have got my head around that. I didn't come along for a couple of years yet.

My mother strove to get the A-levels she needed in order to get accepted for medicine, studied a further five pitiless years, passed her exams, graduated, then never practised one day as a doctor.

Not one single day.

It never made any sense to me. She didn't seem cumulatively

10

frustrated by this as the years went on. I mean, I could have related to it all better had she been hitting the gin by mid-afternoon in her late thirties as her kids needed her less and she wondered where her life had drained away to. Not that she seemed particularly contented either. She was just *there*. Smiling but not cheery, caring but not warm, dependable but not inspiring.

I didn't see it for a long time because I grew up with it and because it was a hard thing to accept, but at some time around my late teens I realised that my mother had almost no personality. As I matured into adulthood, what increasingly bothered me about this – and about the choice she had made in final year – was the question of whether my father had subjugated her, turning a bright young woman into a compliant drone; or whether he had in fact recognised that compliance, that lack of personality, and identified it as precisely what he was looking for in a life partner. For my mother's part, I wondered was she happy to surrender her autonomy, to be annexed like some colonial dependency? Or had her natural timidity made her vulnerable to the manipulations of someone who turned out to be more domineering than she had initially apprehended?

I didn't even know which explanation I would prefer to be true.

There certainly weren't any clues on display in what I witnessed of their relationship. As a child I thought they were everything a married couple should be. My father would come home to find my mother in the kitchen calmly preparing dinner, and would peck her on the cheek and call her 'Dearest Darling', which was sometimes abbreviated to 'Dee Dee'. There never seemed to be any strife, no raised voices, no unspoken words, no simmering tension. (No passion, no hunger, no chemistry, no spark.)

'Dinner was beautiful, Dearest Darling. Thank you.'

'My pleasure, always.'

Even as a child, something about their exchanges chimed wrong, though I was too young to identify what and why. It was only as I got older that I came to understand what my instincts were telling me was off about this. It was like a phoned-in performance, a cargo-cult imitation of intimacy by two people who had seen

11

this behaviour elsewhere and sought to replicate it as a form of civil convention.

Even once I had grasped this much, I still simply assumed that all married couples were like this with each other: that every husband and every wife behaved in a polite, friendly way they didn't really mean, as we do in so many other areas of our lives.

I was the Apple of his Eye. You should note the capitals: this noun was proper. It was not how he saw me, but what he called me.

'How's the Apple of my Eye this evening?'

Or when he was feeling solicitous, merely Apple.

'What's wrong, Apple? Aren't you feeling hungry this evening?'

My younger brothers were proudly addressed as Number One Son and Number Two Son, except when they were in trouble. I always knew that there was mischief afoot and a spike in the domestic temperature if I heard my father address them directly as Julian or Piers.

As a little girl I thought this meant my daddy was jokey, a man who had funny nicknames for everybody, this informality proof of how close we were to his heart. Later on I came to realise that this language of apparent intimacy was actually a way of creating distance. If we were Diana, Julian and Piers, then we had agency: we were autonomous entities with foibles that he had to negotiate, personalities that he had to get to know. But if we were the Apple of his Eye, Sons Number One and Two, then his children were adjuncts to him, defined only in terms of how he regarded us.

Thus our primary role was to reflect well upon him, and we generally made a good job of it when we were young. After that not so much.

Parents can pretend to themselves that their children suddenly change when they hit their teens: that the pubescent transformation caused their offspring to stop communicating with them the way they used to. The truth is that in such cases they never really communicated with them. It's simply easier to project idealised versions on to your children when they are very young, before they start having opinions and making decisions for themselves.

12

However, it was when we became adults that we seriously disappointed him, each in our different ways: the boys because they didn't have the careers he wanted them to; me because I *did* have the career he wanted them to.

I was the Apple of his Eye, his first child, his only daughter, but it was his sons who were supposed to be surgeons. I'm not sure what I was supposed to be, other than born later.

It is said that every time a friend succeeds, a small part of you dies. I've seen it in the expressions of colleagues as they learned of someone else's achievement, and I saw it on my father's face whenever I told him of my latest progress. For a while I thought I was imagining it, but then it became impossible to miss. I could see it in his eyes, eyes that didn't twinkle to match the awkward smile with which he greeted my news.

Everything I achieved, each step I took up the ladder hurt just a little more because it was supposed to be his sons.

So was this hollow imitation of marriage and parenthood the perfect environment in which to nurture a clever psychopath? I guess that's for you to judge. But this much I know for sure: it was what made me determined that I wouldn't be seeking fulfilment in life from being somebody's wife or mother.

THE CARING PROFESSION

The young doctor identified himself to the court, his voice catching in his throat and prompting the fiscal to ask him to repeat.

'Calum Weatherson,' he said.

'And you first started working with Diana Jager how long ago?'

'A year and . . . no, sixteen . . . I think sixteen months, maybe a wee bit less.'

He'd got his name right, even if it had taken two attempts to get it out there. That was a good start: harder than it looks. Now the nerves were really showing as the enormity hit home. As well as everything else that was at stake, he was acting like he was scared he was also going to get done for perjury if it turned out his estimate of how long he'd been at Inverness Royal Infirmary turned out to be a fortnight out.

Jack Parlabane felt for him. He had seen a lot of court cases in his capacity as a journalist and sometimes as a consequence of exceeding his capacity as a journalist. He could tell it was young Mr Weatherson's first time on the stand. There was a tremulous note in his voice, his hands slightly shaky too, and his eyes kept straying beyond his interlocutor, searching the gallery for someone whose approving look would tell him he was doing okay.

Parlabane recalled being the friendly face among an indifferent crowd as a show of moral support when his wife Sarah was on the stand. She had been called several times as a medical witness, which could be an upsettingly adversarial experience when, for instance, the defence counsel decided that the best strategy was to imply that a murder victim may have died due to negligence on the part of an anaesthetist, rather than the fourteen hatchet blows rained down by his client a couple of hours earlier. Such grillings were a breeze, however, compared to the cross-examination to which she

14

was humiliatingly subject during a case brought by Witnesses of the Jehovah's variety. On that occasion his presence in the gallery had begun as a show of solidarity but ended up undermining Sarah's cause when the court heard a typically intemperate newspaper column her husband had written on the subject of the serial door-steppers and their bafflingly stupid objection to blood transfusion.

It wasn't the first time his professional conduct had the unforeseen consequence of raining shit down upon their marriage, and nor was it the last, which went a long way towards explaining why they weren't married any more. That said, the Diana Jager case had given him a whole new perspective on quite how badly a marriage could end.

'And can you tell the court what your respective positions were in January of last year?'

'I had recently started as a, em, that is, I was already a registrar, but I had not long taken up the post after transferring from another hospital.'

Weatherson's voice faltered again. His mouth sounded dry. The fiscal urged him to take a drink of water. He would relax into his narrative in time, Parlabane knew, but those early moments were the most intimidating, especially as the stakes were so high. What Parlabane also knew, to his cost, was that it was when you were relaxed enough to become expansive that the sneaky bastards tended to ambush you.

He had been on the witness stand plenty himself, one time ignominiously as the accused. He vividly recalled the feelings of isolation, vulnerability and impotence as he faced the court, and not merely because on that occasion he was guilty as sin.

For all that the process of justice was supposed to be lucid, open and transparent, once a trial got underway it could seem as though your destiny was in the capricious hands of top-level initiates in some arcane secret order. You could walk in thinking that the evidence all but guaranteed a certain outcome. Then the high priests got into it: meanings became plastic, traps were sprung, and all sense of reality melted into something fluid that they could mould into any shape they liked.

It was almost enough to make him feel sorry for the accused. Almost, that was, until he remembered what the woman in the dock had done: how sociopathically callous and brutally calculating her scheme (in particular how she had even manipulated Parlabane as a crucial plank in her strategy); and how chillingly close she and her secret co-conspirator had come to fooling everybody and getting away with it.

This last was what truly tempered any sympathy he might have now that she was being put on display for the public's revulsion: put simply, it wasn't over. For the reasons he had just considered, he endured a nagging worry that this might not be the slam-dunk everyone assumed. Above all, he remained wary that she may yet have one killer trick left to play.

'Mr Weatherson, can you describe your state of mind on the morning that you first worked with Dr Jager?'

The fiscal asked this in an encouraging, reassuring tone of which Parlabane couldn't help but be suspicious. He had learned the hard way that if a prosecutor asks you what time it is, the question you should be asking internally is: 'Where are you going with this?'

Weatherson remained nervy, talking too fast, tripping over his sentences.

'I was apprehensive. I was new to the department. I had been a registrar for six months, but I had only been in this post for a couple of weeks, and when you're working with a new consultant . . . I mean, when you're working for the first time with a particular consultant, not a new consultant, you start off keen to impress, but then you sort of downshift your goals to simply hoping you don't screw up, which can be surprisingly hard to avoid. Consultants tend to have very individual ideas about how they like things done. You have to tread lightly until you find out everyone's likes and dislikes, not to mention their triggers.'

'And was the prospect of working with Dr Jager in particular making you apprehensive, or was it merely the general anxiety you just described with regard to any new senior colleague?'

'It would be fair to say I was anxious about working with her in particular.'

'And to calibrate what constitutes such anxiety, were you as anxious as you first appeared here on the witness stand?'

Weatherson stole a nervy glance at the object of their discussion. Jager gazed back impassively, as if nothing he could say would make any difference. Bring it on, she seemed to reply silently.

'As I said, consultants have their idiosyncrasies, and surgeons in particular can sometimes be a little . . .' He considered it a moment, choosing his description with care. He took another sip of water, giving himself time. 'Combustible,' he decided.

'You mean explosive?'

'Em, sometimes, yes. The hair-dryer treatment. The operating theatre can be a tense environment, which shouldn't be a surprise given what is often at stake, so it's not uncommon for surgeons to vent when things aren't going as smoothly as they'd like.'

Delicately put, Parlabane thought, if not outright apologism.

What Weatherson was alluding to was that if you ever thought ex-Bullingdon Club cabinet ministers were among the most pompously self-important wankers on the face of the Earth, then you had clearly not been around many surgeons. Parlabane's ex-wife was an anaesthetist, and had regularly regaled him with eye-popping accounts of their rampant inner-toddler behaviour, the most shocking aspect of which was how widely it was tolerated.

Sarah had seen surgeons eyeball-to-eyeball with theatre staff, spittle-flying and their throats going rapidly hoarse as they bellowed their lungs out in fury at some perceived failing or transgression. She had described how instruments were thrown violently at walls or to the floor, equipment smashed and staff reduced to tears by the screaming harangues of individuals who had lost their self-control to such an extent that under any other circumstances they might be sedated, arrested or sent to bed without their supper.

The most commonly cited explanation for indulging this misbehaviour had just been illustrated on the witness stand: that the stakes were high and thus fits of rage were inevitable when such brilliant individuals had to cope with the limitations of working with ordinary mortals. Weatherson was only a surgical registrar, but was already becoming inured to the point where he had ceased to question whether these ridiculous tantrums were perhaps a teensy bit unacceptable.

Weatherson proceeded to avail the court of a few examples of the 'combustible' behaviour he had been at pains to avoid. He demonstrated unquestionably that he had served a few tours before reaching Inverness, and had been inside the blast radius a couple of times already in his new post. Given all of which, you'd have to be asking yourself what made Diana Jager a far scarier prospect than anything the young registrar had faced before.

'And how did your first encounter with Dr Jager work out?' asked the fiscal.

Weatherson cleared his throat.

'I suppose it didn't get off to the best possible start. I had gone in early to do some final pre-op checks on the first patient on the list, and to confer with the anaesthetist in case she had any concerns. It was a bariatric case: the patient was in for a sleeve gastrectomy.'

'What is that?'

'It's a kind of drastic weight-loss procedure. The very big patients can be tricky for a general anaesthetic. Anyway, that was when I first saw Dr Jager in the flesh. She was heading into the ward as I was about to leave. I felt a degree of relief that I had gotten there first, as it wouldn't have looked good to be coming in behind her.'

The relief was reprised in his current expression. He seemed to relax a little now that he realised he wasn't going to be asked anything he didn't know the answer to.

'How would you describe her manner?'

'Fizzing, would have to be my description. It was eight in the morning but she looked like ten people had already annoyed her. I was concerned about what might happen to the eleventh.'

'And was there an eleventh?'

'Unfortunately, yes, but to my relief it wasn't me. She had come from surgical HDU – that is, the surgical high-dependency unit – and discovered that they had no beds, despite management having assured her otherwise the day before. It meant the first patient was going to have to be cancelled. At first I thought I was about to get both barrels for not having been the one who went to HDU and found this out first, but equally I reckoned that if I had been the one breaking it to her, she'd have shot the messenger too.'

'But as you intimated, you weren't the immediate target of Dr Jager's ire.'

'No. She had actually come to the ward to inform the patient that his procedure was cancelled, which she proceeded to do. Very politely, I should add, though she didn't apologise, as it wasn't her fault.'

'And how did the patient respond?'

'He said he wanted a second opinion. She tried to explain that it wasn't a matter of medical opinion, but he was insistent.'

Weatherson took a breath, like an emotion-memory response recalling how he must have winced at the time.

'He said that what he meant was, he wanted to talk to her boss. He was looking at me.'

Ooft, thought Parlabane.

'I was mortified and made a flailing effort at correcting his misapprehension, but Dr Jager intervened and made it clear who was in charge. The patient then accepted that his procedure was indeed cancelled, which was clear from the fact that he began to complain about it, bitterly and at length. I could tell Dr Jager was keen to leave but he was on a rant, most of which seemed to be to do with his having fasted for the operation. He considered this a major sacrifice and clearly didn't fancy having to repeat it. At that point Dr Jager suggested he ought to take a more optimistic perspective.'

Again the remembered wince.

'How so?'

'She said that he had taken the first step, and if he fasted another two thousand days he wouldn't need the procedure at all.'

Ooft again.

'Understandably, he didn't take this too well, and later issued a formal complaint. To be fair, I could tell Dr Jager immediately regretted what she had said. She had clearly been at the end of her tether, but she was furious with herself. I still felt awkward about the patient having assumed I was her boss, and I tried to suggest it might have been to do with the beard I had at that time. I don't know why I thought that would make her feel better, but I felt I ought to say something.'

'And how did Dr Jager respond to your suggestion?'

'It would be fair to say she disagreed. She said my beard merely made me look like Hipster Jesus, and that the principal physical attribute affecting the patient's misunderstanding was my penis.'

'And was this the first time you had been party to such a prejudiced assumption on the part of a patient?'

'Not at all. Patients over a certain age often assume anyone female is a nurse, even if it states their title on their name badge. I've even seen male doctors peg female consultants as juniors because they look young.'

'So it is a common, if regrettable, occurrence. And yet from your response we can tell you were utterly aghast that Dr Jager in particular should be assumed to be your junior colleague. One might even say disproportionately horrified. Would that be fair?'

'It would be an understatement.'

'And yet you had never worked with Dr Jager before. Why then were you so treading on eggshells?'

'Her reputation preceded my arrival in the post. In fact, I had no idea she worked there before I transferred to Inverness, so when I discovered she was in the same department, I was . . . apprehensive, yes.'

Parlabane nodded to himself, as the fiscal's intentions began to come into focus. The journey had been like the corporation bus: it had taken a bafflingly circuitous route, but it was finally getting to its destination.

'Where did you transfer from?'

'I was in Liverpool. My wife . . .'

'Liverpool. So it would be accurate to say that in medical circles there were things widely known about Dr Jager far beyond the environs of Inverness Royal Infirmary?'

'Yes. Very widely. One thing in particular.'

'And what was that, Mr Weatherson?'

The young registrar spoke with coy self-consciousness, like a kid in a primary school classroom who has been told by the teacher that in the interests of getting to the truth, it's okay to repeat the rude word he overheard.

'She was Bladebitch.'

COMPASSION FATIGUE

It was an inauspicious day for destiny to come calling, though it is not in the nature of fate to give notice. The occasions that we think of as life-changing are seldom precipitate. Rather they tend to be mere milestones and markers, events long in the planning, diligently worked towards and keenly anticipated: births, christenings, exams, graduations, job interviews, career commencement.

Weddings.

We recognise the truly significant events – the moments when fate genuinely turns – only in retrospect. This is probably just as well. If you were told in advance that you were about to meet the man who would become the love of your life, then the pressure would be so enormous that most of us would undoubtedly blow it. It would be like a variant of the Heisenberg principle, whereby the act of observation alters that which is being observed. The state you are in during a fateful encounter may be crucial to the outcome, though it is not exactly heart-warming to look back and see that my own chances of finding love may have hinged upon being an exhausted, angry and overwrought mess. And yet I now realise that it was only because my guard was down and finding a life partner was the furthest thing from my mind that he slipped through the barricades.

I wouldn't say I'd completely given up on the idea of meeting the right man, but I was moving ever closer to accepting the notion. That's not the same as saying I had made my peace with it, more a matter of managing expectations. I'd had a few relationships, but the longest of them only lasted a few months, and the last one was four years before the time we're talking about. Well, strictly speaking . . . No. I'm not going to start defining one-night stands as relationships. They were only about sex, about getting someone to make me feel a certain way. I'm talking about the last time there was someone *I* felt something for. So, yes, four years.

The fact that it had been so long actually snuck up on me that morning: one of the many things that conspired to make the circumstances seem so unpromising on the day I would meet the man who changed my life for ever.

I was passing the fish counter when I caught a glimpse of some squat lobsters, which I hadn't seen there in ages. It sparked a memory of buying them the first time I cooked for Dan, a radiologist I started seeing when I first moved to Inverness.

I really thought it was going somewhere, that it would last. Taking up the post at IRI was supposed to be a kind of banishment from the prestigious world of the big teaching hospitals, but it felt like a new beginning after everything that had happened. I'm not sure whether meeting Dan contributed to that feeling, or whether I felt so optimistic about Dan because of how I felt about everything else, but either way, I had high hopes.

Then he found out about Bladebitch. That was the beginning of the end.

It seemed so stupid, so unnecessary. I hadn't changed, but suddenly I could tell he saw me differently. Whatever he had previously projected on to me had been switched off, and replaced with a new projection he was entirely less comfortable with.

Shortly afterwards Dan started seeing someone else: someone less complicated; someone who more readily conformed to his ideals of what a woman – what a wife – ought to be. Her name was Donna: a bubbly but vacuous nurse manager who favoured push-up bras and giddy helplessness as her mating displays.

Dan and Donna were married within a year of us breaking up, and they've already got two kids. That was why it suddenly hit me so hard as I stood there at the fish counter: I realised how long it had been since then, how far on his life had moved, and how little mine had changed. It had been four years since I had anyone I could call a boyfriend, and I was at a stage in life where nobody I considered a friend ought to be describable as a boy.

I'm not saying I thought for sure that Dan was 'the one', by the way. It's simply that back then, I hadn't reached the stage where I was worrying about whether I'd find 'the one'; or even allowing embarrassing phrases like 'the one' to actually form in my head.

I was still young, I thought. There would be time. But then one day you wake up and it doesn't feel like there's time. Being with Dan was the last occasion I could remember contemplating a guy as date material without wondering if he might be my last chance. That mindset has subsequently killed a few things before they even got started: flirtings that might have gone further; conversations that might have led to something else if I wasn't already anticipating the reasons a relationship wouldn't work in the long run.

That's what I mean about being off my guard. If I'd been thinking straight that day, he would never have got in under my radar. But I was a long way from thinking straight that day.

I couldn't remember feeling so low. I told myself it was just fatigue. I'd had a very demanding and frustrating schedule in theatre the day before, but despite my exhaustion, I was too wired to sleep properly. After a few fitful hours I found myself lying awake at about half past four, which was when I decided to cut my losses and get up. A short while later I was pushing my mini-trolley around a twenty-four-hour supermarket, struggling to fill it with enough items to justify having anything bigger than a basket.

Walking the aisles, it was like I was navigating a living, walking (and trundling) theatre list, one that would never end. All around me were future cases, meat-wrapped parcels of symptoms filling their trolleys with precisely the items they needed to exacerbate their conditions.

It was too early in the day for the shop to sell drink, but the guzzling of it was marked indelibly on many of the faces that passed me, their cheeks yellow-tinged and their noses florid with broken capillaries.

Everywhere I turned, I saw, heard and smelled the symptoms and the causes of disease and decay. The place was dotted with overweight and conspicuously unhealthy people loading up on fat, salt and sugar, filling their trolleys with the very pathogens that were poisoning them.

It hit me that I could no longer see human beings. I could only see pathology. I was resentful of the choices they were making, wilfully creating a mess that it would be my problem to clear up.

This happens sometimes. I suddenly see myself as though from the outside, looking down, and I'm someone else: someone I don't like. She is cruel and callous and I have no control over her. Unfortunately I can't say she's someone I don't recognise, because I had been seeing more and more of her back then.

Let me tell you, there are few things more pitiful than having an epiphany in Tesco at five thirty a.m., and one of them is standing in Tesco at five thirty a.m. and being in denial about what the epiphany is telling you.

Yes I was tired. I just wasn't accepting what I was tired of. I had spent so long railing against exclusion in my profession that it had never occurred to me to consider the value of what I was so determined to be included in.

When I reached the fish counter and began thinking about Dan, one of the things that struck me was that I had spent the last ten minutes getting angry about other people's shopping. That's got to be a pretty big indication that I'd bottomed out. But you're seldom so low that you can't fall further, and so it proved when I made it into work.

'Well, you've taken the first step. Another two thousand days and you won't need the procedure at all.'

The second the words were out there it was like I was looking down upon the scene from above, then suddenly had to pilot my body once more.

I felt so ashamed.

What was happening to me? What was I turning into? My very purpose, the thing that got me up in the morning, was to help patients like this one. There was little I didn't know about what life was like for this man and for all the bariatric patients I had

25

operated on before him. Their conditions were a result of the most intractable psychological complexity, their lives miserable and depressed. By the time they had reached me, it was because the procedure I could carry out was their last hope.

It sounded like someone else talking: or at least the someone who lurks inside but is never permitted to surface in hospital. I am used to biting my tongue in these situations, because sometimes dealing with their denial and self-delusion is as much a part of helping them as the operation itself. When you ask them about their diet, it's like asking an alcoholic about how much they drink: you know they're lying to you, but more importantly they're lying to themselves. So you have to handle it subtly. They describe a modest intake of food, so I respond by suggesting that this procedure isn't the right one for them, as it will only help people who grossly over-consume. They usually fess up to a few more Mars bars after that.

I have been outraged by colleagues who have spoken indiscreetly about such patients, never mind to their faces. Such as the anaesthetist who once expressed his incredulity that a woman with a BMI of sixty was a vegetarian. 'What does she eat?' he asked: 'Fucking trees?'

I laid into him for his lack of professionalism and for his insensitivity.

And yet here I was, saying possibly the worst thing I could as the person who was going to operate on this man. I might as well have called him a greedy bastard.

It was inexcusable.

There were mitigating circumstances, but I didn't think 'having an existential crisis' was something I should include in my written response to the inevitable formal complaint.

It was the culmination of a lot of things. My sleep-deprived and brittle state of mind was not improved when I first got to my office that morning and discovered I had been locked out of the hospital intranet. This meant I would have to get in touch with our utterly hopeless IT department and be patronised over the phone for ten minutes, or worse: that it would require an on-site

26

visit and I'd have to endure being patronised in person by Creepy Craig.

That was how things stood by 7.35, before I had gone to surgical high dependency and learned that they no longer had a bed for the first patient on my list, despite my securing a guarantee of this last thing before leaving yesterday evening.

It was fair to say I was ready to blow, and I used up the last of my restraint in not responding when the patient voiced his assumption – despite me having spoken to him several times before – that I was not the consultant and that Hipster Jesus was my boss.

Everybody's got their limits, an endurance of frustration beyond which their composure cracks. But I was doubly angry about what I said to that patient because as a woman in this job, you're judged more harshly if you lose your cool. Women are too emotional, see? Fragile temperament. When a chap cuts a strip off of someone it's because he 'doesn't suffer fools', and it's a sign of strength. When a woman does the same, it's interpreted as a sign of weakness.

So I was in a personal hell of self-flagellation as I worked through the list that day, and just to put a cherry on top, I had a techie visit to look forward to. I had quickly called the IT department to report the problem while the anaesthetist was prepping my next patient, and been given the bad news that it wasn't something they could sort from their end.

For reasons I'm sure you're familiar with, hospital IT personnel were not my favourite people in the world at this point. Obviously the ones at IRI hadn't done anything as utterly loathsome as I'd endured in the past, but nor were they doing much to improve the low regard in which I held their fraternity.

What normally happened was that Creepy Craig would show up, at least twenty minutes later than stated, then proceed to walk me through a sequence of steps intended to determine whether the problem was down to stupidity at my end. He never assumed any knowledge. It was like his brain didn't accept cookies, so he had no recollection of the level of proficiency he could expect in assessing my dealings with the system or with computers in general.

That's my more charitable explanation anyway. The alternative interpretation is that this part of the procedure, with him leaning over my left shoulder (and always my left shoulder), afforded him a sustained opportunity to peek through the gaps in my blouse.

Once Craig had determined that the issue was not going to resolve itself merely as a result of a *man* using the computer *properly*, he would usually proceed to get out his laptop or log into the restricted layers of the system from my machine. After a further quarter of an hour of stinking up my office with BO and halitosis, he would declare the problem solved or else sigh a lot and blame issues further up the chain.

That was what I had to look forward to at the end of this particular day: a little turd garnish on top of a gigantic shit sandwich served with a side of sick.

My list ended early, due to another cancellation resultant of the HDU bottleneck. I longed to go home, but instead I had to wait in my office otherwise I'd still be locked out of the system come Monday morning, when I had a ton of admin to get through.

At around ten past five I heard a knock and felt a shudder run through me. I glanced down at my blouse and wished I had a cardie. The problem was I never thought to bring in such a thing, as it was always cloyingly hot in the hospital, apart from in maternity theatre, where a cadre of menopausal midwives fiercely guarded a thermostat set at twenty degrees.

I was contemplating my mistake in getting changed out of my theatre blues when I called out to Craig to enter.

The door swung open slightly, and a head appeared around it, tentative to the point of apologetic.

'You're not Craig.'

'No. I'm Peter.'

MIGHTIER THAN THE SCALPEL

Bladebitch, as she became known, was the then anonymous author of the now infamous 'Sexism in Surgery' blog, which was already causing controversy among medical professionals before it went explosively – some might even say violently – viral about five years back.

Parlabane first had it drawn to his attention by his then wife Sarah, whose poring over the postings was equally likely to be accompanied by snorts of indignant outrage or cackles of approval, as well as the occasional disbelieving gasp. These last were not to indicate incredulity at the content; rather more: 'Oh my God, I can't believe she went there.'

She called herself Scalpelgirl, but it was the corrupted version that passed into public notice when scandal struck, meaning her chosen monicker became largely forgotten except among the blog's original readership, and eventually even they had to refer to Bladebitch if they wanted people to know what they were talking about.

Scalpelgirl was part agony aunt and part firebrand polemicist. She collated tales of misogyny that had been sent to her by female surgeons from across the UK, passing on their shocking details and responding with sometimes equally shocking invective.

As the blog grew in popularity, the stories started to come flooding into the comments section by themselves, with Scalpelgirl's overview articles sparking off areas of discussion or editorialising over a particular theme that had emerged.

There were copious examples of comments that female doctors had to listen to, which Scalpelgirl categorised as 'low-level harassment', constantly reminding readers that 'the very constancy of this background hum is both its greatest indictment and its greatest threat. The danger is that we'll become so used to it that people will cease to notice how wrong it is.'

Parlabane recalled Sarah delightedly sharing one particular column on this subject with her peers on social media. It was entitled 'Are You Too Cute to Be a Surgeon?', and began by citing a number of quotes from recently posted accounts, including the one that had given the article its title. Looking 'too nice', 'too sexy', 'too homely' and 'too dainty' were all apparently contra-indicated for a career in surgery, according to male colleagues.

This laid the groundwork for male prescriptions upon a more specific area of the surgical female's form. 'I could take her more seriously if those tits weren't so big,' one correspondent had heard said of a colleague. A number of similar remarks were cited, before being contrasted with quotes suggesting that a display of cleavage or a generous bust had played a part in career preferment.

'Clearly, there are profound anthropomorphic implications here,' Scalpelgirl had written. 'We have to ask ourselves: what precisely *is* the optimal breast size for a woman pursuing a career in surgery? Why are there no papers on it? This is one of the scientific controversies of our age, and yet nobody is publishing. According to some sources, we need big tits to get on; and yet according to others, big tits are an impediment to being taken seriously as professionals. The Royal College of Surgeons' ideal standard career-tit has to be empirically defined, and ought to be offered by breast surgeons as a template for reduction or enhancement.'

Parlabane didn't find it as daring or hilarious as Sarah evidently did, but the levels of decorum expected of medical professionals apparently set the bar pretty low for what could be considered risqué. That wasn't what had her punching the air, however. Sarah and her peers loved it because here was a female voice that was saying all the things that same decorum prevented them from saying themselves.

It was also possible that he judged it harshly because he was a tad jealous. It used to be journalists like him whose pithy comments were being quoted and shared, though as it was often by shouting across an office to recommend the piece to others who owned copies of the same paper, the process wasn't quite so immediate or dynamic.

The blog's principal thrust was concerned with themes it considered more substantial than this 'background hum', or even with the frequently busy topic of unwanted touching in the workplace. These were the over-arching issues of career advancement and work-life balance.

'Dressing for the Big Interview' was one of the early articles that first put the blog on people's radars. It started off ostensibly as a discussion of how much more vexed a question this was for women than for male candidates, who knew the answer was simply a shirt and tie. Wearing a dress could make you look insubstantial, it had been suggested. Even a skirt could seem sexualised, apparently, by making a statement of gender.

'Why are women supposed to be sexually neutral in their interview dress code?' she asked. 'Nobody is suggesting men dress in a way that somehow de-emphasises their gender. Perhaps it's to comfort the crusty old golf club bores on the interview panel: you know, the ones who have never gotten over the fact that they no longer work in an all-male profession. So if we all put on a pair of trousers, then if they squint hard enough they can at least pretend that they do.'

She then asked more broadly why women were asked to defeminise themselves in order to practise surgery: why feminine traits were typified as weaknesses, and masculine traits lionised.

'We're always told we need to toughen up. Why do we have to be tough? Scar tissue is tough. It is not sensitive: it feels less. To feel less is not a good thing in a caring profession. Sensitivity is feminine. Compassion is feminine. The irony is that it is this over-emphasis on the value of masculine attributes that tends to make so many of our male colleagues accurately describable as cunts.'

Yeah, he had to admit that one was always going to startle the horses.

Parlabane thought she came across as too snidey and acidic

31

sometimes, but seeing Sarah's reaction and hearing her colleagues talk about the blog, it was clear that women in medicine loved Scalpelgirl because it felt like she had their back. They took pleasure in her takedowns and they applauded her acerbic tone because you kind of want a badass on your side. That's what she was to them: an anti-hero.

Emboldened by Scalpelgirl's forthright style and the discussion she was encouraging, the blog became a touchstone and support base for female whistleblowers in the profession. For instance, interviewers for surgical positions were no longer allowed to ask whether the candidate had or was planning to have children, and the blog allowed women to highlight the more subtle ways in which it remained the conspicuous subtext of their questioning.

'What do you see as your life goals?' they might ask. Not career goals, Scalpelgirl noted: life goals. It was subtle, but once you knew what you were looking for, it was hard to miss. As a result, regardless of their wardrobe choices, she had a suggestion as to the most important thing female candidates could present in order to make the right impression.

'Bring along a uterus in a jar. Your local university anatomical museum will have one, so ask if you can borrow it for the day. What you need to do is slap it down on the table and tell them you've had it removed.'

That particular rant brought forth a torrent of stories from women who had experienced these subtle probings at interview but had previously been afraid to put a name on what was really going on. This in turn led to articles in doctors' publications and a call for the royal colleges to toughen up their guidelines, or at least think about actually enforcing the ones they already had.

But while it was officially not permitted at interview, the subject of women's child-bearing intentions was constantly arrogated elsewhere as fair game for discussion, opinion and unsolicited advice.

'A woman can be a good wife and mother, or she can be a good surgeon. She can't be both,' one correspondent had been told by a cardiac consultant she was training under. 'If you want children, become a GP. Or a dermatologist.'

Other specialities were frequently assessed by senior male colleagues for the apparent benefit of Foundation Year trainees, with the out-of-hours commitments and other demands of each discipline weighed up against the practical implications of motherhood. These 'helpful impromptu careers-advice pep talks', Scalpelgirl noted, never cited any implications for fatherhood. Nor did anyone ever ask how surgery or other specialities might be altered – 'dear God, we mustn't say *improved*' – in order to better accommodate motherhood.

To illustrate what she called 'the blindness of entrenched privilege', Scalpelgirl quoted at length from an email she had received, recounting the regular pontifications of a particularly outspoken colleague.

'You'd think doctors of all people would understand human biology,' he said. 'You can't change it, so why are they in denial about it? They can say it's unfair, but it's a bare fact that it's women who have to be pregnant if a couple wants babies, and it's women who have to breastfeed them and nurture them. That's not some archaic sexist convention: it's the inescapable reality. It is unavoidably going to cause them to interrupt their careers and it is unavoidably going to distract them in other ways: sleepless nights, worrying about their welfare, organising the school run and what have you. They should accept that and commit to a decision. It's not fair on their children and their husbands, and it's not fair on their colleagues and the patients if they're trying to have it both ways.'

The kicker in all of this, Scalpelgirl revealed, was that the surgeon quoted was a father of four. He got to have it both ways. He never had to commit to a decision.

Scalpelgirl could not disclose who had sent the email or where she worked, in order to conceal the identity of her correspondent. Unfortunately this necessary discretion also conferred protection upon the identity of the surgeon quoted. She did, however, reveal that his colleagues secretly called him Leatherface, 'because he leaves his theatre looking like the scene of the Texas Chainsaw Massacre'. He featured regularly on the blog, partly through ongoing correspondence updates, and more significantly when Scalpelgirl established the 'Leatherface Award for the worst instance of family-man hypocrisy' sent in each month.

There was also a Golden Bow Tie Award for boorishly chauvinistic old-school pomposity, and more controversially the Girl-on-Girl Action Award for the worst instance of a female surgeon deemed to have stabbed her sisters in the back.

The inaugural recipient of this emerged from another early rant that helped grow the blog's readership, highlighting attitudes on behalf of female surgeons that Scalpelgirl's piece eponymously damned as 'Our Own Worst Enemies'. Again she was able to illustrate the issue by showcasing the account of another anonymous correspondent to the site, who encountered a less-than-sympathetic response to her pregnancy and subsequent motherhood from a senior female consultant. The young registrar had been put on a run of nights when she was thirty-five weeks pregnant, and then, upon her return after six months' maternity leave, had been stuck back on nights again.

These rota assignments were the work of a female consultant whose unsupportive attitude seemed all the more disappointing when it was revealed that she was a mother of two herself, but her perspective on work-life balance turned out to be most revealing.

'If you're committed to this career, you need to prove that,' she had said. 'I always tell women to stop whining about sexism because it becomes a built-in excuse for failure. I was back at work within a fortnight after my first child, and within seventy-two hours after my second.'

Scalpelgirl suggested that if this self-styled superwoman had a third, she could book to have it delivered by C-section in the morning and then be free to undertake a half-day list in the afternoon.

'Superwoman is our enemy,' Scalpelgirl had written. 'I'm not criticising her choices – there's enough men happy to do that without us joining in – but don't dare tell us that it's normal; don't dare tell the rest of us we should be aspiring towards it. Superwoman isn't pushing the boundaries for women in surgery: she's pulling up the ladder. She's a sell-out, making it harder for the rest of us. And she's legion.'

The piece sparked a wave of highly polarised online debate on doctors' forums, leading to a lot more hits on the blog and inevitable speculation as to the carefully protected identity of its author. As its reach grew, though the website's title remained the same, the contributions saw its remit expand first to cover sexism across medicine, and then sexism in hospitals generally. This, although indirectly, was what led to its downfall.

Scalpelgirl authored what she probably regarded as one of her less contentious pieces, which began as an account of lecherous attitudes from hospital IT techs before broadening into an unfocused rant about the incompetence of hospital IT staff in general. It was, in Parlabane's opinion, not her finest work, with its low point being her assertion that 'considering that IT consultancy remains the most unjustifiably over-remunerated profession of the age, given what the NHS pays, you've got to be the worst of the worst if this is the only gig you can get'.

Nonetheless, something in it proved cathartic to her readers, and set the tone for the torrent of me-too outrage that followed below. Word of this dogpile somehow found its way to hospital IT personnel, and from there spread rapidly to the kinds of forums frequented by guys who demonstrate the internet adage that the response to any article on feminism proves the need for it.

It was actually some of the postings in the unmoderated comments section that had caused the most outrage, describing IT guys as socially inept geeks, virgins, neckbeards, basement dwellers: the full bullshit-bingo card on tech-head stereotyping. However, it was Scalpelgirl whose name was at the top, so as is the way of these things, the Chinese whispers reductionist perspective meant that these remarks soon became indelibly misattributed to her.

Suddenly she was a target, though the death and rape threats we have come to expect from such scenarios were not immediately unleashed. The guys who send that stuff prefer a name and a face before they can really saddle up, but nobody knew who the newly christened Bladebitch was or what she looked like. Unfortunately she had pissed off precisely the constituency most adept at finding out those things.

LOCAL KNOWLEDGE

Sheena Matheson's call was logged as being connected to the first contact at precisely 02.41, and a request to investigate went out from Dispatch shortly after, graded S for significant priority.

PC Ali Kazmi was the responding officer, on routine vehicle patrol accompanied by PC Ruben Rodriguez. It had been a quiet shift, a northerly breeze bringing the wind chill factor down to minus ten and keeping the pavements relatively clear. People didn't hang about outside the chippies and kebab shops when it was cold like that, though the serious drinkers always had their liquid insulation to keep them warm. Only heavy rain kept those buggers off the streets.

It had been an opportunity to break the new guy in gently, give him the guided tour. She had found him standing at the back door, glancing back and forth between the building and the car pool like he had lost his mummy. However, his problem was that it wasn't a woman he was looking for.

She had watched him for a few moments, waiting until she was sure he was starting to feel the cold before she pulled up and slid down the patrol car's passenger-side window.

'You're PC Rodriguez, aren't you? Can I help at all?'

'Yeah. I'm supposed to be going out with PC Ali Kazmi,' he replied. His accent was English: Home Counties generic. 'Have you seen him?'

'Every time I look in the mirror.'

Ali watched his eyes close in brief self-reproach. Some of them acted like it was her fault she hadn't met their assumptions. She decided he looked just about contrite enough.

'Sorry,' he said, climbing in.

'It's short for Alison. But round here, when most folk hear it they think Ally as in Alistair.'

'No, I'd seen it written down. I was forgetting that there's no WPC up here. And in conjunction with your surname, I assumed . . . never mind. I'll quit digging.'

Ali pulled away and commenced her first circuit of the one-way system.

'Are you partly Spanish?'

'My dad is. I was brought up in Wimbledon.'

'You've transferred *here* from the Met?'

She couldn't keep a note of amusement from her voice. It was a career move so unusual as to seem absurd.

'Well, after two of my colleagues were gunned down right in front of me, the PTSD counsellor suggested a change of scene as an alternative to giving up the job completely.'

Ali felt her stomach heave.

'Oh God, I'm really sorry. I didn't mean to . . .'

Then she noticed he was grinning.

'You're a fucking liar.'

'You got to have your fun, I'm giving some back.'

'Fair do's. So what did bring you here?'

'Something only marginally less traumatic. Bad break-up.'

'It must have been. Met to Highland. Though if you've come here thinking it's like *Hamish Macbeth* . . .'

'Your gender aside, I've not made any assumptions. I'm in your hands.'

She stole a look while they were stopped at lights and his attention was fixed on the entrance to the railway station on Academy Street. His father had been generous with his genes: hazel eyes, thick black hair and olive skin. Stick a conquistador's helmet on him and he could have stepped out of a painting.

The brief moment it took to assess that – on a physical level, anyway – she fancied him was also enough to bring her mind back around to the thing she had managed not to think about for half an hour. Maybe he only looked so good to her because she was contemplating a possibility that would rule out dating altogether for the foreseeable future.

Ach, don't be hysterical, she told herself. There were always options. Difficult options, certainly; adult options: a decision that would be difficult to live with, but not as difficult to live with as the alternative.

It was twenty past midnight when Dispatch relayed that there had been reports of a drunk causing a disturbance on Union Street.

'Dispatch, this is Romeo Victor Four. We are one minute away. Will deal.'

'Romeo Victor Four from Dispatch, is that yourself, Ali?'

'Roger, Cathy. Go ahead.'

She gave Rodriguez a knowing look, imagining how this exchange must sound to someone used to the legions of call-handlers at Central Communications Command.

'Aye, well, seeing it's you, it's worth mentioning that, by the sound of it, we're talking Red Dougal here.'

'Understood. Thanks, Cathy.'

Ali swung the car across Academy Street to execute a U-turn, though it turned into a three-point turn instead due to cars parked on the other side. Not that it was a blue-light job.

'Red Dougal,' said Rodriguez. 'Is that a local code?'

'No, it's a local nutter. Mostly harmless. Just need to handle him right, so let me take the lead.'

'You got it.'

Ali drove slowly along Union Street and brought the car to a stop roughly ten yards from where a grizzled old man with a beard like an upturned Afro was sitting on top of a bin, kicking his heels against it. As they climbed out, they could hear that he was singing to himself, thumping his heels in time to the song, though there was an aggression to his cadence. This could go either way. Ali knew him of old; knew him when most of the beard was still ginger, in fact, rather than grey.

They approached slowly. Rodriguez was tensed up, readying his reflexes. She patted him gently and held out her palm, signalling that he should stay behind her.

'What are you singing, Dougal?'

He swung his head around to focus on her, like his eyes couldn't swivel independently.

'Ali,' he slurred. 'Bonny wee Ali. Will I sing for you?'

'Not tonight, Dougal, it's late. Folk are in their beds.'

'Are they?'

Dougal asked this like it was an astonishing revelation and, in his mind, two minutes ago it had been four in the afternoon.

'It's after twelve. *You* should be in your bed. Will we give you a lift home?'

She didn't wait for a response, but put an arm out and helped him slide off the top of the bin.

Rodriguez looked at her like she was crazy, then seemed to work out what was going on. Wrongly, she'd wager.

They helped Dougal into the back, but gave up trying to put a seatbelt on him after a couple of futile attempts.

'You're not going to spew in my car, are you, Dougal? Because that would upset me.'

He shook his head by way of a response, in a manner that left her in doubt as to how much he had understood or even heard the question.

'Drunk tank?' Rodriguez asked quietly.

'As good as.'

Rodriguez looked askance as they took a left at a roundabout. He hadn't been here long, but had evidently established his bearings enough to know that both the nearest station and the regional HQ were to the right.

Dougal began singing again in the back seat.

'Ali, ali, ali bally be, sitting on your mammy's knee, asking for a wee bawbee . . .'

It was hellish, but he was in a world of his own, and they could talk.

'Are we actually driving him home?' Rodriguez asked incredulously. 'Why? I wouldn't even have lifted him. He was a bit pissed, that's all.'

'Local knowledge. The nightclub fifty yards away will be chucking out in half an hour. When he's drunk Dougal sings for them on the High Street. Sometimes he's after money or just attention. Sometimes he's got a wee jag of aggression in him and he's after something else. All it takes is some young guy who's feeling a bit aggro and you've got a mess. Especially if the young guy has mates.'

'So you take him out of the equation and all is calm.'

'On a quiet night like this, why not?'

'We're a long way from Kansas, Toto.'

They drove a couple of miles out of town and dropped Dougal in front of a cottage so ramshackle it looked in imminent danger of collapse. He made an epic journey of reaching his door, but eventually he disappeared inside and a light glowed in the front window, their cue to drive on.

'Now you really are thinking you're in *Hamish Macbeth*.'

'I'm thinking I can't believe that place has electricity.'

'Angus Gourlay, one of the duty sergeants, has known Dougal for ever. Worked alongside him in the rig fabrication yards up at Nigg Bay. Back in the seventies Dougal lived in a decommissioned army pillbox on the Cromarty Firth. He's a rugged old soul: that's why you don't want him getting into any fights.'

'Got you.'

'Angus said that one time he turned up with a seal pelt he was wearing like a scarf. He had killed it for food.'

'Jesus.'

'Angus asked him what it was like, and Dougal told him: "It tastes a bit like badger."'

'All right, now you are making stuff up.'

She wasn't, but it amused her to let him think so.

Around two they were both hungry, so Ali swung by a twenty-four-hour petrol station where the coffee was passable and the microwaved steak-bakes hadn't poisoned her yet.

Rodriguez stayed in the car to monitor the radio while she went inside for the food. He was a veggie, he advised, calling out as an afterthought as she approached the sliding doors.

They were out of cheese pasties and vegetarian samosas, so she went to the fridges to grab him a sandwich. It was on the way there that she passed the toiletries section, stopping to take in the pregnancy test kits, almost mockingly positioned next to the tampons.

It might have made her laugh before, to wonder why the hell were they stocking home pregnancy kits in a twenty-four-hour garage. How could it possibly be something that couldn't wait until the shops had opened in the morning?

Because not knowing was something you never wanted to prolong if you didn't need to, she understood now. Knowing was better than not knowing: as long as the answer was the one you wanted, and not the one you were afraid of.

She wasn't at that stage yet, though. She was only a few days late, for God's sake.

She was brushing pastry flakes off her lap and out of the open door of the car when the call went out from Dispatch.

'To confirm,' she replied, 'it's a significant priority but not an emergency?'

'Caller couldn't say for definite what she saw. It was in her rear-view and she had been shaken up. The car might have left the road but from the sounds of it, it might just have disappeared from sight around the next bend.'

'Isn't this one for Traffic?'

'Nobody available. Fat-acc on the A9 north of Carrbridge an hour ago.'

'Roger. We'll check it out. Uidh Dubh, did she say?'

'That's affirmative.'

A WOMAN SCORNED

The woman on the witness stand now was a senior manager at Alderbrook Hospital in north London. She was confident and clearly spoken, coldly neutral in her account of her trust's most controversial former employee. Her relaxed manner was a marked contrast to the preceding testimony of Calum Weatherson, but Parlabane knew it was always a different story when you had a dog in the fight.

She gave a detailed account of what had happened as a result of the 'Sexism in Surgery' blog being hacked, though the relevance of it all was something the jury were going to have to take on faith at this stage. Parlabane remembered it well, one of those social media mini-storms that seemed so important to everyone following it at the time, but of which the outside world was blithely oblivious.

The first thing the hackers did was leak Diana Jager's name and place of work. Within seconds of these details going public, anyone who googled her was able to discover what she looked like. *That* was when the rape and death threats came flooding in, from what Jager called the 'legions of the angry maggot thrashers: invisible tough guys who wouldn't have the nerve to say boo to me if we were the only two people in a locked room'.

To the first Twitter rape threats, all of which she re-tweeted, she replied with a photograph of a Liston knife, stating: 'You say you'll rape me. I say I'll cut your balls off with this. Let's meet up and see who's bluffing.'

The knife photo was not a stock shot: she had taken it with her phone.

When Sarah showed him these exchanges, Parlabane was aghast. He remembered saying that either Jager didn't realise garnering such a reply would be like a trophy to these bastards, or else she was psychotic. Back then he had meant it as a figure of speech.

She learned the hard way that you don't get into a pissing contest with these people. In the days that followed, the rape and death threats escalated exponentially, but it wasn't only the proliferation that made it far worse. She was fully 'doxed': her home address, landline and mobile numbers were published, then documents and personal photos stored online were posted on file-sharing sites. That was when the police got involved. Anonymous rape threats on Twitter are bad enough, but when you can be sure that they know where you live, it's a whole other thing.

However, it wasn't the threats that proved the most toxic fallout from 'Bladebitch' being unmasked. After Diana Jager was named, there swiftly commenced a retrospective game of join-the-dots, and the picture it revealed was not flattering. With the hospital where she worked widely known, it soon emerged that a male consultant surgeon nicknamed Leatherface worked there too, as did a female consultant surgeon fond of telling colleagues how she had returned to work after the births of her children.

This unleashed a quite colossal shit-storm, as the identities of her disparaged colleagues were revealed and disseminated, with intolerable consequences for their personal and professional reputations. It wasn't only Jager getting hate mail now: Leatherface and Superwoman – named respectively as Terence Horgan and Holly Crichton – were pilloried and humiliated, their lives picked apart in online discussion like specimens on the dissection table.

The ensuing investigation threatened to get more serious still, as questions were asked as to whether patients might also be identifiable now that so much other information was in the public domain. This seemed unlikely, but the true significance of the questions was that they emerged from the Royal College of Surgeons, which had never come out well in the blog, and which presumably hadn't taken kindly to being described as 'institutionally sexist'.

The scalpels were definitely out for her, but Jager stood firm in the teeth of the gale. No evidence emerged that patient confidentiality had been broken, intentionally or by extrapolation. And though she expressed solidarity with her colleagues for the harassment they received, she maintained that she had broken no rules and no laws. She had never named anybody in her blog, other than people who were already in the public domain, and had kept her own identity secret. The naming of Terence Hogan and Holly Crichton she described as collateral damage from an attack on herself.

This was very much in keeping with what Parlabane would later learn about her.

'Diana is never in the wrong,' he was warned. 'She can screw up sometimes, and she can accept responsibility for the consequences, but that's not the same thing. In her mind, Diana is never in the wrong.'

The distinction failed to help her on this occasion. Not having broken specific rules was not the same as being blameless, and there was little sympathy or goodwill on her side as a result of the underhand way in which she had got back at her colleagues.

The charge of gross professional misconduct did not stick, and officially she was not sacked, but only because the terms of her resignation were agreed between her lawyers and those representing the hospital trust. Not only did she lose her consultant post at the prestigious Alderbrook, but the damage to her reputation ensured that no major teaching hospital was likely to employ her again.

One of the conditions of the settlement was that she had to apologise in writing to Horgan and Crichton, which she did, but Parlabane had seen it, and the wording was as careful as it was revealing. She apologised 'for the distress caused them'. She was acknowledging that it was resultant of her actions, but not accepting that it was her doing.

To be fair, the rest of the apology did seem genuinely heartfelt. She did not communicate in lawyerly platitudes, instead writing understandingly and at length about what they must have gone through and how angry they must feel towards her. She seemed acutely conscious of the hurt they had endured, and convincingly remorseful over what they had suffered. But that was something else Parlabane would later be told about her, by someone in this courtroom who had first-hand knowledge.

'Just because you're a psychopath doesn't mean you can't have emotional intelligence,' she had told him. 'And just because you have emotional intelligence doesn't mean you're feeling those emotions. Diana knows how to express the values that put people at ease. She knows how to come across as sympathetic and as empathetic. But what she tells you she's feeling and what she's actually feeling (never mind what she's actually thinking) can be two very different things. It is part of her predator's camouflage.'

One charge she couldn't escape was her dishonesty over the imaginary correspondents to her blog, because that one was heard in the court of public opinion. She had lied about these accounts coming from third parties in order to conceal that these early articles were little more than score-settling. It was a form of what the French call *l'esprit d'escalier*: the things we wish we had said as we descend the stairs after an argument. Rather than argue her case directly, she had hit back in a way that was cowardly and anonymous, and a few observers noted that these were precisely the qualities she subsequently disdained in the trolls who attacked her.

Sly, underhand, scheming and ruthless – that was her MO. If you had made an enemy of her, you didn't know you were under threat until it was too late.

Parlabane glanced across the courtroom to where she sat, her face impassive but oh so much going on behind those piercing blue eyes. He knew from experience that if you were going to go up against this woman, you'd better make sure you didn't leave her standing. She didn't forgive and she didn't forget.

A few weeks after leaving Alderbrook, she quietly slipped back into employment, finding a new start in Inverness, far from the glare and glamour of the bright lights and the big city. Despite the baggage she brought, she was too valuable a prospect for them to pass up, like a provincial football team happy to take on a flawed talent who had fallen from grace at one of the major clubs.

Parlabane didn't doubt she was grateful for the new chance, and she fairly knuckled down when she got there, but nor was there any doubt that she still had a substantial conceit of herself. A couple of years later she gave an interview to a less contentious medical blog, in which she conveyed enduring bitterness about the position she had lost and the circumstances in which she had been forced to give it up.

She had been the principal victim of a crime, she still insisted, and none of the subsequent wider damage would have happened had her computer security not been illegally compromised. She still blamed IT personnel at Alderbrook for the breach, and after the monstering she received as a consequence, it was clear she was harbouring precisely no conciliatory thoughts towards hospital IT personnel in general.

This was why it came as a very big surprise to many people that she ended up marrying a hospital IT tech. And perhaps less of a surprise that six months later he was dead.

A TIME TO CRY

Peter proposed marriage within a few hours of meeting me. He wasn't serious, but given how things transpired between us, it's worth dwelling upon for a moment; though I'll let you infer your own significance.

'I'm in the right place?' he enquired skittishly, remaining in the doorway. 'You are Dr Jager? And you put in a request for IT support?'

'Yes,' I confirmed. 'I'm locked out of the system. Have been since this morning.'

'Okay. Sorry about that. I'll see what I can do.'

The first thing that struck me about him was the thought that he seemed vulnerable and yet shouldn't. Actually, being completely honest, that was the second thing that struck me, but it was directly related to the first. Maybe it was a reaction to bracing myself for the presence of Creepy Craig, but I remember finding him attractive, a rust-stuck part of my psyche still responding at a primal level to the sight of something that pleased me, if only on a superficial level.

He looked early thirties but possibly younger; my judgement on these things was not the best. I had recently got into the consoling habit of trying to convince myself that people were actually older than they appeared. It was my desperate way of making myself believe forty was still young.

Certainly he wasn't someone striving to present an air of grown-up gravitas. His hair was down to his neck, thick and black and shiny, falling across his face when he leaned one way or the other. Though he was dressed in regulation suit and tie, I pegged him for the trendy tech geek sub-genus, lesser spotted in these parts, as opposed to the basement-dwelling pasty-skinned goblin I'd been expecting.

And yet, as I say, I got this meek and fragile vibe from him, something setting off my instinctive damage sensors. It was like coming across an item on sale that may look fine on the outside, but at that bargain price you know there has to be something wrong with it.

'Do you mind?' he asked, and sat at my desk. I was the one looking over *his* shoulder.

He didn't ask me to walk through the process, but started running commands, though his expression suggested he didn't like what he saw.

'Where's Craig?' I asked.

I was concerned that if this guy couldn't fix it, he'd have to call in the boss and I thus wouldn't be spared an encounter with him after all. Yet at the same time, if that's what it took, I wanted it done, and quickly. I needed this sorted, otherwise I'd be back to square one first thing on a Monday morning, because nothing would get fixed over the weekend.

Mainly I wanted to go home. I was feeling so exhausted and emotionally strung out that I had reached the stage where I suspected I would cry if someone said the wrong thing to me. Losing it in front of Craig because he told me my computer access couldn't be restored until next week would be the final humiliation. And what was making me doubly anxious was that 'the wrong thing' might not necessarily be something negative. I feared if someone was solicitous towards me, it might actually be worse.

'Craig? Is that who you normally get? He'll have gone by now. I was the one who drew the short straw.'

Something occurred to him and he looked faintly concerned.

'I don't mean as in dealing with you specifically,' he clarified. 'I just mean it was last thing Friday and everybody wanted to leave.'

He reprised the uncomfortable look, perhaps realising he was only digging himself deeper by implying that there was a reason why I might think this the case.

'Quite,' I said. My tone would have been more acidic had I not been clinging on by my fingernails and trying to neutralise my emotional responses lest the dam burst. 'Why ever would I think otherwise.'

I guess my tone wasn't quite as neutral as I was pitching, because he picked up on it right away. He looked anxious but good-humoured, as though trying to be tolerant of the fact that there was something going on that he couldn't possibly understand.

'Look, I don't want to put my foot in anything here, but they were a bit coy back at the IT hub when I told them the job. Is there something I should know? Have you had a run-in with hospital IT before?'

There was a brightness in his eyes that I couldn't read: either it was innocence openly appealing for a fair shake or it was malice disguised as the first. I was instantly reminded of walking back from one of the few football matches I ever attended with my brothers, the pair of them draped disconsolately in their blue-and-white scarves. A man stopped us to ask the score, and somehow I sensed he already knew, but wanted these young boys to tell him how their team had lost. He had a nasty little smirk as he said: 'Oh dear. Too bad.'

'Are you trying to be funny?' I asked.

He took his hands off the keyboard in a supplicatory gesture.

'I'll interpret that as a yes,' he replied. 'I take it we didn't cover ourselves in glory.'

'You're saying you don't know?'

His hands rose higher, now more like a surrender.

'Don't know, happy to remain in the dark, happy to hear your version of it if you feel the need to vent. The latter might slow down my diagnostic efforts here, but it's your dime.'

I stared at him, still trying to read whether he was bluffing. I decided that if he was, he was very good.

'Does the name Bladebitch mean anything to you?' I asked.

He shook his head apologetically.

'No. Sounds like something out of an MMO.'

'What's an MMO?' I asked, momentarily derailed by his guile-less sincerity.

'Short for MMORPG: Massively Multiplayer Online Role-Playing Game. Like Warcraft, Sacred Reign, that kind of thing. Do you play?'

'Do I look like I play?'

'I honestly couldn't say. Maybe if I saw you in civvies, though even then it's not good form to judge on appearances. So who is Bladebitch?'

'It really doesn't matter. I'd rather not distract you from the task in hand. It's been a very long day and this is the one thing preventing it from being over.'

'I hear you,' he said, his fingers tapping away as he brought down menus and opened windows I had never seen on my system before. 'This job is the last thing keeping me on tie-time.'

'Tie-time?'

'The dress code. They insist. Yeah, I was drawn to computers because I'm naturally comfortable looking like an office drone. I mean, are they afraid of what IT guys would look like if we were left to dress ourselves? Actually, come to think of it, the dress code kinda makes sense now.'

I didn't laugh politely, didn't smile, but I was at least aware of suppressing the latter, though I wasn't entirely sure why.

Despite my reputation, I wasn't immune to male charm, but I certainly could be resistant to it, especially from an experienced practitioner. When I got the impression someone expected women to find him charming, it was shields up. Peter baffled my defences. On a certain physical level he looked like he ought to be boyishly cocky, and that was what initially triggered my resistance. He was not cocky, however, nor even particularly confident, but there was something affected in his manner; just not affected in the way I was on-guard against. Instead his friendly chat seemed like someone putting on a persona in order to overcome shyness. The friendliness was genuine: it was the ability to express it that seemed an effort.

I felt bad about being barely civil to him. After all that had happened that day, it was almost like I needed to be nice to someone even more than I needed to rip someone's head off. I don't know, maybe it was simply because a pathetic part of me needed someone to be nice back. Either way, I tried to be warmer.

'Did you start here recently?' I asked. His accent didn't sound local. I guessed Edinburgh, but I wasn't good at judging. Middle-class Scottish was as much as I could confidently narrow it down.

'Depends on how you define recently. I've been here about three months. I work for Cobalt Solutions, which the hospital trust now outsources its IT to. I got rotated here for the transition.'

'So what's happening to Craig and his team?'

I tried not to betray excitement at the possibility of him no longer being here.

'Their jobs get transferred over to Cobalt, or they can take redundancy. I think Craig is opting for transfer.'

I'll bet, I thought, unable to imagine him getting hired anywhere else.

'So are you into, you know, MORs?' I asked. I felt like a middle-aged auntie trying to strike up conversation with her teenage nephew.

'No. I've dabbled, but there's so much commitment required to reach a level where you're any good. I struggle enough with that in real life.'

'I know what you mean.'

I had often considered how concentrating so much time and energy into one aspect of my life came at a cost to everything else, and I don't only mean family or relationships. I once blogged about it, in fact: how I had failed to take up any hobbies other than a bit of running to stay fit. Part of the problem, I wrote, is the surgeon's mindset, which is hyper competitive. We don't dabble: unless we think we can be brilliant at something, there seems no point in even beginning. And though I am utterly single-minded once I have decided to pursue something, time is always going to be the big stumbling block. They say that in order to master something – a language, a sport, a musical instrument – it takes ten thousand hours. Subtract work, sleep and the basics of subsistence and it might take me decades to accumulate that quantity of free time. I'm not sure I could commit so expressly to one pursuit. I already did that once in life and I was starting to wonder whether it was a mistake.

'I realise how boring this sounds,' I acknowledged, 'but I couldn't imagine pouring in hours and effort to obtain skills that I couldn't utilise in the real world.'

'Yeah, but all your effort has given you amazing skills *in* the real world. I mean, why would you want to hack and slash online when you can hack and slash for real?'

'It's not as exciting as you make it sound. In fact, if it's exciting, that's usually a bad sign.'

'Not exciting, but still pretty amazing. I mean, what other job lets you cut people open without serious jail-time?'

'I must confess I've never looked at it that way,' I said, trying not to sound withering.

'No, I don't suppose you would. But you must still occasionally catch a glimpse of yourself from the outside and secretly think: I am awesome.'

I had been doing well up until then. The conversation seemed sufficiently lightweight and pointless to serve as a distraction from what had previously been building up, but then he went and said that and something inside me gave.

As I had feared, it was him being solicitous that was my downfall, and the fact that he wasn't even trying to *be* solicitous was what slipped through my barricades. I did frequently catch a glimpse of myself from the outside, and it had been a long time since I liked what I saw. The thought of this pleasant and gentle-spirited young man seeing something better, something impressive, suddenly overwhelmed me.

There was nothing I could do to stop the tears from falling. I didn't let out a sob, but my eyes filled and overflowed with irresistible rapidity. His focus was back on the screen, but he noticed before I could reach for a tissue. Besides, there was no way of covering it up.

'Is everything okay? I mean, obviously it's not, but . . .'

'Yes,' I said, waving a hand dismissively as I dabbed at my cheeks with the other.

I hate people seeing me cry, especially at work. I know I shouldn't, and I've written about how we ought not to be masking female traits because they might be perceived as weakness, but as we're a long way from winning that particular culture war, it always feels embarrassing.

It could have been a lot worse, I suppose. It could have been in front of Creepy Craig, or a male member of my department.

'I'm sorry,' I said. 'I'm not feeling at my most awesome right now.'

'And you're desperate to get home. Got it. I'll be out of your hair fast as I can.'

'Thank you.'

He worked swiftly and quietly, his fingers rattling the keys, boxes and panels opening and closing too fast for me to follow. After a few minutes he called up a log-in screen and asked me to type in my username and password.

It still came up as unrecognised.

'Damn. I'm really sorry. Look, just let me try one last thing, and if that doesn't work, I don't know: might have to wave a dead chicken at it.'

'What?'

'Nothing. Geek-speak for desperation. Don't worry, I think I know what the problem is now.'

He worked the keyboard again, then sighed and sat back as code began scrolling in a window on the left-hand side.

'Just recompiling something, and if all goes well, we'll both be able to draw a line under the week. Unless you're on-call tomorrow,' he added hurriedly, perhaps suspecting another way he might have put his foot in it.

'No,' I assured him. 'So I'm not thinking beyond going home and seeing what Friday night has to offer. More crying, I'm guessing, followed by dinner for one and falling asleep in front of the telly before Graham Norton has even flipped anybody out of the red chair. Not very awesome. Sad, in fact. Have you got plans?' I added. Not that I was interested in hearing about someone else's better life, but I wanted to be polite and more pressingly I needed to get off the fragile subject of myself in case I blubbed again.

'Yeah. I think I can actually trump you in the sad and pitiful stakes. I'm heading home to do more work on a pipe-dream project that's never going to take off, then I'll have a quick freshen up before heading out to see Blink-183 at the Ironworks.'

I'm not known for my encyclopaedic knowledge of popular culture, but I was pretty sure this didn't sound right.

'Isn't it Blink-182?' I asked, hoping I hadn't got this wrong and was about to look even more ancient and pitiful than I did already.

'Not at the Ironworks,' he replied. 'That's why I win the sad. I'm spending my Friday night going to see a Blink-182 tribute band. Alone as well. I was meant to be going with a mate, but he's got man flu. I was internally debating whether it was sadder to be going solo to a gig or to stay in alone instead. Deciding factor is I've already spent money on the tickets. Anyway, I'm wittering. Should be done here any second.'

He closed the window that had been scrolling code then opened up the log-in box again, gesturing me towards the keyboard with a hint of a flourish.

This time it let me in.

'You can go home and cry now,' he said, getting up.

'Thank you. Enjoy Blink-182. Three,' I corrected.

I watched him walk out, closing the door softly behind himself.

I sighed, feeling the last of the energy drain from my body now that I could finally afford to stand down. A line had been drawn under the week, as Peter had put it, and under this day in particular: this day of trials that had started more than twelve hours ago, kicking off with a squat lobster prompting a revelation about what a sad, lonely mess I was.

And now I could go home and cry.

Awesome.

Awesome Diana with her amazing skills. Who wouldn't want to be me?

I was reaching for my jacket when there was another brief knock at the door, then it opened to reveal Peter standing there again. He looked even less sure of himself than the first time. I wondered what he'd forgotten, and hoped to God he didn't need to do more work on my computer.

'Look,' he said. 'I was just thinking, and I hope this doesn't seem inappropriate – especially not "harassment complaint" inappropriate – because it's not a pick-up, but I was wondering if you wanted to trade one sad for another. See, I've got a spare ticket for a dodgy Blink-182 tribute band, and after the day you look like you've had, maybe what you need is three guys from Ullapool putting on unconvincing American accents and singing about getting blowjobs from your mom, and I can't believe I just said "blowjobs from your mom". That probably sealed the harassment thing. But, you know, the offer's there.'

Something inside me lit up, and I was aware of feeling it before all of my rational thought processes could bustle in like disapproving relatives.

It was flattering, even though I knew I wasn't being asked on a date: merely the prospect of being out in the company of someone young, bright, attractive and *male* instantly picked me off the floor. For a moment I caught a glimpse of a different self I might be, and I needed to see myself differently right then. I don't mean I was deluding myself about how he might see me, because for all I knew he only saw some tragic older woman who he was trying to cheer up. I simply needed something to change, and I saw a new possibility for how this miserable Friday might end.

'Okay,' I said.

He looked a little surprised, and perhaps I was imagining it, but there was a flash of something in his eyes that suggested he was genuinely pleased.

TERRA INCOGNITA

Three hours later I was regretting my decision, cursing my emotional fragility as I waited alone on Chapel Street, feeling like there was a neon sign above my head spelling out the words 'Stood Up'.

I had spent much of the intervening time asking myself what the hell I thought I was doing. As I cooked and ate, showered and dressed, those glimpses of myself – out having a good time, laughing in easy company – were narrowing, like a constructed future collapsing under the weight of its own implausibility. It was as though the closer time brought me to the reality, the less I could believe in the dream.

I was only going to make a fool of myself, I chided. In fact, I was making a fool of myself already merely by getting dressed and putting on some make-up.

Then I resolved to get a grip. Going out of a Friday evening was not making a fool of myself. Was this how far I had fallen, that I could only perceive myself within a certain context: that of work, endeavour, seriousness and impending lonely middle age?

Nonetheless, I had to pull back six or seven times from ringing his mobile to cancel.

I distracted myself for a while by catching up with my friend Emily on Facebook. We traded some messages, and she told me how things were going with her job and her husband. They were both lecturers at Durham. I replied with some chat about life in the highlands and at the IRI, but I failed to mention that I was going out with a man tonight. I didn't want to invite curiosity or innuendo. It wasn't a date, I kept reassuring myself. Why?

Going on Facebook therefore failed to take my mind off the evening ahead, and inevitably I ended up googling him. He showed up on Facebook and on the Cobalt company site. There wasn't much to be gleaned other than what he had already told me: he was a gamer and a tech geek.

That was when it struck me that he might be googling me too.

So there I was, standing outside the Ironworks, pulling back from ringing to ask where he had got to. I don't know why: he was late, and it was nothing to call and ask what was keeping him. This felt different, though: like phoning up would seem needy or naggy.

I didn't merely feel conspicuously stood up, though: I felt conspicuously out of place, like everybody could see I didn't belong. As a result, I was ridiculously relieved and reassured whenever I saw someone plausibly my age or older going into the club.

Ten minutes ticked into twelve. Six minutes, in my estimation, is the basic margin of error allowing for a three-minute discrepancy either side of the right time on two people's watches. To that I could add bus, train or traffic delays, falling beneath a minimum that was worth sending a text. Though maybe he had sent a text and my phone hadn't received it. That sometimes happened when I hadn't restarted it in a while. Or maybe he had got my number wrong, transposed two of the digits.

I was actually thinking all this shit.

As the time approached fifteen minutes I began to wonder whether it was an elaborate revenge set-up, and that even now he was live-streaming the image of me standing there to a bunch of fellow hospital IT spods. Then I saw him.

Isn't it amazing how turning up late can transform people? How they become a more welcome sight than you remember, or than had they pitched up when they were supposed to? When finally Peter came into view, hurrying along the street in a light jog, I was so relieved to see him that all of my internal doubts as to the wisdom of being here were instantly dispelled.

He was dressed in black jeans and a T-shirt under a leatherette jacket. Somehow he looked smarter than when he had been wearing a collar and tie; or if not smarter, definitely better dressed. He looked right.

I was in jeans too, but I bet he hadn't gone through several changes in and out of them in preference over various trousers that seemed too starchy, too formal, too work-like or too dressy for what I estimated to be appropriate to the venue and the occasion. I had gone through as many changes of top too, with the issue of what looked good proving only a secondary consideration. The principal areas of internal wrangling were the thornier questions of who I was dressing for, what I was trying to say by my choice and whether I was prepared to admit either to myself.

Peter's T-shirt was dominated by a logo that said Blue Sun, above some Chinese characters. It was a fashion line I didn't recognise or a pop-culture reference I didn't get. Neither category would necessarily indicate great depths of arcana.

'Sorry I'm late,' he said. 'I was coding. Lost track of time. Reached what they call a flow state. Thanks for waiting. I was afraid you'd have bailed on me.'

He handed over the tickets at the door, the bouncer giving me the most cursory glance. Whatever he was trained to be on the lookout for, I wasn't it.

We headed inside. I was anticipating darkness but it was fairly bright, coloured lights playing around the walls and the crew still busy making adjustments on the stage. There was music playing but it wasn't too loud to speak. I recall being unsure whether that was a good thing.

'Can I buy you a drink?' Peter asked.

The place wasn't particularly busy: less than a third of capacity, I estimated. I saw two faces I recognised as we approached the bar: a casualty officer called Charlotte and a theatre nurse named Polly. I saw the confusion in their faces as they took a moment to recognise me, thrown by the context with which they normally associated my presence. I guessed that was Monday morning's gossip sorted, but oddly I didn't mind. I wasn't sure what had thrown them more: that I'd be at a Blink-182 tribute show or that I was out with a man, and a younger man at that.

I had taken the car but on the spur of the moment I decided I would get a cab home and pick it up in the morning. Something told me I was going to need more than a couple of mineral waters to get through this.

I was about to ask for a white wine then thought that was probably a bad idea on a number of levels.

'Just a beer, thanks.'

'Pint?'

That didn't sound very me, but I could see that the staff were pouring bottled beers into plastic glasses anyway, so I decided what the hell. I was trying not to *be* very me that night, wasn't I?

'So what were you coding, that caused you to enter this "flow state"?'

'It's a project I've been working on. Rather technical to explain. It's going okay, but . . .'

He shrugged, a rather wistful smile playing across his face.

'What?'

'Ach, just been over this ground a few too many times. I think I'm getting somewhere and then it, well, I think "peters out" is a particularly appropriate expression. That's why I'm in awe of the application it must take to reach where you are.'

'It helps if you're a boring swot with a one-track mind and a pathological stubbornness.'

'Seriously, don't under-estimate it. It takes passion to have a dream and then do what is necessary to really live it. The follow-through, that's my weakness. A lot of grand vision and enthusiasm at the inception, but my past is littered with the debris of abandoned ideas that turned out not to be as clever or as viable as they seemed. I lack your dedication. Guess that's why I can only get a gig in hospital IT.'

He took a sip of beer as he said this, eyeing me over the rim with a mixture of mischief and curiosity.

The part of me that had recently been afraid of an elaborate revenge prank was suddenly on alert, but I didn't have the sense

60

that there was anything malicious going on. More like a gentle dig to see how I took it.

'So you knew all along,' I said, neutrally.

'No, not at all. I googled you when I got home. Had to: I got the vibe that there was something they weren't telling me.'

'I'm not going to apologise to every IT person I ever meet, and I don't need to justify myself over what I wrote,' I told him, feeling myself stiffen.

'So don't. I'm not going to take the huff over what you said about IT guys any more than I'm going to feel responsible for how other IT guys behaved. I just thought I should let you know I was aware of it, because it wouldn't be right to pretend otherwise.'

'Okay,' I said. 'It had to get out there, I suppose. Curse of the age: I hate the fact that people can find out so much about me instantly, all my baggage only a search string and a mouse click away.'

'Yeah, but it's a blessing of the age too, if you look at it differently. It's not some buried mine waiting to be stepped on further down the line. Instead of you worrying about what I might find out, it's out there right away, so we can both get past it instantly.'

'You think?' I asked, indicating my scepticism. I was trying to make him less at ease, more fearful that he had offended me. I don't know why. It was moot anyway, because it wasn't working.

He held up his plastic glass, inviting mine.

I let out a sigh and couldn't help but smile. I tapped my beer against his and we both took a pull to seal the deal.

'Past it instantly,' I said.

'Although we now have to get married,' he replied.

There it is. Read into it retrospectively what you will.

'Why?'

'Because it would heal the rift between our great houses. No longer would surgeons and hospital IT staff be hostages to the bitter divisions of the past.'

'It would never work,' I told him.

'Why not?'

'You told me you're bad at seeing your ideas through.'

'Then eternal war it must be.'

The lights went down shortly after that and the band took the stage, removing the need for small talk. The place was busier than when I arrived, but still less than half full, and the response from the audience was a long way south of rapturous. I didn't imagine a tribute act elicited much hysteria. I had never seen one before, and I had no idea of the dynamic, of what was motivating the people in here who hadn't come along in a genuinely desperate attempt to defer a mid-life crisis.

The sound was discordantly trebly. At first I wasn't sure whether it was supposed to be like that and I was simply too out-of-touch to dig the aesthetic, but halfway through the second number some-body evidently noticed that a cable was unplugged, and the improvement was considerable. It sounded solid and powerful, though I wondered whether the ropey start had the same boost effect upon my perception as Peter turning up late.

It would be fair to say I didn't consider myself au fait with the Blink oeuvre, and not being familiar with the songs, it was difficult to engage. My mind began to drift, though it couldn't drift that far, thrashing guitars precluding any profound contemplation. I asked myself again what I was doing here, and thought about what a waste of my time it was to be watching a tribute act to a band I had no interest in. I wasn't much for going to gigs anyway, so seeing Blink-182 live was hardly on my bucket list. Watching three guys *pretend* to be Blink-182 surely couldn't be of any cultural value that I could discern, so I didn't envisage any way in which this could enrich me, or what meaning I could take away from it. My inner tutor was acutely aware that this was time I could be spending reading up on the latest journal papers, or watching CME-credited online lectures.

The band began singing about getting a blowjob from your mom. I turned to Peter and he gave me a look: part amused, part bashfully apologetic.

The number lasted less than a minute, before the band segued into a song I actually recognised. It must have been popular when I graduated, because it took me right back to that time.

Then something very unusual happened.

I began to enjoy myself.

BLACK WATER

Ali slowed down after passing through the hamlet of Ordskirk. There was frost on the ground and the bends became sharp along this stretch as the road hugged the meandering course of the river.

Rodriguez peered out of the passenger-side window. The water was barely discernible as a slightly more shimmery blackness than all the other blackness surrounding it. It was fast-moving here, rocks jutting above the surface occasionally picked out by the patrol car's headlights as they approached a bend.

'If a car went off the road and into that, we'd see it,' Rodriguez predicted. 'Doesn't look like it would go in deeper than the wheel-arches.'

'Yes, but that's not where she said it happened. This is the wrong side of the waterfall.'

Ali pulled into a layby beyond the signpost Cathy had mentioned. There was a turn-off nearby, a gravel track leading to picnic benches near a viewing point for the falls. Forest trails led off from here too, marked by colour-coded signposts along the way.

She engaged the runlock system to keep the engine turning for the headlights, though there was scant danger of somebody nicking the car out here.

The wind was whipping along the glen, biting into her cheeks. Above it she could hear the white-noise rumble and hiss of the waterfall. Merely the sound of it made her feel colder.

The night was very dark: cloud cover obscuring the moon and stars. They were going to need all the light they could get. She went to the boot and pulled out a couple of torches, though definitely not a pair.

'Why do I get the tiddly one?' he asked.

'It's not tiddly: it's police issue. The Surefire is my own.'

She played the light across the surface of the road. Frost twinkled on the tarmac, which made it easier to pick out the fresh tyre marks.

'Somebody slammed on the anchors pretty hard here,' she said.

Rodriguez pointed his own beam along the marks and beyond, trying to follow the line of where the car's momentum would have taken it. The tracks seemed to indicate that it careered off on the opposite side to the river, which would have angled it into the side of a hill.

'She definitely said the car was approaching from this end?'

'Yes. But it sounded like it fishtailed, so if the skids curve right at this point, then it would have veered left again further on.'

'Can't find another set of fresh marks,' Rodriguez observed. 'Though there are plenty of older ones.'

'It's an accident blackspot. And a well-named one, at that.'

'Uidh Dubh?' he attempted. 'How's that well-named? I can't even pronounce it.'

'It's Gaelic for black ford. But the English name is a phonetic corruption of the original. You hear that rush of water over there?'

'Yeah.'

'It's known as Widow Falls.'

EASY KILLS

I can reasonably consider myself an expert on many things pertaining to the human condition, but relationships are not among them. Nonetheless, I know enough now, from personal experience, to state that anyone who says 'opposites attract' is talking utter rot. It derives from a misunderstanding not only of the concept of opposition, but of the very nature and purpose of gender. Male and female are not opposites. Their relationship is complementary.

I can see where the confusion comes from. In a relationship – in a marriage – it's the things you have in common that bond you, but nonetheless it's the things you don't have in common that fascinate you about one another. This, I suppose, is what people call chemistry. Maybe they should call it alchemy, because it's a far more mysterious and less logical transformative process than could be governed by any chemical equation. I know this because all of the reasons why our relationship shouldn't have worked became all of the reasons that it did.

Peter turned my head. That's what a disapproving mother or a concerned pal says about a boyfriend when they don't understand why a girl is with him. It was true, though. He changed how I thought, how I looked at the world. And I did the same to him. The way I understood it, we made each other believe differently about ourselves, and that made us believe in *us*.

I spent much of that Saturday thinking about him, or at least consciously trying not to think about him; wrestling over how I could interpret last night, and castigating myself for how desperate and implausible some of those interpretations seemed. I couldn't stop it, though, no matter how I was occupied. It ruined my concentration, like I was some silly teenager with a crush.

Last night I had held back several times from calling him to cancel. That day I had to hold back several times from calling on any number of embarrassingly flimsy pretexts, simply to hear what he might say: what clues I might infer as to what, if anything, was going on between us.

Then, around eight in the evening, *he* called me.

Before I answered, having seen his name appear on the screen, I let out an involuntary sound. I believe it was what my young brother Julian would call a squee.

'I was calling on the off chance that you're free tomorrow. My friend who couldn't make Friday night is still down with man flu, so he's cancelled on me for Sunday as well. I know this makes me sound like a complete Billy No-mates but to be fair I've not long moved here.'

'Before I say whether I'm free, am I allowed to ask what you've got in mind? Or does that kind of give away the fact that I am free?'

'Little bit. All I'll say is that you'll need a decent pair of walking boots and outdoor clothes.'

'You can't tell me more than that?'

'Not can't, won't. If I tell you what it is, you'll say no. But I promise: if you do it you'll enjoy it.'

'Like I've never heard a guy say that before,' I told him, surprising myself.

He spluttered.

'Well, fair enough. I'll be straight up: it does involve some pain, but you'll find that does play a part in the pleasure.'

'Okay, now I'm intrigued so much that I'll have to go along just to find out.'

He picked me up early: seven thirty. I dressed in a couple of layers of Trespass gear, and asked him if I'd need more, indicating the heavy jacket I was carrying. It was minus two according to my phone, though the sky was clear and there was barely a breath of wind. He said the jacket would be too much, so I slung it in the back seat, where it landed on top of a sheet of grey canvas. There was something hidden under it, but I couldn't work out what from the shape. I only hoped it wasn't fishing gear.

We talked about what we'd normally be doing at that time of a Sunday. In my case, I'd be out for a run, or at the gym if it was raining heavily. Peter admitted he'd be asleep.

'I had an early night because I knew I was doing this today, but ordinarily I'd be up late. Sometimes I get caught up in coding, and suddenly it's three a.m.; though I'm as likely to be up till three playing games or watching TV. You know what it's like: you decide you'll watch one episode of something on Netflix before bed and you end up watching five.'

I didn't. I really didn't. There were shows I watched, but it was irresponsible to stay up too late if there were cases in the morning. Weekends weren't much different, in that I couldn't sit up watching TV until the small hours because I didn't want to sleep in and miss half the day. I couldn't imagine reaching Sunday night and realising I had got nothing read or written because I'd wasted hours and hours on meaningless distractions.

I didn't tell him this, of course, but I didn't lie either. Instead I nudged the subject on to what shows we each liked, and was pleasantly surprised by some of his favourites. I thought it would be all guy stuff, but he shared my enthusiasm for *Orange is the New Black* and *Borgen*. Obviously he was into a whole lot of guy stuff as well, but there were layers to him, evidently.

We had been driving for about half an hour, heading into the wilds, when I asked him to tell me where he was taking me.

'All will be revealed. You've come this far. Best find out for yourself.'

'Okay, I think I will,' I replied, and reached into the back, tugging at the grey canvas.

'No, don't,' Peter commanded, but it was too late.

It snagged on something, but enough came away to reveal the stock and bipod of a huge and very sophisticated-looking rifle. It didn't look like anything you could legally own. I was sure I spied a machine gun too: a compact automatic with a curved magazine.

I literally gasped, thinking: Oh my God, I'm the clichéd idiot victim of a serial killer. I went along despite him refusing to tell me where we were going, even as we headed into the middle of nowhere.

Peter stopped the car then and there and put the handbrake on so that he could lean back and replace the canvas.

'Need to keep that concealed. Don't want somebody seeing it and getting the wrong idea. Last thing we want is the police sending out an armed response unit.'

'So what is the right idea? What is this stuff? Are we hunting?'

'Kind of. Hunting humans.'

Two hours later, I was face-down in an undulation between two rows of regularly planted pine trees, my body flat to the ground to stay hidden. I was trying not to breathe too loudly but I was panting from the last sprint to temporary safety, my heart thumping from the adrenaline and exertion. Peter was lying a few feet from me, his rifle held along his body out of sight, not daring to raise it right then for fear of giving away our location to the six or seven enemies who were closing in from unseen positions on all sides.

I was a grown woman playing at soldiers: running through the woods firing toy guns, or airsoft weapons as they were known. They were perfect replicas that shot plastic pellets, albeit at three hundred feet per second.

'How are you for ammo?' he asked.

I ejected the magazine from the mp5k slowly, giving it a gentle shake. We could both hear the rattle of only a handful of pellets within. Somewhere to my left I heard the whir of a motor and the rattle of a volley against a tree trunk. It was speculative fire. These guys sprayed off rounds like popcorn, but I was almost out.

Though sweat was running into my eyes, I couldn't take my mask off. The safety protocol would require me or Peter to call out 'mask off, mask off' in order to suspend fire, but that would give away where we were. That would be game over, and I really wanted to win.

Peter was right. I wouldn't have gone if he'd told me it was an airsoft site. I could think of few activities that were less me, but now that I was here, I was losing myself in it. I had initially been concerned that having too few layers would leave me cold, as well as it being more painful when I got hit. After about forty minutes I was so warm I was pondering the trade-off between increasing the pain and streamlining down to a single layer. I reckoned also that the greater threat from the former would make me concentrate more keenly, take fewer risks and think more carefully about my tactics.

Peter counselled against it, warning that at three hundred feet per second, the pellets could leave red marks if there was no thick or baggy material to slow them down. I didn't like the sound of that, and a further deciding factor was that my Under Armour was a very non-camouflage white.

'How you bearing up?' he had asked, as we made our way back to base after the second game ended.

'I'm getting flashbacks to my first tour in 'Nam. It was hell, man.'

'I mean, are you handling the pace? Do you need a break?'

'Not at all. Though I'm getting more exercise than my usual Sunday-morning regime. Lugging all this metal around fairly works the cardio-vascular system. I usually feel I could keep going for longer when I run, but I tend to get a bit bored.'

'This gives a bit of structure and purpose to it, I suppose. Do you not listen to some music when you run?'

'No. I tend to listen to recordings of lectures and seminars, or audio versions of textbooks.'

'Jeez. Do you not want to give your head a rest, let your mind breathe for a while?'

I had blogged about this once, years ago. I felt quite embarrassed recently when I happened upon it again. At the time I sounded as smug about this multitasking as I did evangelical. These days I was conscious of what a zoid I had become. Even my exercise, a supposedly recreational pursuit, had been augmented in a way that would count towards my work.

'Maybe I should. And maybe I should do more fun-for-its-own-sake stuff like this instead, before it's too late.'

'Too late for what?' he had asked, passing me a welcome bottle of water as we came in sight of the muster point where the other players were gathering.

'Too late for me to be saved from being a boring stick-in-the-mud who nobody wants to be around.'

That was my growing fear. You're forced to give up so much to the job that it makes you unattractive: in non-physical ways, though your appearance can certainly suffer too. It becomes a vicious circle. The job is all you can talk about, all you can think about because there is nobody else at home to change the subject, to occupy your time and your thoughts. Then you reason that as it's the only thing in your life, you might as well dedicate *more* time to it, to be as good at it as you can. Gradually you become a machine, and you can lose your humanity. You begin to lose contact with what it is to be a normal person, living a normal day-to-day life, and once that process is in motion, the prognosis is bleak.

'Well, you're not there yet, or I wouldn't have invited you,' Peter assured me.

'You're only saying that because I've got a machine gun.'

'Mine's bigger than yours. And it's all about balance, isn't it? I think I could use a bit more of what you've got. It's been said – not always with the greatest discretion, hence my awareness of it – that I'm a case of wasted potential. Acting the kid too much. If you want to get ahead, you have to get serious, don't you?'

'Well, don't stop acting the kid quite yet,' I told him, reloading my magazine with hundreds of the tiny white plastic balls. 'I'm just getting the hang of this.'

Which was why, sometime later, I was prepared to tolerate the sting of sweat in my eyes and the digging of tree roots into my ribs in order to remain concealed, even when down to my last few rounds.

Peter raised himself up on to his elbows, scanning the trees. I pulled myself into a tight crouch alongside. The woods were so dense that it was dark as dusk, visibility down to single figures and not helped by peering through the aluminium mesh covering the mask's eyeholes.

71

Suddenly there was movement somewhere ahead, a volley of shots. They weren't aimed at us: merely where someone thought we were. Nonetheless, we reacted instantly, rolling back into the trench. I ended up on top of Peter, only for a moment. Our faces were centimetres apart. We had masks on, and couldn't see into each other's eyes, but I think we both noticed I stayed there a fraction longer than natural momentum dictated.

It was a last-man-standing game, and from the complete absence of friendly armbands we had spotted over the past fifteen minutes, it looked like we were all that remained of the red team.

'I think we're done,' he confessed. 'We should surrender, and they can kick off the next game.'

'Sod that. I'm not losing again.'

'Don't worry about it. You're doing great. And remember, Serious Girl, it's just for fun.'

He obviously hadn't met many surgeons.

'Winning is fun.'

'Okay, so how do you plan on doing that?'

'Knife. Give me it.'

Peter reached down to his belt and handed over a foam-plastic dagger.

It had been explained at the start that if you could successfully 'stealth' an opponent and tap them on the shoulder with one of those, they were out, and unlike when they were shot, they could not yell out 'Hit!', as it would give away your position.

'You've got the big gun. Draw their attention. I'll do the rest.'

I grew up with two brothers who would have loved to exclude me from their games, and doubtless would have succeeded had I been younger and smaller, but I wasn't. I became adept at sneaking up on them; at sneaking up on anybody. I learned balance, how weight distribution affected footfalls and other sounds, and in particular I learned to be very slow and very patient.

In this game for bigger boys, I only had to be particularly stealthy once: when I was sneaking back through their slowly closing circle. Then I was behind them as they closed in on where they thought Peter was holed up, their attention concentrated exclusively upon

72

any sound or movement that might give away his position or herald a shot from his rifle.

I tapped them on the shoulder and said: 'Shh.' One by one they fell as I moved in my silent spiral, until only Peter remained. And then I snuck up and tapped him.

He sighed in defeat, then turned around and saw that it was me.

Somewhere in the woods, a guy with a megaphone was announcing that the red team had won.

'You're absolutely lethal,' Peter said. 'Nobody saw you coming.'

'Nobody ever does.'

WASTED

They walked slowly along the side closer to the river, scanning for indications that a car had gone over the edge and down the slope. The water ran twenty feet or so below the level of the road at this stretch, at the foot of a steep banking.

'No crash barrier,' Rodriguez noted. 'Is that not a bit remiss if it's a known blackspot?'

'The previous casualties haven't been people going off the road. It's eejits smacking head-on into oncoming vehicles because they've misjudged the bend, or more commonly round here, they're trying to overtake in a completely inappropriate place. Wait till you've been here a while, you'll see: some of them act as though they've got radar.'

Rodriguez kept crouching low to the ground, running one hand along the top of the grass, the other training his torch a few feet in front of him. Ali was pointing hers down towards the water. The beam picked out tufts and bushes before the flat blackness. It didn't shimmer so much here: it was slow and deep.

'Got tread marks, I think,' Rodriguez announced. 'The grass is flattened here.'

Ali pointed her torch where he was indicating, and then a few feet along. There was a second indentation, around six inches wide.

'Looks parallel,' she said.

They proceeded cautiously, picking out every step with care under the beams of both their flashlights. The indentations were sporadic, vanishing and then resuming again, sometimes visible on one side, sometimes the other, but always the same distance apart.

Ali stopped Rodriguez a few yards from the edge. They played their torches down the rest of the slope, picking out where their progress ended.

'Shit. I'm going to be popular.'

'Why?'

'Because we'll need to scramble a helicopter to search along the river, and we'll need to call out a diving team as well. There's no choice, but I'm about to put a big hole in the budget for nothing. It's what, quarter past three now? That call went out at about two forty-five. Anybody who went into that freezing water half an hour ago and didn't come straight back out is already dead.'

KISS WITH A SPELL

You never forget the first time you kiss somebody. A tender act somehow more intimate than when you first sleep together, because in that moment, you are so utterly vulnerable: it feels as though so much is at stake, like everything can change in one delicate act, one exquisite touch. No matter what happens after that, for good or bad, it is a memory that plays back via all the senses, a point in time you can return yourself to with absolute clarity. It is a precious treasure at the heart of the growing hoard in a relationship that strengthens and endures, and it is the bittersweet remnant you cannot purge from your mind when everything has turned to ashes.

Bittersweet, yes: not merely bitter, because it is the sweetness that burns. It is the feelings of joy and excitement and desire and hope that remain so painfully vivid. If I close my eyes right now I can feel, see, hear, smell and taste everything about that kiss, and I can become again who I was in that moment. I can see the future as it appeared to me then, and remember the two of us as the people I believed us to be.

I wish I could erase all of it, but I can't. I wish I wasn't so easily taken back there by hearing a song on the radio, or catching a scent of curry on damp clothes. But mostly I wish I could delete what I said to him the instant before our lips met, because that is what truly mocks me now.

I felt exhausted but exhilarated as Peter drove us both back to Inverness. In a day replete with me surprising myself, for an encore I realised that I couldn't wait to tell people at work what I'd been doing. In the past I'd have been looking forward to telling colleagues about the seminar or conference I had attended over the weekend, but this prospect was so much more exciting. It was the thought of shocking them, of seeing their perceptions of me given such a shake. I even rather malevolently fantasised about phoning up and telling my father, to appal him. The boys-and-toys factor would have rubbed salt too.

'Thank you so much for today,' I said to him, as we pulled up outside my house. 'And thank you for not telling me. I think I'm starting to remember what fun is.'

'Yeah, if you ever need a dose of enjoyable pointlessness in your life, I'm your man. Honestly, when I have kids, they'll be the ones dragging *me* away from the play-park. That's half the reason I'd want to have them: an excuse to do silly stuff; to just play.'

I caught myself noting that he wanted children. I tried to pretend it was an idle thought, but I was fooling nobody.

'Kids *should* do silly stuff,' he added, looking more reflective. 'I had a little too much seriousness, too much properness in my childhood. That's why my inner kid is a bit too close to the surface: he's finally got the keys, so he's driving half the time. And that's why I'm glad I met you. You say you're boring but I think you're inspiring. You make me want to screw the nut and make more of myself.'

'Thank you.'

I reddened, my fingers gripping the door handle. My instinct was to feel awkward and thus to bail in a heightened moment like this, and then inevitably I'd go away and over-analyse it later. The thing was, right then I didn't feel awkward, and whatever was heightened about this moment, I wanted more of it.

'Actually, and I feel slightly guilty about this, but can I undo my good influence and tempt you not to screw the nut for a few more hours? Pub and a curry? You weren't going to change everything with one evening's programming anyway, were you?'

'That's precisely the internal logic that's kept me from being a millionaire. I like your thinking.'

Despite being the one who had proposed an evening at the pub, I took the car into town. This was for two reasons: one was that

I had a laparoscopic colectomy in the morning and needed to be sharp; but more immediately I wanted my judgement to be as keen the night before. While I was getting showered and changed, I had been struck by an unaccustomed feeling of giddiness, of which I was instinctively wary.

As I took my seat opposite Peter, watching the overspill pool on the dark wood at the bottom of his pint glass, I felt a sense of freedom. Normally on a Sunday evening my mind would be already on the next day's work, yet being in the pub with its sights and smells and the hubbub of chat served to remind me that Sunday evening was still the weekend if I wanted it to be. Emily was often posting on Facebook about going out with colleagues and students, referring to Monday-morning hangovers with what was ostensibly 'old enough to know better' regret, but which I recognised as perverse pride.

I could barely remember the last time I had done this. I used to go out with friends – colleagues – but these days they all had kids or spouses. There didn't seem to be as many girls' nights as there once had been. It was only really at Christmas that the department went out together: big gatherings, trying to show a social side to the trainees. Even then, it tended to be one or two drinks then off to a restaurant where they had a mass booking for about thirty people. To me it seemed to defeat the ends of social- ising to go out in such a huge group, as in practice you only got to talk to the four or five people sat closest to you, and if you were unlucky they were the four or five people you had been hoping to avoid. That said, maybe I was the one that most people didn't want to get stuck with. Certainly the younger trainees seemed rather skittish around me.

But that Sunday night was like the nights out I remembered from when I was younger, when I felt like I was winning. Simply chatting, laughing and enjoying an atmosphere that seemed all the more convivial because of the awful weather that had blown in all of a sudden. There's nothing quite like rain lashing the windows to make you feel snug, and I was feeling particularly cosy that evening. It was starting unmistakably to resemble a date. Apart from there being only the two of us, the conversation was venturing ever deeper into getting-to-know-you territory.

I talked about the whole Bladebitch thing because I wanted my side of it out there, and because, despite our conversation of Friday night, I still felt we had to get past it. He was sympathetic, and by that I don't just mean he agreed with me, or *acted* like he agreed with me in order to keep the atmosphere pleasant. What surprised me was that he had clearly thought about the issues behind the blog, rather than merely the business of my being hacked and exposed. Too many men dismissed the blog as a catalogue of career-specific feminist grievances. Peter understood that it was really about work-life balance.

'I once heard someone say that what you need in order to be happy is something you like to do and someone you like to be with,' he told me. 'The first shouldn't prevent the second: that's all you're saying, isn't it? And the danger is that giving too much to the first makes you forget all the good things about it.'

From there he got me talking about happier times in my career, and I remembered the person I used to be not so long ago, the girl who was taking on the world. For the first time in ages I believed she might be coming back.

It was bucketing down with rain when we came out of the curry house, the crisp clear weather of earlier like a memory of a different day. We made a sprint to my car after I said I'd drive him home. He lived in town, but even at a ten-minute walk he'd be drenched by the time he got home.

He directed me to pull up outside a recently built residential development: twin compact blocks of modern apartments. I had passed them a hundred times and always thought they seemed corporate and soulless, though they looked toasty and dry on a night like this. My own place, by contrast, looked like anyone's idea of a cosy cottage, but it was draughty from so many little nooks that it was a bugger to keep warm.

There was a moment's silence between us after I put the car in neutral and pulled on the handbrake. It was as though we both still had so much to say but were burdensomely aware that time

79

had run out, not only on the evening, but on a very special few days.

It felt like the weekend needed a denouement. A cheerio or a 'see you on Monday' would have seemed so deflatingly banal. I was trying to think of something appropriate to say, but really I didn't want to talk.

Peter spoke quietly, barely audible above the music playing on the car stereo.

'At the risk of blowing it merely by saying this, I want to kiss you. But I'm afraid if I do that, I'll break whatever magic spell is keeping you interested in me. Like the opposite of the princess and the frog: suddenly I'd be changed into someone you want nothing to do with.'

'I don't believe in fairytales,' I told him. 'People don't just transform into something else overnight. So kiss me.'

ACCIDENTS AND AFTERMATHS

'You're a life-saver,' Ali told Rodriguez, instantly regretting her choice of words. He was handing her a polystyrene cup full of steaming hot coffee. It was as welcome as it was thoughtful, but the stark reality was that nobody was saving any lives out here today.

She watched the bubbles appear in sporadic fizzing bursts upon the water's surface. The scuba team had arrived about half an hour back and hit the water by the first light of dawn. When she called it in, she was told they wouldn't be able to get there for at least two hours, so the decision was taken to hold off until morning, as their involvement was never going to be a rescue mission.

Ali had been here all night, spending much of it deafened by the sound of the helicopter as it strafed the riverbanks with its searchlight. Despite the freezing cold, she had actually broken into a sweat from shuttling up and down the slope between the river and the road, clambering over rocks and clumping through vegetation. They were combing the banks either side to see if anyone had crawled from the water and collapsed, or maybe dived from the vehicle before it hit the water.

The search had been joined by as many police bodies as they could spare, which at that time was not a lot. Their numbers were further depleted when Murdo McKay lost his footing near the water's edge and fell in. They got him out in a matter of seconds, but the terror, shock and pain on his face and the deathly blue colour of his lips was a reminder of how futile this search was likely to prove.

They got him out of his wet clothes and wrapped him in a heavy waterproof jacket Ali always stashed in the boot of her patrol car. Some shifts you were barely out of the vehicle, but experience had taught her there was always the possibility you could end up standing outside in the freezing cold for hours on end.

It was when the ground search was declared over and she no longer had the exercise to keep her warm that the sweat started to cool under her uniform and she really felt the need of that coat.

Rodriguez had driven Murdo to the hospital. There were paramedics in attendance but they had to stay at the scene in the decreasingly likely chance that a survivor was found. When he returned, he was carrying two coffees, one of which he handed to Ali.

She hugged it like it was a miniature radiator.

'You look perishing,' he said. 'I thought you natives were used to the cold.'

Natives, he said. He got points for that. He was going by the accent rather than her appearance.

'There's this young polar bear,' she told him. 'Goes up to its mother and asks, Mummy, am I a real polar bear? Mummy replies, Course you are. You've got white fur, you've got claws, you live in the Arctic and you eat fish. Why do you ask? Young polar bear replies, Because I'm fucking freezing.'

Ali didn't have white fur or indeed white skin, but she was a native born if not bred. She couldn't imagine living anywhere else, but she never got used to the cold.

'I'll take that as a warning,' he said. 'And I'll be investing in some thermal undies tout de suite.'

She couldn't help but wonder again what made someone swap a career in London for this. She certainly wouldn't do it the other way around. There was definitely something different about this one, though: some vibe he was giving off that she couldn't quite read.

He said he had shipped out for a completely new start after a bad break-up. That wasn't something guys tended to confide, especially not so soon after meeting you. A male of the species being open about his feelings and crediting her with the vision necessary to respond appropriately? Pinch me, she thought. And wouldn't it be typical if Mr Perfect came into her life right now.

She shouldn't kid herself, though. It was as likely he was the one with the vision to read her as a potential shambles, and he was laying down a marker from the off to explain how he was on the rebound and therefore off limits.

Ali had a dismal track record when it came to reading the signals. Her problem was an over-developed sense of optimism, combined with a bad case of confirmation bias, resulting in a tendency to imagine guys to be a lot nicer and a lot more genuine than the evidence ultimately demonstrated.

Martin had seemed nice. Martin had seemed genuine. Her relationship with Martin, however, was definitely over, even though she might be pregnant by him. In fact it was over *because* she might be pregnant by him. It had been over since sometime around midnight two Saturdays ago, when she realised he had come inside her and that he had said nothing.

The condom had split or rolled off. That wasn't something you failed to notice. And yet he had said nothing: just turned over and fallen asleep, leaving her to lie there horribly awake after she came back from the bathroom, contemplating awful possibilities.

He said *nothing*. Got up the next morning, acting like everything was normal, apart from an unusually pressing need to get out of her flat.

It was amazing how your perception of a person could change in a single crucial moment, with one glimpse of who they really were.

There was a surge of bubbles upon the surface, a black shape emerging from black water. One of the divers was hauling himself up the aluminium ladder they had temporarily anchored to the river bank. He signalled to Ali as he climbed, and she made her way across to where he stood dripping on the frost-dusted grass.

'There's a black BMW down there,' he said, tugging off his mask. 'No occupant. The driver-side door was partially open. I'm thinking when it hit the water he tried to get out before it sank by opening the door, which is actually the worst thing you can do. The water floods in rapid as soon as it's unsealed, and the exterior pressure prevents you from opening it enough to get out. The

83 ·

window was gone, though, so he must have managed to smash it and climb through once the car was submerged.'

'Could you read the plate?'

'Aye, though I can do you better than that. His wallet and his phone were in his jacket. I reckon either he had slung it on the passenger seat while he was driving, or he wrestled it off to give him a better chance of making the surface.'

'And what chance would you give him of doing that?'

The diver grimaced and glanced back towards the river.

'It looks slow because it's deep, but believe me: the current down there is bloody strong. I was kicking flat out against it just to stay in place. Put it this way, it's strong enough to have pulled the car ten yards downstream from where it hit the water before it fully filled up. It jammed against some rocks on the bottom otherwise it would have drifted further.'

'So we'll have to drag for miles?' Ali suggested.

'Aye, but there's nae guarantee that'll turn up a result. If we get lucky, the body might have snagged on something, but it could equally be underneath the Kessock Bridge by now, on its way out into the Moray Firth.'

'Where's the wallet?'

He held up a damp fold of black leather.

'My colleague will be up with the jacket and the phone in a wee minute. Found one of his shoes in there as well. Must have come off as he was trying to get out.'

Ali took it, flipping it open to reveal a driving licence inside a plastic window.

'Hamish Peter Elphinstone,' she said, reading aloud. 'I've heard that name recently. Can't think where.'

'*Elphinstone?*' the diver checked, suddenly gimlet-eyed. Clearly it was familiar to him too.

'That's right. Why does it ring a bell?'

'Maybe because his family owns half of Perthshire.'

BACK TO THE FUTURE

One of the difficulties in listening to any trial unfold was trying to maintain a sense of the chronology. Multiple accounts of various incidents would accumulate further with each new witness, potentially making it very confusing to assemble a consistent timeline. Parlabane had no difficulty recalling precisely when his involvement in this sorry business commenced, having a fairly unmissable landmark with which to orient himself. It was the day he received official notice that his divorce was finalised.

He had opened the door to the postman in a state of bleary-eyed hangover, alleviated by as much anticipation as a man in his forties could feel over the prospect of receiving a mail-order purchase. The postman handed him the envelope then held up a gizmo for his signature. Parlabane scrawled illegibly on the miniature screen and stared at the object in his other hand with curious disappointment. When the postie rang the bell, he had thought it was the new Jimmy Eat World album being delivered. That was about as big an event as he had to look forward to in his life.

Wandering back to his desk, he ripped open the envelope with a ragged slide of his forefinger, thinking of a time when he would not have countenanced such a move for fear of razor blades or hypodermic needles sent in angry revenge for something he had written. He wasn't even annoying anybody these days.

He picked up his mug of black tea from next to his laptop and shuffled towards the windows. He had been surfing in semi-darkness, but figured he should open the blinds in order to see the letter properly. As well as signalling to the world that his flat contained a conscious and functioning inhabitant who was ready for the day, it would be a sight quicker than waiting for the energy-saving bulbs to actually fire some photons. Honestly, some mornings the sun came up quicker.

'Jesus.'

There it was, in black and white, all the more inescapably official for seeming understated. He thought the letterhead for something like this ought to resemble a metal band's logo and the body text look like it was printed in blood on a Caxton press in some ancient dungeon.

Fifteen years of his life, and decades more that he had imagined in his future: this document was the line drawn under the former and through the latter. Truth was, it didn't need anything gothic about it to seem like a headstone.

The death had been slow. It had taken years for his marriage to fall apart, and over that time he had experienced a lot of different feelings about what was happening: regret, anger, helplessness, despair, sorrow. It changed from day to day, hour to hour. Right then, though, the main one was of loss: of a precious thing he once had, and would never have again.

But as he had learned long ago, when life kicks you in the balls, it can always knee you in the face too while you're bent over.

Parlabane looked up from the letter and out of the window, his gaze taking in the newly mown lawns in the centre of Maybury Square before alighting upon the less aesthetically delightful sight of the police station opposite. Aye. That was when he felt the unique emotional splat one experiences when fate decides to burst your nose as a follow-up to having already administered a full-blooded boot in the haw-maws.

He had always known this moment was coming. Admittedly, for a while he had almost convinced himself that he could merely acknowledge how the wheel had brought him back around and that would be that. He'd been here a few days, after all. But this blow had been heading his way from the moment his mate Dunc offered to do him a favour.

He needed somewhere to stay, the short-term lease having run out on the flat he was in. He'd taken it as an interim measure, thinking opportunities might come up that would require him to move elsewhere. Wrong again.

Then Duncan McLean got in touch from New Zealand to say his tenants were moving out, so he had a flat up for grabs. Dunc had lent him it once before, shortly after purchasing the place, when it was halfway through being gutted for renovation. That accounted for the 'wheel coming back around' part. The skelp in the dish part was that this had been the very place where he first met Sarah.

The awareness of this had been lurking in a dusty corner of his mind, waiting to be unpacked like all of the boxes currently stacked out there in the hall. Looking out upon the square had suddenly broken it open, spilling its content of memories across his consciousness and reminding him of a time when the same window had offered a view of a better future.

Strictly speaking, he had first met her in the flat directly beneath, where her ex-husband had lived – and indeed died. Given that things post-Sarah had worked out even worse for Jeremy than they had for Parlabane, perhaps he should nip upstairs and warn whatever poor bastard lived on the top floor to steer clear in case she ended up going for a full house.

Christ, he thought, thinking of the phrase that had always been applied to Jeremy: 'Sarah's ex-husband'. Now that should be *first* ex-husband.

Parlabane sipped at the black tea, realising that the smell and flavour were playing their part in this assault by nostalgia. He'd been making do with black tea then as well. He remembered inviting Sarah into the kitchen and offering her UHT with her coffee. In those days, his excuse was that the flat didn't have a fridge. The place was looking a lot more hospitable now, it was fair to say. There was indeed a fridge; a freezer too; even carpets. So his excuse for drinking black tea this morning was that he hadn't gotten around to hitting the supermarket since moving in, but as his fuzzy head reminded him, he had managed to bring home a six-pack and a bottle of whisky. Priorities, priorities.

That was what happened when you didn't have a wife around

to explain yourself to. Or an office to show up looking respectable at, or a boss to please, or colleagues, or a proper job.

He kept seeing references to himself as a disgraced journalist, a description which was almost a tautology these days, but in his case he had to concede it was more apposite than most. He had once been an investigative reporter who made a name for himself uncovering corporate and institutional malfeasance, notching up a few notable scalps along the way. But then came the Leveson Inquiry, when his professional methods came to light and it emerged that he had employed hacking, burglary, subterfuge and all manner of inventive illegality in order to get stories. What really finished him off, though, was his subsequent desperation to get back to the top of the game.

Even after Leveson, some people may have retained a sneaking admiration for him on the grounds that the ends justified his means: he hadn't been hacking dead schoolgirls' phones or sniffing out tittle-tattle on soap stars, he was going after substantial issues. He knew he was still perceived to have a certain integrity, even if nobody wanted to hire someone so otherwise tainted. But then he made an almighty arse of himself before the whole country, when he became the useful idiot who ran with a hoax story that had been deliberately planted to flush out a leak. Someone in the intelligence services used him like a barium enema in order to expose security compromises within the MoD, and any remaining credibility he might have had evaporated quite literally overnight.

His marriage crashed and burned in parallel with his career, Sarah deciding her own reputation had suffered enough collateral damage from her association with him. Obviously there was a lot more to it than that, but the bottom line was that only a few years ago he had a wife and a career, both of which he loved, and now he had neither.

He sat back down at the laptop with a sigh. This wasn't just his home now, it was his workplace, the boundaries of his world shrinking all the time. He wasn't a journalist any more: he was a 'content generator' for various websites, churning out all manner of vapid filler one step up from lorem ipsum on everything from hotels he'd never visited, to TV shows he'd never watched, to consumer products he'd never laid hands upon.

Everything was virtual and remote. His life was becoming a digitised version of Plato's cave: he was stuck here alone, describing a shadow of a reality that he couldn't touch.

He missed working in a proper newspaper office; missed it more knowing how few journalists still were.

Nah, upon reflection that was bollocks. He had hated being stuck in an office as much as he hated being stuck in a flat. What he truly missed was the man he had been once upon a time, when he first stayed in this flat, when the world before him seemed boundless and when love had been waiting outside in the close.

Just then, the doorbell rang again. He shambled over to open it, and was confronted by a woman clutching a cardboard tray bearing two polystyrene cups. He assumed she had the wrong flat, but then she spoke.

'Jack Parlabane, right?'

'Yes.'

He was unable to keep the surprise from his voice. Her own tone was at once stern and tentative, which made him wonder if he was about to get served.

'Sorry for the intrusion, but I've seen you around, so I knew you lived locally and I wanted to talk to you face-to-face. Someone gave me an address, but it turned out to be your old place. They directed me here. Can I come in?'

'Sure. Who are you?'

'Oh, sorry. My name is Lucille Elphinstone. People call me Lucy.'

He placed her around mid-thirties, maybe older. She was dressed in a rather sweeping black coat, opened to reveal a black blouse buttoned up to a frilly collar. It seemed at once prim and somehow fetishistic, though maybe the latter was in the eye of the beholder. He hadn't been laid in a very long time.

Her black hair was swept back behind an Alice band marked with Celtic symbols. Between that and the garb, she looked like the headmistress had the Tories' Free School programme allowed Marilyn Manson to set up an academy.

The one thing jarring against the overall impression was that she had a folded copy of the *Daily Record* tucked under her arm. She didn't look like the normal demographic.

'I brought coffee.'

There was a dourness in her tone as though she already regretted the gesture but had to go through with it now.

'Thanks. Let's grab a seat.'

Parlabane led her to the kitchenette, gesturing to the two stools at the breakfast bar looking out into the living room. The first time he lived here, the place had been literally twice the size. Edinburgh was getting almost as bad as London that way. They said you couldn't divide zero, but property developers in Hoxton had to be getting pretty close.

'What can I do for you?'

She had a few false starts, seemingly about to speak and then abandoning the attempt. It was as though she was composing and deleting various drafts of the opening line of a sensitive and important email. Up close he could see that she was a few years younger than he first estimated. She looked tired and she looked sad, both of which had aged her. Her eyes were bloodshot: from lack of sleep or from crying or from both.

Letting out a sigh of frustration, she unfolded the *Daily Record* and placed it on the worktop, spreading it open a few pages in. Parlabane noted that the edition was yesterday's.

'This was my brother.'

The headline stated:

TRAGEDY STRIKES NEWLYWEDS AS HUSBAND FEARED DEAD

The story was accompanied by a picture of a smiling couple and another showing a crane hauling a car from a snow-lined stretch of river. Parlabane quickly scanned the copy. He had seen the same story online already. The *Record* was stretching the definition of

90

newlywed to an outer limit of six months, but he couldn't argue with the tragedy part.

HOPES FADED for Peter Elphinstone yesterday as police called off their search for the missing computer programmer, whose car plunged into a river near Inverness in the early hours of Friday morning.

Elphinstone had recently married consultant surgeon Dr Diana Jager, who hit the headlines five years ago over her controversial 'Sexism in Surgery' blog. The pair met at Inverness Royal Infirmary, where they both worked, and were married last summer.

Sources close to Diana say she is devastated.

'They were perfect for each other,' said theatre nurse Abigail Darroch. 'From the moment they met they were barely out of each other's sight. She used to talk about how she was worried she'd never find someone, so when she met Peter it was the answer to her prayers. It was like something from a movie: she had this high-profile feud with hospital IT guys and then fell in love with one.'

One friend of Peter's told us tearfully how the IT whiz worshipped his wife. 'He was so happy, he had everything to live for. He really couldn't believe his luck in ending up with someone like Diana. If ever two people looked like being a happy ever after, it was them. It's just so sad.'

Elphinstone is believed to have lost control of his car at Widow Falls, a notorious accident blackspot near Ordskirk, close to Inverness. He is the son of Perthshire landowner Sir Hamish Elphinstone. A spokesman for Sir Hamish issued a statement asking for privacy at this difficult time.

'I'm so sorry,' said Parlabane, cringing as he always did when a complete absence of context meant he had nothing but platitudes to offer. On this occasion, he guessed context would be imminently forthcoming.

'I came here because . . .'

She bit her lip and then got up from the stool.

'I'm sorry. I don't know what I was thinking.'

'Hey, just take a moment, it's okay.'

He spoke in a register learned from two decades of coaxing nervous sources who either thought they weren't going to be believed or feared he might think them crazy. Putting them at ease was a vital skill of his profession, because very occasionally neither of these things turned out to be the case. 'You might as well finish your coffee seeing as you went to the bother.'

She took a sip, nodding nervously.

'Sorry. I'm a mess at the moment.'

'I can imagine. Were you and your brother close?'

'Yes. I like to think so.'

Her tone indicated someone else might think otherwise.

'We weren't living in each other's pockets, but we were the first person the other called whenever one of us had news, you know?'

Parlabane nodded, thinking of the one person in his life with whom he ever had that kind of relationship. Now there was a letter from her lawyer in his living room.

'I realise you might think that I'm not dealing with this well, that I'm looking for something that's not there because I can't accept it, and you'd most probably be right. In fact I'd hope you were right. But I need to talk to somebody about this and I don't know where else to turn.'

Parlabane said nothing, just lifted the cup she had brought for him, a gesture of complicity.

She looked suddenly apprehensive.

'This is completely confidential, right?'

'It's better than that. Nobody believes anything I say these days anyway.'

She didn't smile, but she seemed reassured by the sentiment.

'I know you've a reputation for looking for the story that might lie beneath the mainstream narrative everybody else accepts.'

'That's a flattering way of putting it.'

He omitted to add that a more common description in the modern parlance tended to invoke hats made of tinfoil.

'I came here because I don't recognise this tabloid version of my brother's marriage, but it seems disloyal or inappropriate to say that out loud to anyone who knows him and Diana. *Knew*, I should say.'

It wasn't unusual for people to feel insulted by the simplistic way in which the press reduced complex lives to fit large-font headlines, but Parlabane didn't see what he could offer her beyond sympathy.

'Nuance isn't exactly their stock-in-trade. What is it that you think they're missing?'

She had another false start, then bought herself a moment's preparation for take two with a mouthful of coffee.

'I don't know how to say this. I'm not sure I can even give voice to this because of what it says about me, but . . . I was worried about Peter before this happened. Peter never likes to admit he's in trouble, or that he's got himself in over his head, so he makes out nothing's wrong – or nothing's all *that* wrong – but something was. A lot was wrong.'

'Like what?'

'The last time I spoke to him, I could tell he was unhappy. Seriously unhappy. I've never heard him sound so stressed. I know he was under a lot of pressure to do with his work, but I'm sure the business was only part of it.'

She reached to her coffee cup again but didn't drink. Instead, she turned it gently on the spot as she spoke, a few degrees at a time, like she was opening a safe.

'Nobody sees what's truly going on in a marriage behind closed doors. It's a partnership, and even when the partnership is failing, the one thing they'll still cooperate in is putting on a united front. You can never know the truth from the outside, but I got a few smuggled dispatches, and it was not the fairytale everybody keeps talking about.'

Parlabane eyed her cautiously. He was curious as to where this might be going, and already worrying about how he was going to let a bereaved but crazy person down in a manner sufficiently diplomatic as to get her out of his flat without incident.

'They had only known each other a few months before they got married. I think that increases the complicity in a united front because they share the embarrassment of people thinking they were foolish. Add to that Peter's aforementioned reticence to admit when things are going wrong and you'll understand why everybody else thought they were blissful. But I know him better than anybody, and he knew there was only so much he could hide from me.'

'What did he tell you?'

'Do you know anything about Diana Jager?'

'A little, as it happens. My wi— my ex-wife is an anaesthetist. I know Diana was Bladebitch, from the blog.'

'Diana is a driven, obsessive person. That's what impressed Peter about her. He said he was inspired by her, and he was very taken that someone so driven should be so interested in him. She'd need to be driven and obsessive to do what she does and to have achieved all that she has achieved. But I think Peter became an obsession too.'

She turned the cup absently again, her gaze aimed in its direction but her focus elsewhere.

'Peter said she kept complaining that he had changed. If you knew Peter, you'd know that's absurd. Anyone else would say Peter's problem is that he doesn't change. I think that when people marry so fast, when it sinks in that it's for keeps they suddenly realise what they're committed to. That's when they finally see all the things they were ignoring or in denial about. I get the impression Diana had this idealised version of Peter, the perfect man who had made her dreams come true, and she was not prepared to tolerate any deviation from that.'

'So you're saying she was smothering him,' he suggested, hoping to hurry things along. 'Is it your concern that he was feeling trapped, and that he . . .' Parlabane paused, allowing time for his meaning to get there in advance and thus permit his choice of words to be sensitively oblique. '. . . maybe did something desperate?'

'That crossed my mind. But here's the thing. It only crossed my mind because of something Diana told me. She said a few weeks back that she was worried about Peter because they'd had an argument while he was driving, and he almost lost control

94

of the car at Widow Falls. The exact same place his car went in the river.'

Parlabane sat up straighter, his story reflexes firing.

'Diana blamed the argument and his state of mind on his work, said it was taking over. She told me about this as if she was confiding in me. Let me tell you, Mr Parlabane, my sister-in-law and I have never been close. She does not confide in me.'

She lifted both her hands, palms-up, in a stop gesture. Whether she was putting the brakes on herself or signalling to him not to press her was unclear. Either way, he could tell she was concerned she had gone too far, and yet Parlabane's instincts told him the opposite was true: that there was something more she wasn't telling him, some deeper reason she should be prepared to share these concerns with a stranger, and a journalist at that.

'Look, I know how all this sounds, and I hate myself for even implying, but I know I'd hate myself more if I thought something was wrong and I never acted. Christ, maybe that's it, though, don't you think? I knew Peter was in a bad way and I did nothing, so now I'm projecting and transferring and God knows what.'

'What is it you think I can do?'

He spoke delicately, aware that bringing things around to the practical was a good way of focusing people when they were upset like this.

'I thought maybe you could look into it a little deeper than the tabloids have. I realise this might be a waste of your time; in fact, with apologies, that would be the preferable outcome for me. Ideally what I want is for you to come back and tell me there's nothing to this, and I'm simply crazy and paranoid and all messed up because I lost my brother. But if there's another story here, I want to make sure it gets told.'

DIFFERENT SELVES

While the memory of a first kiss can still be bittersweet, the thought of the sex now turns my stomach.

I was seduced. Peter seduced me.

I feel embarrassed saying that. I always thought women complaining that they had been seduced were self-deluding and pathetic. Oh, spare us, I would think. You're a grown woman, you abide by your decisions, you make them consciously and deliberately.

I believed I was too smart, too strong and frankly too cynical to be manipulated that way, but in practice I was stupid, weak and naive. I was easy prey.

When people talk about seduction in a relationship, they usually mean sex. They're wrong. The real seduction is not about sex: it's about trust. You don't need to be seduced into sex when you are in love with someone: you give yourself willingly because it is what you both desire. But you only believe it is your desire because the seduction has already happened.

It is an act of deceit, a misrepresentation of the self, and by it Peter seduced me into something far more intimate than sex. He made me love him. How angry would you be with someone who betrayed that?

We kissed for so long in that car, making out like a couple of teenagers as the rain pattered the roof and the wipers beat back and forth. It felt perfect, one of those moments when the world melted away, when the past and the future melted away. We weren't kissing as a prelude to anything else. I knew he wasn't going to ask me to stay the night. We both understood that this was all that was going to happen, and all that we wanted.

Eventually we broke off, both laughing self-consciously.

'I'm light-headed,' I said.

96

'Can I see you tomorrow?' he asked.

'Apart from at work, you mean?'

'Yeah. Oh shit. I forgot. Cobalt need me to go down to Edinburgh for a few days to help out on another project. I'll be back on Thursday, though.'

'I'm on-call on Thursday,' I remembered with a grimace.

'Friday then?'

'Friday, definitely.'

Peter let out a sigh, his expression regretful enough for me to wonder what was wrong.

'It's going to feel like a long week,' he said.

It was and it wasn't.

Every day that passed added disproportionately to what seemed a very long time since we were kissing in my car on Sunday night, longer still since we had first met in my office. Yet the individual days themselves passed quicker than normal. I feared my mind might drift off on daft girly feelings of longing but rather I achieved what Peter had referred to as a flow state in my work. I would watch my trainee finish suturing the patient and see from the clock that three or four hours had passed since I first scrubbed up. The minor and major irritations of the job didn't seem to get to me as much as usual, with only the delays between patients piquing my frustration.

On a couple of the lists I was doubled up with Calum Weatherson, or Hipster Jesus as I had uncharitably christened him back when we first met. He had shaved off the beard since then. I wondered whether I had made him self-conscious about it, but if so I wasn't going to censure myself for bullying. It was a massive improvement. He had a handsome face with a ruggedness about it that was actually lessened by the face-fuzz. When we got talking, I learned that it had been his wife Megan who had prevailed upon him to shave. It was particularly nice to be able to show him that I wasn't the scary nightmare who had pitched up and insulted a patient the day we first met.

He was a good prospect: solid and safe in his work, if somewhat slow and deliberate. We chatted about books as he stitched up, and it turned out we shared a love of Neal Stephenson, though I was keener on his historical stuff where Calum liked the SF.

Peter called every night. There were no games, no strategic posturing. He wanted to talk.

Late on the Tuesday night, he suggested we watch a movie together. We both cued up the same film on Netflix, Skype open in a minimised window in each of our laptop screens as we sat up in bed. We were able to share comments and see each other's reactions. I was going to say it was like a virtual date, but in fact it was more like virtual already living together, and it felt so right.

We did it again on the Wednesday too.

When the movie was over, he told me he had something for me that would make me laugh. He sent me over a file, though when I clicked on it, nothing happened.

'Computer genius,' he chided himself. 'Wrong format. This is why I'm not the next Bill Gates.'

He tried again and this time when I opened it, I saw a slide show of photographs from the airsoft games on Sunday. I hadn't even been aware of a photographer, which was why the shots were so natural. There I was, toting a machine gun; yomping through the trees; prostrate under fire; crouching to take aim; walking back towards the muster point.

I barely recognised myself even in the ones without the mask. I looked so happy.

The Thursday night was always going to be the hardest. I was there until around three in the morning. We had just enough cases to prevent me from going home, but the gaps between them were soul-crushingly drawn-out, rounded off with an emergency bowel repair coming in by ambulance all the way from Skye.

By the time Friday evening came around, it seemed like ages since we'd last spoken on Skype, and this was exacerbated by feeling as though we had been together – if you could call it that – for a lot longer than five days. I'm not too proud to admit I was clock-watching in the hours running up to when Peter was due to arrive, unable to distract myself with journals, papers or even an episode of something on TV.

It would be an understatement to say the date didn't exactly go according to plan. I had made a reservation at an intimate Italian place I'd heard good things about. Peter was going to pick me up and park back at his flat, then we'd walk to the restaurant via a bar where he said he'd had surprisingly decent mojitos.

In contrast to the previous Friday, he turned up about fifteen minutes early.

'I was trying to think of a plausible pretext,' he explained, 'but the truth is I just couldn't wait.'

I was kissing him before I had even closed my front door, and we were naked on top of my duvet by the time he was originally scheduled to arrive.

Between the second and third bouts I managed to make a giggly call to the restaurant to cancel the table. Sometime around nine we ordered in pizza.

We didn't have anything resembling a sensible discussion until after breakfast the following morning, sipping coffee and nibbling croissants in bed. I'd normally be uncomfortable with the flakes of pastry crumbling all over the duvet, but every stitch of these sheets was imminently going in the washing machine anyway.

He was content to listen, like no male I had ever met. He understood what it was to listen, too: i.e. just that, listening, no mansplaining or unsolicited advice.

I realised I was dominating the conversation, or at least the subject of me was dominating it, so I got him to tell me a little about his past. I asked about his family background, but he skirted around it. He mentioned a sister and I asked if they were close. He said 'yes and no', but wouldn't elaborate. I got the impression there was something painful back there, but didn't press it.

Kind of like myself, he was more expansive on the subject of his job. He talked me through what he described as a non-glittering career in computers, in which he had barely succeeded in 'scaling the middle'.

'I could have climbed the ladder in a couple of companies where I was consulting, but I never felt sufficiently engaged with what they were doing or what I was doing for them. My interest would drift and my enthusiasm would get channelled into whatever side project I had going on in my spare time, and I should stress that these side projects were not works of wayward genius that simply needed the right mentor.'

'But you do enjoy aspects of what you do?' I asked, as his manner on the previous Friday afternoon had not indicated a man who hated his job.

'Absolutely. There are things I enjoy on a day-to-day basis, but it's not demanding the best of me. I was never sure whether the problem was that I never found something that truly engaged all of me, or whether I lacked the application and oomph that would make me truly engage. I'm envious of you because no matter what heartaches it brings, you at least know you found the thing you're *meant* to do.'

I had never appreciated what a blessing this was. When you have a vocation from such an early age, you don't give much thought to might-have-beens, and still less to what it must be like not to know what you want to do.

'I like coding, tinkering, *hacking* in the original sense of the word, so people might assume that working in IT is what I'm meant to do, but I've never felt I had the right outlet. Not until quite recently.'

'I take it we're not discussing hospital IT here?'

'No. I've come up with that rarest and most precious of things: a simple idea that meets a need. I was thinking about how you've inspired me to knuckle down, so I wondered whether it was seren-dipitous to have met you now that I've got an idea I believe in, but maybe I'm harbouring this belief in an idea because of how you make me feel.'

'Who knows? Maybe it's like the uncertainty principle, and being sure of one part of the equation means you can't know the other.'

'I'm trying to be serious here,' he insisted, though he was laughing.

'So what's your big plan?'

He laughed again, in a kind of exasperated self-reproach.

'What's funny?'

100

'Uncertainty. I can't tell you much about the project. Its value at this stage is very much contingent upon being first, getting it implemented before someone else has a similar idea.'

'Can't you copyright it?'

'It's more about how being first to market scoops the pot. Put it this way: can you name a competitor to PayPal?'

I got the idea, and I must have looked impressed.

'Don't get excited. I'm not kidding myself this could make me a billionaire, but I do think it's worth pursuing. I'm simply trying to explain why it's confidential at this stage.'

'And you don't trust me yet,' I teased. 'Despite what we just did together. Six or was it seven times?'

He smiled but he did look a tad vulnerable.

'Please don't push the issue, because this stuff is so hard for me. Believe me, I am not good at keeping secrets and I don't have a poker face. But I think I've been dealt a hell of a hand here, and so it would be the worst failure of my life if I didn't do whatever it takes to bring this off.'

'So you'll be spending all your spare time on it from here on in, starting now?' I suggested, putting on a pretend frown and mock absent-mindedly tugging open the top button on my nightie.

'Well, maybe not all my time. And maybe not starting right this second.'

PROFESSIONAL DEMEANOUR

'Don't park in sight,' said Rodriguez. 'I need a moment.'

Ali pulled in short of the cottage, a picture-postcard place on the Culloden Road. The nearest neighbour was quarter of a mile away, so if the patrol car was visible from the house through the trees, there would be no ambiguity over who they were here to visit. For that reason, a moment was all she could give him. This woman's husband hadn't come home last night, so seeing a cop car outside would be a very bad sign, and they couldn't leave her hanging.

Hell of a way to end a shift, right enough. They were tired and should have been home hours ago. Ali had stayed on to see it through, and she figured Rodriguez followed suit because he was the new guy. She felt a little sorry for him, that being the case. She could easily have farmed this out to someone else and been home asleep by now; except that if she farmed it out to someone else, she wouldn't have been *able* to sleep. Sometimes it worked that way. There were incidents she dealt with that were merely process, gone from her mind as soon as her involvement was over, and others that she couldn't help but feel a personal connection to.

It was searching Elphinstone's name that did it. She would have been fine if she hadn't done that. She wanted to check whether the man on the driving licence was indeed related to the landowning family the diver mentioned, because that was bound to bring down greater attention on the whole thing and so forewarned was forearmed.

The search results threw up a number of articles about his wedding, which at first she took to be confirmation of his gentrified background, but that turned out not to be the reason his marriage was considered newsworthy by several tabloids and other gossipy sites. It wasn't so much about him as about his wife. She was a surgeon who had been a controversial blogger until running into career-damaging trouble when she was hacked, apparently as revenge for disparaging remarks about hospital IT personnel.

Ali knew the story was being framed in simplistically romantic terms to make it clickbait, but there was an undeniably heart-warming element to Jager subsequently falling for and marrying a hospital IT guy. Making it all the more poignant, she was described as having frequently written about the clock running out on her chances of finding love due to the demands of her career. Friends and colleagues of both were quoted, saying what a miraculous whirlwind romance it had been, and how perfect they seemed for each other.

They had been married less than six months, and now Ali had pulled up a few yards short of their fairytale cottage with news that was going to devastate this woman.

'You could have said if you wanted to duck this.'

'I don't. I need a second or two to suit up, psychologically, that's all. Need to get my head in the right place, you know?'

Ali nodded, putting the car in neutral but leaving the engine running. It was good that he had such a firm grasp of the gravity of what they were about to do. Some people could be very distant from it, whether out of self-defence or becoming inured to the whole thing. The worst you could be right now was disengaged.

'My mum has a friend whose wife got a really late-presenting cancer diagnosis,' she told him. 'She was only given a few months. What I'll never forget is him saying that sometimes it would temporarily slip from his mind for a few seconds, due to some distraction. Then he would remember again and it was like being punched in the face every time. We're about to punch this woman in the face.'

Rodriguez gave a dry little laugh.

'I've been literally punched in the face on the job. And I've given

103

the death message before too. If I had the choice of which one to go through again, I'd take the punch.'

'So why did you volunteer?'

'Why did you?'

'Good answer.'

Ali drove the car the final few yards and stopped it in front of the cottage. The front of the plot was bordered by hedges tucked tight behind a low stone wall. At the centre, a small iron gate opened on to a garden path bisecting a tidy lawn on its way to the front door. To the left, a larger set of electronically operated gates barred a driveway leading to a substantial stone-built garage abutting the house.

Ali imagined the thing drawn in coloured pencils on a primary-school desk, curly loops of white smoke emerging from the chimney, curtains with tie-backs on the windows. Wee girls always drew those, even if their own houses had blinds. The flat she grew up in with her mum never had curtains, but blinds never looked cosy in a picture.

Ali rang the doorbell with a firm press, hearing it chime some-where deep inside. There was no response for a few seconds, no sounds emanating from anywhere within. She was about to press it again when finally she heard footsteps.

The woman who opened it was in a dressing gown. They had called the hospital when they found out where she worked, and been told she had phoned in sick. Ali recognised her from a photo posted online. She was shorter than Ali was expecting, her expression understandably more defensive and severe than in the wedding snap. Her dark hair hung down over the left side of her face, partially obscuring one eye, but from what Ali could see of her features, she looked like she hadn't slept.

'Dr Jager?'

'Yes? Can I help you?'

'I'm PC Ali Kazmi and this is PC Ruben Rodriguez. Can we come inside, please?'

Jager didn't ask what it was about. She stepped away from the door with a certain weary resignation, waiting to close it behind them like she didn't trust Rodriguez to remember. She gestured to a door on the right of the hall, following them into what turned out to be her living room.

It was bright and tasteful but a wee bit spartan to Ali's eyes. She wondered how long Dr Jager had lived here, as it looked like she had only recently moved in. Possibly it was a rental: when Ali first got a place of her own, the landlord was this totally anal creep whose terms barred her from so much as putting a nail in the wall to hang a picture.

Jager stood next to an armchair, her posture shyly self-conscious. Her body was turned sideways and her head drooped, that lock of hair still draped over part of her face.

'Dr Jager, you should take a seat. We have some bad news.'

This was when you found out who they most cared for, or most feared for: when they asked who you were talking about. Jager, however, still said nothing. She stepped rather awkwardly around to the front of the chair and sat down, still tilting her head. It reminded Ali of half her pals when they were about fourteen, but it didn't seem at all right on a successful professional woman.

'Your husband's car was found submerged in the river near Ordskirk a few hours ago. We believe it came off the road some-time around two forty this morning. We have had divers searching the river and officers working the banks, but we haven't been able to find him.'

Jager put a hand to her head, a look of confusion on her face. She rather absently brushed the hair briefly clear of her eye, long enough for Ali to notice that there was a mark and some swelling beneath it.

'You're saying . . . you think he's dead?'

'We don't know anything for certain at this stage. Just that his car was at the bottom of the river, and that his phone and wallet were inside it. We haven't given up the search, but it is looking increasingly unlikely that we will find your husband alive.'

Jager fixed Ali with a stare, as though looking right through her. For a moment she thought she was about to be accused of lying.

'His car came off the road?'

'That's right. It appears he lost control, according to the witness who called us out.'

Jager stared a moment longer, then something in her seemed to give. Her posture slumped and she let out a soft sigh, as though resigned that this was making sense now.

'This happened at Widow Falls,' Jager said.

Her tone was odd: Ali couldn't decide whether it was a statement or a question. Either way, she and Rodriguez traded looks. They hadn't told her this.

'How do you know that, Dr Jager?'

Jager stiffened in her chair, suddenly that bit more alert.

'You're saying *this* happened at Widow Falls?'

'Yes, ma'am. How did . . .'

'No. I mean, it happened before, nearly: that's what I'm saying. Peter almost lost control of the car on the hairpin bend at Widow Falls. I just . . . I spent so many times wondering about what might have happened that night, and now you're saying . . .'

She sighed again, shaking her head. Ali was reminded of a mother who has told off her kid for something and then watched him hurt himself doing it again. It was as though she hadn't quite taken in the scale of this. It wasn't a skinned knee. Nobody could kiss it better.

'I believe you called in sick today. You look tired. Have you been up all night waiting for him?'

'No. I thought he was working.'

'Working? Where?'

'He has a company . . . he's working on a software project. Sometimes he likes to work late, occasionally through the night. That's where I thought he was.'

'And are you all right physically?'

'I'm okay. I wasn't feeling so good this morning, and when you're a surgeon you can't afford to be spreading infection around theatre.'

'And what about . . .' Ali touched her own cheek by way of alluding to the mark. 'Have you had an accident yourself?'

Jager rolled her eyes in faintly embarrassed self-reproach.

'Oh, this? So stupid. I hit myself in the face opening a parcel. I was tugging and tugging at this piece of packing tape when suddenly it snapped and I . . . Never mind. Last night it was the biggest thing I had to worry about. Jesus.'

Rodriguez offered to make tea. Jager seemed reluctant at first, but acquiesced as if she didn't have the energy to argue. Ali couldn't help but develop the impression that she just wanted them out of her house.

'Is there someone you can call?' Ali asked, once Jager's barely touched tea was way past drinkable. 'Someone who can sit with you?'

'Not right now. Maybe later.'

'You shouldn't be alone.'

'Looks like I'd better get used to it.'

Ali made a further attempt to insist she contact a friend or relative, but she was rebuffed again, and Jager didn't seem like someone who could be easily prevailed upon, even under these circumstances.

They both got to their feet, Ali stating her reluctant intention to leave.

Rodriguez surprised her by walking over to the window and lifting a framed photograph from the table in front of it.

'This is quite recent, yeah?'

Jager nodded, like she was barely paying him attention.

'Do you mind if we take it? We'll scan it and bring it back. It's helpful to have a picture we can give out, to the press or whoever. Saves you from being pestered.'

Jager waved her hand dismissively by way of assent, like it couldn't be more trivial. Ali reckoned they could have asked for the telly and been given the nod if it got them out the door.

SIBLING RIVALRY

In science, they call it the null hypothesis: the search for all the reasons you might possibly uncover that *you are wrong*. They tell you 'never want it to be true'. Instead, test the evidence to destruction, especially when you have actually found yourself asking: 'Is this too *good* to be true?' It applies to medicine as it does to any other field, which makes my gullibility all the more embarrassing. My downfall was that I wanted it to be true.

Though it's small consolation, I was far from the first. We do not, cannot, and perhaps should not apply scientific and empirical principles to matters of the heart, other than those matters falling within the magisterium of cardiology. Let's be realistic: who wants to go looking for proof that they are wrong when they think they have found love?

Nonetheless, there is a difference between seeking out contrary evidence and ignoring it when it is right in front of you. There must have been signs there all along, I'm sure everyone will say, employing that unfailingly accurate instrument we surgeons call the retrospectoscope.

It looks very different at the time, particularly when the time is past your fortieth birthday and you fear you're running out of chances. Don't judge unless you've seen it through that perspective for yourself. Even now I can't fully comprehend the dynamic that is at work there. Do you edit things out when you find a decent prospect at this stage in life because you desperately want to convince yourself it will work? Or do you see the problems with your partner but simply decide that they're not deal-breakers? Do you tell yourself that perhaps these are the compromises people learn over time in successful marriages, and you are exercising the wisdom to fast-forward?

I still don't know, but I do know this much: one classic mistake I *didn't* make was telling myself that if there were things about Peter I wasn't happy with, I could change him once we were married. He made me believe I had already changed him. My folly was not in thinking that the person who proposed to me was perfect, but in believing all the apparently perfect things about him were real.

They were the best days of my life. Who wouldn't want that to go on for ever? I kept waiting for it to fall apart, or for it to at least show signs of strain somewhere, but they never arrived. I'm sure there were many ways in which we were on our best behaviour, anticipating the things that might cause friction, but there has to come a point when that gives way and you either become comfortable with each other's foibles or it's the beginning of the end.

I know I was making myself more available than usual, not only emotionally but practically. I was saying no to lucrative extra sessions and holding off on research projects that might lead to future publications. This was partly to keep my immediate time free for Peter, but if I'm being honest I was also trying to give the impression that my future workload wouldn't be a problem for us. Peter, by contrast, was probably working more conscientiously on his external project than he might otherwise have done, in order to demonstrate to me how much more mature and industrious he was becoming.

Equally, I remember when we had a reservation for a restaurant one Friday night, and we had both been looking forward to it throughout a very demanding week. When Friday evening rolled around I was exhausted, and I wanted nothing less than to get changed and head out, but I didn't want to disappoint him, or to tip him off that this might be a regular occurrence. He called to ask if I was still okay for our date, and I told him I was, but he must have read the hesitation in my voice or maybe just the fatigue.

'You sound knackered.'

'No, I'll be fine after a quick shower.'

109

'You'll be fine after a long soak, a night in and about ten hours' sleep. Why don't you run a bath and I'll come around later with pizza and a movie?'

That's what love sounds like: two people on the phone lying about what they want because the main thing they want is to please each other.

I had that bath. We ate pizza and watched *Belle*. It was bliss.

We seemed to move into phase two so seamlessly that I couldn't tell you when it happened. Weeks piled upon weeks and turned into months, the fastest months I had ever known. Time seemed to accelerate. There would be moments when I couldn't believe I had only known him since January, and in other ways the time before I met him seemed an age ago.

The sex was easy, and by that I mean it was seldom a source of pressure or tension, as it had been in previous relationships. We were relaxed with each other. Peter didn't give me grief about it when I was too tired or when my head wasn't in the right place because of things that happened at work. And conversely, there were many times when a goodnight kiss turned into something I suddenly needed much more than the twenty minutes' extra sleep it was costing me, even if I had an early start and a long day ahead.

The only time we had the hint of a problem was when he suggested we film ourselves, which I was absolutely not comfortable with.

I recall Peter looking apologetic.

'Oh God, I forgot about you getting hacked. But I'm not talking about something that would ever be stored online. And I'd frame it so that your face is never in shot. Or mine, so no chance of being identified. Only we would know.'

There was something oddly cosy and intimate about that notion, and I was tempted for a moment, but only for a moment. I just knew I couldn't relax, couldn't be naked in front of a camera, never mind have sex.

He was fine about it though, and never brought it up again. Equally, I reassured him that I didn't think he was weird or pervy for suggesting it.

Like I said, we were easy together.

What I need you to understand is that our burgeoning relationship wasn't about the spectacular or the escapist: nights out, weekends away, surprise presents. Though all these things did happen, in a way they weren't the highlights. It was the day-to-day, the week-to-week that made it special. It was about me enjoying all that was normal in my life. In the earliest days, the hardest part was getting through work because I was impatient to see him, but soon the impatience wore off and I started to really enjoy my work *because* I knew that I would see Peter when it was finished.

Isn't that what we all want? Someone to be with and something to do?

And yes, as I said, there were times when I couldn't believe my good fortune. I confessed as much to Peter, though only because he said the same first. It was as though we were both terrified of losing what we had.

Peter rationalised it, though.

'Maybe it's more balanced than we think. Maybe when it comes to relationships, we've both had more bad luck than is average, and it's skewed our sense of what is normal. Or, what's thrown us is that our good luck has been disguised as bad luck.'

'What do you mean?'

'Well, if we are each as adorable as the other believes, then we must have had bad luck in order to both still be single when we met each other, so our bad luck then is our good luck now.'

Amazing how bullshit circular logic seems like mystic truth when you're blinded by love.

I used to hate it whenever I heard women say of their latest beau, 'he totally gets me'. But I soon came to understand what they meant, even if that wasn't how I would choose to express it.

I'll never forget the first time he handed me a present, feeling touched and yet almost shaking with apprehension as I clutched what was unmistakably a soft parcel. Clothing gifts were tricky territory in a burgeoning relationship, so it felt like a far more tense moment than he might have anticipated. I unwrapped it slowly, preparing myself, afraid I was about to be confronted with inappropriate underwear, some garment that was far from my taste, or worse: something that indicated he wanted me to look different, with all that implied for what he really thought of how I looked now. Basically it was an unexploded awkward-bomb that had been dropped into my hands.

When I pulled away the wrapping, I uncovered this gorgeous purple dress that was quite similar to one I had eyed up in a department store, and even pored over a few times on the shop's website without ever clicking Buy. I liked it but didn't think I could pull it off. I thought it was for someone more glam than me.

'Oh my God, that's beautiful.'

I teared up, my relief giving way to gratitude and delight, touched by his solicitude.

Peter wasn't with me when I saw it in the store; in fact at that stage I wouldn't have dragged him around the shops for fear of wasting a day better spent doing other things together. Which made it all the more lovely that when he had gone out looking for a present, he happened upon a similar item and, as he put it: 'I pictured you in that and thought it was perfect for you. I might be way out, though, so I've kept the receipt.'

It happened a few times: he would surprise me with gifts that were closer to the taste I aspired towards rather than the taste my more cowardly instincts told me to settle for. Nothing inappropriate, nothing outrageous: just the kind of thing I might consider and then chicken out of. It was as though he saw this better version of me, and helped me become it.

I did the same for him too, though not so much in terms of wardrobe. I kept him to his good intentions with regard to working on his project, even when the selfish part of me would rather have him dedicating all of his spare time and attention to me. I believed in his potential, and the exciting thing was watching him start to believe in it too.

Not that everything simply clicked into place without a hitch. We were proving good for each other, but we couldn't be the solution to all of each other's problems. One of the great markers on the road to serious in any relationship is meeting the folks, but neither of us was in a hurry to introduce the other to their family.

In my case, geography proved a convenient means of avoiding the issue. My parents still lived in Huntingdon, so it wasn't as though they were likely to drop by one afternoon and require an introduction to the young man whose shaving kit was sitting by my sink. Besides, they regarded what happened to me over the blog as a family disgrace and had never once blessed me with a visit in my penitential northern gulag. Christmas aside, I rarely went home, and even then I often volunteered for on-call so that I'd have an excuse why I couldn't come. My brothers Julian and Piers lived in Brisbane and Dunedin respectively (only living off-planet would have further satisfied their need for distance from our loving family hearth), so we weren't going to run into them either.

This mutual reluctance was no surprise to either of us. I deduced early on that Peter didn't want to talk about his family, and I had explained a bit about mine when inevitably the issue came up regarding why I was Doctor Jager.

'Aren't surgeons usually Miss or Mrs?'

'Statistically speaking, they're usually Mister.'

'You know what I mean. They're not usually *Doctor*.'

I told him all about my doll's house, and about my mother, who qualified but never practised, merely married my father and became Mrs Jager. In fact, throughout my life I seldom heard my father call her Veronica. I told Peter how my father addressed her directly as Dearest Darling, and to us in the third person as Mummy, but here's the weirdest part: in front of other people he always referred to her as Mrs Jager.

'Yes, Mrs Jager did enjoy our holiday . . . Mrs Jager has a head cold and won't be joining us . . . Sorry, I'll have to discuss that with Mrs Jager and get back to you.'

It was as though she was defined so entirely on his terms that she had even lost her given name.

That was why, when I went into surgery, I insisted on remaining Doctor Diana Jager. I spent my entire youth longing for that title and all that it signified, so I wasn't giving it up for the sake of convention.

Nevertheless, despite our shared reluctance to inflict our families upon each other, I did meet Peter's sister after we had been going out for about two months. I didn't like her then, and given her squirrelly role in all of what transpired subsequently, it would be quite the understatement to say I fucking despise her now.

We were down in Edinburgh for our first Saturday night away together when we bumped into her on Broughton Street. I noticed Peter slow down alongside me and thought he was about to look in a shop window. He glanced uncertainly at me for a moment, as though he was preparing to say something, and then I heard a voice and saw that a rather prissy-looking female had stopped right in front of us.

Upon first seeing them together, I would never have guessed they were brother and sister. She seemed so buttoned-up, quite literally, while Peter's appearance was always as laid back and understated as his demeanour. He had an effortlessness about how he dressed that sometimes skirted the borders of scruffy and yet always looked right on him. His sister, by contrast, looked like she must take a lot of time and regimented effort about presenting herself, and yet the result was strangely incongruous, like an ageing goth who these days only shopped in M&S but couldn't help resorting to certain instincts.

'Peter, you didn't tell me you were going to be in town this weekend.'

There was pleasant surprise in her tone, but a hint of accusation too. I quickly inferred that she was not merely chiding him over how infrequently they spoke: they had spoken recently and she was annoyed that he hadn't let on he would be on her turf.

'Well, it was kind of a last-minute thing. A cheap hotel deal on the internet.'

This was a lie. We had planned it a fortnight back, once I got my latest on-call rota and knew which coming weekend I would be free.

'Lucy, this is Diana. Diana, this is my sister, Lucy.'

I once met a boyfriend's sister who was unsettlingly gushy: hugging me upon introduction and acting as though we were going to be instant best friends, which paradoxically made me instantly dislike her. I had little fear that such effusiveness was going to be reprised here, but the end result looked certain to be the same.

She gave me the most thin-lipped smile and didn't offer a hand to shake.

'Oh, yes. Peter's told me about you.'

Not Peter's told me *all* about you. It's one tiny word, but in this context it makes a very big difference.

'Why don't we grab a coffee?' Peter suggested. 'Give us all the chance to talk. We were only out for a wander anyway.'

She seemed to think about it for long enough that I believed she might be weighing up whether to fabricate an excuse. I might have been relieved if she had, except that I could already sense how keen Peter was that we should all spend some time together.

'Yes, I'm not doing anything urgent.'

We went to a place in a basement down some steps from where we had met Lucy. I thought it would seem gloomy and claustrophobic, with its windows showing only the brick walls of the stairwell, but it was brightly lit and the décor made it seem airy.

That didn't prevent the atmosphere from becoming oppressive, but it was nothing to do with the location. It was the company.

When I was able to look at them sitting side by side at the same table, there was no mistaking the sibling resemblance, or that there was a complex family dynamic at work. I gathered that she was older by eighteen months, but she seemed somehow more grown-up. Her features were softer, and she might have been pretty if there wasn't a certain severity about her. With the right look, facially she could have passed for the younger of the two, but from her demeanour she could have been ten years his senior.

And despite the palpable awkwardness over Peter not having told her we would be in Edinburgh, now that we were in each other's company, little brother was keen to impress. He seemed almost over-anxious that she should like me. He was talking up my CV like he was my agent, and saying what a positive effect I was having on him. This vicarious immodesty was most unlike him. It was as though he was showing off, proud of how well he had done, seeking an attaboy.

It was not forthcoming. Lucy seemed quite determined to remain politely unmoved. I don't expect everyone to go: 'Ooh, you're a consultant surgeon', but equally I can tell when someone is making a point of not being impressed. I suspected this would still have been Lucy's response had her brother presented a Nobel Prize-winning physicist and supermodel as his girlfriend. It was all about laying down a marker, of sorts, though I had to wait a while for its nature to become clear.

They struck me as a brother and sister who had a close bond but who nonetheless would rather not be in each other's company. I got my first hint as to why when Peter went to the toilet and we were left alone together.

'Peter is very taken with you.'

She wore that thin-lipped smile again, a flimsy mask of politeness. I knew that whatever was coming next, she meant business.

'I'm happy for him. But I'm concerned too. There have been women before you. They've taken advantage of his nature and he's been hurt. He's more fragile than he'd ever let you see. He's open with people and he assumes they're being open with him. He wants to believe you're perfect, that you won't suddenly decide he's not what you're looking for and dump him like they did. So if you're not in it for the long haul, get out now, and let him down gently. Because if you lead him on and then break his heart . . .'

She stopped herself there. I thought she was letting it hang unspoken as a threat, but as I searched, flabbergasted, for a response, she recanted slightly.

'I'm sorry, that was inappropriate. I don't know you and all I've heard about you are good things. But I've only heard them from him, and let's just say it's not the first time I've heard good things from Peter about a girlfriend. I'm only saying . . . I don't know. He's my little brother. I can't stop myself looking out for him.'

Before I had a chance to assure her of my intentions, or maybe tell her she had no right to be demanding such assurances, I saw Peter coming back from the bathroom. I put on a polite smile, both Lucy and I pretending nothing contentious had been said.

WHIFF OF SUSPICION

Ali sat behind the wheel, her fingers resting on the ignition switch, but she didn't turn it. She stared back towards the cottage, her lips pursed in what her mum always called her thinking frown. She'd been doing it since she was about four.

'Something up?' Rodriguez asked.

'Not sure. Just a feeling, you know?'

'Regarding the good Doctor Jager?'

'Yes. I generally like my grieving widows to have a bit more grief on them.'

'Strictly speaking, we don't know for sure yet that she's a widow.'

'Quite, but I can't help getting the notion that maybe she does.'

Rodriguez cast a glance towards Jager's house. It seemed almost incredible how a building remained unaltered when an emotional bombshell had been dropped upon it, offering no clue to the outside world of the damage that had been inflicted. In this instance, there had been scant evidence inside either.

'Playing doctor's advocate, if there was more to this than meets the eye, wouldn't she be hamming up her response to the news, chewing the scenery a bit?'

'True,' Ali conceded. 'Something just feels off, though. Her eye, for one thing: she didn't want us noticing that. Her explanation was odd too. Not the substance of it, the way she said it. It seemed rehearsed, as though she'd run through it in her head and then delivered the lines on cue.'

'I got that too. It could have happened like she said, though. If she was worried about what people might assume when they saw it, it's possible she'd think through how she would tell them.'

'Yeah, fair enough if she was talking to work colleagues on a normal day, but we had just told her that her husband is most probably dead. It seemed bizarre to give us a story about opening a parcel. People elaborate when they're lying, because they're never sure they've given enough detail to convince you.'

'Or when they're reeling and flustered,' he countered. 'Like if you've just been told your husband is missing and realise that an accidental mark on your face might suddenly look rather suspicious.'

'True. But we haven't even touched on the two things that bothered me most.'

'I'm guessing the fact that she couldn't get us out of there fast enough piqued your curiosity. The words "unseemly haste" come to mind.'

'Damn right. That's one. The other was the odour. You might not have picked it up, though: I've always had a super-sensitive nose. Used to freak my mum that I could tell which of her friends had been round while I was out because I could identify their perfume hours later.'

'I'm recovering from a cold. I got nothing. What did you smell?'

Ali turned the ignition and the engine growled into life.

'Bleach.'

THE QUESTION

If I was inclined to be generous (which it goes without saying I'm not), I would have to credit Lucy with her part in turning Peter's project into a viable business vehicle, and thus indirectly laying the grounds for him proposing to me. It was the one instance in which her preferred role of interfering busybody had an unintended benefit.

I met her again a couple of times after our chance encounter in Edinburgh – both times when she was passing through Inverness – and on each occasion we seemed to instantly resume the tension of that moment. Peter was oddly restless around her too, which always made me fear what poison she might have been dripping in his ear down the phone.

'I know so little about Lucy,' I said to him, the second time he told me she would be in town. 'You never talk about her.'

We were driving back from Cromarty, where we had gone for a wander and some lunch one Sunday.

'What do you want to know?'

His tone wasn't exactly encouraging. I could tell by this stage when he was trying hard to be patient.

'The usual things. What does she do, what's her story, is she in a relationship.'

'You mean girl things?'

'As opposed to what music and TV shows she likes, yes.'

'I don't think she's seeing anybody these days. That's not the kind of subject we talk about, to be honest. She's a big sister, so she sees her younger brother as too trivial to want to confide in about her love life. Which suits me, to be honest.'

'So what do you talk about?'

'Music and TV shows.'

'You must know what she does for a living, at least.'

'Vaguely. She works in finance: these days at any rate. She's had as much of a chequered career as me, though the chequers include greater instances of dynamism mixed in with the rudderless drifting. She worked for an art dealership for a long time, and she worked in a museum too. Scaring children away from priceless exhibits, mostly. She did a degree in art history.'

Peter changed the subject after that, as he always did when the conversation threatened to open a route towards my asking about his parents. He seemed no closer to telling me about them, and I had learned it was counter-productive to ask. I appreciated that he indulged me in letting off steam about my parents, but his remained a complete blank. I didn't know what they did for a living or even where they lived, more specific than 'a place in the middle of nowhere out in Perthshire'.

Peter gave the impression that he and his sister seldom talked about anything substantial, but clearly he had gone to her for advice and assistance in setting up his company, perhaps in the same way she might have come to him if her computer was on the fritz. Due to her multifarious connections, Lucy was able to introduce Peter to potential investors, though introductions were the extent of her involvement. I didn't need to worry about becoming jealous that she was party to more information than me, as Peter complained that she had limited comprehension of the mechanics of his plan. The only data she understood was that pertaining to development budgets and potential returns, but her command of that proved sufficient to attract solid investment from people who did grasp what Peter was hoping to pull off. As a result, he was able to form a company and give up his job with Cobalt, allowing him to work full-time on developing his breakthrough software.

He was nervous as a kitten throughout all of the contractual red-tape stuff, terrified of the real and constant possibility that the opportunity opening in front of him could suddenly vanish due to any number of uncontrollable variables. So when the documents were signed and the venture became an official, listed reality, honestly, I watched him grow a foot before my eyes. It seemed like a landmark moment in his life, one for which he was keen to

121

heap credit upon me as the person who had 'inspired him to get serious'.

The only down side, ironically, was that a mutual Non-Disclosure Agreement insisted upon by the investors meant that he still couldn't give me any specifics regarding what the software was ultimately for. There were people I had never met who knew more about this than I did, which I will admit annoyed me, but I wasn't so precious as to miss what the bigger picture was here. These people believed in Peter's idea and in his ability to make it happen, which was why they were backing him with hard cash.

'You have to give me some kind of vague hint,' I pleaded, as he was showing me the sheaves of paperwork that would make the venture official. They were covering all the worktops in his flat's tiny kitchen.

'It's only fair,' he conceded. 'You've put up with me being preoccupied over all this recently, and there's only so many leaps of faith I can ask from one woman.'

He slipped a thick document into a plastic wallet and turned to face me.

'Have you ever thought it would be handy to be able to pay for small purchases, like under a pound, without clicking through Paypal or entering your credit card?'

'All the time.'

'Well, it's a way of doing that. Loose change for the internet. And it wouldn't only be convenient for customers – it could change subscription models. For instance, you might want to see one edition of a newspaper or magazine online, and instead of paying for a month's sub, you could pay fifty pence for one day or ten pence for a single article, but without filling in details forms and signing yourself up for spam.'

'God, that could be huge.'

'Exactly. But only if I'm first. Hence . . .'

He mimed locking his lips. I kissed them.

When the company was launched, Peter took me away for a surprise weekend to celebrate. At least, I thought that's what we were celebrating. On the Thursday night he told me to pack a bag for the following day. Unbeknown to me, he had spoken to the clinical director for surgery and got me swapped from a full-day list on the Friday to a morning only, meaning we could make a late-afternoon flight to Bristol.

'It's not a weekend in Paris,' he said, 'but when it comes to flights from Inverness, you take what you can get.'

The destination didn't matter. I was so moved that he had quietly gone to this trouble when he had so much else to deal with in the chaotic early days of setting up the firm. I had been resigned to an ordinary weekend at home, probably seeing less of Peter than I could normally look forward to due to his new commitments, and instead he had delivered this lovely escape.

He had booked us into a suite at the Hotel du Vin. It was a converted sugar warehouse: all bare redbrick and black metal pillars. Our room was about twice the size of the flat I lived in when I was working in London, with a private roof terrace, a luxuriantly vast bathroom and the most sprawling bed I have ever slept in.

He seemed a little distracted on the Saturday. We took a train to Bath and wandered around the place. Peter could often be quiet that way, lost in his thoughts, but I sensed his mind was drifting somewhere specific: whirring away with the details of his great opportunity and equally great responsibility. I was completely, magnificently wrong.

We were having a bath together late afternoon. The taps were in the middle – a deal-breaker for such things – and we had a bottle of champagne open. I made a crack about finally having his full attention.

'I'm sorry. I guess you noticed my thoughts have been elsewhere.'

'It wasn't a dig. I'm trying to acknowledge how much I appreciate you doing this, taking so much time for me, for us, right now.'

'Except, I have to confess that my distractedness was nothing to do with the project. I've been anxious about something else.'

'What?'

'Remember when I said I wanted to kiss you, but I was afraid of breaking the spell?'

'How could I forget?'

'Well, that feeling has never quite gone away. I can't believe everything that has happened for me since I met you, where I am now compared to only a few months ago. So here I am again, worried that I'm about to make a misstep and lose it all.'

'Peter, what kind of misstep could change how I feel about you?'

As I said it, I was conscious that he looked vulnerable and sincere: very much like he had when he first asked me out to the Ironworks. Suddenly I had my answer, and I knew why he had been talking about my making a leap of faith.

I don't know whether he noticed, but my eyes were already filling up before he spoke.

'The kind where I ask you to marry me.'

FULL DISCLOSURE

We were lying in the afterglow, his proposal in the bath having led to us chucking towels down on the bed so that we didn't get the sheets too damp in our impatience to have sex. Neither of us had said anything for an unusually long time, certainly enough for us both to be aware the other was feeling the gravity of the moment.

'They say it ought to be the easiest question you ever get asked,' Peter said, 'because you should already know the answer.'

'I didn't need to write down my working.'

'But they also say that the question shouldn't come as a surprise. I realise I sprung this on you, which put you under pressure, especially after me saying how worried I was about the possible consequences of asking it.'

'As I was lying there just now, I will confess my thoughts had turned to whether this is all too fast, too soon. That's how my mind works: as a surgeon, my life has been dominated by risk-averse judgement. And yet, the moment you asked the question, I had no doubts whatsoever. None.'

'Maybe it's all the business stuff I've been reading, but I feel like I should offer you a cooling-off period. Give your risk-averse mind time to do its full due diligence.'

'Do *you* need a cooling-off period?'

I was suddenly anxious that he was projecting here.

'No. I've never been so certain of anything. I realise some people might think it's too soon, but I feel like I've been waiting my whole life for this, so now that it's finally in front of us, why delay?'

That was how I felt too. I knew that if I looked hard enough, I would see lots of reasons to wait, but was this about reason? I knew there would be obstacles and difficulties ahead, but marriage wasn't about finding someone with whom you would never have problems, it was about finding someone you could better tackle your problems with. You appreciate what you have built in a relationship rather than what is given to you easily. Anything is possible when you both want the same thing, and I sincerely believed that we did.

There was also, of course, the issue of my biological clock, which we had already wordlessly broached half an hour ago when I pulled Peter back from getting a condom and he came inside me for the first time. There was a significant unspoken conversation in that, about our mutual desire to be parents, and about how we wanted – and pragmatically needed – that to happen as soon as possible.

We had dinner in a restaurant down at the quayside. I think I floated there. I don't remember walking. The food was divine, but I think we could have sat on the plastic benches in the nearest kebab shop and it would have been divine. I do remember Peter had a risotto with a quail parked in the middle of it. I think I had linguine.

Peter sat up straighter once we had both finished eating.

'In the interests of full disclosure, now that you're my fiancée, there's something I need to tell you.'

'Full disclosure? Doesn't that describe something you should have told me *before* I agreed to marry you?'

My tone was jocular, but Peter's expression indicated this was serious; or at least sensitive.

'On this occasion it works the other way round. I needed to know you wanted to marry me before I could tell you this.'

I sat up straighter also, intrigued and, it must be said, a little nervous.

'My real name is Hamish. Peter is my middle name.'

I laughed, thinking the sudden shift to seriousness had been the build-up to a joke, and this the punchline. But Peter wasn't finished.

'Do you know anyone else with my surname? Apart from Lucy, obviously.'

I gave it some thought. It was unusual but not unique.

'I haven't *met* anyone else with your surname, but I have heard of it. I'm pretty sure there was a Professor Elphinstone who authored a physiology textbook. Oh, and come to think of it, there's that Sir Hamish Elphinstone who was in the news a couple of years back, to do with protests against wind farms on his estate.'

That was when it hit me.

'Hamish Elphinstone, with an estate *in the middle of nowhere out in Perthshire*. Oh my God. Is this where I find out that, as well as everything else, you're secretly rich?'

Peter swallowed.

'I'm not rich: that's the crucial part. And nor am I going to be rich unless it's off my own back. My father said that Lucy and I had to learn to stand on our own two feet – just like he didn't.'

His face briefly flashed a sneer as he said this last, perhaps the first time I had seen bitterness etched upon it.

'We weren't given any financial support once we left home, and nor will we inherit anything. He told us that this was the greatest thing he could pass on to us. The irony is that he now *couldn't* give me his money, because I wouldn't take it. I want nothing to do with him. Neither of us even uses the names he gave us. Lucy's real name is Petronella Lucille Elphinstone.'

He took a mouthful of his wine, like he needed it to wash away a bad taste.

'I had girlfriends before: women who affected not to know about my background, but who buggered off sharpish once they found out I was neither rich nor in line to become rich. Please understand: I'm not saying I didn't tell you this until now as some kind of test. Nobody chooses the life you did because they're after an easy route to riches. This is kind of the opposite: I needed to know you wanted to marry me for who I am before you found out about this baggage, because this baggage is not who I am.'

I reached a hand across the table to his and squeezed it.

'My father is not a nice man. In fact he's a truly horrible human being. He has this utterly utilitarian view of people that comes from generations of aristocratic privilege: anyone he perceives as beneath him exists only to be used and discarded, and there are precious few people he doesn't perceive to be beneath him.

'You wouldn't know that if you met him. He is polite to a fault

127

and can be charming when it serves him, but you'd be conned if you believed that his seeming friendly meant he would lift a finger to turn on a hose if you were burning right in front of him. Not unless this action would benefit him in some way.'

'And what about . . . your mother?'

I kept my tone apologetic in anticipation of the answer.

'An expensively dressed and thus elegantly disguised alcoholic. I've never been sure whether she took to drink because she couldn't stand up for us against him, or whether she would have been able to stand up for us if she hadn't been a drunk.'

'I know what you mean.'

The parallels with my own upbringing were not proving hard to find.

'You remember you asked whether Lucy and I were close, and I answered yes and no?'

I nodded.

'This is what I meant. We are close on one level, and yet on another we crave our distance. We were allies: we grew up under the same tyranny but being around each other reminds us of it. People assume we must have had this lovely privileged childhood. It was financially privileged by anyone's measure, but deprived in many other ways. That's why I'm still so much of a child now, and why I want my kids to have a childhood in which they are *allowed* to be childish.'

I gripped his hand tighter and offered a smile.

'I suppose, then, that we won't be needing a long lead-in to plan a big family wedding?'

So it was never going to be a grand traditional affair with a marquee on the lawn, speeches and favours and catering staff offering champagne flutes from silver salvers. That was okay by me. I never had little-girl dreams of 'my special day': I always thought that was for women prepared to settle for being worthy of notice merely for an isolated few hours of their entire lives.

Peter didn't see the occasion as an opportunity to mend relations with his parents. I made the suggestion as gently as I could, in case some part of him wanted and needed the nudge to offer an olive branch, but his response was unequivocal.

'I don't want his presence ruining this. And his presence would be all it took.'

He didn't mind the conspicuous imbalance of me inviting some of my family, but I didn't want some god-awful jamboree with great-aunts whose names I couldn't even remember being wheeled out of nursing homes, or second cousins' children I'd never met scoffing cake and barfing on a hotel dance floor. So it was only my parents, whose collective response (i.e. that of my father, with my mother contributing meek agreement) was typically graceless. Stiffly polite congratulations were offered initially, but the suddenness of the announcement (I hadn't told them about Peter) and the short notice ahead of the event was interpreted as an indication of some further indistinct shame I was attempting to conceal. They gave the impression that their attendance would be more of an obligation than a pleasure, but to their credit at least they did finally make the trip to see me, and it saved me from my plan of lying to people that they were dead.

I missed having my brothers there. It was too big an ask for them to come so far, especially with kids, but I must confess I harboured a secret fantasy that they would show up as a surprise.

Emily was supposed to be there, but she got flu. Not man flu, but the real deal. She was in her bed for a fortnight and later told me she lost a stone. She was skinny enough to begin with, so she must have looked like a corpse.

I remember feeling a little sad when I saw how few names were on the invitation list. Not, as I have explained, because I wanted a big wedding, but because it brought home how small my life had become, how limited my circles. I had almost no friends outside the realm of medicine, and even among that constituency, the list was never going to be long. I had burned a lot of bridges over the years, I realised.

I was sad, but I was also feeling emboldened. This was a new beginning in lots of ways: a chance to make new friends, to live a new kind of life.

What surprised me was that Peter had so few friends on his list also. He was such an easy person to get along with, and had worked in so many places, that I assumed he would have a huge network of old mates who would come out of the woodwork for a thing like this.

I remarked as much to Lucy on the day.

'Peter is far more shy than you perhaps realise. With you he makes a special effort to seem confident and gregarious. You bring that out in him.'

It was the only thing she ever said to me that could be interpreted as a compliment, though she managed to make it sound like an accusation.

It was a modest and intentionally unspectacular affair: a registry office ceremony followed by a meal at a restaurant and then drinks at the adjoining bar for anyone who still wanted to hang around. Inauspicious circumstances for a thoroughly auspicious rite of passage: so began my new life, both of our new lives.

But let's be honest: nobody's here to talk about how my marriage began. We're here to talk about how it ended.

PART TWO

STORM CHASER

Parlabane watched dusty flurries of snow zip from left to right across the A9 north of Pitlochry. The sight gnawed at him, nagging like a disapproving voice as to the wisdom of pursuing this journey, and the voice wasn't only talking about the possible road conditions around the Drumochter Pass.

He was chasing a flyer here, and if he was chasing it through a blizzard in a recently purchased second-hand car of unproven reliability, then desperation was edging towards suicidal recklessness. What was worse was that it wasn't the promise of a story that had set him on the road: it was the alternative. While he was undoubtedly intrigued by Lucy Elphinstone's visit, in truth he wanted a reason not to be in the flat right now. He was feeling boxed in by memories everywhere he looked. Even a trip out to the back court had got him in the gut, when he looked up at the rear of the building and saw the drainpipe he had once scaled when he fatefully locked himself out. Add to that the fact that the place was half the size it used to be and it completed the sense that a big part of himself was missing.

He knew it would pass, but for the meantime it was best to be somewhere else, and besides, he could rattle out filler on his laptop anywhere.

He had called up and agreed to meet Lucy Elphinstone for coffee around the corner on Broughton Street that morning. He told her he wanted to talk things over more in-depth, but mainly he wanted to see if she still felt the same having had twenty-four hours more to mull things over and deal with her grief.

It was a bright airy cafe up the hill from the Barony, the morning sun through its big windows warming the place despite the frost still sparkling where the pavement was in shade. Parlabane had waited for her close to fifteen minutes after their appointed time, and was about to interpret her no-show as a change of heart when she came through the door. She had an air of flustered apology as she took a seat, explaining how an important work-related call came in just as she was about to leave the flat.

She ordered a pot of Earl Grey which she sipped black. She leaned over the cup and breathed in the fumes much as Parlabane recalled breathing menthol vapour to alleviate childhood colds. The fumes alone appeared to have a restorative effect. The flustered air dissipated and she visibly relaxed in her seat. Parlabane felt his own tensions ease, as he was braced for a degree of amateur bereavement counselling and it didn't look as though that would be necessary.

She looked better, like she'd had a good night's sleep, perhaps for the first time in a while. Sheer exhaustion must have overcome the wakeful effects of being wired and overwrought.

Before he could ask how she was doing and whether she still wanted him to go ahead with this, she reached into her bag and produced an A4 envelope, from which she slid out a printed list.

'I've typed out names and contact details for everybody I could think of: people who knew Peter personally or knew him and Diana as a couple. Anyone who might be able to offer more insight than I can into what was going on.'

She came across as businesslike and purposeful, though he sensed that beneath this façade she was still struggling to keep herself together. He couldn't decide whether she was sticking to her purpose despite her turmoil or whether having this purpose was the one thing staving off breakdown. Either way, there was more of a calmness about her, a quiet determination, rather than that slightly frantic neediness he had witnessed the previous day. He reasoned that if she had enjoyed a good night's sleep, was feeling more centred, and yet she still held these suspicions, then it was worth looking into.

She nudged the list towards him across the table. His hand hesitated before picking it up, conscious of what might be inferred from this simple act. It felt as though he was not merely being handed a lead or taking a job but somehow accepting responsibility for this woman and her emotionally fragile condition.

'I looked up more about you too, while I was in research mode. I read that you were married to an anaesthetist, though I gather you're not together any more.'

'We're recently divorced.'

He had never said that out loud before, but he knew he had to get used to it. It felt easier saying it to someone who had worse shit to deal with: a matter of fact rather than some defining catastrophe.

'I'm sorry. I only mentioned it because I assume it means you know a few surgeons. It's just, I get the impression they're a strange bunch and I reckoned it would help that you're familiar with them. I've always found Diana to be somewhat cold and aloof, and I'm curious as to whether she is cold and aloof because she's a surgeon or whether she's cold and aloof *for* a surgeon.'

'My wife called them clever psychopaths.'

The words had come out before he could consider the implications. It was a familiar term that tripped off the tongue without thought: a joke that functioned as a cultural shorthand among anaesthetists. Unfortunately it had sounded very different spoken to a layperson, particularly in this context.

Parlabane put his wipers on but the snow hitting the windscreen wasn't melting on contact. It was like a hard, brittle dust, brushed aside by the blades, which scraped across the glass with a squeak. It wasn't snowing, he realised: the wind was whipping the top layer off what had fallen a couple of days ago and scattering it like sand.

The route would be clear after all, but it was a timely reminder, after recent costly lapses in his professional judgement, to always make sure he was seeing what he thought he was seeing. He was merely looking deeper than had so far been delved in this story: there was no hypothesis in play here.

The biggest reason for Lucy's suspicion was that Diana Jager had mentioned a prior incident at Widow Falls, but the most rational interpretation for this being more than a random coincidence was simply that she had identified a risk and that her husband

135

had failed to learn from his near-miss. She had expressed her concern over the fact that the guy drove too fast when he was stressed and angry, and had mentioned that the previous occasion had followed an argument. That both incidents should happen at the same place sounded less dramatic when you factored in that it was an accident blackspot. Lucy said Peter was in a bad way mentally when she last spoke to him, so the most likely explanation was that his stress had led to a fatal accident, with a further outside possibility that it had led him to suicide.

Nonetheless, he had been sure that Lucy had greater reason for her suspicion than she was prepared to let on. There was definitely something she wasn't saying, but that wasn't the hunch that was urging Parlabane north. It was the fact that they had found the car but not found a body: *that* part had triggered his suspicious-bastard reflex from the first second.

TALE OF THE TAPE

'Romeo Victor Four from Dispatch, do you read?'

The radio seemed unusually noisy, breaking over the comparative silence inside the car. It was mid-morning, Rodriguez at the wheel. This was the first time Ali had been out with him since that initial prolonged shift, and she was patiently navigating as the Londoner attempted to develop his sense of the local geography. The reason for the quiet was that they were slowly making their way through the labyrinthine streets of the Silver Brae housing scheme, a recently built upmarket development where there was little traffic outside of rush hour. In fact, the only other cars they had encountered were learners under instruction, and she was wondering how many they would pass before Rodriguez worked out that she was taking the piss.

He earned points for how he first got behind the wheel. Rodriguez had to be six inches taller than her, which was not an uncommon distinction among male officers. However, they often seemed to make a big deal about adjusting the seat if she had been driving a patrol car. The preferred tactic of such colleagues was to squash themselves in behind the wheel in order to emphasise how close to the dashboard her seat needed to be. Well woohoo, you're tall, she would think. How long did you have to practise to achieve that?

Rodriguez had simply slid the seat back a few notches without fuss and slipped into position. He'd been in the Met, though: maybe they got an awareness course.

'Dispatch, this is Romeo Victor Four, go ahead.'

'Reported break-in at Lower Mills industrial estate. Can you deal?'

'Roger. On our way.'

It took less than five minutes to reach the address: a printing and copying business in a single-storey unit on the outskirts of the estate where it bordered a residential area. The call had come from a woman who was hanging out her washing when she saw someone climb up on to the roof and disappear inside, presumably through a skylight.

They got out of the patrol car and did a quick circuit of the perimeter. There was no sign of damage, and though the premises had been in darkness when they pulled up, there was a light on by the time they made it around to the front again.

Rodriguez rang the bell and a few moments later a squat and slightly sweaty bloke opened the door. He was flushed about the face and breathing heavily. He looked mid-fifties, dressed in a grey suit and a blue tie that he had loosened as though his work day had just finished rather than begun.

'We received a call about a possible break-in?'

Rodriguez's tone indicated that he had already sussed the situation.

The guy rolled his eyes.

'Aye, sorry. My wife's away visiting her mother in Fochabers, and she's gone off with both sets of keys.'

He showed them his driving licence, identifying him as Stuart Preston. The business was called Presto-Print.

He showed them inside to verify all was as it should be.

'They say you only find out how secure your place really is when you lock yourself out of it. And the answer in this case is "not very". Took me about two minutes from realising Audrey had the keys to gaining access through the roof, and I'm not exactly Spider-Man. Just needed to roll one of the rubbish hoppers against the wall and then pull myself up over the gutter.'

'How did you get the door open for us?'

'Spare keys in the office desk.'

The place was well worth breaking into. There were four PCs, two with extra-large widescreen monitors, as well as an array of laser printing machinery.

Ali clocked a photo on the wall of the guy with his wife, handing over an outsize charity cheque for funds they had raised for Cancer Research.

They were done here.

'It's reassuring you got here so fast, right enough,' Preston said.

'PC Rodriguez knows a few shortcuts.'

'Can I offer you both a cup of tea?'

'Oh no, we wouldn't trouble you.'

It was her stock answer. She always felt impolite about refusing. People didn't know it wasn't permitted.

'It's just boiled,' he told them, indicating a kettle in the corner. 'First thing I did. Well, I needed it after hauling myself in like that.'

'That's kind, but we have to get back on patrol,' Rodriguez told him.

The guy looked genuinely disappointed. Perhaps with his wife away he feared being starved of company.

Preston glanced down at the newspaper on top of his desk.

'Hell of a business that, was it not?' he asked, thus confirming Ali's hypothesis. Any excuse to engage them in conversation.

She looked at what he was talking about. The paper was open at a story about Peter Elphinstone.

'Terrible, yes.'

'Not long married, as well. I never knew him, but his wife, she operated on me once.'

He sounded quite proud of this, like it was an achievement. People over a certain age loved to tell you about their operations. Ordinarily, this would have been Ali's cue to get out the door all the quicker, but curiosity got the better of her.

'What was she like?'

'A bit of a cold fish, to be honest. Didn't smile much, you know? Not a lot of chat. But very good. Very professional. She sorted me out grand. I had this problem in my . . .'

They made their way back to the car about ten minutes later, Rodriguez giving her an admonitory look.

'Jeez. We were almost out of there and you had to ask him a

139

question. I now know enough about that man's colon that it could be my specialist subject on *Mastermind*.'

'Sorry.'

'I suppose I'll need to get used to everybody vaguely knowing everybody else.'

'What do you mean?'

'Diana Jager doing that guy's operation.'

'Yeah, that's Inverness for you. Still a village. Never assume your anonymity in this place.'

It was something Ali felt most keenly at times like this, after a break-up. What made it homely and reassuring could also be oppressive. Everybody knew things about you, so when you suddenly realised you couldn't rely on the discretion of someone you once trusted enough to be sexually intimate with, it could leave you feeling horribly exposed.

In recent days she had wanted to melt into the background, but she knew that it was only a matter of time before she ran into Martin again, and into people who knew him. There weren't any particular revelations he could bring to light: it was simply the unsettling knowledge that secret things they had once shared were no longer under joint ownership.

Did guys feel this way too? She hoped so. Mutually assured destruction would be a reassuring threat.

'You still got questions about Dr Jager, then?' Rodriguez asked, putting the car into gear and accelerating with a slow, steady foot.

'Only an open-minded curiosity.'

Ali had left Jager's home with a sharp, instinctive sense of suspicion, but the prospect of presenting her notion to CID showed up its paucity in an unforgivingly harsh light. She could picture that patronising git Bill Ellis smirking as she admitted that the sum of her evidence comprised a small bruise on Jager's cheek and Ali's personal impression that she didn't seem sad enough.

'How are things with that business?' Rodriguez asked. 'It's kind of been off my radar.'

'Slow and annoyingly grey. Still no body, but they've got the car out of the river and it's being examined by our people down at the depot. I have to pop down there later, in fact.'

'What's grey about it?'

'I don't know, just that sense that I'll never fill in all the blanks. For instance, we haven't been able to trace the only witness.'

'The woman who called it in?'

'That's right. Sheena Matheson. Her number was a pre-paid mobile, so there's no details registered to it. When you dial it, it comes up as unavailable.'

'And isn't she listed in the usual . . . ?'

'We've found two Sheena Mathesons in the area, but neither of them admits to making the call. Neither of them live west of Ordskirk either.'

'I suppose it's possible she only moved here recently.'

'True. She said she had a ten-year-old daughter, so she would have to be enrolled in the schools register. Actually, there's a thought. Hang right at the next junction.'

'Where we going?'

'I listened to the recording of the call a couple of times. She said she was nipping out to get Calpol from the garage because her daughter had a temperature. If she was coming in from the west on that road, there's only one place she could have had in mind.'

A few minutes later they pulled up at the twenty-four-hour petrol station where she and Rodriguez had stopped for a late snack the night Elphinstone's car went into the river.

'This is where we were when the call came in. We probably drove right past her on our way to respond.'

Ali recognised both of the people behind the counter: an adolescent called Grieg and the duty manager, Brenda. She was on first-name terms with most of the staff here, as it was a regular stop for nocturnal sustenance.

'Ali,' said Brenda with a smile. 'What can we do for you? The usual?'

'Aye, two coffees would be great. But we're also hoping for a wee look at your CCTV tapes. I'm trying to track down somebody who was in here early hours of Friday morning.'

'No bother. Come on through to the back.'

Brenda led them to a cramped space, no bigger than a pantry, where the CCTV cameras fed into an ageing PC with a compact monitor.

'I can never remember how to work this thing,' she confessed, tapping the keyboard uncertainly.

Ali braced herself for the possibility that she would have to come back later when someone else was on-shift. Nothing about this incident was proving easy or convenient to deal with.

'Oh, no, I tell a lie. I just need to . . . here we go.'

Brenda hit a combination of keys and the live image was replaced by a list of files, each denoting a date followed by start and stop times for the period it covered. They were broken into two-hour segments.

'Early hours Friday?'

'Yes. About three.'

Brenda selected a file running from two until four, fast-forwarding under Ali's instruction. Ali kept an eye on the time-stamp, telling her to slow to normal as it approached two forty-five. She wanted to be absolutely sure they were looking at the right file, and confirmation came as she watched herself enter the shop.

'That's one of our regulars,' Brenda told Rodriguez as they watched Ali on screen lifting some sandwiches from the fridge. 'If she's shoplifting, we've never caught her.'

Ali felt disproportionately conspicuous as she watched herself stop briefly in the toiletries section. She remembered pausing to stare at the pregnancy kits. Her cheeks flushed with heat. There was no way for Brenda or Rodriguez to know what she had been looking at, but it felt as though it must be obvious. Maybe it was displaced anxiety she was feeling. It was three days later and her period still hadn't come.

'Okay, speed up the playback again. And slow it down whenever anyone comes in.'

Nobody did. The recording could have been a still image but for minor flickering, until the door opened shortly before four o'clock. It was a burly male in biker leathers, his helmet under his arm.

142

'It's like that some nights,' Brenda said apologetically. 'You need a good book.'

Ali got her to run the file backwards until reaching her own appearance again, playing at half the speed of before to make sure they hadn't missed even the briefest of visits. Still nothing.

'Maybe she changed her mind and went home,' Rodriguez suggested. 'The crash could have spooked her, especially knowing her kid was in the house alone.'

This was true. On the tape, Matheson said she had told her daughter she would only be half an hour. Having seen the crash and stopped to make the call, had she decided she'd been away too long and turned around? But if her kid was sick enough for her to have ventured out in search of Calpol in the middle of the night, would she really go back empty handed?

It was something else that wouldn't sound like much if she was presenting it to Bill Ellis, but she couldn't help thinking the wrong notes were starting to accumulate.

OLD FRIENDS AND NEW LIES

Parlabane strode up the driveway of a neat redbrick modern detached house in an upmarket estate on the western outskirts of Inverness. His phone had told him the address. It had also told him it would take five minutes to walk from the hotel, but after a brisk ten he checked again and saw that he had looked at the driving time estimate by mistake. He thought the walk would clear his head, but as he approached the front door, clutching a bottle of wine, he was still feeling anxious, awkward and slightly guilty.

Lucy had given him as much information as she could collate with regard to Peter and Diana's work and social circles. The theatre nurse quoted in a couple of press reports was not among the names she supplied, and nor had she ever heard the woman mentioned. It was Lucy's suspicion that she was an attention-seeking busybody who had sought to insinuate herself into the story, but Parlabane had the more prosaic notion that she happened to be the one who answered the phone when a reporter called the hospital. Rather than exaggerate her own connection to Diana, it was likely she said as much as she knew and the reporter made it sound like she was a bosom buddy.

Parlabane wanted to speak to the people who genuinely knew the couple, and the briefest scan of Lucy's notes gave him his first break. The name Austin Waites leapt out at him from a list of Diana's colleagues, as he used to work alongside Sarah in Edinburgh way back when they were both registrars. Parlabane and Sarah had socialised with Austin and his partner Lucas semi-regularly in those days, and had kept in touch at Christmas card level after their respective consultant posts took them elsewhere.

It had always felt like they were more Sarah's friends than his, falling into the category of people he never saw without her. Thus

144

he guessed that whatever they had heard about the divorce, he was unlikely to have come out of the dispatches well.

That covered the anxious and awkward aspects of how he was feeling. The guilt part derived from the fact that he had only made the effort to get in touch after all these years because he suspected they might have information. In fact, it went double because he was pretending otherwise. He had called Austin to say he was staying in Inverness for a couple of days' climbing (lie number one) and had remembered (actually just learned, so lie number two) that he and Lucas lived there now, so would they mind meeting up for a drink.

Austin insisted he come for dinner instead, which reminded Parlabane that Lucas loved to cook. He remembered huge noisy groups gathered around their kitchen table in Marchmont, candles jammed into wine bottles and the Lemonheads on the CD player. Lucas always squeezed in next to Parlabane as a non-medical ally and sole hope of taking the conversation elsewhere. He was a radio producer in those days, working on news and current affairs for BBC Scotland.

They got on well enough, but Parlabane remembered with a further pang how he had always bodyswerved Lucas's overtures towards meeting up at other times because he tended to act like a bit of a fanboy. That was a hazard he'd never need to worry about again.

The front door opened before he could reach the bell, and they welcomed him inside with a warmth he felt he didn't deserve for any number of reasons. It was an indication of how bad things had got after the Leveson Inquiry that he was always surprised when anyone gave the impression they still liked him.

As soon as he walked into their living room, he clocked the photo taking pride of place on the mantelpiece. Suits, smiles and a blizzard of confetti.

'You guys got married?' he asked.

'Soon as it became legal,' Lucas replied, his Canadian accent still not softened by twenty years in Scotland.

'Congratulations.'

Parlabane felt an upspring of emotion that he hoped they interpreted as being all about them.

It wasn't, though: it was merely another thing that brought home the scale of what was gone. Austin and Lucas had been together roughly as long as he and Sarah, but it turned out they had been beginning married life round about the time he and Sarah were ending it. Christ, he wondered: was life fucking with him right now by tossing these things in his face, or was it just that you inferred cruel parallels and painful significance all the more when you were feeling so raw?

At least it turned out he needn't have worried about awkwardness deriving from what they had heard about his divorce, as there was far more awkwardness to be derived from them having heard nothing.

Lucas was setting down their main course on the kitchen table when Austin said it.

'So, how's Sarah these days? She took an academic post for a while, didn't she? But last I heard she was back in the clinical side of things.'

If there was a positive to be gained from the ensuing confessional, it was that it provided plausible cover for him to turn the conversation towards another recently ended marriage.

'Still, there's always someone worse off than yourself. I gather you're a colleague of Diana Jager's. I read about her husband. Must be devastating.'

Austin nodded, finishing a glass of wine and placing a hand over the top as Lucas offered a refill.

'Did you know her?' he asked.

'No. Sarah used to show me her blog. I didn't know she ended up in Inverness until I read about the accident.'

'I've known her for about five years. I saw her today, in fact. It's awful. Awkward too: nobody knows what to say to her. Sorry for your loss? Can you say that? His body may never be found, they reckon. I don't even know how it works: is it still seven years before he can be declared dead?'

'Not necessarily,' Parlabane told him, 'if the police and the coroner conclude that death was probable. But even so, it's a horrible limbo to endure. And you say she's back at work?'

'Yeah. I guess that's how she's dealing with it: staying busy, concentrating on something that will occupy mind and body.'

Kind of ironic, Parlabane thought, given that it all blew up for her over an article criticising a colleague for being back at work too soon after childbirth. He decided it would be politic not to share this, however; nor what it might indicate regarding her being not quite so devastated as people assumed.

'It's so terribly, terribly sad,' Austin said. 'We were all delighted for her when she got married, you know? All the things she wrote in that blog, it was the truth. You see it all the time: women giving the best of themselves to the profession, so they can't find someone, or can't find someone who'll put up with what the profession demands.'

Parlabane wondered if he was being subtly got at here, despite the non-judgemental sentiments offered earlier. If so, these particular barbs wouldn't pierce his armour. It had never been Sarah's job that was the problem. She was the one who had issues with what *his* profession demanded, but given that they were issues unique to the way he chose to exercise that profession, there was still no way he was coming out of this well.

'I gather they hadn't known each other that long.'

'About a year all told. That's what makes it all the more tragic. She found someone and very quickly they both just knew. She was happy. She *deserved* to be happy. And then a few months after the wedding, this comes out of the blue. Bang.'

'Die young, stay pretty,' said Lucas, earning an odd look from his husband and a more guardedly curious one from Parlabane.

'I don't mean Peter,' he clarified. 'What I mean is, they say that about people, but can't it be true about a marriage also? They might have grown old and died together, but equally they could have been broken up within a year. Point is, we'll never know.'

'Why would you say that?' Parlabane asked.

'Ignore him,' said Austin. 'He's winding me up. It's a running gag ever since I once confessed to an irrational insecurity that something would break us up now that we're married, after being contentedly together for so long before.'

'There should be a word for the fear of ironic twists of fate,' Parlabane said, though he wasn't convinced that an affectionate dig at Austin was the whole reason for Lucas's remark.

'We had Diana and Peter here for dinner,' Austin said. 'Maybe a month after their wedding. We squeezed ten around this table, if you can believe it. It was great to see her out like that. She wasn't always the most sociable before then, but she seemed determined to make more of an effort after Peter came along. He had a really positive effect on her.'

Austin looked away and sighed, a glum but searching expression on his face.

'We'll need to try and reach out to her now. Make sure she doesn't retreat into herself.'

By way of drawing a line under an uncomfortable subject, Austin got up and began clearing the dishes. Parlabane ignored protestations to stay in his seat and helped ferry a few items to the kitchen.

'If you're in an obliging mood,' said Lucas, 'perhaps you could spare an hour to give a talk to my students.'

Lucas had explained how he was now a senior lecturer in media studies at the University of the Highlands and Islands. Parlabane knew quite a few journalists who had moved into academia as work dried up in their own fields, many of them doing so with resignation and regret. Lucas, by contrast, seemed utterly content; indeed Parlabane couldn't recall seeing him so enthused in talking about his work. It fitted his longstanding fascination with Parlabane's activities back in the day, which always seemed to exercise him more than the subject of his own endeavours. Lucas, it seemed, was more comfortable as an analyst and an observer of the media than as a hands-on practitioner.

'I don't know, Lucas. It's not something I could do without a bit of preparation.'

'Oh, no, you wouldn't need to give a lecture. Just a kind of Q and A. I would tee you up with the questions.'

Parlabane felt horrible now. He was indebted to his hosts for their hospitality, but strangely uncomfortable about the prospect of what Lucas was requesting, and he couldn't tell him the truth about why. It wasn't inexperience in speaking to students, as Lucas knew Parlabane had done plenty of that during his stint as rector of a university a few years back. It was the fear that this was what awaited him.

With so many doors closing all around him, it had already been in the back of his mind as a possible option offering a regular salary and even the chance to salvage some respectability. But it also represented a final surrender. It would be like being put out to stud, when he wanted to believe he still had races left in him.

'I'm sorry. It's not a good time, you know? Between the work situation and what happened with Sarah, that's why I'm up here climbing: trying to get my head together.'

'That's okay, forget about it.'

But he could tell Lucas wasn't going to. There was a glint in his eye as he spoke, ostensibly of bonhomie but somehow calculating. Parlabane's explanation hadn't cut it.

Austin got to his feet and announced his intention to have an early night as he was operating the next morning. He gave Parlabane a hug, a look of sincere regret on his face as he said: 'So sorry again about you and Sarah.'

Austin headed up the stairs as Lucas crouched down in front of a cupboard and produced a bottle of single malt. He poured them each a generous dram of Glenfarclas. Parlabane recalled a line in a song about clearing your conscience with Speyside. So far the highland air hadn't done it. Might as well let the highland spirit take a shot.

'It really is great to see you again,' Lucas said, sitting down opposite. 'Let's not leave it so long in future.'

'Absolutely. Next time I'm up this way, I'll definitely give you guys a shout.'

'Where was it today? The Cobbler? Angel's Peak?'

The question confused Parlabane for a moment, until he remembered the false pretext he had given for getting in touch.

'The Cobbler.'

Lucas had that glint again. It made him uneasy.

'Ranger service was advising strongly against climbing today due to high winds.'

Lucas sat back in his chair, helping himself to a sip, all the time keeping his gaze trained on his mortified guest.

'Why were you lying to us, Jack?'

Parlabane couldn't bring himself to argue, as that would be to lie again.

'The usual.'

Lucas nodded, thin-lipped and glowering. He let Parlabane shrink under his admonitory stare for a few seconds then couldn't keep it up any longer.

'Sneaky sonofabitch,' he said, with a dirty laugh. 'I goddamn knew it.'

Parlabane gave a bashfully apologetic smile.

'Thanks for not calling me on it during dinner.'

'Didn't want to ruin the atmosphere. But I'm calling you on it now. The price is you're singing for your supper. UHI, Inverness Campus. Shall we say eleven tomorrow?'

'I was serious when I said I wasn't comfortable with it, Lucas.'

'Yes, but I'm offering a quid pro quo, and I know you'll go to any length to get a lead.'

'I haven't told you what I'm working on.'

'Come on, Jack. Inverness may officially be a city these days, but it's still a small town. How many stories could have led you to seek us out after all these years?'

'Touché. So what have you got?'

'First, do we have a deal?'

Parlabane sighed. Ordinarily he wouldn't concede anything until he knew the likely worth of the information, but he owed Lucas what he was asking anyway.

'We have a deal. But this better be worth it.'

'Oh, it's not. But it's marginally better than nothing and I figured you're desperate. My take on Diana and Peter.'

'I'm listening.'

Lucas took another sip of malt and set down his glass, leaning

150

forward. He dropped his voice too, and Parlabane was soon aware of another reason his deceit hadn't been unmasked in front of Austin.

'I like Diana. Let me get that out there so we can be clear where I'm coming from. She's a bit of an acquired taste, granted, and she doesn't exactly bowl you over with her light and warmth, but ultimately her heart's in the right place, I think. She's had to put up with a lot of shit, so I can understand why Austin was so happy for her. Why he wanted to believe *she* was happy.'

'You think she wasn't?'

'I think she settled, that's all, and it was rough on her, coming to terms with that.'

Parlabane couldn't allow for ambiguity around Lucas's choice of words.

'Settled?'

'I mean I think she compromised: dropped her standards and was then in denial about it. What may have made it worse is that she was so high and mighty on the subject. Her blog was notoriously unequivocal regarding the "nobility of a woman being alone" as opposed to putting up with someone unworthy simply to be in a relationship. Unfortunately I think that's precisely what she ended up doing. That's got to be a blow to your pride when you finally realise it: especially if you suspect *other* people realise it.'

'What are you basing all this on?'

'Seeing them together. I met Peter a few times. He wasn't all that.'

'Yeah, but it's not about what *you* saw in him, is it. I know plenty of people who don't get why a friend is with their particular partner. In fact, I'm pretty sure I was "that particular partner" in a lot of Sarah's friends' conversations.'

'Never us, I swear,' Lucas replied with a deliberately coy smile. 'Hey, look, I know what you're saying. It's one thing when you know a guy's punching above his weight, especially if he realises it and ups his game accordingly. But that's not what I saw when they were round here.'

Parlabane sat forward. From Lucas's face he could tell this was something that had troubled him, and yet possibly something he had found difficult to talk to Austin about.

'Here's the thing. We never saw them together before they got married, so I can't compare. Nobody did, really. I remember Austin remarking on it: whenever Diana wasn't at work, she was with Peter, together alone, exclusive. Like a cocoon. He took it to be a healthy sign: who wouldn't? And maybe that built up my expectations, both of what he would be like and how they would be together.

'As Austin told you, Diana was keen to be more sociable after they were married, and we missed the wedding because we were on holiday, so we had a dinner party for them after we got back.'

Lucas glanced over to the dining table, like he could still see them sitting there.

'I was sitting opposite Diana, with Peter facing us both. He was pretty quiet at first. Struck me as naturally shy, so this was understandable in new company; and busy, loud company at that. After a few drinks, he was less reticent, but let's just say he should have stuck with shyness and letting us imagine his unspoken thoughts were profound.'

'Was he crass?' Parlabane asked, thinking it unlikely, but he did remember being at Austin and Lucas's place in Edinburgh once and sharing their unspoken disdain for the improbable new boyfriend who had turned up on the arm of a surgical senior house officer. They had later concluded that she was road-testing this Rangers-tattooed fucknugget for shock value before introducing him to her parents as an act of revenge.

'No,' Lucas replied. 'Just conspicuously out of his depth. His frame of reference was so limited: all internet memes and sci-fi and videogames. It was like talking to a fourteen-year-old. When we were talking politics, he kept bringing it back to *Game of Thrones* and even *Star Trek*. Seriously, the guy could quote Star Federation directives on every issue but was considerably less up-to-date on UK or Scottish government policy.'

'So what?' Parlabane asked. 'I mean, I get that you found it annoying, but maybe Diana reckoned she needed a bit of geek in her life to counter-balance all the overblown hyper-seriousness that we both know comes with the job.'

'It wasn't me who had a problem with it: that's what I'm telling you. It was Diana. She spent most of the evening spinning for him.'

'Spinning?'

'Managing the message. Interpreting for him. Saying "I think what Peter means is that . . ." You know?'

'And how was he taking this?'

'He was looking at her like: what the fuck? A mixture of embarrassment and confusion. He thought he was doing just fine, and here she was, explaining on his behalf. Not only explaining, either. She was quoting him on stuff more than he was opining himself, like he had played his A game elsewhere and she wanted us to see that rather than how he was performing here tonight.'

'Quoting him on what?'

'Gender issues, hacking and privacy, climate change, religious fundamentalism. When these things came up, he'd make a limited or sometimes inane contribution, and she'd be like: "Peter, what was that great thing you said about this that time . . ." He seemed reluctant to quote himself, maybe from being cued up and put on the spot like that, so he'd say he didn't remember, and she would say it for him.'

'And what was his A game like?'

'It sounded a lot like Diana's opinions reflected back at her after being rehashed enough that she thought she was hearing a new angle. Not exclusively, though. She was particularly keen to showcase what he had to say on things she didn't get, like hacking and cyber-crime and cryptocurrency. But even on those, she didn't seem so much like his wife as like a mother who was over-eager for her teenage son to impress in front of grown-up company.'

'Ouch. That sounds like a pretty harsh take, Lucas.'

'Just telling you what I saw, Jack. I may be biased and kinda bitter at having to wait a decade and a half for the state to permit me to marry the man I love, but it gives a certain perspective upon the danger of getting married after a whirlwind romance. While you're distracted by the sex and the excitement, you can deceive yourself about your partner's limitations. After the wedding, though, there's nowhere to run, nowhere to hide. Sooner or later you have to face the truth.'

WIVES AND PARTNERS

When I was twelve, my parents eschewed our usual February half-term skiing trip in search of some winter sunshine in Lanzarote. I hated it. Instead of snow, there was a constant precipitation of black dust, like a cruel inversion of the holiday I would have preferred. Plus I had not long hit puberty, so the previously unproblematic issue of sharing a room with my two younger brothers became a vortex of awkward, made all the worse by getting my period that week too. I got all kinds of grief from Mum and Dad for being grumpy and sullen and ungrateful for this unrequested privilege, particularly over my reluctance to don a bikini or ever take off my shorts and T-shirt. I recall them bemoaning what they interpreted as the first heralds of my becoming a sulky teen, thereby giving a textbook illustration of the term 'self-fulfilling prophecy'.

My one positive memory of the trip was our visit to Cueva de los Verdes, a volcanic tunnel created by a subterranean lava flow. There was no guide, so we were left to explore by ourselves, which made me all the more alarmed when we reached its dramatic central cavern and I observed how the ground fell away in a sheer plunge only inches from the edge of the path. The drop had to be fifty feet, down to jagged rocks and thus certain death, which made me fearful for my heedless brothers who were always wrestling and pushing and tripping each other. I was appalled that there was no barrier, not even a warning sign, and that my parents weren't cautioning us to stay away from the precipice.

Then I realised that it was an illusion. What actually lay inches from the path was a shallow pool, untroubled by the movement of air and thus perfectly reflective of the cavern's carefully designed lighting. But the weird thing was, once I understood what I was looking at, I was disappointed. Now I could simultaneously see

155

the pool and the phantom ravine, but I only wanted to see the latter. That's what is seductive about certain illusions. Even when you know the truth, you can still choose to see things that are not there. You can prefer the illusion to the reality.

I was ready for that Oh my God moment. I knew that things might look rather scary once the honeymoon was literally over, that we might both be inclined to inflate the significance of any emergent problems because we were terrified of it not working, of us having made a huge mistake. But I also knew, as I had told myself when he proposed, that in a marriage, you value what you build, and the dividend is in overcoming difficulties together.

It is not that I was blind to Peter's faults before we were married. More that he concealed them beneath what in myth is known as a 'glamour': a magical disguise that prevented me from seeing who he really was. And once we were married, once the seduction was complete, he discarded it.

The first thing that struck me was that we seldom ate together. Often it was because of our respective schedules, one of us coming home later than the other. Two decades in surgery had prepared me for that, but it made it all the more disappointing on the occasions when we were both home and yet didn't sit down to the same meal. Peter would say he wasn't hungry and slope off to his computer or his Xbox, only to fix himself something or even order junk food a couple of hours later.

He was usually drinking too. Not to extremes, but he seldom seemed to have a dry night, and he would look at me like I was being ridiculous if I ever drew attention to it. I never said anything melodramatic, merely passed comment: 'Wine on a school night?' That kind of thing.

'Jesus, Peter, we're becoming more like flatmates than a husband and wife,' I complained one night, having barely got five minutes of his time between him coming through the front door and disappearing into his den with a can of beer and a McDonald's.

'I'm sorry,' he replied, indignation underlining that he was the opposite of apologetic. 'I've got a lot on my plate at the moment and some things I need to look over before tomorrow, because I need to finish a brief for one of the subcontractors. I've been working fourteen hours straight and I'm stressed out my box, so if your idea of being a husband and wife is to be getting on my case rather than being supportive, then flatmates sounds pretty good right now.'

It was an exchange we had over and over again. One time he apologised and put down the laptop, and we ended up in bed; but mostly he made me feel guilty for being selfish.

'I'm trying to build something here, Diana. I'm trying to do what I've never done before, like you encouraged me to do. And when I get home, if I don't have more work to do, I need space to unwind.'

'I appreciate that,' I replied. 'But before we were married, your idea of unwinding didn't involve retreating into your own company all the time.'

What troubled me was that we didn't talk the way we used to, and by that I don't mean as often. I mean literally the *way* we used to, and in particular the way *he* used to. We would talk about things that mattered, things that made us feel connected. Every conversation was an exploration of who each of us was, pregnant with plans and possibilities of who we might be in future, together. He was articulate, he was engaged, he was passionate.

To give you an example, not long before we got married, I was quite upset about something that happened at work. I had a death on the table, which is fortunately very rare, and even though we had done everything, it was still a horrible thing to deal with. I went over and over the case in my head, all of the decisions I had made and actions I had taken, but could find no way I might have done things differently that would have affected the outcome for the better. It may seem odd, but somehow this only made me feel worse, until Peter said something that made sense of it, and I felt like a burden was lifted.

'It is possible to commit no error and still fail, Diana,' he told me. 'That is not a flaw, just life.'

It was moments like that which assured me I was making the

right decision about marrying him. Where did he go, I wondered: this man who understood me, who inspired me?

I recall we went to my colleague Austin's house for dinner a few weeks after the wedding, and Peter seemed so dull, like a dilute version of himself. I was so frustrated because I wanted everyone to see the real him.

'What was wrong with you in there?' I asked him as we drove home.

'What do you mean?'

'You didn't sound like you. It was like you couldn't be bothered being yourself so you were phoning it in.'

'I don't understand,' he replied, confused and slightly exasperated. 'I am myself. You make it sound like you needed me to suit up and be some alter ego, like you wanted Superman but got Clark Kent. Is that why you kept speaking for me? Explaining what I "meant" to say? Because that was bloody mortifying. Did you want me to be more impressive in front of your friends, is that it? To be somebody else because they might think the guy you've married is beneath you?'

'No, it's precisely the opposite. I wanted them to see the man I married, but he didn't show up. It was like you were afraid to be yourself.'

'Well, maybe I was feeling intimidated about being around so many people you know and I don't.'

Perhaps it was just a difficult time, I told myself. Lucy had warned me Peter was more shy than I assumed, and it occurred to me that he might be experiencing the same Oh my God anxieties about what we might have rushed into. Add to that the pressures of having given up his job and embarked on a new and daunting business venture, and it was inevitable that he would be feeling a little insecure, a little afraid.

And, of course, none of this was made any easier by his mother dying shortly after our wedding.

I had come out of the shower and was walking to the bedroom to get dressed for work when I heard Peter on the phone. He was seldom awake at that time, often sleeping in after a late night in his den, and from his tone I could tell it was something serious.

'Okay. Yeah. Okay. Right. Yes. Okay.'

His voice was monotone, his eyes glazed. He seemed numb rather than shocked, sitting there gripping his mobile for a few seconds after he had ended the call. I waited for him to speak.

'It was my mother.'

His choice of words made me wrongly assume something had happened to his father, or maybe Lucy.

'What's happened?'

'She died last night.'

'Oh, Peter. I'm so sorry.'

I sat down beside him, still damp in my towel. I gave him a hug, but he didn't respond. He seemed stiff and detached, not ready to lean on me, physically or emotionally.

'I'll call the hospital. They can find someone else or they can cancel the list.'

'No, you go to work. There's nothing to be done here. I'll be heading down to Perthshire once I'm dressed, and I'll probably be there a couple of days.'

'But I can't leave you alone when . . .'

'I'm okay, Diana.'

He didn't look it. He was sitting there in a daze, like he didn't quite know how to make sense of his feelings.

I felt terrible about having to leave him and head out to work, but I had a full-day endoscopy list and didn't feel I could cancel all those patients at such short notice when I knew Peter was right. There was nothing to be done, especially if he wasn't going to let me in.

He drove down to the family estate that day and stayed overnight. I spoke to him on his mobile but it was clear he didn't want to talk. I felt shut out but I had to remind myself this wasn't about me. He would talk when he was ready, and this might help us reconnect.

He wasn't much more communicative when he first returned, but he finally opened up last thing at night, after I had put the

159

light out. Maybe it was easier that way, lying side by side in darkness, without exposing his feelings face to face.

'I haven't really known what to feel,' he said. 'At first I felt numb, and then I felt guilty because I wasn't feeling more, I don't know, bereaved. I wasn't expecting it, but it wasn't exactly a shock. I've been losing my mother by degrees. I've barely spoken to her in recent years.'

When he said this it belatedly hit me how estranged they would need to be for a mother not to be at her son's wedding. There was more to it than that, though.

'None of this came out of the blue. She had been ill for a long time.'

'What with? You never said.'

'I told you she was an alcoholic, but I never revealed how far down the drain she had reached. That's where I'm more my father's son than I like to admit, because I was keeping with the family strategy of concealing her condition from any and all outside observation. I think that if she had been born a hundred years earlier she would have been quietly disappeared into an asylum like those embarrassingly incapacitated relatives of the queen.'

I tried to hold him but once again he stiffened. He told me he was tired and rolled away from me.

It hurt, both to see him suffer and to have my efforts rejected, but I think I understood what he was going through. Even though he and his mother were estranged, even though he knew she was dying – maybe even because of those things – some part of him must have believed they would one day make it up. Some part of him must have always thought that whoever she was to him once upon a time, she could yet be that person again, and that he could once more feel the connection they had enjoyed when he was a child.

That is why, when a parent dies, no matter how damaged your relationship, it hurts so much because you realise you can't go home again. In Peter's case it must have truly conveyed that there was no return from the life he had made for himself. Whatever fantasy or denial had coloured his perception of our relationship, from that moment forward there was only this reality.

I therefore took it as a positive sign when he asked if I could accompany him to the funeral, particularly given that this wish would entail overriding his long-standing reluctance for me to meet the in-laws. For all he was in a fragile state and feeling alienated, it must have been sinking in who his real family was now.

As such matters were in the gift of NHS management, to whom human suffering can only be measured in terms of how it affects waiting-list times, I didn't think I had much chance of being granted compassionate leave merely over the death of a spouse's parent. Fortunately I was able to call in a favour from a colleague in order to get someone else to cover my clinic that day. If Peter needed me by his side, I was going to do whatever it took to be there.

We arrived almost but not quite late. We were stuck behind a succession of lorries and caravans on the road south, but this was far from unusual for the A9, so I suspected that it had been a deliberate decision by Peter not to factor in any extra time. It was important to him to be there, but clearly he would rather be a little late than at all early.

We took our seats at the back of his family's private chapel, drawing discreet looks of appraisal from curious eyes as we shuffled our way quietly inside. The chapel was connected to the house but had a separate entrance leading directly outside, through which the coffin had presumably been carried. It was resting before the altar, a single framed portrait photograph of Catriona Elphinstone sitting on top amidst a spray of cards. The shot was of a woman in her late twenties at the oldest, indicating how those present were choosing to remember her. This didn't speak well of the past couple of decades if nothing more recent had been deemed acceptable.

I know it sounds shallow, but not knowing anyone, and never having met the deceased, I spent much of the short service looking at people's clothes and trying to work out which of the men towards the front was Sir Hamish, Peter's father. It was my first close encounter with what would be termed old money, which manifested itself sartorially in attire that looked well made and thus expensive, but somewhat stuffy and drab too. Obviously nobody would be dressing with any flamboyance on such an occasion, but there's black and there's black.

There were only two women who were sporting subtle gestures of personal style. One was Lucy, who was either retreating into her teen self for comfort or conflating funereal with gothic. The other was a lady in the front row, who held herself with a certain self-confident elegance that was a statement in itself, but not as much of a statement as her red-soled Louboutins. She was the reason I guessed wrong regarding the identity of Peter's father, as I had ruled out the gentleman whose hand she held and whose arm she kept squeezing throughout the service.

The service was followed by a burial ceremony a short distance away at what was evidently an Elphinstone family plot going back two centuries, according to the earliest of the headstones. I had expected to feel like I was an outsider tagging along, but as we trailed along at the rear of the small procession, I sensed that the feeling extended to myself and Peter as a pair.

He reached for my hand as the coffin was lowered. Lucy had appeared at his other side by this point, and I noticed that he gripped hers also.

Other than that, there were no great outpourings of grief on display from anyone in attendance. It was all very dignified and restrained in a rather sterile way, a matter of observance and decorum rather than human emotion. I knew I shouldn't be judgemental, though. Perhaps it was indicative of what had gone before, to which I had not been party. Certainly, as we gathered for a reception in one of the grand public rooms inside Elphinstone House, there was an air of relief about the proceedings, a sense of closing a painful chapter. Further, there seemed to be no hint of disapproval emanating from the deceased's side of the family regarding her husband being quite conspicuously on the arm of a new – and much younger – female companion. My impression from the chatter I overheard was of gratitude towards Sir Hamish for his sensitivity and discretion in having stood by Catriona and kept her condition from public knowledge. The unspoken alternative was that he might quite reasonably have divorced her some years back, though Peter did mutter that 'it doesn't have to be official for my father to effectively disown those who are no longer of value to him'.

I sipped on a glass of sparkling water, taking in my surroundings. It was the first time I had been in such a place without velvet rope cordoning off the furniture and a guide keeping a close eye. It was imposing upon first impression but the fixtures and fittings were surprisingly careworn up close. I wondered about the costs and complications of maintaining such a place. What did one do if one's carpet was a hundred and fifty years old and showing its age in places? The options were to live with the frayed edges or call up Behar, and I didn't imagine they would be able to supply a like-for-like replacement. Even harder to imagine was the sight of two young kids ever running around this place. I instantly caught a glimpse of what Peter had been alluding to when he spoke mournfully about his childhood.

People came up and made polite conversation, asking Peter how he was holding up. I soon understood that this was not so much solicitude as the ideal pretext for running the rule over his recent bride. The reason for their having remained unaware of our court-ship and marriage until after the fact remained unspoken in these exchanges, but it was unspoken pretty loud.

By my watch we had been on the estate three hours and we still hadn't spoken to Peter's father. He was on the other side of the room, by a large bay window, where an informal receiving line was in operation. It was not recognisably a queue, but people were gravitating close by and choosing their moment to take their turn at paying their respects.

His new significant other was by his side, a position of unmis-takable significance under such circumstances. I estimated she was around thirty-five: younger than me and yet in her composure and sophistication she might have seemed older. Certainly the effect was that the age gap between her and Sir Hamish seemed less striking, though this was also down to him being younger than I assumed. I put him in his early fifties, which meant he had become a husband and father relatively young.

She was attractive and elegant, but steely too. She would be nobody's adornment, and nor would the phrase 'gold-digger' be crossing anybody's mind. It was obvious she had come from money. She knew her worth and she knew her role too. Those shoes. She didn't mind being noticed, and I rather uncharitably reflected that the phrase 'it's not about you' hadn't crossed her mind this morning.

'Her name is Cecily Greysham-Ellis,' said Lucy.

I was uneasy as it seemed Lucy knew where my gaze had been slyly focused.

'They've been together more than a year. I can't quite believe it. The family used to come and visit here when we were teenagers.'

'She must be barely two years older than Peter,' I said.

'Quite. And of child-bearing age,' Lucy added archly, before drifting away again.

The people talking to Sir Hamish looked like they were winding down the encounter, and there was only one other couple hovering nearby. I was conscious of many guests having left the room, and that staff were no longer circulating to offer refills. The reception was drawing to a close, but Peter had made no overtures towards leaving. Nor had he said anything for a few moments. I deduced that he was preparing himself, and I did likewise, though he at least knew what he was preparing himself *for*.

Sir Hamish glanced our way, the first time I had caught him looking in his son's direction. That was when I realised that Peter's choice of location to loiter had not been accidental. His father would not be able to leave without passing him. Perhaps realising this, Sir Hamish stood his ground. His body language indicated that he was inviting us into his company, though it struck me as a matter of preserving appearances rather than a genuine show of openness. Had there been nobody left to witness the encounter, I suspected we would not have benefited from such grace.

'Peter,' he said, his voice soft but his face unsmiling. 'This is Cecily.'

Sir Hamish added no further details for the benefit of either. He clearly didn't expect them to be seeing a lot of each other.

'Hello,' Peter replied. He hardly gave Cecily a look, averting his gaze from her so conspicuously as for it to be embarrassing. All his attention was focused on his father.

Cecily, for her part, barely glanced at Peter either, perhaps a little overwhelmed by the awkward. She was in a difficult position, I supposed: prospective stepmother, and yet she looked the age of his big sister. Nonetheless, I wondered why she hadn't tried harder to make him catch her eye. They were more like two people who had known each other and fallen out than two people who hadn't met in a long time.

'And this is my wife, Dr Diana Jager.'

Peter spoke to his father like he meant the words to hurt.

'Yes, hello,' replied Sir Hamish, with a smile so fleeting and perfunctory it made the average air hostess seem like a gushy long-lost cousin. His eyes met mine for even less time than Peter had traded glances with Cecily.

She moved in expertly to shake my hand and offer a marginally less cursory greeting. I caught a whiff of her scent and immediately recognised it as Jo Malone Blackberry and Bay, the same fragrance I was wearing that day. Peter had bought me a bottle as a gift. I suspected it was going to be the only thing Cecily and I would have in common.

Even as she spoke her few platitudinous words, Sir Hamish was already looking beyond the two of us and silently beckoning his final two waiting guests. I had seldom been made to feel less significant or more dismissed.

Peter seemed to grow a couple of inches, deliberately blocking his father's view.

'*I said*, this is my *wife*, Father.'

His voice remained low but there was anger thrumming in his tone.

'I heard,' Sir Hamish replied sternly.

Then he turned to look at me once more, his tone sincere but not remotely warm.

'You have my best wishes. And my apologies in advance.'

*   *   *

We walked by the river as Peter tried to calm himself following this encounter. It took a while, but the family estate would have accommodated a six-hour hike's worth of self-composure had he needed it. The discretion for which Sir Hamish was being quietly thanked by his late wife's relatives was partly guaranteed by a combination of geography and privilege. No reporter or photographer was getting anywhere near the house, which had to be at least half a mile from the nearest public road.

'I'm sorry,' he told me when he eventually spoke. 'I should have known better. I at least thought he would try to be pleasant to *you*.'

We had walked in silence for a long time, giving me ample opportunity to think of what tack to adopt. I had decided to nudge Peter towards the prospects of the future rather than the wounds of the past.

'Forget about it. If you have to keep hold of that moment, then do it only so that you can think back to it when we rock up here one day in a Lamborghini.'

I thought that would earn a smile at least, but he was still simmering.

'You don't understand him at all. No matter what I achieve, he'll take pains to convey that he's not impressed. He'll still act disappointed and still look down on me even though he did nothing to earn what he has, other than be squeezed out from the right cunt.'

When we got home to Inverness, we had sex for the first time in a while. It started as a hug, after we had got safely inside and closed the door: my desire to convey to him, physically, that this was his home and this was where he would be loved.

For the first time since his mother died, he let me hold him, and it quickly became something else.

I've heard that people often make love after a funeral. It's something instinctive, clinging on to each other amidst the darkness, having been starkly reminded of their mortality. Maybe even a circle-of-life thing, the subconscious desire to procreate.

This was not making love. It was not warm and tender or even hot and insistent. It was full of desperation rather than lust, fury rather than passion.

I felt something cold about it, like I was being used.

It took him ages to come. He pulled me to the edge of the bed and stood upright, bending my legs back, my heels against his shoulders, pounding away in a state more of frustration than desire. I felt like I was a proxy, and not for another lover, but for someone he wanted to hurt.

What he was doing wasn't painful, but when I looked into his face, into his eyes, for the first time I saw something in Peter that was dark, that was turbulent, that was dangerous.

I saw something in him that terrified me.

MAN TALK

Parlabane inched his car cautiously along the forest track, equally mindful of his axles as of getting completely stuck out here. It wasn't so much potholed as honeycombed, with the few patches of flat ground just as treacherous for being slicked with an inch of ice that looked like Jack Frost had sent his apprentice down to give it a thorough polish. There was no danger of anybody ever skidding off this road and into a river: it was impossible to drive fast enough. It was one of the few thoroughfares on mainland Britain that justified the ownership of a four-by-four wank tank, yet here he was crawling along it in what had seemed like the only standard saloon car left in Edinburgh.

According to the dashboard display, the outside temperature was precisely zero. Far from ideal conditions for an interview that would be primarily conducted outdoors, he thought. Then he remembered that he could be tucked up in a nice cosy room, sat in front of his laptop 'generating copy', at which point he told himself to quit whining. Heading out into the wilds in an inadequate vehicle to meet a guy who might be able to tell him bugger-all about a story that might add up to nothing nonetheless made him feel more like being a reporter than anything he had done in months.

One of the things he had told Lucas's students was that journalism is the art of finding something constructive to do with your time while you wait in hope for people to return your calls. Ironically, he had enjoyed an unusually high strike rate on this particular endeavour. Among the numbers Lucy had given him was that of a guy called Alan Harper, who ran an airsoft site that Peter had attended regularly for several years. He was one of the few friends Peter already had in the area when his job took him to Inverness. Lucy was under the impression that the meets only took place on a Sunday, but when Parlabane phoned, it turned out the guy worked for the Forestry Commission and so was on the site most days.

It vindicated something else he had stressed in his talk: the value of making contact behind the firewall. Direct phone numbers were worth a thousand email addresses, no matter whether they belonged to a CEO or an airsoft geek. Otherwise you were merely somebody else they could ignore, and if they had something to hide, they would ignore you fairly hard.

Having someone supply a few numbers, as Lucy had done, was extremely rare, and having someone vouch for you in advance was rarer still, which was why half the job was about finding ways to bypass the invisible cordons of corporate security or personal privacy. He didn't tell the students that an awful lot of this involved lying to decent people and then lying to yourself that this was okay.

Of course, they could still ignore you with some gusto even when you had their private number, but sometimes it was simply about letting them know you were out there. Parlabane did not expect a long conversation when he called the number Lucy had supplied him for Elphinstone House, and thus he had not been disappointed. It wasn't even Sir Hamish that he got to speak to, but his fiancée Cecily.

'Oh, hi, is that Cecily? I was looking to speak to Hamish,' he said, trying to sound comfortably informal. Giving the impression that you expected to be put through was sometimes effective in making the person who answered believe you already had a relationship with the subject.

'Hamish isn't home right now. Can you tell me who's calling?'

She sounded pleasantly polite but there was a firmness to her tone that immediately told him she was making no assumptions as to his access privileges.

'My name is Jack Parlabane. I'm a freelance journalist.'

'What is it regarding?'

The tone was stiffer now.

'I realise it's a difficult time, and I am aware there's been a great deal of rather mawkish coverage regarding the accident, which is why I'm trying to put together a more in-depth piece about who

Peter really was. His sister Lucy was good enough to give me this number, and I was hoping to talk to Hamish about what kind of son Peter was, the unusual paths he chose, that kind of thing.'

'It *is* a difficult time. And so I don't imagine *Sir* Hamish will be particularly inclined to oblige you.'

Parlabane left his number anyway, and despite the edge of hostility in her voice, he was pretty sure she wrote it down.

Alan Harper had been considerably more obliging when Parlabane called him, but that was because he had been considerably less honest about his intentions. He told Harper he was working on a series of articles about 'the alternative outdoors' for a travel website, and so the prospect of a puff-piece about his airsoft business had prompted him to accommodate Parlabane right away.

Harper was waiting for him in a clearing off to the left of the forest track. He had evidently got there in a flat-bed truck with wheels and suspension built for the underfoot conditions. Parlabane thought about how much easier it would have been had he arranged to meet in town and then had Harper drive them both here in the Land Cruiser, but it was never a good idea to be reliant upon your subject for a ride home when you were planning to ask them awkward questions.

He was a bearded bloke in his late thirties: tall and rangy, with the dark complexion of a man who spent a lot of time in the great outdoors. He wore an unzipped body-warmer and fingerless gloves, sturdy boots on his feet and shaded goggles hanging from his neck on an elasticated strap. The body-warmer bore the Forestry Commission badge, but Parlabane recognised a video-game logo on the T-shirt underneath. It spoke of indoor enthusiasms, as did the rows of holes on each earlobe, the rings themselves presumably left off for safety reasons.

They shook hands and Parlabane let him conduct the tour. He was cheerful and enthusiastic, but suffered from a slight stammer. Parlabane interpreted it as betraying a shy unease in dealing with strangers which he was trying hard to overcome. It was easy to picture him content on his own working out here in the woods, and yet being in charge of an airsoft site took strength of personality.

There could be as many as a hundred participants on a busy day, Parlabane learned: predominantly male and sometimes fairly amped, given the nature of the game.

He led Parlabane along a narrow path into the woods, explaining how he had attended airsoft events at a place called Section 8 in Lanarkshire while staying with a cousin about a decade ago. The organisers had an arrangement with the Forestry Commission, so the first thing he did when he got back home was talk to his bosses about how they could make something similar work on their own turf. It had taken a while to grow, but now they had people travelling from all over the country for their Sunday meets.

Parlabane noticed that everywhere he stepped, there were tiny white balls – or fragments of tiny white balls – underfoot.

'What do your bosses make of these?'

'They're mostly biodegradable. The ammo *we* supply, anyway. Can't pat folk down for what else they might be carrying, but the type of people who come here tend to have an appreciation of the outdoors, so they know where we're coming from.'

'I'm guessing they have an appreciation of gaming too,' Parlabane suggested, nodding at Harper's T-shirt. He was laying the groundwork for introducing the subject of Peter Elphinstone later. 'You must have a lot of players who people would assume to be more comfortable in the great indoors.'

'Aye, it would make an interesting Venn diagram, for sure.'

They came to a wooden hut, set back from the path. The trees had been selectively thinned out in the area around it, making it both sheltered and spacious.

'This is the muster point. Where we organise the teams, get everybody kitted up and give the safety briefing. Have you done airsoft yourself?'

'No. I did paintballing once,' he recalled with a shudder.

Harper assumed it was in remembrance of the impacts.

'Airsoft is less painful.'

'So I've heard. But without visible marking, how do you know who's been hit?'

'We rely on people to be honest. You hold a hand up and say "Hit!"'

'Does that work?'

'Mostly. If you say "Hit", people stop shooting you. I said it's less sore than paintball, but if you've got a couple of folk unloading on you with automatic fire, it's not wise to pretend they're missing.'

'I see.'

'Plus we have a marshal system. Me and my team know this place like nobody else. We can disappear, take position where no one realises. We see what goes on far more clearly than the players ever imagine. If somebody's cheating, we have a quiet word.'

Harper took out some keys and unlocked the hut. He swung one door open, revealing row upon row of weaponry. Parlabane estimated there were fifty or sixty replica machine guns lined up on wall racks, with several sniper rifles ranged in a separate stand.

'Boy toys r us,' Parlabane remarked.

'Yeah, that's the other thing we have over paintball. The kit is more fun. Greater variety too, which has tactical implications. Most of our walk-up guests get the standard HK G36.'

'Heckler Koch?'

He wanted to establish some geek credentials and sound authentically interested. It didn't take much faking. Something about these perfect replicas being essentially toys spoke to his inner kid.

'That's right. They're sturdy, durable, collapsible stock, ideal for the conditions out here.'

Harper grabbed one from the rack and offered it to Parlabane. It was heavy, mostly metal. His host picked up a sniper rifle too and lifted a canvas bag from the floor.

They walked past a makeshift fort: logs, boards and old doors fashioned into walls and barricades. Harper explained more about the rules of the various games they offered, as well as giving him a truncated version of his standard safety briefing. As much of it was about the underfoot conditions as about the weapons. It was a very easy place to break an ankle, and a less easy place to drive an ambulance into.

Parlabane pulled on a pair of safety goggles Harper produced from the canvas bag, then shouldered the HK. He flicked the safety to single shot and aimed into the trees. A light squeeze loosed a tiny white dot whose flight he was surprised to be able to follow. He fired off a couple more. They all pulled slightly to the right.

He flipped the lever to fully automatic and released a volley in a short burst. It was a bit like slowed-down tracer fire, the line of dots easy to track as it arced into the darkness of the woods. He noted minor variations in their flight, even though they were only fractions of a second apart.

Parlabane had a go with the sniper rifle. Harper picked out a target in the middle distance: a tree with a wooden sign pinned to it stating 'Out of bounds beyond this point'. He missed by a foot with the first shot, then compensated and bullseyed the second. It was indeed more accurate but the HK was more fun. He hefted it again and enthusiastically emptied half a clip.

'I'm guessing most people opt for spray and pray. More fun running around than camping in a sniping spot. Better exercise too.'

'You're not wrong. Given the weight of these things, folk end up lashed with sweat even when it's sub-zero. I brought my wife once and she had one of those wrist monitor things, 'cause she's a gym nut. She clocked up about a thousand calories.'

'You get a lot of women turning up?'

He grimaced.

'Not really. I wish we could. Maybe your piece will help. We shelled out for a ladies-only Portaloo. Guys just have to go against a tree and hope they don't get a BB in the boabby.'

'You got kids?'

'Aye, two. Gemma's eight and Graham's six. Too young for this carry-on. My wife sometimes moans that I'm doing this every Sunday because she's got them on her own, but she knows it brings in extra money. You got weans yourself?'

Parlabane shook his head.

'Never wanted them, or . . .? Actually that's none of my business, sorry.'

This was precisely what Parlabane was thinking, but he decided that being a little more vulnerable might provide a plausible route into where he wanted to take the conversation.

'I did want them. Always assumed I'd have them, in fact. But it turned out my wife and I couldn't . . . and then a wee while later she wasn't my wife any more.'

'Ooft, sorry man.'

'I mean, not just like that. It was a long and messy process.'

'Still, didn't mean to intrude.'

'Not at all. I've got the scars but I'm still here. There are worse ways to lose somebody, you know?'

Parlabane let it hang. He was hoping Harper would chip in with a remark about the recent tragedy. It was always helpful if you could make the other person think they were the one who brought up the subject you wanted them to talk about. Unfortunately he didn't respond, but from his distant expression, Parlabane guessed it was what he was thinking about.

He decided to push it.

'Drifting apart is prolonged and messy, but at least it doesn't come out of nowhere.'

Parlabane flipped the safety on and turned to face his host.

'I mean, look what happened to Peter Elphinstone. I gather you knew him.'

Surprise and caution immediately registered on Harper's face. He looked edgy enough for Parlabane to fear he'd moved in too soon.

'We had a mutual acquaintance,' Parlabane quickly clarified. 'She told me he came here for airsoft, said he'd known you a long time.'

'She?'

Harper's apprehension wasn't quite of the strain Parlabane had expected. He didn't seem suspicious or defensive, but he was definitely uncomfortable; plus the way he had spoken suggested there was someone specific he hoped Parlabane's acquaintance wasn't, and that someone was female.

'Lucy: Peter's sister. That's who told me about you and how I got the idea to do a feature on your site.'

Parlabane saw relief in his face, but could tell the barricades were still up.

'How do you know her?'

'She lives near to me in Edinburgh. She was in bits the last time I saw her, to be honest. Do you know her, at all?'

'No, we've never met.'

'How did you know Peter?'

Harper seemed a little pressed, shifting visibly on the spot. He stammered at the start of his response.

'Just . . . just through the airsoft, really.'

'How long had he been coming here?'

Harper glanced away, as though thinking about it, but when he looked back at Parlabane, it was clearly something else that had occurred to him.

'You're not here to do an article about airsoft, are you? You're from the tabloids, doing a piece about the tragedy.'

He sounded disappointed rather than accusatory. He wasn't about to decry Parlabane for being a bloodsucking hack and storm off in the huff, but nobody liked being deliberately misled. Either way the interview had about three seconds left to run, so there was no point in lying any more.

'Firstly, I'm not from the tabloids. I'm freelance, and the fact is I might not be doing a piece about anything. I'm just looking a wee bit closer to see whether everything about this tragedy is quite what it appears on the surface. I'm trying to speak to people who knew Peter and who might have had contact with him recently.'

Harper eyed Parlabane with the most intense scrutiny. He looked tormented and resentful, as though he might indeed stomp off or maybe even grab the HK and start peppering Parlabane's face with it. He gazed back into the woods for a very long time, then finally spoke.

'Can I be off the record?'

As a journalist these were not Parlabane's favourite words, but on this occasion they were music to his ears. This guy had something.

'Absolutely. Right now I'm only casting around for information.'

Harper bit his lip and exhaled loudly through his nose.

'You promise what I tell you here won't come back to me?'

With this question Parlabane understood what had been weird about his apprehension from the second Peter was mentioned. Harper had been carrying something around that he didn't know what to do with.

'I never give up my sources.'

Harper paused a moment more, but Parlabane was patient. He knew this guy *needed* to talk.

'He called me the night he died.'

'Jesus.'

This was considerably more than Parlabane had been expecting.

'I didn't answer. I mean, my phone was in my jacket and I never heard it. He left a message. I'm not somebody who lives on their mobile, so I never got it until the next day, after I'd learned about the accident. Spookiest thing, hearing somebody's voice only a few hours after they're dead.'

Parlabane barely dared ask.

'Do you still have it?'

He shook his head.

'No. I deleted it a couple of days after. Apart from the fact it was freaking me out knowing it was there, I was terrified somebody would find out about it.'

'Why? What did he say?'

'He sounded in a state. Distressed. He said he'd done something he couldn't take back and that he was in way over his head. He didn't say what. Last thing he said was: "I need to talk to some-body", but I wasn't there. Guy sounded at his wits' end. I'd never heard him like that.'

'Why didn't you tell anybody about this?'

'Why do you think? I didn't want the polis all over me, looking for things that aren't there. I had no idea what he was talking about, but I guessed it contributed to him having his crash, or worse, that maybe he even topped himself. Either way, it was nothing to do with me, but I can't get his voice out of my head.'

'Why did he call *you* specifically?'

'That's the thing: I really don't know. Well . . .'

'What?'

'What I mean is, Peter told me a lot of things in recent months, but I couldn't work out why. We'd had a few drinks over the years, but he started acting like I was his best friend in the world: or maybe his only friend.'

'What kind of things?'

'Things that would seriously come into the category of overshares. I mean, don't get me wrong, we weren't sitting in the pub all night talking about his emotions: we were guys. Mostly we'd jaw about airsoft and games: we were both big into old-school Starfire. But a few times he got all candid. It made me uncomfortable until I realised he wasn't looking for advice: he just wanted to unload about his marriage.'

Parlabane would have considered the man before him an unlikely choice of confidant, then thought of Lucas's impression of Peter as a shy and socially awkward IT nerd, out of his depth in sophisticated company. Maybe Harper was right, and he didn't have anybody else to reach out to.

'What about his marriage?'

'Not the fairytale everyone seemed to think. Obviously I was only getting one side of it, but she sounded like a bunny boiler. She became really jealous and obsessive, and I don't mean asking why he was home late. I mean extreme lengths.'

'Such as?'

'Trivial stuff at first. Micromanaging his diet, for instance. She started off moaning about him having take-aways, and when he didn't fall in line she started cooking all his meals in advance and presenting them on the table, all laid out for two.'

'What a bitch. Imagine making your man's dinner for him.'

Harper made a face.

'That was my response too, but he made out it was a lot more intense than it sounds: very passive-aggressive. If he worked a wee bit late and brought home a pizza, he knew she'd be sitting there with dinner for two. She laid out a glass and filled it with mineral water or maybe juice, so that it was an overt act if he opened a beer. From an outside perspective you've got what looks like domestic bliss: a wife and husband sitting down to a dinner she's cooked, but Peter said it was a psychological battleground.'

'Or maybe he was a wee bit immature in his expectations of married life,' Parlabane suggested. 'Women do like to knock us into shape. If I had lived alone all my days, I'd be four stone heavier with heart disease and a drink problem.'

'Oh, I hear you.'

Harper patted a flat stomach. He'd mentioned his wife being a gym nut.

'But I think Diana was unrealistic in her expectations too. From the sound of it, she thought it was always going to be like when they were dating. Didn't realise guys are on their best behaviour when they're trying to impress a girl. You'll sit up all night talking when you've first met, but that doesn't mean you're going to want to do that on a weeknight after a day's work, you know?'

Parlabane nodded his agreement.

'Still, none of this sounds extreme, as you put it.'

'That was just context. It got weirder, fast. Peter reckoned she was trying to track down his exes.'

'How did he find out?'

'Don't know, but he also found out she had been accessing his medical records.'

'Jesus.'

Parlabane had considered the bunny-boiler description excessive for someone who was maybe just curious and insecure over their spouse's past sex life, but this crossed several lines.

'Did he ask why she did it? Did he challenge her?'

'I doubt it. I'd have said he was scared of her, but other times he'd talk about how lucky he was to have her. Peter was a tricky guy to get a handle on, though.'

'How so?'

Harper shrugged, screwing up his face.

'He could talk without ever really telling you what he thought. He would give the impression he agreed with you, but then later you'd realise he was subtly sounding you out.'

Harper looked down at the HK Parlabane was holding; or rather, by this time resting with its stock on the ground and its muzzle leaning against his thigh.

'You can tell a lot about people when you're a marshal: watching them when they think nobody's looking, seeing how they play the game, what decisions they make. Peter acted like it was all fun, and to be fair he didn't cheat, but he liked to win a lot more than he let on. We never had bother with him getting aggressive, like with some players, and he was always friendly and cooperative, but . . .'

Parlabane recognised a reluctance to speak ill of the dead, but one that was overpowered by a need for catharsis.

'Did you ever read *Dirk Gently's Holistic Detective Agency?*' Harper asked.

'A long time ago. Remind me.'

'There was a character described as one of those people who are soft and squidgy as long as they're getting what they want. Douglas Adams said that there's something very hard at the centre of those people, which is what all the soft and squidgy bits are there to protect. That was my impression of Peter.'

'And did you ever meet his wife?'

He nodded subtly, as though carefully measuring his thoughts.

'She came here, about a year ago. Shortly after they met, I believe.'

'What was she like?'

'I didn't speak to her, but I did witness her winning a last-man-standing game single-handed by silently taking out six enemies with knife kills. It was a sight to behold: an unnerving display of stealth, positional awareness, tactical acumen, ruthlessness and one other utterly crucial factor.'

'Which was what?'

'She cheated.'

'How? Did she ignore hits?'

'No. Nobody hit her because nobody saw her. She slipped in behind several of her targets by going out of bounds.'

'Did she know she was out of bounds?'

Harper nodded towards the sign Parlabane had been hitting with the sniper rifle.

'I explain about boundaries before every game. On that occasion I had stressed it because that particular boundary was to keep players away from a public footpath. Don't want unwary ramblers getting shot in the eye.'

'What did you do about it?'

'Nothing. I was the only one who knew, and I decided to keep it to myself on that occasion. Partly because everyone was so amused and delighted with the outcome that I didn't want to spoil it, and partly because it helps for the future to know what you're dealing with. Like I said, you can learn a lot from watching how people play.'

'And what did you feel you learned about Dr Diana Jager?'

'That you would be unwise ever to turn your back to her. And that if you ever pissed her off, you should worry.'

FIREWALL

Looking back, I can see that marriage is a lot like that silly airsoft game he took me to when we first met. There are many ways in which you can cheat without the other side ever knowing or being able to prove it. But unless you observe the rules, then what you yourself are doing within this game becomes meaningless.

Let me stress, it wasn't some ongoing state of attrition. In fact, I think it would have been easier if that were true: I would have seen what was really happening and not gotten sucked into the quicksand. But just when I found myself wondering if I had made the biggest mistake of my life, he would do something to remind me why I fell for him. And, of course, I was so determined to make this work, and therefore vulnerable to believing that we were merely enduring normal bumps in the road.

Tensions would simmer for days, before the dam would break and I would have it out with him. Then he would say precisely the right words and between us we would see a brighter future, immediately before or after some very intense make-up sex.

I hated how I sounded, always moaning about the same things, but that was because those same things didn't change. Peter worked late most nights, and when he was home, he was often too tired or distracted to notice that I lived there too. I went to great lengths to ensure we could at least sit down to a meal together instead of letting him flop out in front of the TV or laptop, but he seemed resentful of my efforts rather than grateful. I worried that he was drinking too much, so I tried to discourage the patterns that led to him cracking open a beer with every meal and then staying up drinking after I'd gone to bed. Sometimes he wouldn't come to bed until after two, then he'd sleep in the next morning and so I wouldn't get to have breakfast with him before I went to work.

My complaints about all of this were merely the low-level background hum of our relationship. The major bust-ups took something else to bring them to a head. Such as the time my laptop crashed, and he was absurdly reluctant to let me use his merely to pay some bills and check a few things online. He made such a fuss, and insisted on hovering at my elbow the whole time, sighing every time I surfed to a new site.

I had tried to get these things done while he was in the shower, but his laptop was password protected, with a lock screen that kicked in if he left it alone for a few minutes.

'Why don't you go watch TV or play a game on your Xbox,' I suggested, irritated by his looming presence as I tried to answer some emails to my Doctors.net account. 'What is it you think I'm going to do to your precious computer? Or is there something on here you don't want me to see?'

He responded testily, like I was being obtuse.

'There's things on there that I *can't* let you see.'

'Like what?'

'Work stuff. What do you think?'

'I wouldn't even know where to find it. And for God's sake, can't you trust me not to go looking?'

'It's complicated.'

He sounded sheepish and yet huffy.

'No, Peter, it's simple. Either you trust me or you don't, and having a password-protected screen saver kick in after two fucking minutes tells me you don't.'

'Of course I trust you. But whether I do or not is immaterial. This is about the NDA put in place by the investors. The conditions dictate that I am not allowed to let anyone else use this laptop or any of my work computers unsupervised. The NDA also stipulates that any portable machine I remove from the office be password protected in sleep mode, and set to sleep after a maximum of two minutes' inactivity, even at home.'

'But don't you see that this is our relationship right now in microcosm? It's like part of you is permanently behind a firewall and I'm not authorised to access it. You're at work all the time, and even when you do come home, either you can't talk to me because it's confidential or you *won't* talk to me because you just want to flop out.'

'You're the one who told me to throw everything at this opportunity. After pissing my career up the wall half my life, I'm finally putting my shoulder to the wheel. Or would you rather have the waster I was before I met you? I'm trying to build something, Diana.'

'And I thought *we* were trying to build something: *here*. A marriage. A family.'

We hadn't been using any contraception since before the wedding. Neither of us had used the expression 'trying for a baby', but it was tacitly understood to be our shared intention. It had been four cycles now and nothing had happened. When my period last came, part of me was disappointed because I thought the prospect of a baby would focus things between us and bring us closer again. Another part of me was relieved, as I was beginning to wonder whether becoming pregnant would be the single worst way to compound a colossal mistake.

'If you've got no time or energy for being a proper husband, how can you possibly expect to have the time and energy for being a father?'

'But that's why I'm *doing* this. I'm trying to lay the groundwork and get the business running so that things will be simpler by the time a baby comes along. There's no way of staggering this: it's not like I'm painting a wall and I can pick up the pace or slacken off at will. There's no prize for second in the race for bringing this idea to market.'

He was pacing, his hands out in front of him like his frustration was an invisible object he was trying to crush between them.

'I'm not the only one who works late and finds it hard to disengage,' he said. 'That's why I thought you of all people would understand. I'm putting my heart and soul into this right now. I'm working harder than I've ever worked in my life, and I could use a bit of support and sympathy rather than being guilt-tripped because I don't feel like recreating how it was six months ago, sitting there at the dinner table making plans for our future. This is that future. I'm executing those plans.'

'Well, maybe if you could even talk to me about what the hell you spend your days working on, I'd feel more like they were *our* plans and not just yours.'

Peter smashed his palms together, like the invisible object's outer resistance had suddenly given. The resultant slap echoed off the walls of the former spare room that had become his man-cave.

I felt a wave of something cold and instinctive pass through me. I wanted to tell myself that my reflexive response was mere startlement at the sudden sound, but deep down I knew that really I was bracing myself for violence.

I thought he was going to scream. His eyes flashed and a shudder ran through him. But then he was calm, as though something had defused the bomb that had looked primed to explode.

He closed his eyes for a second, then looked at me imploringly, a hint of a smile about the corners of his mouth.

'I'm sorry. You're right. You're absolutely right, but that's why I'm finding this so frustrating. I want to be that husband, that father, but I don't think I can be either of those things if I fail at what I'm trying to create here. I want to become the person you made me aspire to be, but it seems the more I work towards it, the further I get from you. I was feeling so trapped right now, but then I suddenly thought: there is a way out of every box, a solution to every puzzle; it's just a matter of finding it. Things are only impossible until they're not.'

I melted when he said that. My fear was instantly forgotten, retrospectively absurd, even denied. Something else flooded through me: warm and passionate. His words made me feel like I *had* made the right decision. It made me feel that together we could overcome anything, that he was the man I had believed him to be. I wanted him to father my children, and I wanted that process to start right that moment, up against the wall of his den.

That was how it always went. We'd clear the air and it felt like everything was better: then after a few days, I would come to realise nothing was. All that happened was I cut him some slack and we had shagged a few times, but his own behaviour hadn't changed. He hadn't found a solution to any puzzle: he'd simply got me to stop bothering him for a few days.

I tried to make my peace with what he said: biding my time, hoping to see signs that he had 'broken the back of the start-up stage' as he put it, and that our domestic arrangements would seem more like a married couple and less like flatmates with benefits.

Then one night I finished late at work – massive complications meant a case that ought to have taken forty minutes ended up taking three hours – and I had a bit of an epiphany. My own working day having been arduously extended, I was feeling a sense of solidarity with Peter, and I realised that I was guilty of what used to annoy me about so many of my male colleagues. They saw their own jobs as all-important, expecting their wives to tolerate late finishes, on-call and all the psychological effluent that went with it, but at the same time regarded their spouses' jobs as comparatively trivial.

He was right: I ought to know what it was like to be in a demanding job with no option to dial down the intensity. My classically arrogant medic assumption was that surely *his* work wasn't so important that he couldn't slacken off if he really wanted to.

I decided to surprise him at the office he had rented on my way home. I would show him that things could work differently by suggesting we go out for dinner. He could get a curry and a few beers, and I could get to sit down with him for a couple of hours.

As he was effectively a workforce of one, I had initially queried why he was paying rent for an office when he had his den at home, but as well as (inevitably) the demands of the NDA, he said he

185

needed an environment that was solely about work, away from the comforts and temptations of the house. Also, he needed a business premises for lots of other practical reasons, not least the larger computer systems he was running. He needed space for all his kit, and the energy bills alone were something that demanded to be accounted separately from any domestic tariffs.

He got a cheap lease on a place in Sunflight House, an eighties-built block on the outskirts of a light industrial estate about ten minutes' walk from the city centre and a five-minute drive from the hospital. At one point it had been the regional admin office for a travel firm, but the internet had done for them and now it was subdivided into individual units for small businesses.

It was shortly before eight as I approached, but I could see no lights on in the building, and no cars in the car park. Typical: the night I decide to do this, he's already finished up and headed home. However, when I got back to the house, Peter's BMW was not in the driveway and the cottage was in darkness.

I called his mobile and got bounced to voicemail.

He showed up around eleven, with a pizza and a six-pack, the first can of which he had opened and was supping from even as he came through the door.

'Where have you been?'

I tried to keep my voice as neutral as I could. I wanted to sound interested rather than accusatory.

'Look, don't start tonight, please.'

His words were imploring though his tone was anything but.

'I had a major headache with the servers and I've been firefighting for about nine hours straight. That's why my phone was off and why I didn't ring back when I saw I had a missed call from you.'

'You've been stuck in the office all night?'

'Yes. Which is why I just want to eat my pizza and chill out, and I'd appreciate not being given a hard time about it after the day I've had.'

The room seemed to alter around me. So much had changed in one small moment. Logic dictated that I challenge him with what I knew, but I said nothing, as I was reeling too hard from the implications of what had happened.

I felt my face flush, and worried that he would register my response, but there was no danger of Peter paying me enough attention to do that. Instead I took myself off to bed, where I lay in the darkness and didn't sleep.

THE HEIGHT OF SUSPICION

Peter Elphinstone's black BMW 3 Series was sitting on its own inside the open-fronted workshop building at the far end of the depot, a few yards in front of a hydraulic lift. It looked like it was waiting to be worked on, but the whole point was that it *hadn't* to be worked on.

Lynne McGhee was in charge of examining it. She was waiting in the warmth of the workshop's back office when they arrived, spotting them through the grimy window. Lynne was a petrolhead who drove in forest rallies in her spare time, so Ali pitied any bloke who had tried to patronise the wee woman from Forensics with advice about examining a car.

Ali's role here was to be walked through the report on-site before signing off on the vehicle's release.

'Isn't it technically a write-off?' Ali asked.

'That's between the insurance company and the owner: or in this case the owner's wife. Theoretically it should run okay once it's had time to dry out, though it really depends on the electrics. They might need completely replaced. Freshwater means fewer long-term concerns over the bodywork, but if it was me, I'd want nothing to do with it.'

'I can't see Dr Jager wanting to hold on to it,' Ali mused. 'Any indicators as to what might have happened? Dodgy treads, worn brake-shoes?'

'No. The car had passed an MOT a few weeks ago and appears to have been well maintained. The treads indicate the rear tyres have been replaced since the vehicle was purchased, as I'd expect a lot more wear going by the mileage on the clock. That's moot if there was black ice on the road that night, but I'm not led to believe that was the case. In fact I'm not inclined to think that skidding was an aspect of this.'

She squatted down next to the rear driver-side wheel and pointed to the outer rim of the tyre, drawing an imaginary circle all around it.

'A major skid caused by going around a bend too fast would leave damage to the tyres – nothing huge, but visible if you know what you're looking for – and the lateral momentum would put particular stress on one side. I'm not seeing that.'

'The witness said the car swerved on to her side of the road,' Rodriguez told her. 'Then over-compensated and swerved again.'

The witness who also said she was going to the garage to get Calpol, Ali thought: the witness we now can't find.

Lynne made a face.

'Rear-wheel-drive vehicle like this, there's a danger of fishtailing if you over-compensate in a dramatic steering correction. I'd still expect to see *some* evidence of skidding.'

Lynne opened the driver's door, affording Ali a clearer view inside. There was a musty smell, sediment coating the floor, the seats and the material of the deflated airbags. It looked like the dashboard had been sick. Ali now understood why Lynne was in overalls: it wasn't always about protecting the evidence from contamination by the forensic tech, but sometimes the other way around.

'You couldn't take this one down the local car-wash and expect a full valet job for twenty quid,' Lynne said.

She climbed inside and sat behind the wheel.

'As you can see, both airbags deployed upon impact with the water. The car flooded and became submerged. The driver may have accelerated this process by opening the door in a panicked attempt to get out. What we do know is that he did get out at some point, either by opening the door once the pressure equalised or through the window, which was rolled down. In the latter case he was lucky that the electrics didn't short out before that, but I suppose under the circumstances "lucky" is not the appropriate word.'

Lynne talked them through some more details regarding the state of the interior. Most of these were obvious to the untrained eye, but that wasn't why Ali had stopped listening. She was looking at Lynne, tucked neatly behind the steering wheel, and was reminded of Rodriguez earlier that day, sliding the seat back to accommodate his greater height.

'Nobody's adjusted this seat, have they? I mean, could it have been moved as a result of the retrieval process?'

'No. These things are designed to stay in place even in a crash. They won't move unless you release the lever.'

'How's the position for you if you were driving? Can you reach the pedals okay?'

'Fine, yeah. A wee bit close, if anything.'

'What height are you, Lynne?'

'I'm five foot three. Why do you ask?'

'Because Peter Elphinstone was five nine.'

MUTE

I tried to convince myself to let it go, that I was doing myself no favours by allowing this to grow in significance in my mind. As you're taught in medical school, when you hear hoofbeats, look for horses, not zebras. This didn't have to mean all that I was worrying it might. Besides, did I really want to admit to myself what the worst-case explanation entailed? Because the moment I did was the moment I had to start living in that reality, that version of my marriage.

I couldn't bring myself to broach the subject with him, partly out of fear of what I might learn and partly because of the arguments we already had over trust. It was eating away at me though, so I called him on the office number the next time he was working late.

'Hello?' Peter answered, sounding surprised to be disturbed this way, before the caller had even identified herself.

'It's me.'

'Is something wrong?'

'Em, no. I'm sorry, I didn't mean to call. I hit the wrong button on my phone.'

'Okay.'

I realised afterwards that this gambit was as futile as it was pathetic: Peter probably had the office landline set to divert to his mobile when he wasn't in anyway, so he could have been anywhere. I thought I heard music in the background. Did he play music while he worked? He didn't when he was working at home. Did that mean he was somewhere else? I came close to getting into the car and driving past the office to check he was there, but it felt too overt an act. I told myself this isn't me. This isn't who I am and this isn't what we are.

But not all acts are so overt, or require the level of agency that makes you feel you are crossing a line. Some acts can be a matter of omission. That is where true temptation lies when one is in a state of suspicion, and I did something unworthy, whose dividend was also its punishment.

It was the following Saturday morning when the phone rang. Peter didn't hear it at first because he had headphones on, sitting in his office playing some game on the computer. He usually left the phone for me to answer anyway, as most of the calls to the landline tended to be for me.

I picked it up on a handset in the kitchen and heard a confident, cultured male voice that sounded familiar and yet tantalisingly hard to place.

'Oh, hello, I assume I'm speaking with Dr Jager?'

'That's right. What can I do for you?'

'Well, firstly, you can very kindly forgive me for my rudeness when we were previously introduced. This is Hamish Elphinstone.'

'Oh.'

'I was not at my best, given the circumstances, though that is not to make excuses.'

Except you just did, I thought, resisting the easeful temptation to be politely reassuring.

'Relations in our family have been . . . a trifle complicated, particularly between myself and Peter. I allowed my feelings to get the better of me that day, and for that I apologise.'

'It was your wife's funeral.'

I chose my words carefully. It was as much an acceptance as he was going to get, particularly as I noted that he still hadn't acknowledged my status as his daughter-in-law.

'That's very decent of you.'

His reply inferred a response I hadn't actually given. That was the aristocracy for you: they assume a version of the world and then proceed as if it were true.

'Now, if you wouldn't mind, I'd like to speak to Peter, if that's possible.'

'I'll go and see.'

I deliberately left the outcome ambiguous. I had absolutely no way of knowing how Peter was going to respond.

I pushed the Mute button with my thumb and knocked on the door. Peter turned in his swivel chair and slipped one headphone off.

'It's your father on the phone.'

He looked surprised, confused and then rather grim, all in the space of half a second.

'I'll take it here.'

Peter lifted the handset that sat in a charging dock next to the modem router.

It was as he turned away again, rotating in his chair that I realised what an opportunity was dangling before me. My thumb was still on the Mute button in the handset I held.

'I'll leave you to it,' I said, closing the door as I withdrew.

I knew I should press the red button to disconnect, but I also knew that as long as I kept it muted, Peter wouldn't be aware that I was listening in.

I justified it to myself in any number of disingenuous and morally contorted ways, but my thumping heart was proof that I knew it was wrong. It was beating hard with anticipation and with the fear of somehow getting caught. I had kept the phone muted so that neither my breathing nor the sound of background echo gave me away, but I imagined Peter would have heard the cadence in my chest if I hadn't gone all the way to our bedroom at the far end of the hall.

Initially I feared the extension had automatically disconnected when he picked up, as I was met with silence. I'm not sure whether Peter was making Hamish wait or preparing himself to speak.

'Hello, *Daddy*.'

His father ignored the sarcasm. His tone was stiff and formal. He was like a cabinet minister giving a statement about an unpopular but obstinately maintained policy. There was no attempt at small talk, no query after his son's well-being, his new progress into married life.

'Peter. I feel it's your right to know that Cecily and I are engaged to be married. We are planning our wedding for the spring of next year.'

'So should I check the post for an embossed invite?'

His father's patient silence said they both knew the answer to this question.

'Why spring? Do the etiquette manuals stipulate a statutory minimum time after your first wife is cold before you can marry again without anyone's moral disapproval?'

'I am doing you the courtesy of informing you, Peter.' Hamish sounded stoic and unrattled. 'I am not looking for your blessing.'

'I appreciate it. To be honest, I'm surprised you and Cecily didn't announce it at the funeral while you had everyone assembled. I'm sure all Mum's relatives were in no doubt that you were already shagging her, so they'll appreciate this concession to propriety.'

'Your mother's relatives understood our situation a lot better than you did.'

'Yes, no doubt it was a great comfort to them knowing that you weren't alone of an evening while she wasted away down the hall.'

For the first time, Hamish sounded a little testy.

'Well, none of us gets to choose the circumstances under which we fall in love, do we?'

His tone remained measured but the temperature was unmistakably hotter.

'I didn't think you were interested in who I fall in love with, Father. I got *married*, remember? *I have a wife.* You may recall being an utter thundercunt towards both of us when I introduced you recently.'

'I apologised to her for that a moment ago, but it was my earlier apology that remains most pertinent. She has no idea what she's got herself into. If you had any honour you'd . . . well, that's it precisely, isn't it? If you had any honour we wouldn't be having this conversation.'

'You know nothing about Diana or about who I am these days. There's only two of us – for now – but this is what a real family looks like. We are husband and wife, and sooner or later you'll have to face the truth of that.'

I felt ten feet tall, wanting to go and hug him but aware that I couldn't, as I'd have to confess why.

Then I heard Hamish sigh.

'This doesn't change anything, you being with this woman: you being *married*,' he added with scornful distaste. 'It didn't work the last time and it won't work now.'

THE ROAD TO PARANOIA

When you're feeling scared and vulnerable, you go back to what you know, so once again I immersed myself in work. I tried not to dwell on the irony. I used to worry that my job was an impediment to having a healthy and satisfying home life. Now it had become a haven where I could retreat *from* my home life.

I realised that I was spending longer talking to certain of my colleagues than to my husband, and the conversations were more open too. I had a heart-to-heart with Calum, and learned that his marriage wasn't without its complications either. His wife Megan was a registrar too, working in paediatric medicine down in Carlisle. It was a difficult but common arrangement among married junior doctors: spouses often had to take training positions at different ends of the country, particularly after the implementation of the disastrous 'Modernising Medical Careers' trainee-placement system. It was a matter of toughing it out with their eyes on the long term; the crucial thing was to find consultant posts in the same city when the time came.

As a consultant it is incumbent to take an interest in the trainees' welfare, but to be honest it was a distraction to listen to someone else's worries and preoccupations. Work was the only place where my mind was sufficiently occupied as to keep it from obsessing over the answers I needed to the questions I could not ask.

Had Peter been married before? And if so, why hadn't he told me? Why hadn't *anyone* told me?

I clung on to his defiant words to his father about acknowledging our marriage, about us being a family, but they were constantly undermined by the thought that they were no more than that: defiant words to his father. Why was Sir Hamish so scornful of the very notion of us being married when it was an incontestable fact? And why had he sounded so arch when he made that remark about not choosing the circumstances under which we fall in love?

I was in danger of driving myself mad with this stuff. It was no way to live, and I knew I couldn't go on like this. Either I must have it out with him or I should lay my fevered imaginings to rest, but neither of those seemed an easy or tempting prospect. I couldn't ask him about his conversation with his father because it would be to confess to my own deceit and distrust, yet at the same time, Peter's behaviour remained perplexingly secretive.

Every time I ventured into his den, he would hurriedly pull his laptop closed, concealing the screen from view and automatically putting it into sleep mode.

'You know, you should really knock before you come in here,' he snapped at me one time.

I had only come in to bring him a coffee and one of the whole-meal muffins I had gone to the trouble of baking so that he wasn't snacking on supermarket cupcakes. This was the thanks I got.

'Why, Peter? In case I catch a fleeting glimpse of some impenetrable machine code? Who is even going to know? Do the investors have cameras in here? Or is there something else on that laptop that you don't want me to see?'

'Like what?'

'I don't know: that's the point. I never see you so much as read your email or browse Facebook if you think I might be reading over your shoulder. Not everything on there can be covered by the fucking NDA. You're acting like you've got something to hide.'

'Maybe you should take a step back and have a look at what *you're* acting like, Diana. The road from legitimate suspicion to rampant paranoia is very much shorter than we think.'

'Well I suppose if it's rampant paranoia to wonder why you keep hiding your computer screen, then it must have been legitimate suspicion back at the beginning of the journey when you lied to me about where you'd been all evening.'

It came out before I could stop myself; or maybe I no longer wanted to stop myself.

'When?'

197

He stiffened in his seat. I couldn't decide whether he looked shifty or taken aback.

'A couple of weeks ago. I finished late and came by your building. I was going to take you to dinner, but you weren't there. Then when you showed up back here at about eleven, you said you'd been in the office the whole time. Sorting out a server crash,' I reminded him, my tone dripping scepticism.

His mouth fell open.

'I . . . And you said nothing? Rather than ask me what happened, you let this simmer and you've spent all the intervening time thinking I'm a liar?'

'You *are* a liar. You weren't there. The whole building was deserted and the car park was empty.'

'Jesus Christ. I went out to PC World because I needed a part. A fan had broken down on one of the mainboards.'

'What, at eight o'clock at night?'

'Yes. They're open until nine.'

I felt the ground drop, my assumptions suddenly revealed to be foolish and paranoid. There was brief euphoria in there too, in my relief that it wasn't true, but the essence of euphoria is that it is fleeting and false.

I might have been wrong about one incident, but that failed to change the most crucial thing: I didn't trust the man I had married.

He wasn't merely secretive about that laptop: he was defensive. And sod the bloody NDA: nobody involved in that would ever know or care whether I had caught a glance of some email or whatever. Which was why I instinctively began to suspect that it was something else entirely that he didn't want me to see.

A horrible, haunting thought began to take shape: a fear that went to the heart of everything I had been afraid of since first meeting him. It was the same fear that flashed through my mind outside the Ironworks: that his interest in me had something to do with my blog. Given all that had happened, I knew it sounded even more insane now than it had then, but its very awfulness was what made it impossible to completely dismiss.

What didn't Peter want me to see? Had he been lying when he

said he knew nothing about the whole Bladebitch thing? Surely his colleagues would have mentioned it when he was dispatched to help me that day. I thought back to the way he had been thrusting into me that night, after the funeral: that had felt like anger, like vengeance.

I had so many questions regarding what Peter might be concealing about himself, the biggest of which concerned his marital history. But perhaps a bigger question still was what was I capable of doing about it?

TARGET ACQUIRED

There is a moment in every James Bond novel in which Bond and the villain first meet, giving them the opportunity to size each other up. Much is mutually understood but nothing is overtly declared or conceded. According to Auric Goldfinger, the first such meeting can be considered happenstance. The second is coincidence. The third is enemy action. Parlabane's first encounter with Diana Jager did little to evoke the grand theatre of Caribbean hotels and Riviera casinos, taking place as it did in an Inverness hospital car park, but he would have occasion to look back and ponder the retrospective significance of it.

He was there to talk to a couple more names on Lucy's list, and as a pretext to hand out a few cards so that anybody who wanted to talk about the story could easily get in touch. He'd had a batch of them printed a few months back, bearing his contact details and a QR code. At the time he had suspected it was a pointless extravagance, as most of his income these days came from churning out copy that didn't require him to speak to anyone. Maybe he wanted a physical object he could touch that still said his name with the word 'journalist' underneath.

She was striding out through the main hospital entrance as he was approaching it from the forecourt. In retrospect he might have kept his head down, more deliberately chosen his moment to confront her, such as when he had more of a hand to play. He had only a fraction of a second to decide, and instinct urged him not to let the opportunity pass.

'Dr Jager?'

His enquiry caused her to stop and look up. Her eyes narrowed, taking him in, scrutinising him intently.

He caught a scent of perfume now that she was close, welcomed by his nose out here where the desperate smokers sought respite and shelter immediately beyond the doors. The bouquet was warm and complex, something more expensive and sophisticated than all the samey-smelling brands that pumped so much money into hilarious TV spots every December.

He proffered one of his business cards.

'My name is Jack—'

'I know who you are. Austin warned me that you were sniffing around.'

Parlabane wondered whether 'warned' would have been Austin's description of it, or whether she was trying to psych him out by implying that Austin's loyalty to her as a colleague trumped any Parlabane thought he enjoyed as a friend.

'I'm just looking for the real story here. Human emotions tend to be more complex than the Hallmark card version the tabloids are punting.'

'I know what you're looking for, Mr Parlabane. I know what you are.'

He expected her to walk away at that point, but she stood her ground. Interesting.

'I've spoken to someone who believes your husband was under a great deal of stress before the accident. Intolerable pressure, in fact. Is that something that you were aware of, or that you'd care to comment upon? Were you concerned about his state of mind?'

He hated himself for doing this, given that in all probability this woman had done nothing wrong and had recently received a crushing and extraordinarily painful blow. He never liked being that doorstepping ghoul, getting in the face of a hunted-looking subject and asking them questions he didn't expect them to answer. In this case, it was nonetheless a valid move. It was about letting her know she was on his radar, and seeing how she reacted to that information.

She looked at him like she could see all the way down to how small he felt right then. And when she spoke, her voice was quiet, searching: like she couldn't decide whether he was stupid or insane, but neither could excuse it.

'Why would you think someone in my position would possibly answer that?'

Then she walked away, though not without taking his card.

TICKET TO RIDE

It's terrifying to consider what can hang upon the smallest quirks of happenstance: how much might be different but for the most minor confluences. I have no way of knowing for sure – we can't run the events a second time and compare – but there is a strong case for saying that I would not have ended up where I am now but for a paper jam in a printer. I might have gone on deluding myself until it was too late, and might never have deduced what I so crucially did about my husband: the revelation that made previously unthinkable actions my only choice.

It was a Thursday evening. Peter was still at work (and had taken to calling me to say so; partly as a considerate reassurance and partly as a gentle dig). We had made firm plans to have a sit-down meal on Friday come hell or high water, as I was on call Saturday and he was going to London ahead of a meeting with his investors on Sunday morning.

I was preparing a seminar for the surgical trainees, and trying to print a bullet-points hand-out to distribute, but got an error message telling me there was a paper jam. The printer was a wireless beast Peter insisted on buying to replace the 'coal-fired museum piece' I had owned since about 2002. It sat under a table in Peter's den.

I slid out the tray and sighted the crumpled end of an A4 sheet caught between the rollers. I pulled it free with a firm but smooth tug, mindful of the consequences should it rip. There was nothing important on it: it was one of those infuriatingly wasteful second sheets bearing one line of meaningless blurb that got spat out if you wrongly assumed a document only ran to one page.

Once I slammed home the feed tray again, the print-heads hummed into life. I waited for my hand-outs to slide forth, but there was an outstanding job in the print queue. It was a ticket for rail travel, followed by a second wasteful blurb sheet. Peter had printed an extra copy by mistake, presumably because the printer had been set to produce two copies of the previous job.

I lifted it from the tray so that it didn't get mixed up with my hand-outs, and I was placing it on Peter's desk when I noticed the date and destination. It was a ticket to Glasgow departing Saturday, when he had told me he was flying to London.

I felt those same horrible pangs of paranoia as had plagued me before, but this time I recognised them for what they were. I wasn't going to make the same mistake again.

When he came home, I waited until he was settled in front of the TV and brought it up casually.

'There was a sheet jamming the printer earlier, by the way. I cleared it all by myself.'

'Worrying times. You women will be opening jars next, and that'll be the end of my gender.'

'It was a train ticket for Glasgow on Saturday. I left it on your desk. I thought you were going to London. Has it changed?'

His eyes widened.

'Eh, no. I mean, yes, but the other way around. I mean, initially the meeting was going to be in Glasgow, but they changed their plans and by that time I had already booked the train. They said they'd reimburse me, but you know what it's like: they need receipts for everything, so I was printing out the ticket to give them on Sunday.'

'Okay.'

There you go. I got my explanation, and it was innocent and plausible, same as before. So why was I not reassured? Why did I not believe him?

My calmer voice cautioned against extrapolating, and it had one strong argument in its favour. There was no reason to lie. If Peter had business in Glasgow, even if it was not the business he claimed, there was no need to make me believe he was going to London.

However, they say when you're telling the truth, you keep your answer brief, and you don't give out more details unless pressed for them. The more detail you volunteer, the more it betrays that you are trying to convince, and Peter had been conspicuously elaborate in explaining that ticket. But mainly what had troubled me was something more instinctive: that tiny initial response, that brief moment of alarm in Peter's eyes. There was something here that he wasn't expecting. Something he had overlooked.

The accidental second copy.

My calmer voice's argument could be turned in on itself: lying when you don't need to is a very bad sign.

Sunday morning was an odd time for a business meeting, was it not?

And suddenly I *could* think of a reason to make me believe he was in London. He hadn't known my rota when he made his arrangements. If I hadn't been due to work Saturday, perhaps I might have suggested we go to Glasgow together and have a night out and a stay in a nice hotel. Would that have been inconvenient? Was there a reason he wanted to travel alone?

I had a horribly restless night. I know I slept a few hours because there were unquiet snatches of dreams, but I never felt like I was deeply under. All night and throughout the next day, I changed my mind as to whether I believed him, speculating sometimes soberly and sometimes outlandishly as to what might be going on.

Perhaps I was over-reacting again. That look of alarm in his eyes didn't have to mean what I had inferred. It could simply have been Peter thinking: Oh Christ, here we go again. The same went for his over-elaborate answer. Perhaps he was ladling on the reassurance because of my track record. And indeed was it really that over-elaborate?

Perhaps it was as well I was on call Saturday, because if I had been free I might have concocted some embarrassing scheme to follow him.

We had dinner on the Friday night as agreed. I tried to act normal but all the time I was scrutinising what he said, his body language, anything that might give me more clues one way or the other. I had no idea how corrosive suspicion could be.

The unspoken subtext of us having dinner was that we would have sex later, another tilt at the so-far elusive prize of pregnancy. At my age I feared it was unlikely to happen swiftly, so I had to skew the odds by making sure we did it during the right time in my cycle. That weekend fell smack in the middle of the most fertile time, hence the importance of that Friday night, but there was no way I could let him inside me while I was feeling this way.

I worried that he would ask why I wasn't in the mood, but in the event, he didn't make anything in the way of overtures. Despite my efforts at covering up how I was feeling, maybe he sensed that something wasn't right.

He was still asleep when I got up for work on the Saturday morning. He stirred just enough for me to give him a kiss and wish him a good trip. I faked it like a pro, running a hand through his hair as my lips lingered on his. I was hedging my bets. If it turned out he was telling the truth, I wanted to conceal my suspicions; but if he was lying to me, I wanted it to be the full Judas.

NSFW

Weekend on-call can be a real lucky dip. Sometimes there's cases backed up from the night before, so you're busy from the moment you walk in the door. Occasionally it's quiet, which I hate, because although it allows me to go home, I can't settle to anything because I know the phone could ring at any moment to summon me back in a hurry.

On that particular Saturday morning, there were only two cases lined up. When I examined the patients I was satisfied that neither was particularly complicated, so I was happy for the trainee, Calum, to take them, and he was happier still for the practice.

I supervised the first case, which he handled with competence, if rather ponderously. The second was particularly straightforward, and I couldn't face the prospect of sitting in the passenger seat as Calum carried out another procedure at the same excruciating pace, so I decided to head home.

I will confess that another motivating factor was the opportunity to be around to observe Peter's departure. Annoyingly, the train and flight times were close enough to require him to leave the house around the same time for both, but there had to be clues, didn't there? His choice of clothes, for instance: Peter opted for trousers that didn't need a belt when he was flying, and sneakers rather than boots, to cut down on the number of items he'd have to 'remove at the security area in tribute to Allah,' as he put it.

I didn't see or hear him when I stepped into the hall and hung up my coat. That generally meant he was in his den, so I popped my head around the door, which was unusually ajar. His laptop was on, with the screen upright and the browser running, but his chair was empty.

A possibility presented itself and I brushed the trackpad to ensure the laptop didn't go into screen-saver mode.

I walked on soft feet towards our bedroom, but before I reached it I heard the sound of water running in the shower. I didn't know how long he had been in there, but it was less than the two minutes it took for the laptop to go to sleep. Peter was usually under the spray for at least ten, and that was before he shaved.

I checked my watch and returned to the den, leaving the door open so that I could listen out for signs of Peter emerging from the bathroom.

I went to his internet history first. If he was paranoid about what I might catch a glimpse of when I came in without knocking, then I figured he would be at his least guarded when he thought I was out of the house for the day.

I honestly can't say what I expected or even feared I would find, but in the event there was nothing to raise an eyebrow. He had been browsing sci-fi fan forums and watching a video-game reviews podcast, which made me jump because it started blaring from the speakers when I clicked the link. I hoped the water was still running in the bathroom to drown out the sound of theme music mixed with explosions.

Opening the full history and scrolling backwards chronologically, I saw little among the web addresses that was concerning or inform- ative. Why was he so protective about it then?

I searched the list for hotel sites, hoping to find out whether he had made a booking in Glasgow or London, but nothing leapt out at me amidst the endless sprawl of forum pages and YouTube videos.

I looked at my watch. I had been on for three minutes. I listened carefully to the silence from the hall, realising it sounded slightly different. The boiler had been firing and now it wasn't: a low background white noise one only noticed when it ceased.

Shit.

I opened his email client and scrolled his inbox for the few seconds it took me to realise this was a task that would require hours, even if I knew what I was looking for. Was there any way to copy this, I wondered. I had a USB stick in my bag, but I recalled the time I backed up my email folders, and it had taken about forty minutes to export them.

In a moment of either desperation or inspiration, I ran a search for all files or programs accessed that day, in the hope that I would maybe turn up a PDF with hotel details or a Word document listing Peter's travel itinerary. London or Glasgow, I couldn't say at that point which I would have preferred to find.

The search results listed several image files and two videos, the most recent of them accessed only minutes before I got home. I clicked on one of the jpegs and the screen filled with an image of a woman sitting on a bed, naked. Her back was resting against a headboard, her legs slightly apart. The shot was cropped so that she was only visible from the neck down. I clicked the forward button and the image was replaced by a picture from presumably moments later. The composition was the same, but her legs were slightly wider, a hand resting on her stomach with her fingers brushing the top of her thin strip of pubic hair.

I almost laughed that the explanation should be so prosaic. He was just checking out porn: not every time my presence caused him to shut the laptop, I sincerely hoped, but this morning, when he knew for a fact I was out.

I clicked on one of the video files. The screen now showed an almost identical shot, but in motion this time. The colour was slightly washed and the definition lower, it being video, but it appeared to be the same session. The woman's head was still out of shot. She fondled her own breasts in that way no woman has ever done except on-camera for male pleasure, then spread her legs slowly. I turned up the volume but only heard background hiss. I thought maybe there was no sound, but then she moaned as she began to masturbate.

That was when I asked myself why Peter would be looking at one faceless cropped woman for his jollies when he had the entire internet at his disposal. A knot formed in my stomach as I remembered the time he asked if he could film us. He promised to keep my face out of shot so that I couldn't be identified. Both of our faces, in fact.

Peter had taken these pictures. Peter had shot this video.

I clicked on the other video. It was from a different occasion, maybe a different room, but though her head was still cropped out, I was sure it was the same woman: same breasts, same navel, same landing-strip pubes. She was sitting on a table or a desk this time, having sex with an also headless male who was in a standing position as he thrust away. There was no question but that it was Peter. I didn't need to see his face: I was familiar enough with all the other parts that were in shot, and with the sound of his pleasured moans and grunts.

I reduced the video window and right-clicked on one of the jpegs to see when the file was created. I braced myself for what it might disclose, but bore in mind that the data might merely show when the image was copied to this laptop.

It indicated that the photo was taken almost two years ago, and the first video displayed the same date. The second video was older by three months. This was someone he'd been with before he met me.

I experienced a moment of relief that lasted only until I asked myself what he was doing poring over this stuff now. Was this someone he still wanted? Was this something that wasn't over? Was he going to meet this woman in Glasgow, today, tonight?

I was shaken from my thoughts by the sound of the bathroom door opening down the hall, and reacted automatically. I shut the video window and stepped out of the den, just as Peter was stepping from the bathroom. He had a towel wrapped around his waist, rubbing at his hair with another. He bridled at the sight of me, shock in his expression and a wave of fright causing him to shudder. I remembered that he didn't know I was home.

'There you are. I thought you were in your office,' I said, by way of explaining my own emergence from the den.

'Jeez, the fright you gave me. I didn't hear you come in.'

'Sorry. Things were quiet at the hospital so I decided to pop back, see a bit more of you before you go.'

I followed him into the bedroom as if keen to talk, though it was the last thing I wanted right then. It was my attempt to seem

210

natural; the desire to act natural, of course, only coming when one fears one is acting suspicious. It was once I was in there that I remembered I hadn't put the laptop into sleep mode, which was how Peter would be expecting to find it by the time he was finished his ablutions. I knew it was unlikely, but nonetheless it was possible that he might head back there before getting dressed, maybe to check his email or type out a note. I had seen him do both such things in a towel before, some thought having struck him while he was in the shower.

I started prattling about my morning, pouring out all manner of uninteresting guff so that he couldn't politely leave the room for the next two minutes. But even as I spoke, all I could think about was that faceless woman, and the fact that the man in front of me had been watching himself fuck her moments before I came home.

Had he been jerking off in the shower thinking about her? Was that why he'd been playing those videos right then?

The thought compelled me in the oddest way. I strode across to where he was standing and put my hands around his waist.

'Sorry, I'm wittering away here while you're standing in nothing but a towel. A shocking waste, especially as you'll be away all weekend.'

I pulled myself against him, running a hand over his chest, delicately stroking his nipple. I gave him a long kiss and slipped my hand slowly down beneath the towel, cupping his balls then running my fingers along his penis, which was rapidly in the process of becoming erect. This told me he hadn't been masturbating over the images, because I knew he couldn't get hard again so soon. I found this strangely reassuring. It changed the complexion of what I had seen. There could have been other reasons why he was looking at these old images. I was the one he wanted to be with now, for God's sake. I was the one he had married.

But then that word reared up at me, tapping into all that I didn't know. Was I the *one* he had married? Was this woman in the pictures his first wife? Was this woman someone he *wished* was his wife?

Then the worst of it hit me. Of course he wouldn't be masturbating over pictures of someone if he was going to meet up with her for real – for sex – a few hours later.

I watched him dress, looking for clues. He eschewed the linen trousers he generally favoured for flying, instead pulling on a pair of black jeans. However, I noticed that they were held up by a belt with a plastic buckle, the unusual material allowing for the clasp to be in the shape of some video-game logo. The belt wouldn't need to be removed at security, and nor would the sneakers he pulled on at the front door, suggesting he was flying after all.

He gave me a warm kiss goodbye, then climbed into a waiting cab. If he was deceiving me, right to my face, then he was doing a coolly convincing job of it. I didn't detect anything strange in his manner, and remembering how conspicuously fervent I had felt after looking on his laptop, I realised this was not something easily achieved.

I told myself to stop searching for things that weren't there, but after an hour of self-counselling and attempting to rationalise, I still couldn't think of anything but the woman in those images.

I called the taxi firm and got the dispatcher to give me the mobile number of the driver who had recently picked up from my address. He answered after two rings, easy listening music audible in the background.

'Hi. You picked up someone from my house a short while ago. I've just realised he's left his phone here and I was hoping to catch him up before he gets too far. Can you tell me where you took him?'

'A Mr Elphinstone, was it?'

'That's right.'

'Aye, dropped him at the station about forty minutes ago.'

CONTAMINATED SOURCE

Parlabane was sitting in his car just down the street from the hotel, thumbing through emails on his phone, when a well-honed instinct began to whisper a warning that someone was watching him. There was an older-model black Porsche parked on the other side of the road, lights off inside and out, a solitary figure sitting at the wheel in the dark. He had been there since Parlabane got into his own vehicle, and Parlabane hadn't paid him much heed, but years of experience had told him to trust his gut on things like this.

He had checked out of the hotel upon returning from the hospital, figuring it was quiet enough to check back in if he decided there was reason to stick around. He had one more thing to look into – involving a sit-down with a former colleague of Peter's – but unless it turned up something remarkable, he would be driving back to Edinburgh later that night. He wasn't meeting the guy for more than an hour, so he decided to go for a spin, see whether the Porsche followed.

Sure enough, no sooner had he pulled away than the headlights came on and a subsequent glance in his rear-view showed the nineties-vintage 911 swinging across the street, performing a U-turn. Parlabane's knowledge of Inverness wasn't great, but he knew he would hit a roundabout fairly soon if he stuck to the main routes. He encountered one about a quarter of a mile along the dual carriageway, where he executed what the cops called a reciprocal. He went halfway around and doubled back, allowing him to see the Porsche approach on the opposite carriageway, but it was too dark to get a look at the driver. Whoever he was, he didn't recognise the implications of Parlabane's manoeuvre for his attempt at covert surveillance, because he reappeared in the rear-view a few seconds later, heading back the way they had both come.

Parlabane was congratulating himself on having baulked the guy when it occurred to him that maybe his surveillance wasn't meant to be covert. Could be he had recognised the implications entirely but didn't care because he wanted to be noticed. With that in mind, Parlabane headed back into the city centre and let the one-way system and the traffic lights put sufficient vehicles and distance between himself and the Porsche until he was happy he had lost him. Then he headed out of town. He still had time to kill and there was somewhere he wanted to take a look at.

He let his sat-nav direct him up the hill past the hospital and out beyond Culloden, towards Diana Jager's address. He wasn't going to doorstep her, especially after their earlier encounter, but he wanted a feel for the place, and if the lights were off, it might be quite a close feel too.

Parlabane pulled in short of the cottage, closer to the neighbouring house but near enough to see that Jager's home was in darkness. He turned off the engine and killed the headlights. There was a faint glow visible now to the rear of the cottage, but he couldn't tell if it was a light on at the rear or whether it was perhaps coming from another property abutting Jager's garden. He would check it out anyway: he was practised at staying hidden when the circumstances required it.

He gripped the door handle but before he could open it, another vehicle appeared, approaching from the rear. It stopped about twenty yards behind Parlabane and its headlights darkened, which was when Parlabane recognised it as the Porsche. The driver was too far back to be identified in this darkness, but he could see that the figure inside was on the phone.

Maybe ten minutes passed, a long ten minutes. Neither of them made a move: they both sat there in a silent stand-off. The driver wanted Parlabane to know he had eyes on him. Either Parlabane had been mistaken in thinking he had shaken the surveillance, or the guy knew where he was likely to go. Either way, it was bad news.

The deadlock was broken when another vehicle appeared, arriving from the opposite direction. It was a patrol car, with two officers inside. It swung across into the single carriageway and stopped in front of Parlabane, nose to nose. At this moment the Porsche growled back into life, executing a three-point turn before heading back the way it had come so that Parlabane was once again denied even a passing look at the driver.

Two cops got out of the patrol car: a tall white male and a short female of Indian or Pakistani descent. They approached Parlabane's car, the bloke indicating to Parlabane to roll down the window. He complied.

'Can I help you, officer?'

'We're responding to a report of someone acting suspiciously,' said the female officer.

This sounded conveniently vague to Parlabane, a favoured police method of warning you off. The more nebulous the transgression, the more scope they had for claiming it applied to you if you didn't take a hint.

'I've only been here ten minutes, if that. I think someone's messing with both of us. Who made the complaint?'

'That's not something we can disclose.'

'May I see your driver's licence please?' her colleague asked, his accent English.

He sighed and produced his wallet. The male officer examined it and then handed it to his colleague.

'What is your business here, Mr Parlabane?' she asked.

Parlabane looked blankly at her.

'That is *my* business.'

'He's a reporter,' said the male.

The woman's look seemed to be asking how he knew this. Meantime Parlabane's silence was confirming it.

'Is that right?' she asked.

'Yes. So now you know I'm just doing my job. Not bothering anybody.'

'I'm not sure about that,' said the male. 'I can guess what you're working on, and after all she's been through, Dr Jager could do without press harassment.'

'So you guys know she lives here. Have you been involved in the case?'

Neither of them answered, the pair sharing a mutually worried look that betrayed they knew they had screwed up by giving away something they didn't need to.

'I'll take that as a yes. See, I've been speaking to a few people up here and I've been told that Peter Elphinstone was under extreme stress in the run-up to the accident. I've also been told the marriage was not quite as harmonious as everyone believes. Have either of you got any comment regarding the ongoing investigation into the crash?'

The woman handed him back his wallet.

'You need to move along, Mr Parlabane.'

Half an hour later, Parlabane was returning from the bar with two drinks, reflecting briefly that this was how outsiders used to imagine much of journalism was conducted: buying drinks for strangers in dingy bars in the hope that they might tell you something useful. It was certainly a far cry from the reduced modern circumstances of cribbing press releases or copy-pasting from Twitter, and though he was often nostalgic for the lost days of smoky press bars and the booze-fuelled cultivation of contacts, those outsiders would be wrong if they thought it sounded like an easy gig. For one thing, you had to spend a lot of time and money entertaining insufferable throbbers such as the turd-sculpture sitting opposite him right now.

Craig Harkness was one of Peter's ex-colleagues in the hospital IT department, another of the names on the list Lucy had given him. He was a sweaty wee bowling ball of a man, sitting there in a Motley Crue T-shirt and a denim jacket he couldn't even have got away with twenty years ago. He reminded Parlabane of the green one-eyed character in the *Monsters Inc* movies, though only via his build. Nobody was ever going to compare him to Billy Crystal in terms of wit and charm. He was an unpleasant and contradictory mix of self-satisfaction and resentment, combined with a wild over-estimation of his own conversational appeal. The upside of this, from a journalistic perspective, was his bumptious indiscretion. The downside was having to listen to the bastard.

He spent much of the time complaining about his lot, and a vast proportion of this involved framing his plight as the wise old hand surrounded by idiots and incompetents who didn't appreciate his genius. It seemed everything was particularly awful since the IT department got swallowed up by outsourcing firm Cobalt Solutions, and he'd been forced to transfer into their employ. Before that, everything apparently hummed like clockwork in his wee IT fiefdom, which he ran with judgement and precision in the face of the chronic stupidity of the doctors, nurses, managers and indeed anybody who was not Craig Harkness.

Making it worse was the fact that Parlabane was on Irn Bru to keep his options open, while this guy was happily necking free pints. He had been leaning towards driving home tonight, and sitting with this fud was cementing his decision. On the strength of what he had heard so far, he was already looking forward to being in his own bed in a few hours; his own home, such as it was.

The fact that Lucy had put this guy's name on the list showed that there wasn't much to find. He hadn't even worked with Peter for long: only a few months either side of the marriage. She was grabbing at air, hoping rather than expecting Parlabane to find anything.

He would call her from the car on the drive south later, once he had decided what it would be kindest to share. It was possible her brother had killed himself or had a stress-related fatal accident. Whether the pressure he'd been feeling was related to work, his marriage or a combination of the two, it didn't alter the fact that his death was not suspicious. Maybe it would be best if she made her peace with it and stopped looking for someone or something to blame.

'So, did you have a lot of dealings with Peter's wife?' Parlabane asked, opting to go direct. There was no need to pussyfoot around the point of interest with someone so self-obsessed, and he had already decided he wanted this wrapped up. He certainly wasn't buying this sphincter-lozenge another pint.

'Did I ever.'

Harkness gave a dry chuckle.

'Snootiest bitch in the whole place. One of those smart-arsed cows who can't take the fact that they need your help. She really thinks she's something, that one. Acts like it's beneath her to even have you in her office when she's got a problem needing fixed.'

'I gather hospital IT guys weren't her favourite people in the world. Apart from the one she married, obviously.'

'No shit, Sherlock. Do you know about the blog she wrote?'

'I heard about it, yeah.'

'The cheeky cow said that if we were any good we'd have a job somewhere else. Well, what does it say about Vinegar Tits that she ended up here in Inverness? If she was hot shit like she makes out, she'd be at Barts or wherever, wouldn't she?'

He knew it was best practice to let the guy talk, but there was only so long he could listen to a blowhard puffing himself up. Parlabane hadn't approved of Scalpelgirl's scattergun disparagement but he suspected Harkness's own outrage – and conspicuously insecure self-praise – was rooted in the fact that in his case deep down he knew she was right.

'I believe her previous consultant post was at the Alderbrook, in an internationally leading surgical department. It's my understanding that she had to leave that position due to the fallout from her being hacked: not only was she identified as the author of the blog, but as a consequence so were some of the colleagues she had alluded to. I assume that's why she was uncomfortable with anyone else working on her PC.'

'Yeah, but that's the whole point, isn't it? She was tarring us all with one brush in her blog, and then doing the same when she got here. Never gave us the benefit of the doubt. I didn't know how Peter could stick her, to be honest, but they do say love is blind. Deaf as well, it would seem.'

'So Peter was aware you didn't have a high opinion of her? And presumably she let him know that it was reciprocal.'

From the brief moment of doubt and injury on Harkness's previously smug face, it hadn't even occurred to him that his colleague and his wife might ever have been comparing notes on what a wanker he was.

'Peter was always making excuses for her being such a torn-faced midden. If someone moaned about how snippy she was, he would tell us she'd been through personal tragedy, blah blah blah, not to mention the hacking thing, like that was our fault.'

'What personal tragedy?'

'He never said and I never asked. What do I care? Don't see what difference it makes. I know plenty of people working in that hospital who've been through bad shit in their lives, but they can still manage a fucking smile. And as for the hacking thing, yeah, okay I get that it was out of order, but let's face it, it was nothing compared to what *could* have happened.'

'What do you mean?'

Harkness gave him a knowing and approving grin.

'Don't stick your dick in a hornet's nest. Or in her case, your tit.'

Harkness had chosen his words precisely. He was referring to internet security firm HBGary's deliberate provocation of Anonymous and the hacker collective's entertainingly punitive response. In online lore, the firm's actions had been described as above.

'She pissed off the wrong people. She should be grateful all that happened was she had her personal details leaked. Just as well she didn't have a sex tape back then, or it would have been public domain.'

He looked smugly satisfied about this notion, and the worst thing about it was that he clearly assumed Parlabane shared his satisfaction.

'You know, what has always confused me about these kinds of leaks is why guys are so desperate for porn of women they claim to detest.'

Harkness looked at him with amused confusion, as though Parlabane was thick or Harkness was expecting an imminent declaration of homosexuality.

'Because it knocks them off their high horse. Especially someone like Dr Diana: she acts like she's so superior, like she's above mere mortals, and definitely above the male of the species. Sex tapes prove women like that still love a good hard cock when it comes right down to it.'

There was that nasty grin again, like he knew a secret. Amazing, mate: women like sex too. What a scoop. Right enough, it probably did seem like a revelation to Harkness, as Parlabane couldn't imagine women had ever provided any evidence that they liked sex when he was around.

'So had you heard about her before she pitched up here in Inverness?'

'Course I had. Everybody in hospital IT knew about her: that's how the hacking thing came about. Not that I was involved, you understand.'

He gave a throaty chuckle and touched the side of his nose in a hush-hush gesture. He was inviting Parlabane to think he *was* involved, but Parlabane saw the obvious truth. This helmet wouldn't have had a clue where to begin but he wanted to make out he was badass and connected. It was frankly pathetic.

'How did everybody know about it?'

'Her blog first got mentioned on a support forum for one of the big database management packages we use. A lot of hospital IT folk are on there, as well as sys-admins from firms using the same software. There's the main support bulletin board and there's more informal sub-forums for general moaning and gossip. It went viral from there.'

'So Peter knew all about this stuff before he met her?'

'No. It's probably significant that Peter was the only guy in our department who *didn't* know about it. I guess that gave him the chance to make his own impression, or for his dick to take control before his brain found out what kind of cunt he was dealing with.

'Peter wasn't part of hospital IT before Cobalt brought him here, and the blog-hacking thing was four or five years ago, so I don't know what he was working on back then. Also, Peter was kind of unto himself: a bit unworldly sometimes, you know? If you'd asked him about Bladebitch, he'd have probably thought you were talking about someone in a comic book.'

'Did he tell you what he went off to work on?'

'He was designing some kind of app, to do with small-value transactions, I think. He wasn't giving much away: coy to the point of shifty. One time I asked him about it and he said: "I could tell you, but then I'd have to kill you."'

Harkness rhymed this off with an admiration indicative that he thought this was a hell of a line, one his audience would surely never have heard a thousand times before.

Parlabane decided he'd heard enough. He drained his Irn Bru and got up. Harkness remained where he was, still nursing half a pint. Parlabane wished he'd been running a tab. He'd have no qualms about fucking off after telling the barman that the sweaty flange sitting opposite had agreed to pick it up.

ACCESS PRIVILEGES

Starfire.

That was the name of the videogame whose logo was depicted in the coloured-plastic buckle Peter was wearing when he left the house that Saturday. I mention it because I came to realise how much it bothered me that I knew. When I first met Peter, I thought it was refreshing that I was becoming exposed to things that were outside of my over-serious bubble, vicariously appreciating passions and enthusiasms that didn't begin and end with work or research.

In time, I became resentful that I knew about all this crap. I could recognise the logo of a nineties videogame, same as I could name minor characters from superhero comics and recite the lyrics to juvenile Blink-182 songs about prank calls and blowjobs. It was like there was this sacred canon of Peter's personal culture in which I had immersed myself in order to become closer to him, in order to share something with him, and now I was seeing it for the worthless trash that it was.

There's nothing makes the scales fall from your eyes quite like realising you're being lied to by your husband.

I was still reluctant to accept this, of course. After I finished speaking to the cab driver, I immediately began constructing other explanations; or at least explanations that didn't involve the faceless woman in the photographs and videos. None of them were convincing, or even particularly plausible. When I started speculating that maybe the ex-Inverness flights were full and Peter was actually flying out of Glasgow, that was when I knew I was reaching.

I felt sick: physically sick. I was light-headed and my stomach was churning. I had to sit down. I made myself a cup of tea and sat numbly sipping it in the kitchen, beginning to confront the reality I had been presented with.

I read an email from Piers on my phone, telling me that his daughter Ellen had won a karate tournament on the Gold Coast. Ordinarily this would make me feel a warmth at the thought of my niece and a tang of regret that I saw so little of her. Right then I was too numb to feel anything.

Mercifully, my bleep didn't go off. At other times, my ability to shut out all distractions as I concentrated upon a procedure had offered me valuable respite, but on this occasion, if I had been called back into the hospital, it would have been torture. I felt the need to take action, to engage physically in dealing with what I had learned.

I went to Peter's den. I had been increasingly tempted in recent weeks to go rooting through his things, looking for clues to what he might be keeping from me. There had been other overnight stays, all-day airsoft meets and oh so many evenings when I knew he wouldn't be home until late. I had not wanted for opportunity. But it was as though there had been an invisible forcefield in place, preventing me from entering: a line I could not bring myself to cross because of the person I would be – and the marriage we would have – on the other side of it.

It would be fair to say that on this particular on-call Saturday, the shields were down.

Principally I was looking for documentation of where he was staying in Glasgow. He wasn't due back until Monday, so if I could find out what hotel he was booked into, I could drive there the next day, as soon as my on-call was over.

I didn't go indiscriminately wading through the place like an inquisitive toddler. I took my phone with me and photographed anything I was planning to touch. I didn't want to tip him off that I was on to him, because if he still thought I was swallowing his lies, he might let his guard down further.

I went through his desk and every drawer in his plastic filing stack without finding anything remotely suspicious, which made me realise that Peter wasn't relying upon an invisible forcefield to protect damning evidence from his wife's discovery. Chances were he was keeping anything he didn't want me to see in his office at

Sunflight House. Accomplished deceivers are naturally suspicious, so my enthusiasm for the task diminished as my fruitless search endured. Nonetheless, I needed to stay occupied, and right then I had nothing better to do.

I opened the big double-door wardrobe that stood against the wall at the far end of the room. It had come with the house, an ancient and ugly built-in affair the vendors couldn't be bothered ripping out and moving. Peter kept his airsoft gear inside it, but I was sure I had seen him stick a concertina file in there once as well.

I spotted it near the bottom beneath a shelf, stashed sideways on top of a lever-arch file and behind a sun-faded blue cardboard box that must previously have been stored in direct sunlight. The blue box was considerably heavier than I expected, its weight being used to keep the over-stuffed concertina file from springing open. It was when I placed it down carefully on the carpet that I noticed the logo and text on the lid: it was an old laptop, held on to and lovingly stored like I had learned Peter did with anything electronic.

I flipped it open and pressed the on switch, but there was no response. Typically, an old machine being dead was no reason for Peter to throw it out. But then I noted the power cord and transformer tucked neatly into their polystyrene housing and realised that the battery might merely have run down in storage.

I plugged it in and tried again. It hummed into life and booted up, so tantalisingly slowly as to suggest the thing had a sense of the dramatic and was milking the moment.

It was worth waiting for.

There was no password screen, so I had carte blanche.

The first thing I did was search for files created around the dates of the images and videos I had seen previously, as they were old enough for earlier copies to have been stored on this machine. Sure enough, I found the same photos and clips, as well as more featuring the same woman: always with her head out of shot. I was hoping to find others taken by Peter, less explicit and therefore more revealing. There was nothing, though: only a few phone shots taken at airsoft meets and what I resented recognising as a Star Trek convention.

224

I fared better when I booted up his email client. The most recent email was from eighteen months ago, when presumably he had moved on to a new laptop. I had access to all messages, sent and received, going back almost two further years.

I moved the laptop through to the kitchen table and scrolled patiently, opening messages whenever I came to a female name. These were conspicuously rare among Peter's contacts list, and I struck gold when I discovered his correspondence with a woman named Liz Miller. Reading through these emails and others that they were both copied into, it was clear that these messages marked the early days of a relationship. The exchanges dated from a little more than two years ago, and were therefore concurrent with the time the videos were taken.

I launched the old laptop's browser and scoured his favourites until I found his Facebook page. Unfortunately it didn't automatically log me in, so without his password I couldn't access his Friends lists. I was hoping for a photo, any nugget of information about who she was, but with her first name and surname being so common, there was no point in putting them into Google.

I decided to copy her email address so that I could try a search using that. It was when I clicked on the contact details that I saw that her mobile and landline numbers were listed also.

I felt the hairs on my neck rise in primal response, and watched gooseflesh form on my forearm. I knew that I could dial one of these numbers right now and that Peter could be sitting feet away from the woman who answered.

I glanced again at the landline. It wasn't a Glasgow number: the area code was 01382. I looked it up: Dundee.

I felt a surge of relief, then realised it meant nothing. If this was a dirty weekend, they might both be away from home.

My fingers trembling, I dialled the number and it began to ring, my heart thumping as I heard the syncopated electronic purr. I had no idea what I would say if she picked up, or indeed whether I could bring myself to say anything. I just needed to know.

CAMOUFLAGE

He called Lucy first thing that morning, having got home from Inverness late the night before. The flat might be half the size it used to be, but it felt all the more empty, despite all the crap he had in boxes he was unlikely ever to open. They were like unexploded memory mines dotting the floor. He felt a compelling need to talk to somebody, and in her case he had an excuse to call.

It was almost a week since her brother's accident. She sounded brighter than at their meeting at the café, though there was an underlying sincerity to her voice that didn't indicate she would be cracking jokes any time soon.

'Mr Parlabane. I was just thinking about you,' she told him, which he had no intention of misinterpreting. 'How are things?'

'Busy. I was calling to update you on what I've been finding out.'

'I'm actually going to be in a meeting in about, let me see, seven minutes. How about we catch up this evening when we can talk at a bit more length.'

'Sure.'

'And how about we make it a bar. I think I owe you a drink.'

'You don't really, but I won't say no.'

Parlabane reckoned it might not be a very large drink if she was buying on the basis of what he had discovered, but it might make things less tense and awkward if they were talking in more sociable circumstances.

'I think I do. You're the only person I feel I can be honest with at the moment. Plus it seems only polite. You're running around the highlands on my behalf and I've been so wrapped up in myself that I've never even asked how you're doing.'

Parlabane said nothing for a moment. It had taken him aback that it even occurred to her to care.

'That wasn't a question, by the way, so don't answer,' she said, as though anticipating a response that he wasn't actually about to give. 'I'll ask you later when there's time to talk.'

They agreed a rendezvous, but before she hung up, Parlabane managed to tap her for some information pertaining to the one area he still needed to look into.

'About Peter's firm, MTE Ltd. I found the details through Companies House. What do the initials stand for?'

'Micro Transaction Executables.'

'That's not very revealing. What was he actually working on?'

'I can't say.'

'Can't say as in you don't know? Because I see you're listed as company secretary.'

'Can't say as in bound by a non-disclosure agreement. It's to protect the investors and what they have staked in the project: even with Peter gone, there's still the possibility they can find someone to build on his work.'

'I'd like to know more about how the project was going, even if we have to avoid specifics.'

'That's not me, I'm afraid. My involvement only went as far as finding the investors and helping get the company set up.'

'There are three directors listed,' Parlabane noted. 'Apart from Peter, there is a Courtney Jean Lang and a Samuel Patrick Finnegan.'

'Lang is the epitome of the silent partner. Lives abroad, seldom comes to the UK. We've never actually met. I got in touch via a friend of a friend. The ideal investor, you might say: gives you the money then isn't looking over your shoulder and demanding progress updates all the time. You'd have a better chance of talking to Sam. He's in Glasgow.'

As a journalist, Parlabane had heard 'fuck off' more times than most people in this life. He considered himself a connoisseur, able to detect the finest nuance that distinguished individual varieties of the sentiment, and he was able to recognise it even when it came encoded within words that were ostensibly benign and even purporting to be helpful. Sometimes 'fuck off' was screamed directly into his face from the spittle-flecked mouth of someone in the throes of vein-bulging fury. Yet the message could be equally unambiguous and implacable when delivered in the mellifluent tones of a fresh-faced and smiling young woman as she politely enquired of him: 'Do you have an appointment?'

Lucy had given him the address of an art dealership Sam Finnegan owned just off Great Western Road. She had worked in the art business herself, which was how she knew him, but she cautioned Parlabane that their connection wasn't a guarantee that Finnegan would speak to him. Thus her words 'a better chance' indicated how difficult it might be to get in touch with Lang. And thus Parlabane was able to interpret the true meaning of the receptionist asking whether he had an appointment.

What the receptionist didn't realise was that she was also telling him her boss was around. When she went through the mummery of calling upstairs and telling Parlabane that Finnegan was 'unavailable all day', he reciprocated with his own pretence of giving up and leaving. Instead he sat in his car, parked with a view of the entrance, and did something all good reporters were trained in before the era of churnalism had taken hold.

He waited.

Within the hour he saw two figures emerge from the shop: two men he had definitely not seen enter, for he could hardly have missed them. The older one he took for Finnegan: a tall and chiselled-looking middle-aged bloke with a dandified and haughty air about him: a well-dressed and immaculately coiffured individual whose healthy conceit of himself was evident merely from his gait and posture. He was accompanied by a younger guy who looked a less natural match for his duds: taller, more muscular, easier to picture in a sleeveless vest and sweatpants than a good suit.

Parlabane strode into Finnegan's path, card pinched between his fingers, offering a smile and a chirpy tone.

'Mr Finnegan?'

Finnegan looked at him with mild surprise and calm composure. If there was annoyance there, he masked it well, and Parlabane was damn sure there was annoyance there. Image meant a lot to this guy: that was clear.

'I was wondering whether I could have a wee word with you about your involvement with the late Peter Elphinstone and his company, MTE.'

His expression remained relaxed. He looked like he was thinking about it, as though internally checking his schedule.

'And you are?'

He proffered the card.

'Jack Parlabane. I realise there's an NDA preventing you discussing details of the project, but I'm interested in how it was progressing generally.'

Finnegan took the card and examined it like it was a delicate artefact, turning it over slowly between his leather-gloved fingers. He looked back at Parlabane and gave him a cold smile.

'I don't discuss my businesses with anybody not directly involved.'

Those words, also, said 'fuck off'.

'I was wondering when you last spoke to Mr Elphinstone, and how you felt things were between you at that time.'

Finnegan made the tiniest of gestures: a brief movement of his eyes that was intended to be perceptible only to the individual who was presumably paid to be looking for it. On this occasion, Parlabane was looking for it too.

The bigger guy took a step: not so much towards Parlabane as slightly to one side, thus shielding his boss and ushering him past. It was subtle and controlled: defensive rather than offensive, but unmistakably a demonstration of power.

It told Parlabane a great deal. Finnegan was a man who didn't want to make a brash display of deploying muscle, but muscle he had, and presumably muscle he needed. He was wearing a very expensive winter coat, beneath which Parlabane could see fine tailoring and a flamboyantly colourful silk tie. He was dressing like a man of parts: businessman, art dealer, cognoscenti, but the other thing Parlabane identified beneath that coat was a Glasgow gangster.

Finnegan opened the door of an immaculately preserved vintage

Bentley. Not for him the absurdly ostentatious modern sports version, ubiquitous vehicle of choice for the successful Scottish drug lord. No, Finnegan wanted something more classic, that spoke of taste and refinement rather than just power and money.

As he pulled away, Parlabane wondered whether he owned a classic Porsche 911 as well.

GLADIATORS

Liz Miller answered the phone after an excruciatingly long number of rings, though maybe it only seemed long to me in my desperation to have her location confirmed. Certainly it was time enough for me to consider hanging up, but I knew I would only end up calling again two minutes later, then over and over. I couldn't afford that: if she was away overnight with Peter, I didn't want her handset's history to show a dozen missed calls from the same number: his home landline, where he lived with his wife.

'Hello?'

Her tone was inquisitive when she finally responded. I wondered if she had been looking at an LED display and read this number before picking up.

'Is that . . . Liz?'

'Yes.'

So she was home in Dundee, not in Glasgow with Peter. But I had a lot more questions I'd like to ask her.

'Em, sorry to disturb you. I'm calling because I need to talk to you about Peter Elphinstone.'

'Oh.'

There was a long pause, which I was about to fill, but eventually she spoke again.

'Has something happened?'

'No, nothing like that. It's just, I believe you were in a relationship with him a couple of years ago. Is that right?'

Her tone became more defensive.

'Hang on, who is this?'

'My name is Diana Jager. You don't know me.'

'How do you know Peter?'

'I'm married to him.'

'Oh. *Oh*. I see.'

She sounded as curious about me as I was about her. I don't think either of us was prepared to talk about it over the phone, however, so we agreed to meet the next day.

I was called in for a couple of hours shortly after midnight: an emergency splenectomy. I doubted I was missing sleep through it. My mind was too busy to shut down. Sometime during the evening it had occurred to me that I had no reason to trust this Liz woman, nor to assume that she was in the clear regarding Peter's deceit. Her phone could have been set to relay calls from her landline to her mobile when she was not home, like the phone in Peter's office. That might have been the reason for the delay in her answering, so it was possible he was sitting right there with her when she spoke to me. Perhaps the reason she agreed to meet me the next day was in order to ascertain precisely how much I knew.

I drove to Dundee first thing on the Sunday morning, getting there around lunchtime. It took me about three hours.

She was waiting for me inside the café. I was hungry from the journey but I felt instinctively vulnerable at the notion of eating in front of her. Part of me didn't want to look weak or awkward, though I couldn't have told you why those things would have applied to having a fruit scone.

It felt important to look composed, to look dignified, and generally to look good. I didn't acknowledge it to myself at the time, but I must have spent more time getting ready that morning than I ever did for a date with Peter.

She was wearing black jeans and a tight wool sweater with a white linen collar. I couldn't decide whether it was sexy or frumpy: Japanese schoolgirl or ageing schoolmarm.

If she noticed me sizing her up as I introduced myself and took a seat, then she didn't know the half of it. She was around my age, probably a little younger, with shoulder-length dyed blonde hair, but it was her build I was most interested in taking in. She was slim, I guessed an inch or two taller than me, and from the moment I laid eyes on her I began trying to imagine what she looked like naked as I considered whether she was the woman in the videos.

'I looked up your phone number,' she said, rolling a sachet of sugar between her fingers. 'That area code is for Inverness. You've driven all the way down here on a Sunday morning.'

'That's right.'

'To talk about Peter Elphinstone.'

'Yes.'

'Your husband.'

I nodded.

She was eyeing me with a look of intense scrutiny, as though sternly evaluating the honesty of my responses, a human polygraph. It was not quite as though she didn't believe me; more like she was untrusting of my motives.

'Of how long?'

'About four months.'

She looked away briefly, the judge considering what she had been presented with so far.

'And where is Peter today?'

I don't know, I didn't say. *I was hoping you could tell me.*

I knew I mustn't show my hand at this stage, and that it might end the encounter right there if I came out and accused her.

'He's in Glasgow for the weekend.'

She nodded, evaluating this neutrally.

'But he told me he was going to London.'

Our eyes locked across the table. If she was in on Peter's deceit, then I knew I wasn't divulging anything she couldn't already assume simply from my being here, but by making it explicit I was changing the terms of engagement.

'That's a hell of a thing to admit to a stranger,' she said.

She regarded me in silence for a long time, a very long time, her words hanging in the air all the while, demanding our mutual contemplation.

Then at last she spoke again.

'Are you hungry? You must be hungry. All the way down from Inverness. Order something to eat. You can eat and I can talk. I'll tell you about me and Peter.'

THE PREFERRED OUTCOME

In a parallel universe, only marginally askew from Parlabane's present reality, this might be an evening to cherish. In both worlds it was Saturday night and he was meeting a woman for a drink: sitting in his favourite pub, nervousness gnawing away at him as he awaited her arrival; the sense of flattery that she had sought him out also feeding into an anxiety that he might fail to meet her expectations.

One of those realities was full of openings and possibilities. In one of those realities, the evening might end in laughter, in kisses.

He felt a low dread at the prospect of the encounter, recalling her crushed countenance when she doorstepped him only a few days ago. She had picked up since then, but the anticipation of what he might reveal could have been a factor: something positive for her to focus on, a distraction from her turmoil. He reflected that, under the circumstances, perhaps the only thing worse than disappointing her was giving her what she wanted.

He checked his watch: he was early. He distracted himself by trying Catherine McLeod on his mobile. He had called her earlier, hoping to get the Glaswegian Detective Superintendent's take on Sam Finnegan. It had gone to voicemail and he hung up, intending to phone again later, but it had slipped his mind until now when he had a moment to kill.

It went to voicemail again. This time he left a short message, clicking off as Lucy strode into the Barony in a flowing black coat, her gaze searching the tables. To his surprise, he felt a rush of brightness, of pleasure, at the sight of her walking through the door. Maybe it was mere instinct: in any reality, there were worse ways to spend a Saturday night than meeting an attractive woman for a drink. And he did find her attractive, he realised. She smiled when she spotted him. That always helped. She wasn't exactly beaming, but she was no longer looking post-tearful and exhausted by shock and hurt.

She batted away his offer to go to the bar and returned with drinks for both of them. She was taller than he remembered: she had seemed hunched before, shrinking from the world in her grief. No longer reeling, she carried herself with what he couldn't exactly call grace – it was too straight-backed and formal for that – but certainly a confidence often instilled in the high-born.

She folded the coat and placed it on the chair opposite Parlabane, but sat down next to him on the bench against the wall. It felt unsettlingly intimate until he realised that she didn't want anyone eavesdropping on this conversation.

She wore a patterned silk blouse with a high collar and frilly cuffs. It wouldn't work on everyone, but somehow it did on her. She had her own style, consistent with his first impression: prim and yet fetishistic. Now that he was presented with her in this context, he realised he had seen her in the Barony over the years: someone he had taken notice of, occasionally wondered about, but never had occasion to speak to.

Such an occasion was here now, but it wasn't the one he'd have chosen or envisaged.

She was hungry for details, eager and anxious for answers that he couldn't give her. He told her everything he had learned over the past few days, after first appealing to her to stop addressing him as Mr Parlabane.

'Please call me Jack. Whenever I get called Mr Parlabane it's usually because I'm in trouble.'

'Sorry. I didn't realise I was doing it. I think because I've asked for your help, subconsciously I was trying to be respectful. But it sounds terribly formal, doesn't it?'

'I suppose it does keep a professional distance,' he admitted.

'It feels wrong, though. What you've done for me seems more like the kindness of a friend. Kinder than that, since you agreed to it without knowing me at all.'

'I wouldn't have done it if I didn't think there might be a story in it. Believe me, Lucy, I'm nobody's white knight.'

She looked at him with a wistful sincerity.

'You're the closest thing to that I've had in a long time.'

They held each other's gaze for a moment longer than Parlabane was comfortable with. He needed to get things back on surer footing, so he turned the conversation to the matter at hand.

He laid out the details soberly, keen that she should not infer anything dramatic in his findings.

'You're right that it wasn't the perfect marriage as reported in the tabloids, but it wasn't anything that surprising either, considering we're talking about two people who perhaps married in haste. I get the impression it's like you suggested: she was a bit obsessive about trying to knock Peter into shape, making him conform to the ideal she thought she was marrying. But I think that simply explains why she said Peter had changed and you said his problem was he never did.'

'Did you speak to Diana personally?'

'Only briefly. She was as forthcoming as I'd expect of someone in her circumstances.'

'But did you find out anything about her from anyone else?'

'Not much that wasn't already public knowledge. One person I spoke to mentioned a personal tragedy in her past. Do you know anything about that?'

She nodded, a slightly strained look of frustration in her expression: of the question she never asked when she had the chance.

'I remember Peter alluding to that once. He didn't mention what it was about and at the time I wasn't interested enough to ask. Something that happened when she was a student, I think. Did you speak to my father?'

'I spoke to Cecily.'

Parlabane figured this reply would require no elaboration.

'In that case I wouldn't be on tenterhooks waiting for him to ring back.'

'An iron fist inside a velvet glove if ever there was one.'

'And soon to be my wicked stepmother.'

'They're engaged?'

'Yes. And you don't know the half of it. She's *my* age.'

'I see. That sounds . . . awkward.'

'Creepier still, she used to visit with her family when we were kids. She was always a bit aloof, acting more grown-up than us. Peter had a real crush on her when we were teens. I think there might even have been something going on between them behind the scenes at one point. And now she's marrying my father. They'll be parents together within a year of the nuptials, mark my words. She'll be shagging him every which way until she's provided a fresh new heir, and she'll see the sprog gets a sweeter deal than we did.'

'How so?'

'People assume Peter and I must be loaded, but our father gave us bugger-all. Said it would be the making of us, the hypocritical bastard. That was why Peter was giving everything to make his software idea come good. Peter made out he was done with our father and wanted nothing from him, but I don't think that was ever true. In fact I always suspected he had this naively optimistic notion that if he somehow proved himself, he'd be back in the good books. And by good books ultimately I mean the will. Of course, the reason it took him so long to even come close was that it's hard to believe in yourself when your father has been telling you you're worthless and undermining your confidence your whole life.'

'Certainly a hell of a catch-22. Did you believe it was possible? That your father would change his position?'

'Not enough for me to go chasing after his approval, but occasionally I did wonder . . . That was before Cecily came into the picture, though. I'm sure she'll be, ahem, stiffening his resolve with regard to the finances. And once they have a child, she won't stand for what our mother did.'

'Are you saying she's a gold-digger? I thought she was from quite a rich background herself.'

Lucy looked at him as though pitying his naivety.

'Just because you come from money doesn't mean you're not a gold-digger. In fact, wouldn't appearing to be uninterested in money be the perfect cover for a gold-digger?'

'Are you talking about Cecily now, or does that go for Diana too?'

'I don't know. I've thought about it, I confess, but I don't see how it would work.'

'Take it from somebody who was married to a doctor for fifteen years: they don't put themselves through all that shit because they're driven by avarice.'

Lucy seemed surprised, even a little concerned.

'Fifteen years. That had to hurt. How long have you been divorced?'

Parlabane gave her a wry smile.

'Papers came through the morning you rang my doorbell.'

'Sorry. It must feel like such a loss, regardless how you felt about each other in the end.'

Her words were warm, the balm of feeling that someone else understood.

'It was a slow demise, eventually irreparable, but yes. I lost something – we both did – something that was more than each other, if you know what I mean.'

'I think I do. I've always thought a relationship should be about creating something greater than the sum of its parts. I think that's why I was always protective towards Peter in that regard: wanting to know what the other half is bringing to the table. I was rightly suspicious in the past: he was bitten more than once by women who buggered off once they found out there was no fortune.'

'But from what I've found, that's not Diana. If she believed Peter was secretly rich, she wouldn't have encouraged him to stake so much of his time and energy on this project, would she?'

'You're right.'

Lucy took a slow sip from her glass of white wine.

'But that brings us back to how hard he was working and that message he left this Harper guy about being in over his head. He said he'd done something he couldn't take back. Surely that suggests . . .'

She sighed, holding up her hands in a gesture of frustration.

She couldn't define what that suggests, which was the very nub of this.

Parlabane spoke calmly.

'We don't know what it suggests. Yes, Peter was apparently under pressure: whether from his work or his marriage or a combination of both, we simply don't know. It doesn't mean anybody was to blame. It doesn't mean that the accident wasn't what it looks like.'

He chose his words delicately, not overtly including the possibility of suicide, but not excluding it either.

Lucy's face looked strained: like part of her felt obliged to keep fighting but the other half didn't believe in the cause any more.

'But what about her telling me he almost lost control of the car at the same place? Doesn't that sound suspicious?'

He reached out his hand and placed it gently around her forearm.

Lucy looked back at him, fragile and yet somehow grateful, craving his reassurance that it was going to be okay. A hint of a tear glistened in one eye.

'If you look long enough into any sudden death, any accident, you'll start seeing strange coincidences, and there's a temptation to start joining dots. It's like seeing faces in the clouds. Unless, that is, there's something you're not telling me.'

She gazed away for a moment then shook her head sadly. She seemed shrunken again, crestfallen. He had to show her that she was seeing it wrong.

'We both know I could start looking deeper: start pulling at the frayed edges of what I've found, but I'd only end up ascribing imaginary significance to incidents or remarks. I know you came to me because I've got this reputation for finding hidden conspiracies, but I've learned the hard way about looking too hard for things that aren't there. Sometimes you've got to take comfort in the anthropic principle.'

'Which is what?'

'It is what it is.'

She gave him a half smile. She understood. The tear spilled and she wiped it. She moved her arm and he thought she was pulling it from his grasp, but instead she took his hand in hers, gripping it tightly.

'Lucy, when you came to see me the other day, you said your preferred outcome was that I would come back and tell you there's nothing to this. Well, that's what I'm offering you here.'

She gripped tighter, squeezing, her fingers stroking the back of his hand. Then just as he thought she was going to let go, once again they held each other's gaze a moment too long.

She leaned forward and kissed him.

The parallel realities crossed over.

Two seconds ago, he'd never have seen this happening, but a moment can change everything. Even as she began to lean towards him, he knew what he wanted to happen, and miraculously it did.

He felt himself fade from the room, fade from the physical. The sounds of conversation, music, clinking glasses and laughter all muted. He hadn't kissed another woman like that in fifteen years. She smelled like cinnamon and lemon grass: natural and warm.

And then when she pulled back, the spell was broken.

What was he thinking? This was all wrong, in so many ways. She was grieving and vulnerable. There was also a professional relationship in play here. She wasn't in any formal way his client, but nonetheless, there were huge implications for his judgement.

She must have clocked the look of regret on his face and misread it. She sat back further from him along the bench, looking flustered.

'I'm so sorry. I don't know what happened. That was inappropriate.'

'Don't worry about it,' he said, but evidently she would not be reassured.

'No, you've done so much for me, and . . . Well, maybe that's just it. I'm a wreck at the moment and at times like that I can get overcome by somebody being nice to me.'

She gathered up her coat and got to her feet. She glanced at his pint glass, still more than half full.

'I'll leave you to your drink. Thanks for all you've done, but I'd better go.'

*   *   *

240

He could have stopped her, he realised, as he walked home from the pub in the rain roughly a pint and a half later. He could have persuaded her to stay, told her she wasn't the only one feeling overcome. Told her how much he had wanted her to kiss him.

Why didn't he?

Because he was terrified, was the answer.

He hadn't been in a relationship of any kind since it all fell apart between him and Sarah. The nearest he had come was with Mairi, his late friend's younger sister, who he had known as a teenager then not seen in two decades. They had become close when the singer of a band she managed went missing and he helped find out what had happened.

He had come up with so many crappy reasons not to pursue that, many of which were sounding familiar: she was in a vulnerable place; they had a sort of professional relationship; they were confusing stressful emotions for something else. But the main one had been that he was kidding himself it wasn't over with Sarah.

He had spoken to Mairi online but she had barely been in the country for months. It was only once she was gone that he realised how right she was for him; how daft, how cowardly he'd been not to pursue it. Maybe it wasn't too late, though. He and Mairi had left the door open before she went travelling with the band, so perhaps that had been a factor in letting Lucy walk out of the pub.

He recalled the taste of her, the smell of spices, the touch of her hand. Then he pictured her lifting her coat in flushed embarrassment. That was when he realised what he had just done. He had held back from Mairi because he was telling himself Sarah was still possible. Now he was holding back from Lucy because he was telling himself Mairi was still possible.

The rain was turning to sleet as he trudged along Maybury Lane, making it seem all the more dark and narrow. It hit his face in big wet blotches, like airborne slush. Sometimes cold water to the face was exactly what he needed.

Get real, he chided himself. As if he could possibly end up with some aristo offspring whose full name was Petronella Lucille, for God's sake. As if.

But as he came in sight of the square, he realised he was trying to make himself feel better because he was worried he'd blown it.

He was starting to have feelings for her and that scared him. How long was he going to stay damaged by what happened with Sarah? And at what point was loneliness going to scare him more?

His close came into sight and he fished in his pocket for his keys. As he pulled them out he heard a scurry of movement at his back and then suddenly all was black. A thick sack was yanked down over his head and arms from behind, while at the same time a fist drove into his gut. The blow wasn't particularly powerful, but the surprise of it was enough to double him over. He felt a drawcord tighten at the mouth of the sack, tethering his wrists to his sides as hands drove him forward along the pavement. His knees rapped against something solid and he pitched forward, off-balance, then he hit what felt like chipboard: the floor of a van. He was dragged inside then heard the doors slam closed.

He couldn't see and he could barely breathe from the blow and from sheer panic. He felt the pressure of human weight pinning him to the deck. Someone was kneeling on his back, hands gripping one of his legs, holding it in place. Other hands were tugging at the bottom of his jeans, then he felt the tiny cold sharpness of a needle in his calf.

The rear doors opened and closed again. A few moments later he heard the sound of someone climbing into the cab at the front, then of a diesel engine ticking into life. The last thing he was aware of was a swaying sensation as the van began to move.

THE OTHER WOMAN

'For a long time I really thought he was the one.'

Liz Miller began speaking as I surrendered to my hunger and bit into the hummus wrap that had been placed in front of me a short time earlier.

'And by that I don't mean I was worried I might never find someone. I mean I didn't think I was ever going to be capable of a relationship again. Well, to be honest finding someone was always going to be difficult too, but I didn't even think I was ready to go looking.'

She shifted in her seat, sitting up straighter. These remarks were clearly an overture to something. Her eyes flitted back and forth, as though checking how close the nearest other customers might be to earshot. We were seated by the window, with a view of the Tay suggesting our words would be swallowed by the wind, and yet it was a compact little place, the tables close together. If the music suddenly shut off, I felt my voice would be audible from the kitchen.

'This is a hell of a thing to tell a complete stranger too, but in my case it's a matter of public record. I went to prison ten years ago. I served four years for stabbing my partner.'

'By partner do you mean . . .?'

'My boyfriend,' she clarified, though evidently the word made her shudder. 'Common-law husband, as the law would have it, given we were living together, though to this day I don't know how it ever came to that. The signs were all there before we started sharing a home, but I was kidding myself, maybe thinking I would change him once he was under my roof.'

'He was violent? He abused you? And you stabbed him?'

She nodded, a grim but unapologetic sadness in her face.

243

'Good for you.'

The impulse of solidarity had come through before I could censor myself.

'Actually, not so good for me as it turned out. He came in from the pub one night and he had this look about him, one I recognised as flashing with all the warning signs. He could barely see straight and he was full of poison. I tried to make him go to bed but he followed me into the kitchen, intent on starting one of those conversations where I knew there were no right answers, just different routes into the inevitable. I had been there before and I knew I should have left him afterwards: that's why I was so scared. I thought I'd had my chance to get away and this was my fate for not taking it.'

'So you killed him in self-defence?'

I was trying to deduce the charge and mitigation from the sentence she had served.

'No. The fucker survived, and the blood-alcohol level recorded at the hospital ended up getting used against *me*. It was my word against his, and the prosecution said I had taken advantage of his inebriated state to attempt to kill him while he was vulnerable. A couple of pints fewer and it would have been me who ended up in Trauma, or worse, but because he was too pissed to beat me up properly, I went to prison.'

Liz's voice broke a little towards the end and she swallowed, taking a moment to recover from the effort of telling me this. Her hands were clasped together on the table. I saw that they were shaking.

'When I got out I thought I'd never allow a man to get close to me again, or allow myself to trust one. But then a couple of years ago, I met Peter. He had recently moved to the area, and we met when he joined the gym where I was a member. There was a group of us having coffee after a spin class. I mentioned I was having computer problems and he offered to fix my laptop if I brought it along next time. It started from there.

'He didn't ask me out for a while, which is just as well, as I would have backed off. He was very patient, so much that I didn't

244

think he was interested that way. We went for a bike ride together. He called me before the spin class and said the weather was too good for being stuck in the gym, so would I like to join him. We rode for miles, and got talking properly for the first time, one to one, when we stopped for water up near Monifieth.'

The shaking of her hands had ceased. Talking about Peter seemed to calm her, an effect that was less pacific to me.

'Peter is a gentle soul. You'll know that.'

I nodded, encouraging her to go on, though I wasn't sure I liked how it was developing.

'He was good for me. He was solicitous and unassuming. He listened to me. He built up my confidence. He was everything I needed in order to believe I could have a relationship again, to believe I could trust a man again. But both of those things were mere by-products of the most important thing: he made me believe in *myself* again.'

All of this was sounding unnervingly familiar. I wondered how far the comparisons would endure.

'And what did you do for him?'

I was careful not to make it sound suspicious.

'I confess I never stopped to ask. I was so happy, and it was like aviation: I didn't want to think about how it worked, in case somehow it didn't any more. I did wonder sometimes how he could be still single, but I knew he was shy, and that was before I learned about how he had been hurt before, by the women who thought he had money.'

She glanced at me to confirm I knew what she was talking about. I gave her a solemn nod.

'I mean, he wasn't the absolute perfect catch. He was a shambles in a lot of ways, particularly career-wise. He had a hatful of abandoned ambitions, but the bastard I went to jail for was a driven individual, so it would be fair to say it wasn't the trait I most prized in a man. Peter made me feel happy, and loved, and safe. Those things were far more important. And then he asked me to marry him.'

I felt my breath stop, the world stop. Was this what Sir Hamish had been alluding to?

245

She flashed a wistful smile, recollections of happiness mixed with regret. The big question was *what* she had regretted: saying yes or saying no?

'I thought about it a long time. It was one of the longest sleepless nights of my life, and believe me, the bar is pretty high when you've had my life. But in the end I turned him down. It felt too soon. I said let's wait.'

Sensible you, I thought bitterly.

'How did he take it?'

'He said how about we move in together, see how it goes. I wasn't so sure, but he was quite pushy about it; uncharacteristically so. I think he was also quite hurt, and that's probably why I caved in. That proved to be the beginning of the end, though: vindicated my decision and then some.'

I had this slight sense of relief that maybe I had found an explanation for Peter's behaviour. If he was still looking at the videos they made together, then maybe he was dealing with how marriage closed the door for ever on past might-have-beens. Marriage is about choosing one path, one possibility, and when you did it as quickly as we had, the implications could be a while catching up.

Nonetheless, this didn't address the far bigger question of why he was in Glasgow, and lying to me about it.

I leaned forward, dropping my voice. There was a mother and baby at the table nearest us, and she seemed entirely captivated by the process of spooning puree into the tot's uncooperative mouth, but as I could hear every shriek and gurgle I couldn't assume the woman wasn't paying us any heed.

'This is going to sound a little inappropriate, so forgive me. But did Peter ever take intimate photographs of you?'

She bridled less than I might have expected, but then she knew she was talking to Peter's wife, so there was a sorority of sorts that excused me.

'He asked, but I wasn't comfortable with it. My ex leaked intimate images of me while I was in prison. There was no way I was going to put myself in that position again.'

I barely heard the end of her explanation, as I was already calculating the implications.

She stared hard at me across the table. Finally I felt like the one who knew something.

'Why do you ask?'

'He asked me too.'

I said it as though that ought to suffice. I couldn't tell her the truth: not yet, because if she didn't know, I had no right to bring it to her door.

'Why did you end it?' I asked, preventing her from further pursuing the issue.

She took a moment, eyeing me with that same scrutiny as when we first started to talk.

'I discovered he was seeing someone else.'

She fixed me in her gaze, analysing my reaction. I tried to remain impassive, but I don't know whether I carried it off.

'How did you find out?'

'There were signs that I tried to explain away, but eventually I stopped kidding myself. He had always seemed so open before, but once we moved in together he seemed, I don't know, furtive, secretive about things that there seemed no reason to be secretive about. Then one day I saw travel documents – a boarding pass and a hotel reservation – that he had booked in the name of another woman. I looked up his computer. She was all over it. No emails, but he had her Facebook page bookmarked, as well as blogs she had posted.'

'Facebook? So you saw what she looked like?'

'No. She posted lots of photos, but never any of herself. Her profile picture was a cartoon character. I didn't recognise it. It could have been a caricature of her, I suppose. I'm pretty sure she lived abroad. France, I think.'

'How did you get access to his computer?'

She shrugged, like she didn't understand the question.

'I looked through his laptop when he was out.'

Clearly he had learned since then. Now he had the NDA as a cover for his secrecy, otherwise it would have been more suspicious

247

to be password-protecting his laptop from the woman he lived with.

'I felt so angry. I had this huge sense of betrayal because of everything he had made me believe about him, and about myself. He had made me trust again.'

I watched her knuckles whiten as she squeezed her fists. This was still sore, still raw. And this was why she had agreed to meet me.

'For a long time I worried Peter was too good to be true. It turned out I was right. He's cheating on you too, isn't he?'

'I found some . . . intimate images. They were taken around about the time you and Peter would have been together. I think he's still in a relationship with this woman, or at least still obsessed with her.'

Our eyes met in a moment of acknowledgment: we were allies here. Sisters.

'I used to think I was damaged,' Liz said. 'And that I would never be put back together. Peter helped me repair myself, and I'll always be grateful for that. But he also helped me realise what a truly fractured soul looked like. I came to realise that *he* was the damaged one. He's not a bad person, but he's not a whole person either.

'He gives the impression he's there for you, that he's the most kind and giving person you've ever known. Then you realise that giving is not the same as sharing. You realise you know almost nothing about him, apart from trivia, superficialities. I couldn't tell you who Peter really is, but what's always troubled me is that I'm not sure Peter could either.'

I had one last, obvious question. The fact that she hadn't already mentioned it made me fear she didn't know, but I needed to ask.

'Do you remember what this other woman was called?'

'Remember? It's burned into my memory like a scar. Her name was Courtney Jean Lang.'

RETURNED ITEM

As the van had accelerated and he felt the injection begin to take effect, Parlabane had spent a horrifying few moments imagining the places he might find himself when – and if – he woke up again. He would have to admit that his own bed did not feature on the torture-dungeon playlist.

He came round in instalments, his eyes opening the window into consciousness several times only for it to fall shut again. He had no gauge for how much time elapsed between these glimpses: it could have been seconds or it could have been hours.

As he approached a waking state, he struggled to focus on two consecutive thoughts, like all the lines of connection in his brain were temporarily disabled. Even the eventual awareness of his location took a while to register its significance. This wasn't his bedroom, he thought: this was his bedroom from years ago. His current bedroom was in Glasgow, with his wife Sarah. Why was he back in this one? Was he dreaming this? Or was it still the nineties and he had dreamed everything that happened since?

Fragments began to coalesce. Shit. He knew where he was. The location made sense. Other things did not. He was cold. He was face-down on top of the duvet, naked. Why had he gone to sleep like that? *How* could he have gone to sleep like that?

He wasn't ready to physically move yet. His body felt too heavy. Memories were starting to form, but they were blending into each other. One stood out, though, jarringly distinct: pain and fear. He had been attacked. There had been a van, a sack, a needle. Must have been an intravenous sedative.

There had been a woman, a smell of spice, a kiss. Why had she attacked him? No, he realised: the woman with the spice smell was earlier, at the pub. A different woman attacked him. A different smell: one he had smelled before. There were two of them bundling him into the van. Why did he think one of them was a woman? He wasn't sure yet. Maybe he was still confusing moments, blending time.

Neither of them had spoken, not a word. If you abduct somebody, even if you dump him back in his own bed, it's got to be to send a message. Why would they say nothing when they were sending a message? It had to be to conceal their identities, going a stage further than the sack. They were worried he would recognise their voices, or maybe in one case their gender. Yes. One of them was definitely a woman. It was the smell. Not the spice smell, another smell: a smell that had been familiar to him. He just couldn't remember from where.

He tried to open his mouth and discovered with some alarm that he couldn't. There was a tugging upon his upper lip and his chin: tape. He reached a delicate hand to his face and found the corners of a strip of duct tape. Why had they gagged him if he was going to be rendered unconscious?

His head still swimming, he slowly sat up and braced himself for the act of pulling off the tape; childhood memories of Elastoplast removal bubbling up unhelpfully. He loosed enough to get some purchase then pulled steadily but not too fast: if some skin began to tear, he still wanted to be able to apply the brakes. The action was swifter than he anticipated, suddenly accelerating at the stretch immediately covering his mouth. Less of the tape there was in direct contact with skin because there had been a small object fixed over his lips.

He looked down at what he had removed. Even with his bleary vision he recognised it as one of his own business cards. Somebody had used it to stop his mouth.

The message wasn't subtle.

But who was sending it? He couldn't think straight enough yet. Then he recalled handing a card to Sam Finnegan earlier the same day. He remembered the heavy who had been in tow, and Finnegan's quiet but determined words:

I don't discuss my businesses with anybody not directly involved.

There had been a woman involved too, though. Hadn't there?

He wished his memory would clear. This was worse than any hangover. No matter what anyone said, even with the heaviest of those, you could always remember what happened: it was just a good excuse not to.

Parlabane screwed up the tape and card into a ball and threw it to the floor, which was when he noticed that there were loads of them scattered on the carpet, next to his discarded clothes. The intruders had contemptuously emptied a whole box of the things. As he drew his hand back, an unexpected scent wafted from his fingers.

Perfume, transferred from the card. The one he had smelled last night, in the back of the van.

It struck him that in the multiverse of parallel worlds, he was surely only a few short removes away from having had one hell of a good night. Here he was, woozy on a Sunday morning, with vague memories of an evening involving booze and drugs that had left him naked in bed with evidence that a fragrant-smelling woman had ministered intimately to his lips. Tweak a couple of those things and he'd have few complaints, though his drug of choice wouldn't be Benzodiazepine.

That was when he worked out where he knew the perfume from.

He had smelled it outside a hospital, in the presence of a woman who would have no problem getting hold of sedatives or hypodermics.

He had given her a card too.

Diana Jager had more letters after her name than in it, had published umpteen papers in a dozen different journals and was an undisputed expert in her surgical speciality. However, in keeping with the tunnel vision surgeons tended to exhibit with regard to other fields, she had just demonstrated that she understood bugger-all about psychology.

251

PATIENT HISTORY

I couldn't even wait until I reached home to start googling her name. I tried to centre myself and let the journey calm my spirit. Having part of my brain occupied with the business of driving usually filters the flurry of agitated thoughts and lets the subconscious work silently on what is truly germane. On this occasion, however, my brain was in overdrive, churning through every permutation of the available data and impatiently demanding more.

I pulled into a layby after less than an hour and keyed 'Courtney Jean Lang' into my phone. There was a Facebook page, but the account was private so I couldn't see any of her details as she hadn't friended me. Simply seeing the page, even with its cartoon placeholder instead of a headshot, was an unsettling jolt: providing a tangible – if digital – corroboration that what Liz Miller said was true. I had no reason to doubt her, but mere words were never the same as confronting the undeniable and inescapable fact of this woman's existence.

I found a WordPress blog too, the most recent entry linking to a local news story about a school in Bordeaux being demolished. It might have been due to my French consisting of little more than remnants from my own schooldays, but I couldn't work out from the blog whether she had been educated there or had taught there: it just said something about 'all the years I had toiled in the place'.

She was on Twitter too, most recently a flurry of tweets during Saturday's rugby international, bemoaning the French side's performance against Wales as it unfolded. I wanted to follow her, but I would need to create a new anonymous account to do so, which would have to wait until I got home.

By the time I reached Inverness I had no recollection of the rest of that journey, which truly frightened me. I had been almost literally on autopilot, my thoughts so dominated by the mystery woman that I was taking in nothing else. I told myself that my instincts would have responded had there been the need, but I felt as though I had been asleep at the wheel.

As I lay alone in the dark that night, I was haunted by the question of where Peter was lying right then, and who with. Had she flown over from France for the weekend? Was she in Inverness the night Peter claimed to have been out at PC World when I drove by the office?

These thoughts offered nothing but pain, so I endeavoured to banish them by trying to further analyse what I knew for sure, organising the evidence in my mind and cross-referencing it, searching for connections. I came up with nothing new, but one unanswered question taunted me more than the rest. I kept hearing Sir Hamish's sneering tones towards Peter as I eavesdropped on their telephone conversation.

This doesn't change anything, you being with this woman: you being married. *It didn't work the last time and it won't work now.*

It was the last thing I remember before exhaustion forced me to sleep, and the first thought to greet me when I woke the next day. Had Peter once been married to this woman, and if so, why was he still seeing her around the time he proposed to Liz Miller? And why was his father so disparaging of the match?

In my angst and desperation I thought of a way I might find out more. Unfortunately it was as unethical as it was illegal. Even worse, these were the only two obstacles in an otherwise short and simple path, and I doubted I had the willpower to stop myself.

I could access Peter's medical records from the computer in my office. Nobody would ever question it, and in the unlikely event that they did, I could say that I was checking something on my husband's behalf; most importantly, there was no way he would ever know. Next of kin past and present might be on the system, depending on how much of his information was digitised and how recently the files had been updated. It was possible to look up patients' records and see them listed as being married to people

253

they had divorced years ago, if they hadn't been seen by a doctor in the intervening time.

It was equally possible I would find out nothing. Deep down I don't think I seriously believed Peter was married before. I think what I was really looking for was the reassurance that he hadn't been.

I had a busy list that day, and didn't get to my office until after five. I knew Peter would be already waiting for me at home: his 'flight' having been due in mid-afternoon. I had wrestled with the morality of my intended actions all day, but it was a catch-weight contest. None of the ethical objections was a match for the justifications I could stand against them. Peter had forced me to this. He had lied to me, and left me no other means of getting to the truth. I was trying to save my marriage, I even told myself. But accessing those records proved to be the action that effectively ended it.

I didn't find out whether Peter once had another wife. Instead I found out that my husband once had something even more devastating: a vasectomy.

OUT OF THE LOOP

The supermarket manager asked again if Ali and Rodriguez wouldn't like a cup of tea or coffee before they left. She was never sure whether it was better to explain that they weren't permitted to accept rather than politely declining as usual. The former at least assured people that it wasn't your choice to refuse, but it also took away a certain human element if they learned that you were restricted in terms of your normal interactions with the public.

They had been called out to take details and statements over some criminal damage outside the rear of the store, which appeared to be evidence of an attempted break-in. They had taken a look around the exterior and then been invited into the manager's office where they could chat further out of the blustery rain that was whipping around.

It was on their way back out through the store that Ali's eye was drawn to another batch of home pregnancy kits on a shelf in the toiletries section. It was irritating how her subconscious seemed to home in on these things that she had previously never noticed: in recent days she couldn't nip out for a pint of milk without catching a glimpse. It was like she was being stalked.

She knew why, though. Using one would answer the question, and she wasn't sure she wanted to know. It was Schrodinger's pregnancy right now: there were still two possible futures until she opened the box, meaning she could still cling to the possibility that it was a false alarm. And yet why didn't the confirmation that it was a false alarm strike her as an equally probable outcome? If it had, surely the peace of mind the test potentially offered would have driven her to take it by now.

She knew she couldn't run from it for ever, but she would rather run from it a wee while longer.

The rain had become torrential by the time they reached the front doors. They decided to stay inside for a few minutes to see if it would lighten. Ali's eyes strayed to the news and magazine stands nearby, which was when she was reminded of something from the last time they were on-shift together.

'That guy outside Jager's house: Jack Parlabane. How did you know he was a reporter?'

She meant to ask Rodriguez this after she told the bloke to move along, but when they got back into the car, they had been called out to an emergency. There was an alarmed report from a motorist that it appeared a woman was about to throw herself off the Kessock Bridge. They had driven there, blue lights and sirens, but when they arrived it turned out to be an inflatable doll dressed up and tied to the rails. Someone had put it up as a jokey sign to mark a friend's fortieth birthday, knowing they would be driving past it in the morning.

'I recognised the name. Think I'd seen his picture too. He was in the news around about the time I was going through the worst of my break-up. Irritating how things stick in your mind like that: you think you're cocooned in your problems but you're actually gathering little mementos.'

'He was *in* the news?'

'Yeah. Remember that business with Sir Anthony Mead, the MoD civil servant?'

'Vaguely. A scandal, something about a leak. You're saying he's a political reporter? So what was he doing up here?'

'At the time I assumed the usual: another tabloid tragedy angle. But now that you ask, I'm not so sure. He's best known for looking into criminal conspiracies.'

Ali looked out into the rain, which only seemed to be getting heavier. She reached for her radio.

'Dispatch, this is Romeo Victor Four.'

'Hello, Ali. What's up?'

'A wee favour. That call we responded to the other night, report of a suspicious vehicle on Culloden Road. Do you have an ID on the caller?'

256

There was a pause, the clacking of a keyboard.

'Here you go: the complainant is listed as Dr Diana Jager.'

Ali looked at Rodriguez to confirm he had heard.

'The guy claimed he had only been there ten minutes,' he said. 'I'm starting to think he was telling the truth. He was just sitting there when we arrived. Can't imagine he was doing anything conspicuous, to have drawn attention to himself. Jager knew he was out there and she wanted rid of him.'

'Begging the question: what does he know that we don't?'

SELF-CONTROL

I sat gaping at the screen. My reaction would have been comical had what prompted it not been so heartbreaking. I remembered Peter showing me clips of people reacting to a gross-out video from the grim depths of the internet. That's what I must have looked like: aghast, horrified, disgusted, incredulous. My head was swimming and I had to scurry on unsteady feet across the office to the plastic waste-bin because I feared I was going to throw up.

My mind echoed with all the times Peter had talked about wanting to have kids, the earnest sincerity in his voice as he described the childhood he intended to give them. It was one of the things that sold me on the idea of marriage when I was worried it might be too soon. We both wanted children, and time was running out for me.

The lying bastard had his tubes tied the whole time.

I now had to go home and face this man. I had to pretend I didn't know this most grievous of secrets, had to pretend I didn't know *any* of the things I had discovered since his printer made its fateful intervention on Friday. Then I remembered it was far worse than that: we were supposed to be going to my colleague Suzanne's place for dinner, over at Kingsburgh. I would have to inhabit this role, play my part in this fiction, all evening.

Looking back, the hardest thing about that moment, and about my lonely and dread-filled short drive home from the hospital was that there was nobody I could talk to about this. Nobody to pour my heart out to, nobody whose wise counsel or mere sympathy would help me deal with it. Isn't that why you find a partner? A husband? So that you can share your worries, your fears and your woes with someone who knows you best and soon start to feel better merely from knowing you're not alone in this?

258

Instead, walking through my front door and standing in the presence of my husband, I had never felt so lonely, so utterly isolated. I had to stand there and listen to his lies about how his London trip had gone.

He was strategically heading off my enquiries by saying it was all boring business stuff and barely worth relating, so he wouldn't have to invent anything that might trip himself up. I could have pressed him for more details, but I knew he could always hide behind the NDA.

I couldn't challenge him about Courtney Jean Lang or the fact that I knew he had actually been in Glasgow, because I'd have to say how I discovered these things. It would all have to come out, and then he'd know precisely how much – and perhaps how little – I truly knew. I didn't have a hand that would force him to show his.

I thought many times about calling off dinner, but I didn't have a pretext. Suzanne had seen me in the corridor as I made my way to my office following my list, so she knew I wasn't ill. I had no option but to suck it down.

Somehow I got through the evening, as so many women before me must have done: acting as though there was nothing wrong, bizarrely press-ganged into a silent conspiracy to conceal the damaging lies that my husband had told me.

That would never be me, I had once promised myself: the cowed and meek wife, living out a lie for fear of public shame. But as I played my part, sipping wine and conversing, smiling and laughing, I saw how easily such fictions could become everyday reality. Maybe for some women the lines gradually became blurred until they started to forget the difference between the public ideal of their marriage and the tawdry truth they lived with.

If there was one crack in the façade, it was that I drank more than I normally would. More than I ought, for sure. Perhaps it wasn't noticeable to everyone else, or perhaps they put it down to the fact that Peter was driving for a change. I don't think my behaviour was conspicuously tipsy, but tipsy I most definitely was. At dinner it helped me hide my torment beneath a mask of bonhomie, but it was later, on the road out of Kingsburgh, that it got the better of me.

An intoxicated woman is vulnerable to seduction, and on this occasion it was denial that took advantage and got its hand up my skirt. The medical records had to be wrong, I told myself. I'd seen plenty of misfilings in my time: the wrong name keyed into a data field, an overburdened secretary mixing up cases. It simply couldn't be true. But I had to hear this from Peter, spoken from the same lips that had so often told me how he looked forward to us raising a family together.

I came up with a reason for why I had seen his records. It seemed plausible enough to me at the time, though my bar wasn't high: I just needed something that would embolden me enough to bring up the subject.

'Peter, I need to ask you something important.'

'Fire away.'

'Have you had a vasectomy?'

I saw the tiniest of shudders pass through him, a flash in his eyes like when I asked him about the rail tickets.

'Why would you ask that?'

His reply was defensive, agitated. Nothing he had done or said so far sounded like a denial.

'I saw your medical records. I was thinking about you while I was looking up a patient's files and I absent-mindedly keyed your name into the search instead of his. Suddenly I'm looking at a page telling me you had a vasectomy in Edinburgh back in—'

'You looked up my medical records?

'It was an accident.'

'Was it hell an accident. You've never done anything absent-minded in your life, Diana. You're telling me you took advantage of your professional position to go snooping into my private—'

'That's hardly the major issue, Peter, is it? Regardless of how I found out, I think the more relevant matter is that you told me you wanted to have kids when you've had a medical procedure to ensure you bloody well *can't* have kids. You lied to me about one of the most important things in our lives.'

I saw his knuckles whiten as his body tensed and he gripped the steering wheel tighter. His right foot became heavier too, gunning the engine in a surrogate growl.

He said nothing for a while, his silence confirming my discovery. I didn't feel any sense of vindication about having finally cornered him on one of my now many suspicions; I only felt anger doused in cold misery.

'You're right.'

His voice was low, coming from somewhere deep and dark within him.

'I misled you. But only because I didn't think you'd have me if you knew the truth. I wanted to be with you always, and I was afraid this would be a deal-breaker. I was planning to try having it reversed, and then you wouldn't need to know it ever happened, but everything has been so hectic.'

Only a few days ago, I might have fallen for this, a willing confederate in my own deception. Now every word he spoke was suspect, and the more solicitous it sounded, the less credence it deserved. Nonetheless, little as I could trust the answers, I still had questions, one above all:

'Why the hell would you have a vasectomy in your twenties?'

Again the engine spoke his initial reply, accelerating incautiously until we were right on the tail of the car in front.

'You don't understand. Before I met you . . . Things looked different. If you knew about my father . . . If people knew about my father . . .'

We hit a straight stretch of road. I could see headlights approaching, but Peter floored the pedal and overtook the slower car in front. The oncoming vehicle had to brake, I was sure, and sounded its horn in a sustained blare of rebuke.

'Well, why don't you tell me? I'm your wife. You complain about me not trusting you, but you've never entrusted me with these things that I might be able to help you with.'

He shook his head grimly, eyes blazing. Ahead, the road curved and snaked as it hugged the course of the river. I started to get worried. I thought of my own autopilot drive the day before and

261

realised how detached Peter might be from the task in his hands.

'You don't have the first idea. My father has power and reputation, connections. There are people who can't afford to . . . That's why I can't let anyone know. They'll find ways to damage me. They'll smear me so that my word counts for nothing. I've lived with this shit for years: you've only been in my life five minutes and you think you've got the right to start pulling it apart from the inside.'

He was rambling: furious and increasingly incoherent. He turned it back to me, raging indignantly about my transgression in looking up his medical records. It sounded like deflection, a way of getting away from the subject he had strayed on to. Deflection or not, his anger was genuine, still gripping him as fiercely as his hands gripped the wheel.

I asked him to slow down, but he responded by accelerating faster. I realised that he wasn't detached: he was using the car as his instrument, his voice. Signs flashed past, warning of the S-bend we were approaching too fast.

Suddenly the car began to drift, forward momentum taking it into the opposite lane as the road curved sharply left. We came within inches of skidding off altogether, and it was only luck that there was nothing coming towards us.

He slowed right down after that, the terrifying moment of lost control having thrown off the demon that was possessing him. He looked shaken but still angry. He wasn't the only one.

When the initial fright had worn off, I was furious that this infantile abdication from self-control could easily have killed us both. I could have died due to nothing more than a temper tantrum.

It shocked me to have such a stark perspective on how precarious life was when you were at the wheel of a car. A moment of anger and resultant carelessness – emotions that consumed Peter for a second or two and would ordinarily have receded again – could easily have snuffed out my life; both our lives.

It stuck with me. A revelation like that takes a long time to fade.

THE FRAGILE AND THE DAMAGED

There comes a point when you realise that lying to yourself isn't an act of self-defence but of self-harm: not a bulwark against hurt but a barrier to your potential happiness. Parlabane reached it when he came out of the shower, heard his mobile ring and saw Lucy identified as the caller. He caught himself trying to play down how this made him feel, to rationalise the surge of hope and excitement that thrilled through him merely at the sight of her name and the knowledge that she was getting in touch.

This woman made him happy. He had to stop running away from admitting that. Merely by calling, before he even knew what it was about, she had improved his mood, inspired thoughts of pleasant possibilities. Was he so fucked up by Sarah that he couldn't let himself enjoy that?

He cradled the phone against his shoulder while he wrapped a towel around his waist, wondering what she would see in him if she walked in the door right now. He considered himself to be in good shape, but that was good shape for a guy in his forties. She had to be ten years younger than him.

'Hi.'

He tried to sound friendly but not over-eager, at the same time wondering what it said that he was concerned about how much might be inferred from his intonation of a single syllable.

'Hi. Look, I'm calling about a couple of things.'

She sounded anxious and rather businesslike. Now how much could he infer and project on to a few short words?

'Firstly, I wanted to apologise for running out on you like that last night. It was nothing you did or said, and I'm sorry if I left you worried that it was. I was just freaked out by my own behaviour and I didn't trust myself, so I thought I should leave before

I did any damage. Then I started worrying that *by* leaving I was doing damage. What can I say: I'm a mess right now.'

'I understand. But there's nothing to apologise for. I freaked myself out too.'

In a good way, he failed to say: in a way I enjoyed and would like to repeat.

What was stopping him?

Well, by her own admission, she was a mess. It wasn't right. But then, by anyone's reckoning, he was a mess too. Wouldn't it be good for them to be a mess together?

'It's all been too intense.'

'Yeah.'

As he spoke he could see her slip away from him. Part of him felt this was the right thing to do. Another part wondered when that first part would ever grow a pair again.

'You've been great, though,' she added, and he felt something in him soar. 'That's the other thing I'm calling about. What you said last night, I've come to realise you're absolutely right. I need to accept that I'm getting the preferred outcome and quit starting at shadows.

'Walking back from the pub last night, I convinced myself there was somebody following me. I kept thinking there was someone there, then I'd look back and see there was nothing. I came to realise that I don't want to live in that world, you know? I can stay in a dark place full of paranoia and suspicion or I can move forward into the light.'

Whatever had been soaring in Parlabane crashed back to earth with no survivors. He had learned unequivocally that there was substance to Lucy's suspicions, but to tell her that would be to take away the peace she had found. She was moving forward into the light, while it seemed the only way to be close to her would be to drag her back into the darkness with him.

Equally, would it be right to hide the truth from her: particularly if ignorance might potentially put her at risk? At least it wasn't her who had been physically attacked last night, but whoever had done it, she was in their sights. She was Diana's sister-in-law, and she had also been the one who brought Finnegan into contact with Peter as an investor in his project. Lucy was directly connected to both Parlabane's suspects for last night's abduction, but the outstanding question was what connected Jager and Finnegan.

He wasn't letting this go, but he'd have to tread delicately.

'That sounds wise,' he told her.

'I'm sorry for dragging you into this and wasting your time.'

'I got a kiss out of it. Seems fair.'

There was a tortuously long moment of silence, then finally she responded.

'Are you saying we could maybe meet up again, under different circumstances?'

He just about managed to keep his voice steady.

'I'd like that,' he replied.

'Me too. Although I can't promise I won't stray into old territory. I said I'm moving *towards* the light: I think it'll be a process of degrees. I mean, even lying awake last night, telling myself I was letting it go, stuff still kept bubbling up in my head.'

'Like what?'

'Well, you mentioned Diana having some tragedy in her student days, and I remembered Peter saying there was a friend she was still in touch with from her time at Oxford. I think he only meant Facebook and the like: I don't think she was at the wedding or anything.'

'What was her name?'

'That's just it: I don't remember. All these fragments of useless crap are going to keep bothering me until I can get over this.'

'I know what you mean. I've been living it for days, looking for the tiniest connections. Once your mind gets into the habit, it's hard to shut it off. I even found myself wondering what kind of perfume Diana was wearing when I met her, and I couldn't tell you why it struck me as remotely significant.'

He was glad they were talking on the phone and not face to face. It was easier to make this sound like a matter-of-fact remark, and not the question in disguise that it surely was.

'For what it's worth, she wears Jo Malone: Blackberry and Bay.

265

I know because I asked Peter what he had got her for Christmas, and he went off and read me the label. That's in case you thought I had encyclopaedic knowledge and a parfumier's expert nose.'

Parlabane wanted to tell her he liked how *she* smelled. He wanted to say he liked her nose too. However, he didn't want to come on too strong. And his thoughts were already moving on to other things, following his own nose.

A BESTED RIVAL

As soon as he was dried and dressed, Parlabane began searching for Diana's student-years pal, cross-referencing her Facebook friends with lists of contemporaries from the medical faculty at Oxford. He was allowing an overlap of four years either side to account for friends or flatmates who were on the same course but different year groups. If the person Lucy was talking about had studied something else, he'd be struggling, but he knew from Sarah that medics were phenomenally insular during their undergrad years and only became more so thereafter.

After about ninety minutes of trawling archives and databases, he had a match: Professor Emily Gayle, senior anatomy lecturer at the University of Durham. They had both graduated in the same year, so if anybody could tell him first-hand about Diana Jager's student days, it was her.

Parlabane drove south early the next day, ahead of the Edinburgh morning traffic. It was probably the soonest he could be sure he was safe to get behind the wheel, given the after-effects of the sedative he'd been slugged with. The rest of Sunday had been a bust: after the rush of adrenaline following his conversation and subsequent web search, he'd been beset again by the sleepiness he was trying to shake with a shower when Lucy called.

He had established that Professor Gayle was timetabled to lecture at ten thirty on Monday, and his plan was to buttonhole her after that. There were contact details for the department, but even if he was able to get past the bureaucracy, this was not a conversation he could risk to the vicissitudes and easy get-out excuses of a phone call. He would be a lot harder to ignore if he showed up in person.

His phone rang somewhere around Berwick, Detective Superintendent Catherine McLeod of the Glesca Polis getting

267

back to him from a couple of days ago. He wouldn't go so far as to say she owed him a favour, but he had pissed off a few of the right people, as far as she was concerned, so they were on good terms. For now.

'I'm sorry I missed you Saturday. I just got back on duty. Wasn't urgent, I hope?'

'Aye, someone said my pants were smelly on Twitter, and I was wanting the cyber-crime team to get right on it.'

'So not urgent.'

Her tone indicated she was precisely as much in the mood for levity as one might expect of a Monday morning.

'I was wondering what you could tell me about a gentleman by the name of Samuel Finnegan. Is he "known to the police", to use a favourite euphemism?'

'Yes and no. We know what he's all about, but he's not the kind of guy we'd ever be hauling in for selling tenner bags in a club toilet.'

'Yeah, I get the impression he's management rather than floor staff. I gather he fancies himself as a man of the arts.'

'Snobby Sam, he's nicknamed. Most Glasgow drug dealers have aspirations towards respectability: he's got aspirations towards something higher yet. He cornered a niche for himself selling to the luvvie market because he was able to move in their circles and speak their language. Now he has an art dealership and a controlling interest in an auction house. He's got a lot of friends among artists, but his eye for fine talent extends to forgery and counterfeiting. Why is he on your scope?'

'Maybe something, maybe nothing. He's an investor in a software company whose programming visionary was Peter Elphinstone.'

'Why do I know that name?'

'His car ended up at the bottom of the river outside Inverness the other week. His body was never recovered.'

'Well, ca' canny in dealing with him. Don't assume a sense of refinement precludes more brutal proclivities. There's a reason nobody calls him Snobby Sam to his face.'

Parlabane had trouble getting parked anywhere near the building he needed, and had completely lost his bearings in a one-way system in his increasingly frantic search for a space. He consequently found himself roughly quarter of a mile away from where he needed to be at the time Gayle's lecture was scheduled to end, and by the time he was watching her stride briskly away from the building, he was flushed, sweaty and breathless: maximising the sleazy reporter look.

'Professor Gayle,' he implored, pulling alongside her.

'Yes?'

She regarded him with bemused curiosity. She was six inches taller than him and way ahead in the gravitas stakes too. At this point he reckoned his best hope was that she took pity on him.

'My name is Jack Parlabane. I'm a journalist. I was hoping you could spare some time to talk to me about Diana Jager. I gather you were at Oxford together.'

He could see the barriers go up the second he mentioned her name. He wasn't so downhearted, however. These days a frequent problem was them going up when he mentioned his own.

'I'm not prepared to talk to reporters about—'

'No, no, please understand. I'm not here to intrude and I'm not pursuing some mawkish human-interest angle regarding what happened recently. But the story did rekindle my enthusiasm for Diana's "Sexism in Surgery" blog of a few years ago.'

She looked at him with continuing scepticism, but she was listening, at least.

'Believe me, after fifteen years married to an anaesthetist, I can assure you I get where she was coming from, one hundred per cent. So when the subject of the blog inevitably pops up again in the wake of the tragedy, I'd like to be able to set the agenda and make sure it's about the issues and not the hacking.'

He could tell she was softening. Perhaps the red-faced sweatiness had worked for him, lending an air of sincerity through his desperation. He wondered why he was so careful in the wording of his vicarious medical credentials, though. He was reluctant to misrepresent his marital status, yet had no problem misleading her as to his overall agenda.

It was the sense of shame, he realised. Not being married to Sarah any more felt like a failure, a huge debit in his credibility as a human being. He didn't want to admit to Professor Gayle that he only had an ex-wife in her profession, and yet he couldn't bring himself to lie about it either, because for some reason that seemed like it would hurt all the more.

'Would you be prepared to talk to me, maybe give me some background on Diana's early career?'

She made a face.

'You're catching me on the hop. Perhaps later in the week, I might be—'

'I've come out of the blue, I know. I wanted to call ahead but it was the weekend and I knew your department would be closed. See, the thing is, I took a chance and diverted here because I'm en route to an interview on another story later today. I'm only asking half an hour over a coffee.'

She glanced at her watch and let out a sigh. Then she nodded. 'Okay.'

She told him he had roughly forty minutes as they sat down in a noisy and bustling campus café. This was as honest as it was generous, he appreciated. She had another lecture coming up at twelve and she was giving him all the time left in between. He watched the clock carefully as he got her talking, partly to ensure he got to the goods before time ran out, but also in order to bring up the crucial subject just as things were drawing to a close. People tended to let their guard down most when they were mentally packing up to leave. They felt less defensive when they knew they were about to get rid of you.

He teased her out from guarded generalities into a warmer expansiveness on the subject of Diana's character and personality during her student days.

'There aren't a lot of war stories to tell. Not much in the way of student high jinks or adolescent excess. We were both monastically studious to the point of being pathologically boring. It's why we got on, to be honest. We were outside all the cliques, both of us terribly serious about our studies: driven, ambitious and occupying

270

a dizzyingly exclusive percentile of the no-fun scale. Looking back I alternate between feeling sorry for my younger self and feeling embarrassed for her. It's why I look out for students now who are showing signs of the same, and I tell them that university is about learning to live a well-rounded life as well as getting your degree. Doctors aren't going to be much good at relating to patients if they don't know what a normal life looks like. Diana still bemoans her tendency to become consumed by the job. That's why I was so happy about her getting married.'

'These were themes the blog touched on,' Parlabane observed. 'Work-life balance. Were the two of you similar in personality back then?'

'In a lot of ways. The main difference was that Diana has always been more driven. Smarter too, to be absolutely honest. And fiercely, fiercely competitive. She always had a robust sense of her own worth, which is why she kicked back hard later on whenever she got the sense she was being slighted: whether for her gender or anything else. Let me stress, I don't merely mean competitive with regard to her studies – though she was always in the running for prizes – I mean everything. She's a bit calmer now, but in those days Diana turned into a different person when pride was at stake: she seldom came second at anything, which was just as well, because she was a nightmare afterwards when she did.'

'What kind of thing are we talking about? Sport?'

She smiled, amused by the memory.

'Honestly, if it was a pub quiz, that would be enough to put her in the zone. But she was into sports, yes. Quite outdoorsy. She did orienteering and rowing. And, well, canoeing.'

Gayle made a strange face as she said this last. Odd phrasing too, Parlabane noted. There was something there.

He saw that he had about ten minutes and began winding it down, thanking her for her time and calling for the bill. Then he made his play, speaking like it was an afterthought.

'Oh, one last thing. Can you think of anything that would maybe show how resilient Diana was in her student days? Did she have to fight any battles back then, overcome any barriers?'

271

'God, did she ever.'

Gayle's expression was a mixture of pride and indignation.

'I suppose we both did, really, but the impact was much greater on Diana because she was directly involved. Our flatmate was killed in a canoeing accident in our third year: third term, not long before the exams.'

'Jesus. What was her name? Or was it a he?'

'Her name was Agnes: pronounced Ann-yes. She was Belgian. Agnes Delacroix. The three of us shared a flat when Diana and I both moved out of halls at the end of second year. Diana knew her through the canoeing club. She was studying medicine too, but it was a big year group, so I didn't know her before that, apart from seeing her name, usually up at the top of results lists. She was very clever. She'd have done great things, I'm sure.'

Gayle looked sorrowful at the memory, but Parlabane surmised that her regret seemed more nuanced. Something about this was complicated.

'What happened to her?'

'She and Diana were away at a river event one weekend, up in Yorkshire. Some white-water thing. They were sharing a canoe: I don't recall what you call the discipline. Anyway, there was an accident. The canoe flipped over and Diana managed to get out like they practise and swim to shore, but it turned out Agnes had hit her head on a rock.'

'Jesus. What a thing to deal with. Were you all close?'

Gayle swallowed, a strained look on her face.

'The difficult thing is, Agnes wasn't a very nice person. She was extremely clever, but these days she'd probably be diagnosed as being on the Asperger's spectrum. I'd have said she was Diana's principal rival for academic prizes, but rivalry has to be a two-way thing. Agnes wasn't competitive, in the same way robots aren't competitive: you need to have emotions first. She was like a machine.'

'Not an easy flatmate?'

'A nightmare. I won't dredge up what would only sound like petty incidents, and even more churlish given what happened, but believe me, she had the morality of an insect: function and survival, nothing else. Diana and I wanted to leave after a few weeks, but we were stuck with this lease we couldn't get out of.'

She sighed.

'I felt so guilty. When someone you don't like, someone you wanted rid of suddenly dies, it's a dreadful and confusing thing to cope with. Worse for Diana, of course. Not only was she there when it happened, but people started making nasty jokes because they knew there had been tensions between her and Agnes. Don't get on the wrong side of her, they'd say, or she'll take you canoeing and you'll never come back.'

'And how did she respond to that?'

'Damn well, if you ask me. She never let the bastards see it was getting to her. I'm sure she was in turmoil underneath, but from the surface you'd never know she was giving it a second thought. The accident itself bothered her, though. Diana has always been fastidious about safety and planning.'

'So what went wrong?'

'It was simply a freak accident. All the safety protocols were followed, the inquest said. Agnes had a helmet on, but when the canoe got tossed in a section of rapids, it was her face that got smashed into the rock. She fell out, lost consciousness and drowned. It was just Sod's Law that it happened on a stretch of the river where there was nobody else around to intervene.'

Quite, Parlabane thought.

Or to witness.

SHARPEST EDGE, FINEST LINE

It might have had something to do with the fiscal holding up a lethal-looking blade for the jury to examine, but Parlabane felt an acute sense of vulnerability on behalf of the witness for the prosecution who was currently sitting cross-legged on the stand. She seemed so small from his perspective in the gallery, certainly smaller than when their paths first crossed up in Inverness; though on that occasion her professional stature and the advantage of being on her home beat meant she had loomed larger as she sent him on his way.

Perhaps it was what she represented that heightened his anxiety: they both wanted to see a guilty verdict, they both had played their crucial parts in bringing the accused to trial, and they both knew to take nothing for granted, ever wary of who they were up against.

The showy bastard waving that blade about wasn't helping. The fiscal had important points to make, but all Parlabane could see was the juxtaposition of a deadly weapon and this woman seated only feet away, one hand resting protectively on her little round belly. She had to be four or five months pregnant, he estimated, meaning she must have conceived around the time that this all went down.

Right then she was regarding the fiscal with studied calm as he asked about the object in his hand, which he had identified to the court as a Liston knife.

'Would it be fair to say that a blade such as this would be ideal for the swift and efficient dismemberment of human limbs?'

'In the event that you had a body you needed to render more easily portable, if you happened to have one of these sitting around the house, I imagine it would get the job done.'

Parlabane could tell he was not the only one who felt slightly

274

woozy at the mere thought of this. Indeed, the court had been learning all about the history of this type of blade. More pertinently, the court had also been learning how Diana Jager received just such a knife in a presentation case as a gift from her father, to mark her passing the post-graduate exams that conferred her Fellowship of the Royal College of Surgeons. It had taken pride of place on her mantelpiece for many years, before being more recently pressed towards defeating the ends of justice.

That this hadn't been achieved was largely down to the determination of the pregnant woman on the witness stand. Thus it wasn't merely the fragile life growing in that womb that gave Parlabane a sense of the precarious, but the thought of how one misstep by the mother-to-be might have prevented the truth from coming out.

WANNABES

Ali spotted Tom Chambers walking towards her as she and Rodriguez made their way in from the car park. It looked like he was coming from the interview rooms. He had a plastic cup in his hand and didn't appear to be in any particular hurry. He lifted his head to acknowledge her as they passed, which was when she decided to seize her moment. Tom was an affable sort and more likely to give her a fair hearing. Ideally she'd have given herself time to mentally marshal her resources, but sometimes opportunity trumped preparation.

'Tom, have you got a moment? There's something I think we ought to be taking a closer look at. It's Peter Elphinstone. I'm not sure his accident is everything it first appeared.'

Tom looked ambushed, like this was way more than he expected to be processing on this short trip between the interview suite and the vending machines.

'Eh, that sounds intriguing. But I've got a wee chancer in Three who's about ready to give up his mates in a car-ringing op. Just letting him simmer a minute. Can you come and see me in a couple of . . .'

He glanced behind her, over her head, giving someone a beckoning nod.

'Oh, no, tell you what. Here's Bill Ellis. Bill, you're free to talk to Ali here about something, aren't you?'

'For lovely young Alison, I'm always free.'

Fuck.

Ellis sat leaning back in his chair as Ali laid out what she had. His eyes kept gazing upwards, flitting back and forth as though there was something fascinating about the ceiling. She couldn't

276

decide whether he looked like he was evaluating what she was telling him or distracting himself from a growing irritation, though the most likely interpretation was that the former was necessitating the latter.

When she was finished he let a silence hang for a few moments then leaned forward, clasping his hands with his elbows on the table. He looked at Rodriguez.

'So, do you reckon there's something to this?'

It was like she wasn't even there. Yeah, why not defer to the less experienced officer, who is only in the door a fortnight, because he's a guy.

'Absolutely.'

Ellis nodded.

'Aye, that figures,' he said wearily. 'These things are always worse when there's two of you reinforcing each other's daft notions. I mean, correct me if I've missed anything, but you're telling me what you've got is a woman with a black eye that apparently constitutes motive enough to kill her husband of only a few months, hide his body and fake his death in a car crash. Your primary evidence for this consists of the fact that she seemed insufficiently upset when you broke the news and that her house smelled a wee bit of bleach, the latter being particularly pertinent because clearly there could be no other explanation for it. Is that about the size of it? Oh, no, hang on, I'm forgetting about the first ever instance of uniform not being able to trace a witness, a state of affairs so conspicuously anomalous as to make anybody suspicious.'

'You're forgetting about the position of the driver's seat,' Rodriguez protested, though Ali knew Ellis had made up his mind and further engaging him was only going to make things worse. 'It couldn't have been Elphinstone who was driving.'

'Couldn't it? Did you ask Lynne McGhee about the elevation of the seat or just the horizontal position? Some people like to stretch their legs out low to the floor, others sit higher and bend their knees. And you've completely missed the other possibility, which is that someone else was driving while Elphinstone was in the passenger seat, in which case we've actually got another death we never knew about.'

'The witness didn't say she saw two people in the car,' Rodriguez reminded him.

'You mean the witness who appears to have vanished from the face of the earth? The witness whose testimony you were suspicious of five minutes ago? See, what we've got here are classic symptoms of frustrated CID-wannabe syndrome. You're seeing crimes that aren't there because you've already got the story mapped out in your head, and you're looking for evidence that fits it instead of a story that fits the evidence.'

'Surely the ambiguities here at least warrant further investigation?'

Ali felt there was something to be salvaged if she could justify herself in terms of procedure.

'In a fantasy realm of infinite time and resources, maybe. Here in CID we have to make decisions according to the real world. Do you know how much money this bloody car crash has already cost us? It's become the most expensive fatal accident in the history of Highland policing. And that's all it is, hen: a fat-acc.'

A PERFECT MARRIED COUPLE

Desperation's fuse burns slow. It is a gradual, drawn-out process of doors closing, options being withdrawn, possibilities disappearing, amidst a growing sense that only the negatives prevail. Then there comes a moment when you realise that your hopelessness is absolute.

My marriage was over. It ended on that car journey, when Peter confirmed what I had discovered in his medical records. I didn't consciously acknowledge it to myself right then, but something in me knew from that moment forward that there was no repairing the damage.

It wasn't merely a response to my feeling hurt at Peter's lies and betrayal, but something more fundamental: this desperate awareness of a door closing, of my hopes for becoming a mother suddenly disappearing. That was why I absolutely knew we were finished, because in that same moment I understood that I would have to move on and leave him behind.

We literally didn't speak for two days, our silence thawing only into a stiff forced civility. Eventually Peter broke the deadlock with an impassioned plea that we should rally together, delivered with a concern and sincerity that was now paradoxical in its effect upon me: the more heartfelt he sounded, the less I trusted him.

'Marriage is for life, for decades, generations. You don't bail out because of some bumps in the road this early in the trip. It's riding these things out that brings us closer and prepares us for the long-haul together.'

And where does Courtney Jean Lang fit into our travel plans, I wanted to ask him.

In the days that followed, it shocked me how easy it became to inhabit a house and to politely negotiate everyday practicalities while feeling so utterly isolated from one another. It wasn't that different from normal, really. Peter was out most of the time, working late (or at least saying he was working late), staying up into the small hours and waking after I had left in the morning.

I started saying yes to every management request for someone to cover extra sessions for colleagues who were off sick or on annual leave. I volunteered for waiting-list initiative sessions, which ran late into the evenings and all day at weekends. I was probably working more hours than at any time since my house-officer years, my regime becoming a sad parody of the work-life balance aspirations that had driven the 'Sexism in Surgery' blog.

I was hurting so much inside that I was starting to feel numb, as though there was a buffer between myself and the outside world. Under those circumstances I might not have expected to notice anyone else's pain, but conversely it seemed my radar was more sensitive, picking up on signals of emotional distress to which I would have previously been oblivious. Or perhaps I was drawn to help someone else with their suffering as a proxy means of dealing with my own.

I was on-call from home, with Calum Weatherson resident in the hospital as my first line of defence.

I had put my head around the door earlier in the day, checking how he was getting on with a solo case. He wasn't his usual chirpy self: tersely monosyllabic in his responses. I put it down to his feeling under pressure about doing an elective list unsupervised, or maybe he was resentful about having me look over his shoulder and thus effectively rendering it supervised after all. Trainees could get tetchy about these things, and they were never alike: some hated the thought they didn't fully have your trust, while others got jumpy if they thought you'd abandoned them.

The next time I spoke to him was when he called me at home around eleven, to tell me about an emergency that had come in: a case of peritonitis that required a laparotomy. He described the symptoms and the general health of the patient, and I decided I had better come down and take a look for myself rather than give him the nod to forge ahead on his own. It was as well that I did.

When I opened the patient, there was gross faecal contamination from a perforated carcinoma. It was a total mess, and Calum didn't have the experience to deal with it.

As he stitched up for me at the end, I tried again to engage him in non-clinical conversation, but he was gloomy and joyless, barely making eye contact. I put this down to him being annoyed that I had come in and taken over, compounding his resentment about what had happened earlier in the day.

When I was content that the patient was comfortable, I checked to see whether there were any other cases in the pipeline, either needing attention immediately or likely to require my return shortly after I got into bed. There was nothing: it was set fair for a quiet night. I was about to leave when I bumped into Zeinab, one of the anaesthetic registrars. We chatted briefly about how our respective evenings were going and I mentioned how I thought Calum was in the huff with me.

'It's probably not you. His wife was up for a consultant post down in Bristol. She was being interviewed yesterday. I'm guessing she never got it.'

I was approaching the hospital's main entrance a few minutes later, heading towards the car park, when suddenly I changed my mind. I had been relieved to learn that it wasn't something I had done that upset Calum, but the thought of going home for the night while he was resident until morning sparked something in me.

I knew what it was like to spend the night in an on-call room when there were worries troubling your soul and no work to distract you. Sleep never came on nights like those. Or maybe it was me who knew I wouldn't sleep and couldn't face the prospect of lying awake with my own troubled thoughts; me who didn't want to go home to find Peter still up, doing God knows what online; me who didn't want to have to pretend to be asleep when he finally came to bed stinking of beer and single malt.

I knocked on the door of the on-call room and opened it when Calum responded. He was sitting at the battered and Formica-peeling desk next to the bed, scrolling Twitter on a laptop. He looked surprised and a little concerned by my presence.

'I thought you might need to talk to somebody.'

'What? No, I'm fine. Thinking of grabbing some kip, actually.'

'Come on, Calum. You're so conspicuously in pain that even the orthopods might notice.'

That made a scratch in the ice, at least. I closed the door and walked across to the desk, leaning with my bottom against its edge so that we were facing each other, side by side. He rolled his chair back and folded his arms.

'I heard Megan was up for a consultant post down in Bristol. I take it the news wasn't good.'

He sighed.

'Probably for the best,' he said.

'It must be tough on you guys, being apart so much of the time. They say what's for you won't go past you, so maybe the right post is just waiting for her, for both of you. Or did you have your eye on Bristol too?'

He looked at me for a while before responding, like he was evaluating whether to answer at all.

'No, I didn't. But you're getting the wrong end of the stick. She got the job.'

I didn't quite follow.

'Right. So you're not sure you want to end up in Bristol?'

He gave a weary laugh.

'I'm sure Bristol's great, but that's not the problem. It's that I'm not sure we want to end up with each other.'

I tried to think of reassuring things I might say, but this wasn't a young trainee in need of a pep talk. My role here, if I genuinely wanted to help, was simply to listen. I said nothing, just nodded in a way that I hoped seemed sympathetic and an invitation for him to go on.

'We've seen so little of each other over the past two years: just weekends as long as one of us isn't on call. They say absence makes the heart grow fonder, but it's also true that distance provides perspective. We've been growing further and further apart.

'Her applying for a job at pretty much the opposite end of the country: you can't miss the subtext there. We both know it's not working. It's not even like there's animosity between us. It's something far worse: indifference. We don't love each other any more. Today just made it official, somehow.'

He touched a hand to his cheek, seeming surprised to discover tears there.

'I'm sorry,' he said with a sniff.

'Not at all, Calum.'

'I just realised my head has been on the verge of bursting for weeks, months, because I couldn't tell anybody about all this. You must have got more than you bargained for when you knocked on my door.'

'I could tell you were in a bad way. I only wish you had come to me sooner.'

I reached to where his hand sat on the desk in front of the laptop and gave it a squeeze.

'Not how us guys do it, though, is it?'

'Not generally, no.'

'Plus, you're probably the last person I'd have expected to understand.'

'Why? Because I was Bladebitch? My point was never that men should be the ones who sacrifice their happiness for their partners' careers. It was about balance.'

'I understand, but that's not what I was getting at. I meant because you've made sacrifices and bided your time and now you've got what you wanted: marriage and career on your own terms.'

Part of me wanted to laugh, and for a moment I thought I might. Instead I felt my eyes fill and a swelling in my throat.

'Oh, Calum. You've no idea. My marriage is crumbling into dust in my hands.'

As I spoke my eyes overflowed and I thought my voice would crack, but instead it remained steady. I felt a surge running through me, a relief like Calum had just described at sharing something I had been unable to tell anyone who knew me.

'I understood it was a risk not knowing a lot about someone before deciding to get married. What I didn't anticipate was that I would know less about him now than I did six months ago. He's a cypher, a shadow. It's not merely that I think our marriage is finished: it's that I don't think it was ever real in the first place.'

I wiped my cheeks with the back of my free hand. The other remained interlocked in his.

'Christ, look at the pair of us.'

'Do you need a tissue?' he asked.

'No, I need a hug.'

I leaned into him and he stood up from the chair so that our posture wasn't so awkward. I felt his arms around my shoulders, resting my head on his chest. We stayed there for a long, comforting few seconds that I was in no hurry to see end. I'd seldom felt so much in need of human contact.

Eventually, reluctantly, I pulled away before the duration became unseemly. When I lifted my head, I found his eyes looking into mine. They stayed locked like that for a moment, then he leaned forward and kissed me.

For a moment I felt like I was falling. All kinds of instincts told me this was wrong and I tensed up, pulled away.

I could see Calum was in the early stages of being appalled at himself.

'I'm so sorry. I don't know what . . .'

As he took a step back from me I felt like I was watching a ship pull away, the last ship leaving for a place I desperately needed to be.

I grabbed him by the back of his head and all but launched myself on to his lips: not passive and unready like before, but greedy, lustful and abandoned. I pressed against him, my hand holding his head to mine as my fingers tangled in his hair. I didn't want this to be an innocent snog, a tender if confused encounter between two overwrought people misinterpreting the emotion of the moment. I wanted this to go too far.

I remember unbuttoning my blouse. I remember taking his hand and pulling it down the waistband of my trousers, inside the elastic of my knickers. I remember how I bucked when he touched me. I remember all heaven broke loose.

DRIVEN BY INSTINCT

Ali could feel the heat in her cheeks as she strode briskly to the car. There was a whooshing in her ears, like all the blood was rushing to her head, muting the sounds of the outside world and exacerbating her feeling of isolation. The fear of breaking down in front of her colleague was the hardest thing to deal with right then: that would put the tin lid on it. She'd be okay, though: crying would have been more of a danger had she been alone in her humiliation and Rodriguez was offering sympathy. The fact that she and Rodriguez had shared the ordeal would make it easier. They could drive around in a pact of silence, mutually aware of what they weren't talking about and why.

But when she got behind the wheel, everything she'd been dealing with seemed to crash in upon her and she found herself in floods of tears.

'I just need a minute.'

'Don't mind me.'

'I wish I could, but you're here, aren't you? Nothing personal, but I resent letting anyone see me like this.'

'I'm going to take a flyer on the basis that this isn't how you normally react to a setback and ask if there's something more that's troubling you.'

She was about to bat him away with the standard denials and assurances, then she figured what more did she have to lose? Plus, she already had a good sense about this guy. He was different.

'I'm late.'

'Late?'

It took him a moment.

'Oh. How late?'

'About a week.'

'I see. And I take it you and your boyfriend don't have ambitions towards parenthood?'

'Would it answer your question to tell you there was a burst condom and the bastard acted like it never happened? He didn't acknowledge it. Hence he's no longer my boyfriend, but I'm afraid I'm carrying his kid.'

'Are you religious?'

It struck her as rather tangential but then she sussed where he might be going with it.

'No. Though with my face I might as well be, given the assumptions people make. They say that down in Glasgow, if you tell folk you're an atheist, they ask if that's a Catholic atheist or a Protestant atheist. I don't have a moral objection to abortion, if that's what you're getting at.'

'No. I was just wondering about family background.'

'And thereby hangs a tale. My mum is originally from Birmingham. She got pregnant after a one-night stand and her family pretty much disowned her. She decided that suited her fine and moved about as far away as she could, raised me here on her own. I know how hard it was for her, and she'd hate to think of me ending up in the same situation.'

'It doesn't sound like she'd judge you harshly for it.'

'I know, but I would feel like I'd let her down.'

'My sister was almost a full cycle late once. More than once, in fact. Same kind of thing: she had a little accident, with a married man too. She later reckoned it was actually the stress of worrying about being pregnant that was messing with her body. Apparently when you're under extreme strain, your uterus can suspend normal service.'

'So you're saying the more I worry, the later my period is likely to be?'

'Quite possibly, yeah. But the important thing is that the reason for the lateness doesn't have to be pregnancy.'

'Though acting hormonal by bursting into tears probably isn't a good sign.'

'Same rules apply. The cause is as likely to be worry as it is pregnancy.'

She let it sink in, a comforting thought flowing through her like the buzz from that first gulp of white wine.

'Thanks. That helps. Though just as an aside, if you're going to be a polisman in Scotland, you should probably avoid ever saying "same rules apply".'

'Why?'

'Never mind. I feel better now. A million times better than I would have thought possible two minutes ago, anyway.'

'It's nice to be actually of some use to a woman for a change.'

'Ooh, now that sounds like a harsh judgement. Are we talking about your previous relationship here?'

Rodriguez glanced away, an awkward wee smile on his face, like he didn't want to go there but had to be polite about it. Fair enough. Just because she had opened up to him didn't mean he had to reciprocate, or that he should feel he could trust her.

'Hey, do you know where that photo is,' she asked him. 'The one Jager gave us of her and her husband?'

'Sure. It's in the case folder back inside.'

'Can you nip in and get it?'

'Why?'

'Because fuck Bill Ellis, that's why. I'm going to take another pass at Jager, and returning the picture can be my excuse: routine follow-up visit, nothing to raise her suspicions. Or are you not going to "reinforce my daft notion"?'

Rodriguez opened the door of the patrol car.

'Speaking as a frustrated CID wannabe, I'll be right back.'

SLEEPING WITH STRANGERS

I don't think anybody would ever describe me as a sexually wanton individual. I had certainly never behaved like that with anyone else. Who knows how far it would have gone in that cramped little room, yards along the corridor from the nurses' station, if his bleep hadn't gone off.

We didn't speak as he composed himself and reached for the phone to find out who was paging him. I don't think either of us knew quite what to say. It didn't feel like something we had been doing so much as something that had overwhelmed us.

I headed for home, feeling light-headed to the point of faint. It was around two thirty as I undressed and climbed into bed alongside my already sleeping husband. I was jangling with adrenaline and other hormones, and I knew there was so little chance of sleep that I might as well be back in theatre all night.

I had never been unfaithful, in any of my relationships. I wasn't used to deceit; wasn't used to wanting someone else. I didn't know yet what I felt for Calum, but I was sure what I felt for Peter. It had come out in that on-call room: something I was able to tell another person but had been previously unable to admit to myself.

It's not merely that I think our marriage is finished: it's that I don't think it was ever real in the first place.

I thought back to the man I fell for. Where did he go? My mind kept returning to my irrational suspicions that he had always known I was the detested Bladebitch, and his interest in me had stemmed from that. I knew this still sounded crazy: who would be so hell-bent on payback over some internet postings that they would make it their whole life to punish the perpetrator? But I couldn't escape the notion that the Peter I had met and married was a fiction. In which case this meant I was lying in bed every

288

night with an impostor, and anyone prepared to engage in that level of deceit had to mean me harm.

I must have nodded off eventually, and as my bleep didn't go off, I slept so long that Peter was awake before me. He was sitting up in bed fiddling with his mobile when I came round.

He scrutinised me as I blinked into consciousness.

'So, anything exciting happen last night?' he asked, his gaze intent and curious.

It took me a bleary moment to recall the events of the previous evening, but when I hit the highlights I felt my cheeks flush and I sharpened up fast. I suddenly feared he knew something about last night; that he could somehow see through me. I knew this was ridiculous and that he was only making conversation by enquiring as to whether some dramatic case had kept me at the hospital, but the impact of my initial fright was already manifest.

I realised I would have to get better at lying. I intended to get practice. I intended to give myself reason to lie more often.

I had no lists the next day, the rota allocating me two non-clinical admin sessions, so I didn't need to go into the hospital. This was for the best, as it was the last place I wanted to speak to Calum. I did desperately want to speak to him though, and I guessed he would feel the same. We couldn't let this hang.

I knew I could be wrong, however. He might be freaked and mortified by what had happened, and in need of a few days' distance before he could possibly face me. Ordinarily I might have let this kind of worry tether me, but that evening, when Peter rang to say he'd be home late, I acted immediately.

In the recent past I'd have consumed myself with wondering what Peter was really up to; instead I didn't care. I was too occupied by plans of my own.

I got Calum's mobile number from switchboard at the hospital.

'Are you at home?'

'Not long in, yes,' he replied cautiously. 'Why?'

'I need to talk. *We* need to talk.'

'I can meet you in town whenever. I'm just out the shower, so I'll throw some clothes on. Name a pub.'

Yes, I was picturing him. And why would he offer that detail, if he didn't want me to. I think we understood each other.

'No, I'll come to you. This is delicate and I don't want to risk being seen by prying eyes.'

It sounded like a plausible reason for coming to his flat. Much like there was no subtext to him saying he was just out of the shower.

I've never had sex like I did with Calum that night. I frightened myself. It reminded me of whatever Peter had been doing to me when we had sex after his mother's funeral. I was lost, consumed by a mix of lust, abandon and ecstasy, but there was rage, hatred and violence in it too. However, unlike what I felt when Peter was doing it to me – used and alienated from whatever was going on in his head – Calum was as consumed by it as I was.

After sex like that, when the passion is spent and the clouding mists of need and desire have cleared, that's when there comes shame, embarrassment, regret. I felt none of these things. I felt this had been my right. I felt this *was* right.

We found something in each other. We *unleashed* something in each other.

We did it in my office – *in my office* – late on a Friday afternoon when there were still people working nearby. We started kissing, pressing into each other as we stood next to my desk. I could feel his erection through his trousers, pushing against my stomach. I reached inside his waistband and—

'Jesus. You can't do that here.'

'Never tell me what I can't do.'

Giggling, I made him shag me at my desk, next to the computer that had been the occasion of my first meeting Peter. We heard voices in the corridor, which spooked Calum more than a little, but I made him do it: as much as you can, I insisted. I told him I wouldn't let him do this again if he didn't do it right there, right now. We both knew I didn't mean that, but it added something. My command, his compliance.

I had to bite my arm to keep the noise down as I came. I came so intensely I wanted to scream down the building.

Does it need to be said how un-me this all was? I guess not. After what Peter had duplicitously brought out in me, I had learned to be analytical of my own behaviour.

Was I ambivalent about getting caught? Perhaps I was looking for a way to precipitate a blow-up, to bring things to a head because I couldn't prove any of Peter's deceptions. Perhaps I reckoned that if I had an affair, it would help bring our marriage crashing down. Was I just angry, just needy?

But what did it matter? Even if my reasons were wrong, I could never have believed the outcome would be so right. However I fell into this, it caused me to finally discover something that had been in my sights the whole time. And that is why I wasn't lying when I told you how that dreadful, fateful Friday was the day I first met the man who would change my life for ever.

It's just that the man concerned was not Peter.

A LETHAL INSTRUMENT

Ali stopped the car right in front of Jager's cottage this time. She glanced towards the photograph Rodriguez was holding delicately in two hands and told him to pocket it. It was cover for why they were there, but they didn't need to simply walk up and hand it over.

There was a car in the drive that she didn't recognise from before: a black two-seater Porsche 911 with nineties plates. Jager drove a silver Audi A5, which was presumably in the garage.

As they stepped through the front gates a man emerged from the house, pulling on his jacket as he made for the Porsche. He was saying polite cheerios to Jager as she stood on the doorstep but there was something flushed about him that gave Ali the instinctive feeling that he was leaving in a hurry. This was compounded when Jager strode forward to engage them, as though distracting the cops while her visitor got away.

'It's PC Kazmi, isn't it? And PC Sanchez, right?'

'Rodriguez, ma'am.'

'Sorry. What can I do for you?'

'It's just a routine follow-up, Dr Jager,' Ali told her. 'Do you mind if we come in? Or is this a bad time?'

'No, not at all.'

She led them to the living room again. All the other doors in the hall were closed, but Ali could smell roast potatoes, pastry and something dark and rich, like a wine sauce, wafting from the kitchen. She doubted Diana was cooking for one.

'Who was that?' she asked casually.

'Oh, that was Calum. He's one of the surgical trainees. He popped in to ask how I was doing. All of my colleagues have been very supportive.'

Some more than others, Ali thought. The bloke who just left had smelled of shower-gel and aftershave. He was all scrubbed up as though for an evening out, but maybe it was an evening in that she and Rodriguez had interrupted.

They sat opposite her on a sofa, Rodriguez with his notepad out. He had the photo tucked underneath it, sitting on his left knee.

'We want to bring you up to speed on our investigation,' she said, then went through a deliberately dull breakdown of procedure since the futile search-and-rescue operation. Jager nodded with stoic patience throughout, like this was some kind of mourning rite she was obliged to observe but wasn't feeling.

'Obviously we're still fumbling in the dark for an explanation. And I'm sure the uncertainty's been a source of much difficulty for yourself. If it's not too painful, can you maybe give us some insight into your husband's state of mind in the days preceding the accident?'

'Sure. He was stressed. That's the one thing there's no uncertainty about. He was under pressure from work, putting *himself* under pressure. He had his own company: it was a one-man show, but there were investors and he was always fretting about them. He was working extremely long hours. I was getting worried about him, to be honest; though in retrospect maybe not worried enough.'

'How about your own relationship with him? Was he happy at home?'

'When he *was* home, sure. When we actually saw each other and he wasn't exhausted, it was fine. His work was a major source of tension, though. That was the only thing we ever really argued about, if you could call it arguing. Neither of us was much good at confrontations.'

As Jager spoke, Rodriguez subtly drew Ali's attention to what he had written, lifting the notepad and thus bringing the photograph into view. It said: 'Spot the difference.'

Ali glanced at the fireplace then back to the picture. In the photo, there was a large knife in a glass case sitting right in the centre of the mantelpiece. She couldn't remember whether she had seen it there on their last visit, but it definitely wasn't there now.

'We've brought back your photograph,' Ali said. 'Thank you for the use of it.'

'No problem.'

Rodriguez stood up and walked a short few paces across the carpet to hand it to her.

'Out of interest, what was the knife in the display case?' Rodriguez spoke with deliberately boyish curiosity. 'Was it a surgical thing?'

'It's a Liston knife. It was named after the nineteenth-century Scottish surgeon Robert Liston, whose proficiency with it was such that he could amputate a leg in two and a half minutes, and was said to have once amputated an arm in twenty-eight seconds.'

'Sharp, then.'

'Indeed. Given that anaesthetics at the time usually consisted of a stick to bite on and a bottle of whisky if you were lucky, the speed facilitated by this implement's sharpness was quite a mercy.'

Jager lit up as she warmed to her subject, eyes twinkling with enthusiasm.

'That said, the combination of speed and sharpness wasn't always so merciful. Liston once operated on a patient who subsequently died of gangrene, and during the procedure managed to lop off two fingers from his young assistant. He died of gangrene too, these being the days before antiseptic. But to round it off, Liston also sliced through the clothing of a spectator who was observing the operation. The poor chap thought he'd been stabbed and in his mortal terror had a heart attack. He died too. It went down in surgical legend as the only operation to have a three hundred per cent mortality rate.'

Ali didn't know any surgeons, but she was troubled by how much pleasure this woman appeared to be taking in talking about death and dismemberment.

'I can see why you would keep it in a glass case Where is it now?'

Jager paused, apparently needing time to think about it.

'Peter hated it, so I stuck it away in a cupboard. I suppose I can put it back now.'

Was Ali imagining it or did she say this with a certain satisfaction? She certainly didn't sound regretful about the notion.

'Can I take a look at it?' Rodriguez asked with eager enthusiasm.

'Em, sure. I'll just go and look it out.'

Jager was gone for several minutes. It felt like a long time to retrieve an object from another room in a house this size.

When she returned she was empty-handed.

'I'm terribly sorry. It doesn't appear to be where I thought I'd put it. Another time, perhaps.'

Count on it, Ali thought.

VOICES AND ECHOES

Clever psychopaths: that was how Sarah and her anaesthetist colleagues often referred to the surgeons. Admittedly, professional tensions played a part in this jaundiced impression, an element of Sarah letting off steam after being forced to bite her tongue in theatre throughout temper tantrums and other histrionics, but Parlabane got the impression she was only ever half joking.

'They love to cut,' she told him. 'They *live* to cut. Some of them look so crestfallen when a non-surgical solution gets the nod. The reason we put up with so much shit from them is that we're worried if they couldn't do it in theatre, they'd be doing it elsewhere.'

Diana Jager had even blogged about it, directly referencing the 'clever psychopaths' slur in the posting's headline. She talked about how it was normal for people to be horrified by the prospect of slicing open another human being, and thus not everybody was capable of it. Do we learn to cut, she asked, or are we born to cut?

Either way, those of us who practise surgery are afforded a transformative perspective upon the human condition. We see human beings differently when we are so tangibly familiar with what is under the skin. We feel overwhelming responsibility when it is in our gift to cut out disease, to repair damaged tissue, to preserve life. And yet to be in the position to act upon that responsibility requires us to be given enormous power over that life, life that is literally in our hands.

Once you have operated, there is no going back to how you used to regard your fellow human. Seeing a patient opened up by one's own hands, it fills one with awe at both the complexity and the fragility of our form, and even more so at how we have transcended it. It seems astonishing that something so easily

296

damaged can have survived so long and built so much. And yet at the same time one can't escape the awareness that the greatest minds and the most remarkable individuals – be they kings, popes, poets, lovers – are nonetheless reducible to so much meat.

She seemed aware there was something abnormal about the way she looked not only at the human body, but at people generally. How abnormal, was the question. Parlabane was contemplating the possibility that this was a woman who had got rid of someone during her student years by killing her and making it look like an accident. Same as Peter Elphinstone, Agnes Delacroix had apparently died from drowning.

Delacroix had been an intolerable flatmate and an academic rival. Parlabane could see the psychopath logic in deciding to get rid of her, but was still struggling for a motive as to why Jager would kill Elphinstone. In their different ways, Lucas Tudek, Alan Harper and Craig Harkness had depicted a woman who was obsessive in her behaviour towards a husband who was not living up to her love-blind or deluded ideals. Psychopath or not, it seemed a stretch to think she would escalate from nagging him about his diet to murdering the guy.

These things more typically turned out to be crimes of passion, Parlabane reflected, which was when his thoughts instinctively flashed to the second party in his unexpectedly eventful trip home from the pub. The perfume on his business card told him Jager had been present, but he knew she had enlisted the help of an as-yet-unidentified male in pulling it off. So far, his prime candidate for this had been Sam Finnegan or someone working on his behalf, but truth was he couldn't see how Jager and Finnegan's paths crossed, far less how the pair of them fitted together.

So what if it was nothing to do with Finnegan? Whoever her accomplice was, she didn't need to tell him what motivated the stunt: she could have made up some story about press harassment. Therefore it didn't follow that he had been in on Elphinstone's death, but nonetheless there were huge levels of trust and commitment required. Regardless how she coloured it, what they had done to Parlabane on Saturday night could bring down charges of kidnapping and false imprisonment. You'd have to be pretty close before you asked someone to come on board for something like that. Very, very close indeed.

Jesus, could it be that simple?

He was driving north, having just left Durham. His original destination was a return to his flat in Edinburgh, but this latest deduction meant he might be heading to Inverness again, for an old-fashioned stake-out-and-follow job.

Diana Jager had a lover, and Parlabane intended to find out who.

On the trip down he had begun playing back the conversations he had recorded since commencing this investigation. It was partly to refresh his memory and partly an opportunity to re-evaluate everything he'd been told, in case previously insignificant details took on new meaning in the light of subsequent disclosures. So far it hadn't thrown up anything dramatic, other than a guilty feeling at his own creepiness in recording Austin and Lucas without them knowing, particularly as he had done so even as they extended their hospitality. He had relived his evening at their house and his morning on the airsoft site with Alan Harper, their voices booming through the speakers so crisp and clear he could picture all of them as though they were sitting in the car.

It made him think of the voice he most wanted to hear right then, and not recorded, but live. Lucy: talking, confiding, sharing and especially laughing. She hadn't done much of that when they were together; and neither had he of late, for that matter. He wanted to change that. *Together* they might change that.

Parlabane wished he could call her but he didn't have an excuse. He had some new information, granted, but he wasn't sure of its worth, and he didn't want to haul her back into the darkness unless he knew for sure it was where the truth lay.

That said, he continued to wonder about what had been behind Lucy's earliest suspicions, what had driven her to such dreadful unknowing that she would seek out a washed-up journalist in her desperation to find out more. The sudden loss of a brother she felt responsible for was a powerful blow, but it was a hell of a leap to so quickly suspect foul play.

When Lucy first came round to the flat, he had got the impression there was something she was holding back. There had to be a specific fear that underpinned her paranoia. He recalled how she had sounded on the phone when she told him she 'didn't want to live in that world'. She was relieved and yet still wary. There was a reason Lucy was still afraid her suspicions were true.

As though to underline Parlabane's distance from hearing the voice he truly desired, the next recording his phone skipped to was of Craig Harkness, the IT guy from Inverness Royal. It was tempting to shut it off and trade it for some music, but a grim sense of duty stayed his finger from the button.

Peter was always making excuses for her being such a torn-faced midden.

As his braying and bumptious voice filled the car, all bass tones and self-satisfaction, Parlabane was forced to picture him again, sitting across that table, belly stretching his Motley Crue T-shirt.

Don't stick your dick in a hornet's nest. Or in her case, your tit.

Harkness really was a silver-tongued devil.

She should be grateful all that happened was she had her personal details leaked. Just as well she didn't have a sex tape back then, or it would have been public domain.

Parlabane listened to himself respond by asking why guys were so desperate for porn of women they claimed to detest, and was amazed at his own professionalism in remaining so calm. Part of him wished he had chucked the bastard's drink all over him.

Something nagged at him though. He vaguely remembered it nagging him in the pub too; he couldn't quite isolate what it was. Reluctantly, he skipped back a few seconds and listened again.

Just as well she didn't have a sex tape back then, or it would have been public domain.

Hang on, he thought. Was that what he thought it was?

He played it one more time.

Just as well she didn't have a sex tape back then.

It was subtle, but he was sure Harkness's tone placed the slightest emphasis on those last two words: *back then*.

Parlabane remembered the smug grin as Harkness had said this, the cat who creamed his trousers.

Diana Jager had a sex tape *now*. And Harkness had seen it.

CARPET BURNS

They had a quiet time of it after leaving Jager's place. It was about two degrees outside, with a blustery wind whipping the steady downpour about the almost deserted streets. Consequently the evening passed slowly, the highlight being their rescue of a damp, shivery and thoroughly confused American tourist who couldn't find his hotel. Ali couldn't find it either, until it became apparent that the bloke thought he was in Fort William, where his whistle-stop tour party had been staying the previous night.

Ali spent much of the shift mulling over their visit to the perhaps not so good doctor, and was nursing a growing sense of frustration. There was nobody she could approach regarding her suspicions, even as the clues began to mount up. The only option would be to go over Bill Ellis's head, but that would backfire disastrously unless she came up with evidence that made the case look 100 per cent nailed-on. The catch-22 was that there was no way of amassing that kind of proof without enlisting greater police resources, and that would require going over Bill Ellis's head. Plus, she knew that even if her instincts were proved right, by doing that she'd be making an enemy for life.

The shift finished at ten. Ali and Rodriguez were walking in the rear entrance when she noticed the duty sergeant, Hazel Glaister. She was hovering beyond the vestibule, arms folded and a face like thunder. Ali was wondering what fun and games they'd missed while out on patrol when the sergeant sent a searing gaze her way.

'Hey. Mulder and Scully.' She jerked a thumb. 'My office. Now.'

Glaister said nothing on the short walk, Ali feeling that burning sensation restored to her cheeks, like she had left it here earlier and it had resumed its effects upon her return. She told herself she had no idea what this might be about, but she wasn't buying it.

The sergeant shut the door with a bang then rounded on the pair of them.

'I've had the Assistant Chief Constable on the phone.'

The words instantly turned Ali's insides into cement.

'He was called at home – *at home* – by Dr Diana Jager, who is not only a consultant colleague of his wife's, but who also performed his gall bladder op two years ago. Jager was phoning to ask him if she was under investigation, because she just had two officers round the house asking her questions about the state of her marriage and the psychological condition of her husband prior to his recent death.'

Ali could feel the walls in the office moving closer, like they were theatre flats. Hazel was only a couple of inches taller than Ali, but right then she looked like a giant.

'I have subsequently learned from DC Ellis that you pair have been busy convincing yourselves of some far-fetched nefarious murder plot, despite the absence of a body, a motive, or indeed any substantial evidence whatsoever, not to mention the absence of ANY REMIT TO BE DOING SO. DC Ellis has also informed me that you were directly instructed not to pursue this theory any further only a matter of hours ago, and yet the first thing you did was go round to Dr Jager's house and harass a woman who has recently and suddenly lost her husband in a road accident.'

Some defensive instinct in Ali prompted her to counter with the revelation of what they had discovered as a result of this visit, but even as she thought of it, its previously profound significance seemed to evaporate. Was she going to stop Sergeant Glaister on the warpath by telling her how a bereaved woman couldn't find a presentation case containing an antique knife? A knife she had been only too happy to tell them all about, describing its capabilities with helpful enthusiasm. If the knife had been used for the reasons Ali was imagining, surely Jager would have been less openly chatty on the subject.

What was the more likely explanation, she belatedly asked herself: that Jager simply couldn't remember where she had put it, having stored it elsewhere some time ago because her husband didn't like it; or that she had recently used it to kill her husband and consequently needed to dispose of it? She was a surgeon, after all: if it was a murder weapon, wouldn't she know how to perfectly clean the thing, then put it back in the display case and thus beyond anyone's curiosity?

As the sergeant laid out the extent of the emotional trauma the woman had already been through, only to have her suffering exacerbated by the suggestion that she might be under suspicion, Ali felt doubly awful for having let her down. Hazel had been so supportive of Ali since the moment she first showed up as an eager but anxious probationer, always taking an interest in her progress and offering a sympathetic ear when she was feeling insecure.

Thus her shame stung all the more for it being Hazel who had been put in the position of doling out the lashes, but that wasn't even the worst thing about this. That distinction went to the horrific realisation that Bill Ellis was right. She had looked only for evidence that supported her theory and willingly interpreted it in ways that fitted her take on the story.

Suddenly she could see alternative interpretations not merely of Jager misplacing the knife, but of everything that had previously pointed only to one explanation. The black eye, the position of the car seat, even Jager's muted emotional response to the news. Doctors dealt with horrendous stuff every day: as a police officer, Ali should have appreciated that. A practised impression of calm or detachment didn't mean she wasn't silently screaming with despair beneath the surface. And now Ali in her naivety and inexperience had gone and made it so much worse.

Ali could see all of her accumulated career progress and future ambitions disintegrating before her eyes. She was looking at disciplinary action, and she'd deserve it; even worse, she had dragged the sensitive, charming and all-round lovely new guy into the mire with her.

In case she needed another lesson in how things didn't always turn out to mean what they appeared on the surface, suddenly there was a knock at the door before Bill Ellis barged in without waiting for a response from the sergeant. Ali thought that it was proof no situation was ever quite so bad that it couldn't get worse.

It was actually her salvation.

'Sorry to interrupt, Sergeant, but I'm just off the phone to Detective Superintendent Catherine McLeod down in Glasgow. I think you'd better dial back on the bollocking until you hear what she said will be in tomorrow's paper.'

FILE SHARING

Parlabane pulled off the A1 at Morpeth and drove around until he found a café with Wi-Fi. He ordered a coffee and booted up his laptop in a corner booth, where he sat with his back to the wall. If he found what he was looking for, then he didn't want anybody catching a glimpse over his shoulder.

A call to Cobalt got him the name of the database management system used in Inverness Royal and at a large number of hospitals around the country. It was called Holobase, and as Harkness indicated, it had a large and busy support forum where system administrators and other IT staff could search for solutions, give feedback, trade tips and less formally shoot the shit on everything from TV shows to recipes.

Parlabane keyed the names Diana Jager and Bladebitch into the search field, already thinking ahead to the filters he would have to apply in order to narrow the results. Instead he found himself disappointed by the paucity of the response. There was only a handful of posts, all of them returned due to the inclusion of the word Diana. There were none for Jager or Bladebitch.

Parlabane noted that all of the Diana results dated from the past couple of years. He tried searching for what he anticipated to be universal terms, such as Windows and Android, reverse ordered by date. The earliest posts were from no further than five years ago. Evidently there had been a purge of forum content around about then, and he didn't think the time frame was coincidental.

According to Harkness, this had been where the feeding frenzy over Jager's blog got started, and Parlabane suspected the admins had been busy cleaning up the aftermath, protecting Holobase itself from any fallout.

He had a trawl through the more gossipy sub-forums, from

where it was clear that, like any bulletin board with a long history, it had evolved its own in-jokes and arcana among regular users, including contextually baffling terms employed to get around content filters. They could be posting about Jager in the thread that was open in front of him now and he wouldn't know that was who they were referring to.

There was a list of users currently online at the bottom of the page, one of which jumped out at him: Kickstart_My_Heart. It had never sullied Parlabane's turntable, but he recognised it as a Motley Crue song. He checked his watch. It was early afternoon on a weekday, meaning there was a strong chance that this was Harkness.

The forum had an automated registration system, so in a couple of minutes Parlabane had created an account under the name Theatre_of_Pain and validated it from a disposable email address.

He was then able to send a direct message to Kickstart_My_Heart.

> Hey Craig, got locked out my account due to a server glitch so I'm on a temp log-in. Can you hook a brother up with a link to those Dirty Diana goodies? It's for a thing. There's a pint in it for you.

Parlabane sipped his coffee and waited, hitting the refresh button every few seconds, though he wasn't sure that was necessary.

A few minutes later he got a reply.

> For a thing? Well seen there not for a wank, because she isn't worth one. Anyhoo, here ya go m8.

Parlabane followed the link pasted beneath the sub-literate message. It took him to the first post on a thread entitled 'An old friend like we've never seen her before [NSFW]'.

The post consisted of another link to a file-storage site preceded by a single line of text, stating simply: 'Bookmark this for home viewing, peeps!' Its author went by the online handle of KwikSkopa.

Parlabane right-clicked on the link and saved the target to his laptop. It was a video.

He glanced up briefly, taking in the café. It was busy, people sitting at the tables adjacent and opposite. They couldn't see his screen but he felt as self-conscious as he did shifty about doing this here. Nonetheless, the alternative was to wait until he got home, which would be a couple of hours at least, and he was damn sure he couldn't do that.

He launched the playback. Immediately he was looking at Diana Jager performing oral sex. The angle was roughly level with her head, taken a few feet away from the bed she was lying on. The recipient was lying flat, roughly perpendicular to her, the camera positioned so that his face was out of shot.

Parlabane quickly muted the sound, glancing over the screen in case a waitress might be approaching the table. He felt a disorienting mix of arousal, curiosity, anxiety and shame.

The video cut crudely to show Jager straddling the guy, rocking back and forth on her haunches. The angle was the same, taken from a position a few feet to the left of the headboard. Again it showed a clear view of her from head to groin, but kept her lover's face out of shot.

He had to turn it off. Parlabane knew nobody would ever describe him as prudish, but he couldn't watch any more. He felt party to a violation. This was not merely a stolen, hacked or revenge-leaked sex tape. There was no movement of the camera to indicate the use of a phone, no glances into the lens. Jager was being filmed without her knowledge, and the only person who could have done that was her husband.

This represented a double violation, of which the hacking and posting was the lesser second part. It was a despicable combination of intrusion and malice, but it was only made possible due to the greater crime that preceded it, which was a betrayal of the most sacred trust.

The big question was whether Jager had become aware of it, because if so, Parlabane might have his motive.

He tabbed back to the forum and checked the date KwikSkopa

started the thread. The video had been posted the day before Elphinstone's crash.

Parlabane clicked on KwikSkopa's profile. He had been a member of the forum for three years, and a search of his content showed that he had posted sporadically over that time, mostly technical stuff. There was nothing to indicate any connection to Jager, but clearly he was aware of her significance to the forum, so perhaps he had previously been a member under another alias. As far as background details Parlabane might glean, he offered slim pickings: only a few posts griping about the traffic in Birmingham, and an offer of spare tickets for an air show in Shropshire.

Predictably he was scoring lots of kudos for having delivered this scoop, but scrolling down the thread Parlabane noticed that after the initial flurry of congratulations, he was starting to receive jokey warnings about reprisals. The content of these was oddly consistent. Many respondents made allusions to KwikSkopa imminently requiring blood tests, others posting images of hypodermic needles. Several recommended he speak to a poster called BoA for safety tips.

Parlabane wasn't the only one late to this party. A few baffled posters enquired as to what they were missing, but they were evidently unfamiliar with bulletin board psychology. Asking for such information was to self-identify as a hapless newbie and thus condemn oneself to be toyed with until the trolls got bored, with no prospect of ever getting closer to the answer.

He scanned the online users list again but failed to spot the name BoA, and putting the term into a member search delivered no results either.

It was possible the name was an abbreviation. He tried listing all members alphabetically and began scrolling down through the Bs, which was when he found it: Ball_or_Aerosol. It was a reference to an old gag about buying deodorant in a Swedish chemist shop.

Ball_or_Aerosol had been a member of the forum for seven years. He was offline right now, but had last logged in an hour ago. According to his profile, he had racked up thirty thousand posts. There was no time to sift through that kind of volume, but Parlabane was confident he didn't need to. This, he was sure, was the guy who hacked the Sexism in Surgery blog, and he might not have gotten away with it quite as scot-free as most people assumed.

BEGINNING OF THE END

I got better at lying, though the sad truth was I didn't need to. I came to learn that it is easy to keep an affair secret from a spouse who is paying you so little attention. Granted, I had the excuse of being on-call (even when I wasn't) to explain my being out overnight, but at some point I stopped telling him and he never asked.

When you say 'affair', people assume it's all about sex, but it wasn't. Not even at the start. It was about companionship. It was about two people who had everything in common, two people who appreciated the preciousness of this second chance they had been unexpectedly gifted, and who would do whatever it took to nurture it. But chief among the things we understood it would take was patience.

I recall lying on Calum's couch, resting my head in his lap as I read a book. He was sitting up straight, idly stroking my hair with one hand while he scrolled a tablet that was lying on the arm of the settee. It felt like we were living together, that we had been for years.

'This is bliss,' he said, as if he'd read my mind. 'Simply this.'

'Except that I have to go home again in the morning.'

I didn't want to ruin the moment, but until the thought occurred to me, I realised I had actually forgotten. Reality crashed back down so hard that I had to vocalise it.

'You don't, though. You can leave him any time. Or you can tell him to leave. Either way, you don't need to keep living out this charade.'

I sat up.

'It's a lot different for you, Calum. Your wife is in Bristol. Your marriage has been on life support for two years and is just waiting for one of you to switch off the ventilator.'

'Whereas by your own admission, yours was never alive in the first place. You're living with a stranger to whom you owe nothing. Why don't you tell him it's over?'

'Because it's . . . delicate,' I told him. 'I need time.'

I'll admit among the things that held me back was a mixture of cowardice and shame. I didn't want to admit to anybody that my marriage had failed. I couldn't face my friends and colleagues finding out: couldn't face their solicitude and sympathy; couldn't face the idea of the secret vindication they might be feeling for the doubts they had always held. I felt foolish and embarrassed. I was the proud and haughty woman who wrote all those uncompromising things as Scalpelgirl, then went desperately and blindly chasing a dream of love and marriage only for it all to fall apart within a matter of months. I wasn't yet strong enough to cope with that, so the truth is I hid: living apart together with Peter in a state of limbo, waiting for something to give.

There was also the practical consideration that I couldn't simply tell Peter to move out. For one thing, he had nowhere immediately to go, but more importantly, he was in a fragile state of his own, and he seemed to be unravelling in front of me.

I came in close to eleven one night, after a major case ended up taking nine hours. I was exhausted, stressed and hungry, and when I opened the fridge, there was nothing to eat: not even any fresh milk for me to make myself a cup of tea.

Peter was sitting on the couch in front of the TV, playing some game on his Xbox.

'There's no milk,' I said, and admittedly I made it sound like an accusation.

'Yeah, I just had take-away and a beer.'

'But I said to you this morning I would be working all day and into the evening.'

'I was working too. I didn't get back until nine.'

'You couldn't have popped into Tesco on your way home?'

'I forgot, I was tired.'

'And you couldn't have nipped out again when you saw there was nothing in the fridge for me to eat? Instead you're sitting here playing games?'

This last seemed to trigger something. He put down the controller and stood up, the look of huffy resentment replaced by something more animated. More worrying.

'The supermarket's open twenty-four hours, Diana. You could have gone in on *your* way home. You could still go now.'

'I've been on my feet in theatre since half eight this morning. I couldn't leave. You can nip out of your office any time, like when you need something from PC World.'

He didn't miss the subtext here, but as soon as it came out, I wished I hadn't said it. He seemed to grow in front of me, his back straightening and his posture tense.

'Yeah, because my job is piss-easy, and I can pick it up and put it down any time. Is that what you think?'

'No, but—'

'I'm working all the hours God sends, and yet you're resentful of me doing something to unwind during the few hours I have to myself. Maybe you could do with unwinding, Diana. All *you* do is work. You're doing more on-call and more of these waiting-list initiative sessions all the time. All those blogs you once wrote about work-life balance, yet I hardly see you because you're working more than ever. And what's worse is that you turned me into a mirror image of yourself. You got what you wanted, Diana: someone just like you, consumed by their job, someone as *unhappy* as you.'

His voice was getting louder, his eyes wide. I was reminded of how he appeared when we had the near thing in the car: possessed by anger, detached from his surroundings.

He strode across to the TV and pressed a button on the Xbox. A disc ejected from the console and he took it in his hand, holding it up in front of me.

'Is this the problem? These games I'm spending time with, these games that give me pleasure, give me escape?'

He gripped the disc in both hands and snapped it.

'Will this make it better, Diana? If we've both got nothing but work?'

He reached down and grabbed another game, popping open the

case and snapping the disc. I saw a tiny spray of blood, a jagged edge having scored the fleshy part of his palm.

He ignored it, opening another and snapping that disc too, then tossed the case and the debris to the carpet.

I was utterly paralysed. I had seen fits of temper in my life, but I had never been so close to this much anger, already spilling out into acts of violence and destruction. An instinct said run, but I felt powerless to move, as though hypnotised by my own fear, utterly at his mercy.

He ripped a fistful of cables from the back of the console, dropped them to the floor and then stormed out, slamming the front door behind him. I heard his car start a few moments later, by which point I realised I was physically shaking.

I knew he had been drinking, though I didn't know how much. Alcohol wasn't the biggest danger, however, having seen what almost happened a few weeks ago.

I remember thinking that if he killed himself, I would be relieved.

I confided in Calum about this and he assured me that if I was ever scared, I only had to pick up the phone and he would come running. It was the zero option, because I knew it would trigger all the other things I didn't want to deal with. Yet there were also times when Peter was pathetically needy, as if he was in a state of denial about the condition of our marriage. It was like he thought we could still save this; that we would both *want* to save this.

And then, of course, there was the project itself: this occult malevolent entity that had consumed more and more of Peter since we got married and which was now threatening to devour him. Now that he no longer had me nagging him about eating together and spending time with one another, he could dedicate himself entirely to his work, and yet he seemed more stressed about it than ever. I would hear him on the phone to investors, contractors and God knows who else, talking about how the developers making the user interface were behind schedule, or there was a bottleneck with the server traffic or some other jargon-heavy problem I didn't understand. The one thing I did grasp was that all of these things

313

were costing more time and more money, and he was evidently running out of both.

On one occasion I saw the bathroom door close down the hall as I was passing Peter's den. I snuck in and observed that his laptop wasn't locked out, his email client open on the screen. I clicked on several messages, skim-reading the first few lines in the preview window then moving on to the next. It was all techy or video-game-related. But just as I heard the sound of the flush, I previewed an email from someone called Sam Finnegan, three words of which leapt out at me before I returned the cursor to the first message. Finnegan appeared to be one of Peter's investors, and he wasn't happy.

> The longer this thing takes to deliver a return, the more it is costing me. If I am laying out more up front, then I want that reflected in my share of the back end. Don't forget that what I know about Courtney Jean Lang could make things very awkward in the near future.

If I had any lingering doubts about my feelings for Peter, then that was the moment of truth. Before I began my affair with Calum, catching a stolen glimpse of that name on an email would have sent my mind and my pulse racing, condemning me to hours of obsessive speculation and yet another fitful night's sleep.

Now, I realised, I didn't care. It didn't matter who Courtney Jean Lang was or what she meant to Peter, past or present. I was moving on. All the questions that had previously consumed me would only be of relevance if I was trying to salvage this. Instead my priority was finding an exit strategy.

That was why it was difficult – though I knew it was right – to remain circumspect about our affair. I knew that if some indiscretion or mere happenstance caused it to be discovered, then it would force the issue. I think deep down I wanted something to come along and take the decision out of my hands.

Careful what you wish for.

WOUNDED

Before he left the café, Parlabane had sent Ball_or_Aerosol a direct message, figuring the guy would get it whenever he logged on to the forum.

> My name is Jack Parlabane. I am a journalist. I urgently need to talk to you about your dealings with Diana Jager. This will be off the record and in the strictest confidence. You don't need to identify yourself. We can do it by phone, Skype or whatever you find most secure/convenient.

His phone steadfastly refused to ring on the journey up from Morpeth.

He was already booting up his laptop as he got out of his car at Maybury Square, watching it connect to his Wi-Fi network as he climbed the stairs to his flat. There had been no attempt at contact via Skype or email. He logged on to the Holobase forum. There was no reply to his direct message, but he could see that BoA was online. He messaged him again, including a link to the Elphinstone car crash story.

> I have seen the video posted by KwikSkopa. It was filmed by Diana Jager's husband without her knowing. Two days after it appeared on the Holobase forum, this happened: http://tinyurl. com/d9r87vb
> I am not convinced it is quite what it appears and I think you may have an informed perspective. Please get in touch.

Parlabane got a Skype notification ten minutes later, followed by a message stating BoA would call in two hours. 'Can't talk about this at work,' he explained.

No shit.

The connection was stable and clear, which was a surprise and a relief. Parlabane's dealings with a notorious hacker known as Buzzkill had him anticipating complex shenanigans involving voice disguisers and speech synth, but instead he found himself in normal, civil conversation with a nervous and diffident-sounding young male.

'I won't be identified?' he asked.

'I only know you by your online name,' Parlabane reassured him. 'Anything else you choose to volunteer is up to you, and if you subsequently decide you want to withdraw anything, I'll respect that.'

'Okay. It's just that, I know it was all a long time ago, and I don't think anything can be proved, but I'm not proud of what happened. I've got a wife and a baby now.'

Parlabane could hear a conscience at work. This was good news.

'As I said, I don't need specifics at this stage. Tell me what happened at Alderbrook.'

'Okay. First of all, this is not who I am now, yeah? I was twenty-five. I was single and I'd been through a few girls but I wasn't any kind of ladykiller.'

'Sure.'

Parlabane tried to sound like he understood but in truth this was far from where he expected it to go.

'We went out a few times, a matter of weeks start to finish.'

'You went out with Diana Jager?'

'Yeah. She was older but she was fit. I was flattered that she'd be interested in me, so I brought my A game, man. Turned up the charm and probably made myself out to be someone I wasn't. That's why I realised it was never going to last. I ended it, and it looked really bad because it was only a couple of days after we had slept together.

'She was pretty pissed off, saying I was only after her for one thing, but that wasn't how it went. Sometimes you have libido-vision. You can't see what a person is really like or how a relationship isn't feasible until you've cleared that mist, but up until that point you've convinced yourself it's gonna be great between you, you know?'

316

'It's been a while since I was out there. But I get what you're saying.'

'It was obvious we weren't a good match. We both knew the sex had been awkward, for one thing. The spark wasn't there. But she made out that was my fault. She said like I should work harder on our relationship and everything would get better. My psycho alarms were going off, telling me to get clear pronto. The blog piece about IT guys ran shortly after I broke up with her.'

'So you're saying it was personal?'

'It's never not personal with Diana. Just like the other stuff in the blog that turned out to be more about payback than principles.'

'Were you aware of the blog, then? Did you already know she was Scalpelgirl?'

'No: to both, man. Why would I be reading a medical blog? Someone on the forum posted about it, getting in a right lather, and when I read it, I couldn't believe my eyes. She never revealed where she worked and everyone was given nicknames, but I knew exactly who Scalpelgirl was talking about right away and it took me two minutes to suss her identity: a hundred and nineteen seconds of which was me being in denial.'

'Denial about what?'

'That this was really her: being so vicious, so disrespectful. I know she was writing about IT guys generally, but I felt she was getting at me personally: making out I was stupid, immature, not good enough to get a better job. I don't mind telling you, man, I was wounded. I was pissed off. And I did something rash as a result.'

'You hacked the blog and revealed her identity. How?'

'I put a keylogger on her office PC. Sussed her password. This stuff is off the record, right?'

'I don't need the technical details.'

'Okay. Cut a long story short, she used the same password for WordPress as she used for her hospital log-in, and that opened the door for me to have some juvenile fun.'

'And what happened next?'

He sounded chastened, like he was appealing for Parlabane not to make him relive it.

'You know what happened next, man. But you have to believe me, it was never my intention for her to get dogpiled like that, or to end up losing her job.'

'I'm not talking about the part everybody knows. I mean what happened to you?'

THE NEW YOU

I received the email minutes after I got home from work. I had just switched on the coffee machine when I heard the chime from my phone, and I glanced at it to see who it was from. Unless it was highly intriguing, I wasn't going to open it until I'd sat down to a latte and put my feet up for a few blessed minutes. It had been a long day and I could feel the strain in my calves that came from too many hours bent over the operating table.

The 'From' field listed the sender as 'The Worst of the Worst', the subject line stating simply: 'Hello again.'

I tensed up immediately, recognising my own words from the blog that had disparaged and enraged hospital IT staff: *you've got to be the worst of the worst if this is the only gig you can get.*

I thought about deleting it unread, thinking 'don't engage, don't feed the troll', but some instinct told me this was worse than that. It would be unwise to ignore a potential threat. I needed to know what I was dealing with.

I tapped the message to reveal a single short paragraph and a hyperlink.

All your old friends in hospital IT are loving this image of the new you. Whoever would have guessed an uptight frigid bitch could suck cock like a pro.

I sighed, feeling more irritated than threatened. It was annoying that they had found out my email address and were having another pop at me after all these years, but as I clicked on the link I wasn't bracing myself for anything worse than yet another Photoshop sticking my head on a porn actress. There had been a time when I saw so many of these things that I was almost

319

surprised to look down and see my own breasts whenever I took a shower.

This was no Photoshop, however, and nor was it a mere still.

I dropped the phone as my fingers turned to rubber. It clattered off the edge of the table and landed on the tiled floor. The screen was cracked but it had landed face up, still showing the most intimate of footage, shot in my own home. My own bedroom.

My first terrified thought was for the implications. Whoever was behind this knew where I lived. They knew where I fucking lived. Someone had broken into my house and placed a hidden camera in my bedroom.

I forced myself to look again, and saw from the angle that the video had been shot from the table in the corner where I often sat my laptop. Another possibility took shape, no less horrifying. An intruder hadn't physically invaded my house, but he hadn't needed to. Some anonymous stranger had remote control of the camera on my computer, and by extension access to God knows what else.

Then I realised that I was wrong, and the truth was actually something worse.

It hadn't been a stranger. It had been Peter.

He asked to film me and I refused. He had done it anyway, secretly, using my own laptop, and now some hacker had accessed the footage.

There are simply not the words to describe how I felt.

Instantly I was reliving all that I endured when my blog was hacked, but amplified a hundredfold. The shock. The helplessness. The humiliation. The fallout radiation of other people's hatred. The isolation. The vulnerability. The shame.

The nakedness.

The whole world might see this; for all I knew, the whole world already had. And back then, as now, all of those emotions were soon consumed by fire: overwhelmed by the flames of a searing, blazing rage.

Even as the storm was whipping around me at Alderbrook, I was taking refuge in my vengeance. I knew who had hacked me and

I knew why. It was Evan Okonjo, an attractive but cocky young IT consultant with whom I'd recently had an ill-judged and predictably short-lived fling. I was foolishly flattered by his interest, enough not to realise that this interest wouldn't extend beyond a notch on his bedpost. I'll admit that the sour taste this left may have played a part in me subsequently committing my unflattering impressions of his peer group to print.

He was trying to make a point: proving that IT guys in general – and himself in particular – were smarter than me, as payback for what I had implied in the blog. All Evan had proven was that he knew more about computers than I did. I would demonstrate that it didn't take long for me to catch up.

In the days immediately after Scalpelgirl's identity was leaked, I scoured a few sites and gave myself a crash course in hacking, quickly deducing how Evan had got my password. Stupidly I had used the same one for multiple accounts, including my hospital log-in. It was one of those things I had always meant to rectify, but it never seems imperative until it's too late.

I scanned the computer in my office at Alderbrook with some specialised software I had downloaded. Within seconds it had located a keylogger program lurking on the hard drive, installed shortly after my IT article had gone viral, according to the file properties. It was recording every keystroke I made, which on any given day would begin with my password, and its logs were presumably retrievable from elsewhere on the local network, particularly for IT techs who had all kinds of access.

This constituted proof of how, but not of who.

I waited until lunchtime the next day, when I knew the IT guys would all be down at the canteen or even across the road at the pub. I had been in there a few times, getting shown around when Evan was turning on the charm. I had observed that despite the near-hysterical security and confidentiality measures that were imposed upon clinical staff in using our computers, the IT guys just left theirs up and running all the time. Presumably their log-ins didn't have access to medical records, or it was simply another typical NHS instance of 'do as I say, not as I do'.

I sat down at Evan's computer and checked his browser history. I found my own blog page, the log-in screen automatically filling in the username and password fields from local memory.

I screenshotted it, saving to a memory card, then took a photo on my phone, showing unmistakably that it was his desk and monitor.

None of this would be sufficient proof to raise proceedings with hospital management. He could say I logged on to the site from his computer myself, and there was no way of proving he had installed the keylogger (nor even that I hadn't put it there myself to frame him). However, this was never about proof that would satisfy a third party. This was between two parties only.

I couldn't prove to anyone else what he had done to me. Same as he wouldn't be able to prove to anyone else what I was about to do to him.

PAYBACK

'She called me up,' he told Parlabane. 'It was soon after it had all kicked off about the blog and those people at the hospital had been identified. She sounded calm, professional; very "let's not mention the elephant in the room" of us having slept together, while at the same time actually playing on it. She said she wanted to be sure she couldn't get hacked again, so she needed someone she could trust to come around to her office and check out her computer security.

'Seriously, man, I had no idea. I was actually feeling a bit guilty that she seemed so clueless, that she should be coming to me of all people to sort it out. My main concern was how I'd keep a poker face if she started unloading about what had happened to her.'

He was earnest to the point of insistent. The guy sounded to Parlabane like someone who was still spooked by this experience, nearly five years down the line.

'I go in there and she shuts the door, saying something about making sure nobody could see in, as she was paranoid about her new password. The screen was blank, in sleep mode. I gave the mouse a nudge to wake it up and suddenly I'm looking at the log-in screen for her blog, with the password field all asterisks. I couldn't believe how clueless she was: I honestly thought she was gonna ask me to show her how to set up a new password.

'She said it wasn't responding when she clicked the log-in button, so I had a go and nothing happened. Then I noticed the desktop background was exactly the same as my own. That's why it wasn't responding: I was clicking on a photo. She had filled her entire display with a screengrab from my computer.'

'Awkward,' Parlabane suggested.

'She had a photo on her phone too. She said, "I know you did this." I was shitting myself, but thinking fast. I knew she couldn't prove nothing with this, and I told her that.'

'How did she respond?'

'She said I was right. She said she couldn't prove I had hacked her blog, but that we both knew it was true. I'm thinking, she must be recording this or something, trying to get me admitting it on tape, so I said nothing. Next thing I know, she fucking stabs me.'

'With a hypodermic?'

'Yeah. That was the first time I noticed she had surgical gloves on. She moved like lightning: fucking found a vein too. Half a second later the syringe is gone again, palmed out of sight.

'I said: "What the fuck you doing? You fucking stabbed me." That's when she tells me: "We both know that's true, but you can't prove anything."'

'Touché.'

'No, mate, that wasn't the half of it. She tells me she got the hypo from a sharps bucket down at A&E: that's why she wasn't handling it without gloves. You should see A&E at Alderbrook: it's wall-to-wall junkies half the time. She advised I get tested for hepatitis and HIV as soon as possible, then showed me the door, like I was her patient. I swear she never even raised her voice the whole time.'

'I take it the tests were okay.'

'Yeah, man, but it was a long couple of weeks before I got the results back, truth. Worst two weeks of my life. I know it's likely she only said all that about A&E to mess with me, and the needle was actually fresh, but the scary thing is I'll never know.

'I accept I pulled a shitty move, but her response was off the scale, seriously. And when I found out she was getting bagged from her job over the blog, I was kacking it in case she decided I was due some afters for that too. This is someone you do not want to fuck with. This is a woman who will make it her purpose in life to settle the score. They say payback's a bitch? Then believe me: you don't want payback from the Bladebitch.'

THE FINAL BETRAYAL

I couldn't face the prospect of sitting there alone, watching the minutes crawl agonisingly into hours without knowing how late Peter would stay at the office that night, so I sent him a text and an email. They both stated simply: 'Get home now.'

When he came in, he found me sitting in the kitchen, my laptop open on the table in front of me. The screen was blank from having gone into sleep mode, and I was reluctant to wake it until I absolutely had to. I had the video saved to the desktop, and even the automatically created thumbnail icon showed an image that made me ill. There wasn't a single frame of it that I would want another human being to see, but I intended to show it to Peter simply because I was so shaken that I didn't think I could bring myself to speak.

As he walked through the door, I doubted whether I could even go through with that, but I didn't need to. He could see it in my face. He glanced at me, then at the laptop, and his expression of confused concern, stemming from my insistent text message, turned immediately into one of alarm.

'Oh my God.'

He was breathing heavily all of a sudden. He put a hand on the doorframe, like he needed to steady himself or perhaps was even thinking about closing it and running away.

'Diana, it's complicated. You have to let me explain.'

I'm all ears, I wanted to say, but I couldn't get the words out. I still couldn't bring myself to speak to him yet. I simply stared at him, feeling the anger kindle inside me. Anger would animate me again, beyond this mute paralysis of shock and injury.

'I've been under so much pressure and my judgement has . . . I've been desperate. I know what I did was unforgivable, but I thought I could get it dealt with and retrieve the situation before you found out.'

As soon as I heard his floundering babble, my voice was restored in response not merely to what he was saying now, but all of the lies and excuses I had fielded since we got married.

'What do you mean you're under pressure? What has judgement got to do with anything? How could you possibly deal with this before I found out? You can't put this kind of genie back in the bottle. I got sent a fucking email by a complete stranger. It's out there, Peter. It's out there for *ever*.'

'What's out there?'

He looked dazed.

'What the hell do you think? The sex tape. The sex tape you made, of us, in our bedroom, without me knowing a damn thing about it. You filmed me going down on you, *fucking* you. You filmed it secretly using my own laptop, and now somebody has hacked in and copied the file.'

'No. No. Somebody must have planted a Trojan and got remote access to your computer. They can do that. It's how Russian gangsters steal people's credit card details.'

'Oh, fuck you, Peter. How stupid do you think I am? You asked me if you could film me, and I said no. Then you did it anyway. And I'm not the first, either. I've seen the files on your own laptop: you and this woman you're still obsessed with. Who is she, Peter?'

'Files? I'll admit there might be some old porn on there, but . . .'

'It's you in the videos, you lying shit. You cropped your head out, like you did when you filmed us, but I know what you look like naked. The only difference was that you cropped *her* head out too. You granted her an anonymity you didn't extend to your wife. Why was that, Peter? Was it my punishment for saying no? What's so special about Courtney Jean Lang?'

I saw his eyes widen the way I had come to recognise. It was as good as a sign that lit up saying 'Busted'.

'It's not what you think.'

'I don't know what to think. Tell me what to think, Peter. Give me a fucking clue as to why you were in your office watching videos of yourself screwing another woman while you thought your wife was out at work.'

He held up a palm, which I observed was trembling. By contrast I was feeling steadier by the second, but only because my growing fury was emboldening me.

'Okay. She's an ex. And definitely an ex. We had a thing for a while, but it was before I met you. Way before I met you.'

'Was it before you proposed to Liz Miller? Because according to the dates, that sex tape was made while you were supposedly head over heels in love with *her*.'

I watched him swallow. It was all unravelling: lies within lies, yet still I had no answers. And still he tried to shore up the old lies with new ones.

'The dates? No, the calendar was never properly set on the camera I used. Courtney and I were over well before I knew Liz, I swear. How did you find out about her?'

'I've been finding out a lot of things, darling. It's what happens when you can't trust a word your husband says.'

He looked like he wanted to run. He seemed exasperated and panicky, like he didn't know where the next shock was coming from. Welcome to my world, I thought.

'Diana, you have to understand. I know it looks bad with the video and everything, but it's not what you think. Courtney is an investor in the company. She was putting the squeeze on me over something, and I admit that despite our affair – maybe because of it – I still find her intimidating. I was watching the videos of us having sex to make myself feel better, gee myself up for dealing with her.'

'You need to stop lying Peter, because you've no idea how much I know. You were going to see her that weekend, weren't you? I saw your tickets. You weren't flying to London, you were taking the train to Glasgow. I even got the cab driver to confirm he dropped you at the station, not the airport.'

His breathing was quickening. His hand gripped the doorframe all the tighter, knuckles white. His back was pressed against the other side of the arch like he feared he would fall over. He looked cornered, but I noticed his back straighten and his eyes briefly blaze.

I recognised that look, and climbed to my feet, moving slightly backwards from the table. He was barring the way out.

'No. I swear. I know I kept things from you, and I've tied myself in knots, but I was trying to . . .'

He breathed in, closed his eyes for a second, composing himself. When he breathed out he looked calmer, but the strain of staying that way was unmistakable.

'That weekend, it's true I went to Glasgow. But I made out I had a meeting in London because the real reason for my trip to Glasgow was to see a urologist about getting the vasectomy reversed. I was doing it secretly so that you wouldn't find out I'd had it done in the first place.'

'That's bullshit. That's utter bullshit. If that were true, why wouldn't you tell me that's where you had been when we were having that argument about it? Instead you said you'd been meaning to reverse it but hadn't gotten around to it. Or is the problem that you can't remember which lie you told when?'

His head drooped, gaze flitting back and forth, unable to look me in the eye. Finally it appeared he was out of lies.

'Shall we try again, from the top? Don't I deserve an explanation as to why, as well as an Oxford medical graduate, a Fellow of the Royal College of Surgeons, the author of a dozen papers and a consultant of ten years' standing, I am now also an amateur porn star? Do tell me how you were planning to, as you put it, "retrieve the situation"? What, were you going to track down everybody who has downloaded the video and ask them politely if they wouldn't mind deleting it?'

Even as I said this I realised that its sheer impossibility was too absurd for even Peter to offer up as an excuse. That was when it struck me that this was not what he meant.

'Oh my God.'

My words were a mere breath. This was, incredibly, about to get worse.

When I had first confronted him, he thought I was talking

328

about something else. He had looked shocked, really shocked, when he walked in and found me sitting there. He knew I had discovered something quite disastrous, but this was before he learned it was the sex tape.

'This isn't what you thought you could retrieve.'

I caught him glancing anxiously at the laptop, unable to prevent himself.

'What did you think I was talking about? What were you trying to sort?'

He strode forward and made to grab for the computer. I was closer, though. I snatched it up from the table and clutched it to my chest, backing away.

'It was only temporary,' he said, pleading. 'I was going to pay it back.'

'Pay what back? What have you done, Peter?'

I was barely able to speak above a whisper as my mouth was suddenly so dry.

'Give me the laptop, Diana,' he commanded.

He was chillingly calm now, like the ocean is calm before a tsunami.

Peter was standing between me and the kitchen door. I had to get away from him and I had to be alone with the laptop so that I could confirm whether this was as bad as I feared.

'Stay away from me.'

I opened the door that led down three concrete steps into the garage, grabbing the keys that were dangling beneath the handle. Glancing back to see Peter was already following, I slammed the door behind me, locking it with my right hand as I clutched the laptop with my left.

The Wi-Fi signal wasn't great out there, but it was enough. I didn't have the remote for my car with me, so I couldn't sit inside it. Instead I placed the laptop on the bonnet and launched my banking app.

It rejected my password and PIN combination. For a moment I worried I really had been hacked by Russian gangsters, but I realised it was more likely down to my fumbling fingers mistyping in my tremulous anxiety. I logged in at the second attempt, impatiently navigating past an annoying service announcement to reach the accounts summary.

When I saw the numbers, it was as though I began to drift out of myself. Even remembering it now, my recall is of watching the scene from above, like the emotions were so overwhelming that some defensive system had kicked in and detached me from feeling their full impact.

Forty thousand pounds had been transferred from my accounts into MTE. He had moved the money into his company in four instalments over the past week. To do that he didn't merely need my password and my PIN: in order to set up and approve a new payee he would have needed access to my bank cards and my card reader too. He must have done it while I slept.

This man I had loved and trusted above anyone else on this earth, this man with whom I shared a bed: this man had filmed me having sex on that bed, and had then robbed me while I slept in it.

THE FATAL BLOW

It seems bizarre, but one of the first rational thoughts that came into my head was that I had been remiss in letting so much money accumulate in those accounts. That was where my salary went, and I had been meaning to deal with the surplus, but had never gotten around to it. It's what happens when you're well paid for an all-consuming job. You end up with no life outside of work and no time to spend the money you're making. I only had to look at my surroundings for an illustration of how dominant my work had been. When I bought this place, I had all kinds of plans for renovating the garage, turning it into an extension maybe. Four years on I hadn't even gotten around to throwing out the ancient tools rusting on the wall-rack alongside the car.

After the financial crash, I had been wary of letting too much build up in one place, having heard that it was only guaranteed up to a maximum of fifty K. So in those first few moments of shock, part of me was giving myself a hard time for my negligence in letting the pot fill up. But then the garage door opened and this weird reflex of self-recrimination was blown away in the icy blast of air that whipped in from outside.

Though it could only have been a couple of minutes, it was as if I had been cocooned in there, alone with my laptop and its revelations, deluded as to its sanctity. I forgot Peter could come around the front, or maybe I simply hoped he would be too ashamed to disturb me.

I heard the scrape of wood catching on the uneven concrete, an undulation caused by a creeping tree root, and saw Peter step through the gap. The night was black behind him, freezing and blustery.

He had followed me in here, but he was the one who looked

cornered. He seemed wracked, in a state of torment like he was suffering a slow electrocution.

'You have to let me explain. I know I was stupid and I should never have gone behind your back like this.'

'You didn't go behind my back, Peter. You fucking stole my money.'

His eyes were bulging, his expression simultaneously haunted and insistent.

'I'll put it back. I mean, I can't put it back now, but I'll pay you back, everything and so much more. I'm getting squeezed by my investors. The project is behind schedule and over-budget, and they'll only front more money if they can get a bigger slice of the back end. I'm so close to delivering something amazing, and the more of the company I can keep in my own hands at this stage, the more money we'll have when the product starts to roll out.'

'The more money *we'll* have? There is no "we", Peter. If there was, *we* would have talked about this. *We* would have agreed on how to deal with it. Instead there is me, a victim, and you, a criminal. I should go to the police, and you should start praying that it's only the theft I tell them about, because you could end up on the sex offenders register for what you did.'

I was thinking out loud with this, and on reflection I should have kept my thoughts silent and let my actions speak later, but I wanted to see him reel, like I had been reeling from blow after blow since I got home and heard that fateful email ping.

The slow electrocution seemed to jack up a few hundred volts.

'NO!'

Peter balled his fists as he yelled, his spine straightening out of its previously craven posture.

'I was desperate because I've come this far and I can't afford the whole project to fail. Don't you fucking understand? I only did this for you. I only did any of it for you. Perfect fucking you who never screws anything up, perfect fucking you for whom nothing's ever good enough. I wanted to be good enough, Diana. I needed to pull this off so that you'd respect me, so that I'd be the husband *you* wanted.'

His eyes were blazing: they were fixed upon me and yet it felt like he was looking at something else. It reminded me of how he had been when we argued in the car: consumed by his emotions and increasingly detached from awareness of his circumstances, of his actions.

We weren't in the car now, and I was in no state to mollify him. I wasn't letting him have his tantrum. I wasn't letting him justify himself. I yelled back, right in his face.

'I wanted a husband I could trust. I didn't want a pervert. I didn't want a thief.'

That was when he hit me.

PART THREE

FEARS AND CONFESSIONS

Parlabane hung up the call and placed the mobile down next to his laptop, a long sigh breezing between his lips. The final version of the copy had been cleared, and they weren't merely running the story: they were leading with it.

He felt drained, the tension and frantic effort of the past couple of days finally spent.

He already had Professor Emily Gayle on tape, and a few calls to local papers in Oxford and Yorkshire provided him with details of what was documented regarding the death of Agnes Delacroix.

He had recorded the Skype conversation with the individual he had been able to identify as Evan Okonjo. Given that he knew when the guy had worked at Alderbrook, a bit of digging had thrown up a limited number of possibilities as to his name, after which it was a lot easier to sift those thirty thousand forum posts for relevant details. As promised, he wasn't going to name him in the piece, but confirming who he was and where he worked meant Parlabane could stand up that part of the story.

After that it was a question of sounding out who might want it, and he wasn't short of takers.

He thought back to what a patronising cop had said to him a few months back, when he had made a nationwide arse of himself chasing a story that had turned out to be a flushing-out exercise waiting for a useful idiot to take the bait.

'You were trying to get back in the game with one swing.'

Well, it had taken a sight more than that, but he was back in the game for sure, and not with a swing, but with a splash: a front-page splash.

He had given Catherine McLeod advance notice, in case she wanted to move on the information before it went to press. She told him he had banked another favour, and it always felt good to know he was in credit with a senior poliswoman.

He ought to be elated, but as he sat staring at his laptop, at the copy that was now out of his hands and soon to be landing on newsstands up and down the country, he felt torn. There was one call he still had to make, a warning of collateral damage to the person who had called in the airstrike.

Lucy.

She had come to him seeking answers, though really, he knew, she had been seeking peace. She even thought she had found it. But then he had delved into the darkness at her request, and now he had to tell her that her fears had been right on the money all along.

He had tried to call her earlier, before he filed, but her phone was off. It wasn't like he was going to hold the story if she had an issue with it, but he would have felt better about it had she been given the heads-up before he was talking details (not to mention money) with the news editor he sold it to.

He tried again, and this time it rang more than twice without being cut off for a voicemail message.

'Jack. What's up?'

She sounded bright. He could hear a hubbub of voices and the echoing tones of a PA in the background.

'Where are you?'

'London. I just got off a plane. Heading for the Heathrow Express.'

'Look, I need to let you know: you were right about Peter. I don't believe his death was an accident. I've discovered some things. There's going to be a newspaper story.'

'A newspaper story. About Peter.'

Her voice was blank, neutral, drained of its previous emotion.

'You okay?'

'I need a seat. What did you find out?'

Parlabane told her about Agnes Delacroix and Evan Okonjo, about his abduction on Saturday night, and finally about the sex tape.

'Oh Jesus.'

He could hear her breathing, the phone pressed close to her cheek. He could imagine her feeling exposed, sitting in a public space when she most needed somewhere private to speak and probably to cry.

'Oh Jesus. Peter.'

'Look, I know this is awful, and I wish I was with you rather than doing this over the phone, but there's something I need to ask you.'

'It's okay, Jack.'

Her voice was dry and croaky.

'I mean, it's not okay, it's fucking awful, but you know what I mean. What do you need to know?'

'When you first came to my flat with this, and a couple of times since, I got the impression there was something you weren't telling me. Maybe because you didn't want to believe it or . . . I don't know. But everything is coming out now, Lucy. This is going to press tonight, so if there is something that I ought to know, you need to tell me.'

He heard only breathing again for a few seconds. Then she spoke.

'Okay. Okay. There was something. You're right. I didn't want to admit it might be relevant, but that's not the only reason. It's not something you ever want to admit about someone you love, even when he's gone.'

She paused again, this time like she was holding her breath. He could hear a tannoy announcement in the background warning about unattended luggage.

'Peter could be violent.'

'I see.'

'I don't want to overstate that. I don't mean frequently or uncontrollably, and I don't mean he was remotely dangerous, except to himself. It was an impotent rage, really. As a kid, he would sometimes strike out when he felt cornered or under too much pressure. I think subconsciously it was a form of surrender. He would only do it to someone he considered stronger, and who he knew would

339

hold back from retaliating too much, whether that be his parents or his big sister.

'I thought he would grow out of it, but he's done it in adulthood too. He hit me once a few years back when we were arguing, and it was like he forgot he was stronger than me. In his head I was still his big sister. There was an incident at work too, in one of his previous jobs. He was being serially got at and he felt trapped. He got suspended and ended up leaving soon after. My concern was that it could have been much worse. The guy he hit read the situation for what it was and didn't over-react. But I always had this fear that one day Peter would lash out at the wrong person, and it would cost him dear.'

ONE STRIKE POLICY

I grew up with two boys. Rough and tumble was a part of living with my brothers. Throughout most of my pre-teen childhood my arms and legs were seldom free of bruises. We would all lash out at times: loss of temper, loss of control, a desire to strike back, a desire to punish. It was usually a thump on the upper arm that I was on the receiving end of, sometimes a kick to the shin.

A girl at school once slapped me on the cheek. I can't remember why, but I do remember that my outrage was greater than my pain.

I had never been hit in the face with a closed fist before.

Peter punched me on the cheek, below the eye socket. There was a flash of light then a dull, solid pain, a pain that was putting down foundations and starting to build.

I fell against the car, knocked off balance in that narrow channel between my A5 and the wall. My hand shot out and grabbed the edge of the workbench before I lost my footing altogether. Some instinct took over, dictating imperatively that I must not end up on the floor.

I recall turning around, gripping the workbench with both hands as I steadied myself. I recall seeing the wall rack and its rusted tools. A pair of pliers. A hacksaw. A claw hammer. A monkey wrench.

I worked a year in A&E when I was a house officer. I remember treating a woman who had 'fallen down the stairs' late on a Saturday night. She had a broken nose, a hairline fracture to her cheekbone and a number of bruises on her forearms indicative of a defensive posture against further blows.

There was a nurse working with me that night who I will never forget, a redoubtable Irish woman by the name of Dymphna Flaherty. She asked the woman calmly if she wanted us to call the police, to which the patient responded with an insistence that it wasn't what it looked like.

The husband had brought her in, all shocked concern over this dreadful accident, and was outside in the waiting area while we treated her. His performance was authentic enough that I bought it at first, until I saw her arms. I was sure his contrition and promises that it would never happen again would be equally convincing.

Dymphna sat on the edge of the bed and spoke to her gently but firmly.

'What I've got to say doesn't really apply to you,' she told her, 'because you only tripped and fell down the stairs. And we can all have a nasty accident, can't we? Nobody knows that better than us here in Casualty, because we deal with it every day. None of us sees that nasty accident coming. None of us thinks it'll happen to us. But seeing as you're sitting there a moment, let me say this anyway: this thing that doesn't apply to you.

'If a man ever hits you, it's over. That's what my mammy told me, and it was good advice. Not that it applied to me either, if you know what I'm saying. But good advice nonetheless. No second chances. No matter how much he apologises, the truth is it's only become more likely – even inevitable – that it will happen again. Once the line has been crossed, it only becomes easier to cross it the next time. And I remember saying to my mammy that everyone deserves a chance at redemption, and that maybe unique circumstances can contrive to make a good man lose control. She asked me this: if it was a twenty-stone, six-foot biker with five mates that he was angry with, would he lose control then?

'So it's sad, because you don't want it to be over, and you think it doesn't have to be. But it is, and it does. It's like he's died or he's dumped you, or cheated on you: turned out not to be the person you thought he was. Do you hear what I'm saying?'

The woman nodded, weeping silently as she did so, but when we finished treating her, she went home with her man.

I can still see her walking through those double doors towards the street, his muscular arm supportively placed around her tiny

342

shoulders. I knew Dymphna was right. I knew that same arm would be driving his fist into her face again: it was only a matter of time.

As I watched them leave, I vowed that I would never be in similar denial about Dymphna's advice. If a man were to raise his hands to me *once*, I would ensure the bastard could never do it again.

CORNERED PREY

Appropriately for a surgeon, in the end it was blood and bone that gave away Diana Jager.

Ali had been part of the team combing every inch of her property for the proof of what had really happened to Peter Elphinstone. She had seen the tents erected in front of Jager's house and garage, flagstones hauled up to give access to the drains, but it was actually in the boot of her A5 that they found the most crucial forensic evidence.

She had been present at the arrest too: her and Rodriguez. Once Catherine McLeod had informed Sergeant Glaister about what was about to appear in the newspaper, the whole picture changed. It was made known that their insubordination hadn't been forgotten, but was at least being backgrounded for the moment.

'You got lucky this time,' Hazel warned them. 'Your instincts were vindicated, but that doesn't mean your conduct can be excused. We don't work on the basis of instinct in this job any more than we rely on luck.'

The sergeant's tone had been as stern as Ali had ever heard, underlining the importance of the lesson she wanted them to learn. Nonetheless, she interpreted it as something of a pat on the head that she and Rodriguez were asked to sit in on the interviews, watching on a monitor in an adjacent room.

Admittedly a larger consideration in this was probably the fact that they had been the primary point of contact with Jager throughout. It was they who had broken the news of Elphinstone's accident to her and seen how she reacted; or more significantly, seen how she barely reacted. As such it was hoped they would be a useful barometer for Bill Ellis and Tom Chambers to refer to as they braced their suspect.

It was always odd watching on a relay. Even though the interview was taking place right then, only a matter of yards away, they could have been watching a recording from a station in London filmed ten years ago. It was disempowering not to be able to contribute or intervene, but that didn't spare them the tension, or the feeling that Jager knew she was being watched.

She was as cool and detached in the interview suite as she had been in the comfort of her living room, and little Ellis or Chambers said appeared to penetrate her façade.

Only the mention of the sex tape had made an impact. She kept her expression impassive but Ali saw her eyes fill as the implications sank in: these men had seen it.

'Have *you* seen it?' Rodriguez asked.

Ali could hear the sympathy in his tone, though whether this was for Ali's sensibilities or for Jager's suffering remained unclear.

The answer was yes. She guessed he had too, and she was suddenly grateful she had seen it alone. Watching it with someone else in the room – someone male in particular – would have made it even worse.

'Working Traffic, I've been to RTAs that made me less queasy,' she said. 'And it's not because I'm prudish: I've seen my share of porn.'

'No, I hear you. It made me feel horrible too. It felt like something beyond voyeurism and beyond betrayal. It was consensual sex and yet I was watching a violation.'

Ali nodded. She had been with guys who asked to film it and she always refused. This was what happened when they didn't take no for an answer: a different kind of rape. She thought of how she had felt when Martin pretended not to notice that he'd come inside her. Multiply that by a thousand, she thought, and you'd get how it would feel if he had leaked a non-consensual sex tape.

'No wonder Jager killed the fucker,' she said.

On the monitor, Ellis was in full flow, speaking with his signature calm and slightly patronising authority.

'We have found a small quantity of blood and powdered bone fragments in the boot of your car. DNA analysis has proven both to match that of your husband. A wee drop of blood, we couldn't get ourselves too excited about that. A scraped knuckle opening the boot, helping you in with the shopping, perhaps. Any number of reasons why that might be found there. But it's the powdered bone mixed in with it that really intrigues us, Dr Jager. Apparently it's the human equivalent of sawdust. Do you have any ideas as to how that got there?'

Jager didn't respond, didn't look to her lawyer, didn't even shake her head.

'Well, as you're feeling a wee bit reticent, why don't I have a go? You argued, quite understandably, about this sex tape Peter had made: this surreptitiously obtained and mercilessly candid video of things that should be kept between two trusting people. It must have been more hurtful than any of us can imagine, and you must have been uncontainable in your anger. But then to make it worse, rather than get down on his knees and plead for your forgiveness, he hits you. He punches you in the face, leaving you with the black eye that PC Kazmi and her colleague PC Rodriguez observe the following morning.'

Jager glanced up briefly. Did she look to the camera, Ali asked herself, or was she imagining it? Did she even know the camera was there? It certainly felt like it, but maybe this was merely a hangover guilt from her previous compulsory voyeurism.

'That was what pushed you over the edge,' Ellis went on. 'You were angry and you were probably scared too. Who wouldn't be, in your position, having learned what depravity your husband had stooped to? You had no idea what else he might be capable of. So you had to take drastic steps. You had to act on the spot, in fear and in the heat of the moment. Did you grab what was to hand? Where did it happen? Did you hit him on the head with some-thing, then realise you'd hit him harder than you meant to? Did he maybe hit his head on something as he fell?

'Or was it more instinctive than that: you're a surgeon after all. Even without thinking, your hands would know where to put a blade to inflict the most damage in the shortest space of time: a small woman with a limited window of opportunity against a bigger man who was bound to strike back. Again, were the consequences greater than you had intended? Because we could easily be talking manslaughter, self-defence even. But I need your input, and so far you're giving me nothing.'

Jager simply stared at him with unnerving detachment, like she was the one in Ali's role: listening intently, observing, taking mental notes.

'Whatever happened, you realised it had gone too far. Though it surprises me someone of your experience and resources wouldn't take steps to recover the situation. If there was a man lying there who had received a life-threatening injury, the one person most people would want on the spot would be a surgeon. But maybe it happened too fast, or you froze in shock and didn't recover your faculties until it was too late.

'Again, if it had been a regrettable accident or a heat-of-the-moment reaction with unexpectedly dire consequences, this is when I'd have expected you to phone for help. Maybe you did, though, eh? Just not 999.'

That got a glimmer of reaction, Ali noticed: the tiniest flinch.

'I think we just spied a chink in her armour,' said Rodriguez, confirming he had picked up on it too.

'Because here's what I think happened,' Ellis resumed. 'You're a smart woman, quick at thinking on your feet. You decided you could cover this up, and you came up with a plan. First priority would be getting rid of the body while it's still dark. It's not easy to move a dead weight, one that's heavier than yourself, and not easy to dispose of it either. But you're a surgeon, and you've a Liston knife just sitting there: damn handy for lopping off limbs.

'You dismember your husband, probably wrap the parts in plastic, and put them in the boot of your car. You clean up the mess – Officer Kazmi smells the bleach the next day – but there's one wee drip oozes out, maybe in the tiniest hole in the plastic. So small you don't notice it, especially not in the dark. Dries in practically the same colour as the fibre in the lining of the boot. Nobody's ever going to see it without Luminol and a blacklight.

'You take the Audi wherever and you dispose of the contents.

347

Can't be too far, because we know you had other things to be getting on with. Now, this is the part where we could really do with a wee bit of decency from you, Doctor. Believe me, it will go easier for you if you tell us where we can find the remains. It's the one area of cooperation a judge is always going to look favourably upon.'

Chambers leaned forward, making one of his rare contributions. He spoke in that warm, reassuring baritone of his: a voice that always promised the suspects understanding, catharsis and absolution after Ellis had softened them up with his snarky hectoring.

'Where is he, Diana? Just tell us that much. Because however angry you were with him, whatever he did to you to force your hand, Peter meant something to other people, and those other people did you no wrong. They deserve to have him back so that he can be laid to rest.'

It was the one time she spoke.

'I don't know. That's the truth. I don't know where he is.'

Chambers sighed, laying on the air of disappointment. He wasn't guilting this one into anything, though: Ali could see that.

Ellis took it as his cue to wade in again.

'Never mind. We'll find him soon enough. What you did with the body is only half the battle though, isn't it? Because you can't simply tell people Peter walked out on you when you know he's never going to be heard from again. You need a better story. Drowning. That's worked before, hasn't it? People can have terrible accidents when water is involved, can't they, Doctor?'

There was no flinch this time. Jager had been pre-warned by reading the news story.

'So you drive Peter's car to a known accident blackspot: one you happen to mention to PC Kazmi a few hours later, as a matter of fact. "This happened at Widow Falls," you said initially. Then you had to backpedal to explain why you knew the location. You told her Peter had almost lost control of the car there recently, when he was upset. Must have stuck in your mind: a plausible spot for a wee tragedy. Again I'm wondering quite how spur-of-the-moment this all was, but maybe that's for the jury to decide. The point is,

348

you fake the accident. You drive Peter's car to the edge of the embankment and then roll it into the river. I wonder at what point you realised you had forgotten to slide the seat back?'

Ali was already watching closely, having anticipated where Ellis was going with this. She saw another tiny flash of emotion in Jager's stone-set features.

'But of course, nobody's going to simply discover a car at the bottom of the river, so you need to make sure the police know to look for it. That's when you phone up on a disposable mobile, using the name Sheena Matheson, and say you've just witnessed a BMW going out of control. You even have a story as to why you can't hang around and wait for the cops: something about a sick kid at home. Perfectly plausible, except that it directed us to check the CCTV cameras in the twenty-four-hour garage you said you were going to.

'The main thing is it gets the job done. PC Kazmi and PC Rodriguez are dispatched to investigate. All that remains for you is to get home, which admittedly is now problematic seeing as you don't have a car. Did somebody give you a wee lift? And was that *all* this somebody did? Who can you call for something like that in the middle of the night? It would need to be somebody you were close to. Somebody you trusted *intimately*.'

Ellis pressed this a little longer but Ali could tell he was pissing into the wind. Jager had reacted the first time he suggested the idea of an accomplice, but after that she had assimilated it into her calculations. And there were a lot of calculations going on, always. She never seemed distraught or scared or defeated or angry. Instead she was quite unsettlingly calm, in keeping with how Ali had witnessed her before.

'Is it just me,' Ali asked, 'or do you get the impression Jager is biding her time for something?'

'No, I know what you mean. They're nailing her to the wall but it's as though she still has some genius move to make, a card yet to play that nobody is going to see coming.'

'It would have to be a hell of a card. What we've got on her is looking pretty conclusive.'

'Except there's still one important piece of the puzzle missing,' Rodriguez reminded her.

That was the real reason Ellis and Chambers had been talking about cooperation and pleading for decency in a concerted bid to get her to open up on one particular front. It wasn't for the sake of Elphinstone's bereaved relatives: it was that nothing is guaranteed in a murder case when you don't have a body.

AFTERSHOCKS

Lucy was waiting for him in a café on Broughton Street, the same one where they had met for the second time. Parlabane spotted her through the window and felt something tingle inside him. He admitted it freely to himself; enjoyed the sensation, even. She was wearing a silver-grey coat and a mariner-style cap, her look a modern evocation of Victoriana that was definitely more steam than punk.

She looked up in response to the sound of him coming through the door. His breath paused in anticipation of her reaction, craving a sparkle in her eyes. Instead she gave him a sad and fragile smile.

The first time Lucy came to his flat, she had brought coffee and a copy of the *Daily Record*. Both things were present on the table in front of her, the latter seeming no less incongruous second time around, and once again it bore the reason for her mood.

BLACK WIDOW screamed the front page. It was his story, though he'd never have gone with that headline.

Diana Jager had been charged with Peter Elphinstone's murder. She had been interviewed by detectives in Inverness and was now being held on remand. The cloying report about tragedy striking fairytale newlyweds was recalled in a rag-out miniature of a previous page: 'deception of a gullible tabloid' being an unofficial addition to Jager's charge-sheet.

They traded small talk as he ordered, tentative and cautious steps on neutral ground. It exclusively consisted of him asking about her.

'When did you get back? What were you doing in London?'

That kind of thing.

The reciprocal questions about what he had being doing lately represented harsher terrain.

351

A waitress in a nose-ring and a Savage Earth Heart T-shirt put down his double espresso with a smile, then glided away like she was on roller skates. He took a sip and placed the cup down, his action an overture they both understood.

Proper questions now.

'How are you?'

'I'm okay. I'm fine. I'm okay.'

She nodded affirmation but her expression contradicted her: full of doubt, certain of nothing.

They both sipped at their coffees, conspicuously filling the silence. Parlabane could hear people at other tables having easy conversations. It served to underline how awkward this suddenly felt. Whatever had ignited between them a few doors down at the Barony now seemed a guttering flame. A draught from an open door could extinguish it.

She put down her cup, ran a finger along the rim.

'Jack, the reason I called you here . . .'

He stiffened in his seat, swallowed involuntarily.

'I want to say thanks. For everything.'

He loved the sound of her voice. That cinnamon scent. Her clothes. She'd never looked so good, in fact, as right then. But they say a woman never looks as beautiful as when she's walking out of your life.

'You're welcome. I just wish I hadn't been so successful, if you know what I mean.'

'Entirely. And that's why this is hard, but I need some space right now. I'm trying to come to terms with all of this. It's like my feelings have been on hold, or I've been having kind of place-holder emotions since Peter died. And now bang, here comes the real thing. Pain, anger, shock, and the grief of losing him all over again, only it's so much worse because this time I know she hurt him.'

He thought she might cry, but her voice remained steady, if feeble. His instinct was to reach out a hand, but it didn't feel right.

'I understand.'

And he did. He understood that she was always going to

associate him with this. He understood that the only thing to do was give her that space, let her find that distance.

They finished their coffees in silence. Someone at a nearby table was talking about the story: the usual mixture of speculation and judgement, an ideal accompaniment to a mid-morning cuppa. It was a stark reminder to him of how much harder this was for Lucy. It wasn't a story to her, or a paycheque. It was her world. He had delved into the darkness for her, but now she was the one who had to live there.

'I'd better go,' she said.

'I know.'

He watched her walk out, felt a draught as she opened the door; pictured that flame going out.

That was when he realised it was only over if he allowed it to be. He wasn't going to make the same mistake he did with Mairi, appreciating what had been in his grasp only once he'd let it go. This was worth fighting for.

He stood up and looked out his wallet, putting down a tenner. He wouldn't wait for change. He was going after her.

Then his mobile rang: a number he didn't recognise. To other people, that aspect would immediately bump it down the priority list. To Parlabane, it was always a potential lead, a story waiting to be told, a summons he was compelled to obey.

He pressed Answer with his right thumb as his left hand reached for the handle on the café door.

'Hello.'

It was a woman's voice, querulous and uncertain.

'I was looking for Jack Parlabane?'

'Speaking.'

'Oh, right. Okay. Well, my name is Keira Stroud. I'm Diana Jager's lawyer.'

That stopped him where he stood, quickly running a mental fact-check on everything he had filed.

'I think it's the polis you should be worrying about. My story stands up one hundred per—'

'She wants to talk to you.'

'Aye, very good.'

He was already searching for some kind of legal trap.

'Listen, I'm not finding it any easier to believe than you do. I'm the one supposed to be defending her and she's giving me absolutely nothing. Instead she says she wants to speak to you, in person.'

'About what?'

'She said to tell you – and I am quoting precisely here – "you alone will discover the secret of what happened to my husband".'

'Sounds like a set-up.'

'Sounds like an exclusive, but that's not my call. I'm only the go-between, it would appear.'

'Why would she tell me? I'm the one who dug up all this stuff that helped put the bite on her.'

'No point asking me, Mr Parlabane. Diana's the one person who can answer your questions. And good luck with that, because she's answered precious few of mine.'

THE ADDRESSEE

When morning came around, I called in sick as soon as I knew the department secretary would be there to answer the phone. I was in no condition to go to work: mentally or physically. I wasn't ready to face anybody, and nor did I expect to be for a while yet. My hands were still trembling, for one thing, so there was no way I could hold a scalpel.

I hadn't slept and I had to deal with the police on my doorstep before I was even dressed. I remember feeling like a zombie, totally detached from the moment. They ushered me gently into my own living room like I was an invalid, then told me about Peter's car.

One of them – PC Kazmi – asked me about my face, which I'd actually forgotten about at that moment. I suddenly realised how it might look, to say nothing of how embarrassed I felt to be sporting a black eye from my husband. I lied, gave them a story I had already thought up to tell my colleagues, about bashing myself while opening a parcel. I thought it sounded stupid and embarrassing enough to be true.

It felt like they were there for ages. I couldn't understand why they wouldn't leave. I desperately, desperately wanted to be alone, to sit in silence and gather my thoughts about what had happened. They asked if there was someone who could sit with me, which was when I remembered how different it must look to them. From their perspective they had just told me about the likely death of my husband, but from mine, I hadn't learned anything new. I remember a cold part of myself thinking Peter had been dead to me for weeks. I wanted them out of my house. I wanted the future to start as soon as possible, the rest of my life to commence.

I went back to work after what some would consider an unseemly brief period, but when you're in distress, you go to what you know.

Work is always where I've sought refuge, and I knew it would be easier if I was busy than stuck at home. It wasn't without its trials, of course. I was forced to play the widow, a role I never envisaged for myself. The hardest part was the awkwardness of having to endure people coming up to say how sorry they were for my loss. I didn't feel bereaved. I had already got over being cheated of the husband I thought I had married; I had long since come to accept that he never existed.

But then a few days later, the police came back. It was about seven in the evening. Dinner was in the oven and Calum was about to open a bottle of wine. I had to usher him out, telling him I'd give him a ring when the coast was clear. I had recognised that it was the same two cops, including the woman who had asked about my black eye. I told them he was a junior colleague solicitously popping by to make sure I was okay. I didn't want to provide fuel for her imagination by spelling it out that my lover was round for a romantic evening only a matter of days after she'd told me my husband was dead.

They were there on the pretext of returning a photograph, but when PC Rodriguez asked me to retrieve the Liston knife he had seen in the picture, that's when I knew I was in trouble.

I called up the Assistant Chief Constable, Angus McLean. I work with his wife, Janice, and I'd actually operated on him, so I had some leverage; or at least his home number. He said he knew nothing about me being under investigation, though I guessed he wouldn't tell me if I was. I wanted to lay down a marker: let them know that if they were going to investigate me, I wasn't going to make it easy on them.

But then there was the newspaper article. Front page, no less, digging up what happened to poor old Agnes and my revenge on young Evan. Once I saw that, I knew it was only a matter of time before I was in custody.

They didn't haul me out in my underwear, at least. It happened by degrees.

First they showed up with a warrant to search the place. I was taken away to be questioned, informally. I knew that while I sat there in the police station, drinking rotten tea from a plastic cup, they would be scouring through my home, taking the place apart. I hoped I'd done as good a job as I had assumed in cleaning up.

I guess not.

That informal interview was when they began asking me the questions they would return to over and over, from different angles, different interlocutors. Despite the official caution about it 'harming my defence', I knew it was easier to remain consistent if I didn't tell them anything.

You might argue that it's easier to remain consistent if you're telling the truth, but I knew the police weren't going to listen to the truth. They were never going to understand what I needed to say. As I sat in a succession of waiting areas, interview rooms and cells, I came to realise that if I was ever to get out of this, I was going to have to take unexpected measures. Some might say desperate measures.

I needed to tell my story not to these detectives who already thought they knew everything, but to somebody who would relish the idea that there might yet be one more twist in the tale. Someone with a sharper ear for nuance. Someone who appreciates that the morality of these things can be, shall we say, fluid. And someone who believes that it's possible to be deceitful in the service of honesty.

With all of that in mind, I gave specific instruction to my lawyer, Keira Stroud, to make contact.

And now here you are, Mr Parlabane.

MATING PORCUPINES

He could almost feel the air electrified by Jager's presence, a centred energy about her that quietly filled the room. Parlabane had seldom sensed such a controlled strength of will emanating from a person, a constant reminder not to be misled by her clothes or her circumstances.

Ironically he was here ostensibly to assist with her defence, that being the reason given by Stroud in order to facilitate his accompaniment during this sustained period of access to her client. They sat in a drab but over-lit room, on ugly plastic furniture pocked by an acne of cigarette burns. Jager was in prison-issue sweatshirt and slacks, her hair pulled back carelessly into an untidy ponytail. She bore scant resemblance to the woman he had spoken to outside the hospital in Inverness, but he couldn't let that distract him from a vigilant awareness that he was dealing with a formidable intellect and a thoroughly dangerous individual.

He waited a few moments to be sure she had finished speaking, and to digest what he had learned. It was a lot to take in, and he remained as wary as he was unsure of where he fitted into it.

'So,' he said. 'What can I do for you?'

'First things first. The initial story you wrote, about Agnes and Evan and your little adventure on the way home from the pub. I'm assuming that's how the police got all of that information. Was it also you who told them about the sex tape?'

'Yes.'

She fixed him with a piercing look.

'I thought so. In that case I would like to thank you for keeping that part out of the paper.'

'The editor probably won't when he finds out, but I like to think I've still got some integrity. A crime was perpetrated against you and I didn't want to be party to worsening the damage. I only granted you a stay of execution, though. It will all come out in court.'

She angled her head, as though evaluating something. She didn't seem too disturbed. Maybe she had already made her peace with it. What difference does it make how many strangers see a thing like that?

He was wrong, though: that wasn't why she seemed sanguine.

'This won't be going to court. You're going to see to that.'

'I am? Why?'

'Because I didn't kill my husband. There's a scoop for you.'

THE DEPARTED

I pulled myself to my feet. I was shaking but there was something deep within me that had turned to steel. I recall being hyper-aware of my surroundings, as though everything was amplified. The light seemed brighter, the colour contrast enhanced. I could distinguish individual scents: diesel from my car, fabric conditioner from my clothes, the tang of Peter's sweat. I could hear both of our breathing, the distant sound of a train.

Peter was shaking too. He was looking at his fist like it didn't belong to him, as though it were some alien appendage.

I put a hand tenderly to my cheek, checking for blood. There was none: only a growing throb.

I turned around, raised myself up straight, and looked him in the face. From some chasmic depth inside I summoned my voice, and it came: firm, low and grave.

'Nobody gets to do that to me twice.'

Peter stared, hollow, drained. It was like he'd woken up from a trance.

'You leave now, and you never come back. You can collect your things another time when I'm not here, but right now, get out of my house. I don't care where you go. I never want to see you again.'

He stared at me a moment longer, fear and confusion on his face, then left without another word.

GREATER CRIMES

Jager folded her arms, holding Parlabane in her gaze, silently challenging him.

'He left?'

'It was the last time I saw him. The next morning, when I learned about the accident, I assumed something had happened like when we were on the road that night we argued about his vasectomy. I didn't think he had committed suicide, but I knew what that loss of control could have led to. While he might not have set out to kill himself, I thought maybe he had been consumed by that same reckless abandon that meant he didn't particularly care whether he lived either.

'I was numb when the police came that morning. I was still so angry with him. At that point, I didn't have it in me to feel sorry for him, never mind bereaved. I was too churned up, too confused. I acknowledge I may have seemed a little cold to the police, because at that point I literally didn't know what to feel. I wasn't exactly distraught that he was dead, but I didn't kill him.'

'Why didn't you tell the police this?'

'Is it convincing you?'

'No.'

'There you go, then.'

'And yet apparently you think I can help you. How? Have you got any evidence?'

'Not on me here in this room, which is why I need your help. I can point you in the right direction, though. Let me start with your abduction that Saturday night, in case you're harbouring any personal resentment towards me over that. According to the report and to the police, you never saw your attackers. How did you deduce that it was me?'

361

'I recognised your perfume. Jo Malone: Blackberry and Bay.'

She rocked her head back, considering.

'I can't imagine I'm the only woman in the world who wears it. In fact, you may recall I mentioned that Cecily Greysham-Ellis smelled of the same perfume at Peter's mother's wake.'

'Are you suggesting *she* abducted me?'

Parlabane tried to make it sound like he thought the notion absurd, but only to disguise the fact that wheels were turning in his head. He felt there was a possibility he had been missing, always just out of focus. He recalled Lucy talking about Peter having a crush on Cecily when they were teenagers, and of Jager's account of their awkward mutual blanking at the wake.

'I honestly couldn't say. I only know that it wasn't me. I have an alibi.'

He reeled. He wasn't expecting this.

'Seriously? Well how about you give me the name and I'll check it out.'

'I can't.'

Parlabane couldn't help but let out an irritated scoff.

'Patient confidentiality, you see. I can't give you his name, but I do have half a dozen witnesses that I was wrist-deep in his colon around the time you say you were being bundled into a van and stuck with a hypodermic.'

'You were working?'

She nodded, a hint of a smile forming on her lips.

'Okay, that would cover you for the Saturday night. But it's a previous date that's a bit more problematic, don't you think?'

'My current situation would certainly suggest so.'

'So if you weren't trying to warn me off, how come there was a guy tailing me around Inverness in a black Porsche? Or are you going to tell me you know nothing about that?'

'No, I know everything about that, starting with the fact that it was a dark blue Porsche. Austin had warned me about you, which made me rather anxious, and then you suddenly turned up at the hospital. I don't think you appreciate how intimidating that feels.'

Parlabane found it difficult to imagine Jager feeling intimidated, but maybe that served to underline her point.

'I asked a friend to keep an eye on you, for my peace of mind. And you can imagine what it did for my peace of mind when he called and told me you had parked yourself outside my house.'

'So you called the police.'

Jager said nothing, as though there was no need to confirm. She leaned back in her seat and placed a foot up on the table.

'What do you think of these trainers? Not really me, are they? Velcro straps, like I'm a kid. Do you know what that's about?'

'They took your laces away.'

'They took my *boots* away. I remember it struck me as such a strange and arbitrary act. At first I wondered if it was deliberately so, to rapidly convey my complete absence of agency, of free will in this place of confinement.'

'They thought you were a suicide risk.'

'That's right. I loved those boots. Peter bought me them. You remember I said before we were married he would surprise me with gifts that were closer to the taste I aspired towards rather than what I tended to buy for myself? They were a perfect example. He didn't always get it right, though. He bought me a faux leather biker-style jacket once that was way too young for me. Had to get a refund: there was no way I was going out the house in it.'

She set her foot down again carefully.

'I put it out of my mind. But recently I noticed Annalise, one of our surgical trainees, wearing the same jacket. Annalise was up at the house shortly before Peter bought it for me. She lives out on the Nairn road, and she picked me up one time on the way to a department night out, so that I could have a drink. I wasn't quite ready when she turned up, and I remember her asking if she could use my laptop while she waited. She was planning a shopping trip to Glasgow that weekend and was surfing some clothing sites in advance. Can you see where this is going yet?'

'He was spying on your browsing history to see what you were considering, get a handle on your taste.'

'You're quicker than me. It was only when I was banged up in here that I managed to put it together.'

Parlabane was unable to see what Peter's great crime was here.

'It's underhand, but some might call it solicitous.'

'What you're forgetting is that this started before we were living together. He knew what I was browsing before he ever had direct access to my laptop. He sent me a file over Skype quite early in our relationship, remember? One that apparently didn't do anything when I opened it, so he sent another, full of photos from the airsoft meet. I think the first file did plenty. I think he had remote control of my laptop from that moment on, including access to my webcam. He was spying on me almost from the moment our relationship began.'

'Ah.'

This changed things just a bit.

'My life was probably open in a live feed on his laptop whenever he wanted to look, which would be icky enough if this was merely about voyeurism, but that's only where it begins. Take a moment to consider what a research job he was doing on me. He had access to all the information he could possibly need in order to make himself appear the perfect man. In order to *make me fall in love with him.*'

She swallowed, the only time so far he had seen her feelings rise to the surface.

'That's cold. Clinical. Like there was a contract out on you.'

Parlabane offered a smile. He could tell she was hurting, and though he was stepping cautiously, he couldn't keep too much of an emotional distance. He needed a reading on her at all times, some kind of a connection.

It worked. She loosed a tear from her left eye with a gentle nudge of a knuckle.

'Quite,' she said. 'One minute he's using this covert surveillance to seduce me, and a few months later he's moving money out of my accounts. The police don't know about that, by the way. I thought if I told them it would only further support the motive in their existing theory. They would think that Peter's greatest crime was stealing from me. How could that even come close to the crime of *marrying* me?'

She looked at him pleadingly, like she needed him to understand. He did, but only her pain.

'See, that's where it breaks down for me,' Parlabane told her. 'It's a hell of a long haul for forty grand, or for however much more he might have taken before being caught. And he would have been caught: there was no mystery about where the money was going. But the main thing that I don't get is the same one that's burning you: why would he marry you? If he was scamming you, he could have done that way back, without moving in, never mind proposing. I don't see what his endgame could have been.'

She was nodding her acknowledgment, her expression still appellant.

'I don't know. I don't know. I don't know. There are so many things I simply don't understand about what happened between Peter and me.'

'So what exactly am I doing here? Your lawyer sold me this visit on the promise that you would tell me what happened to your husband.'

'No, you were told *you alone would discover the secret of what happened to him.* You're here so that I can tell you where you might find it.'

Parlabane reined in a sigh, masking his exasperation. Despite a few minor shocks, he was developing a strong suspicion that she was manipulating him, and it would require something pretty solid to dispel that.

Jager sat up straighter, hands clasped on the table in front of her.

'The police are working on the theory that my husband didn't die in that car crash. They think I killed him, disposed of the body and then faked the accident to cover up my crime. They're right to think that, on the basis of all the available evidence. But only, Mr Parlabane, because somebody has gone to a great deal of trouble to make it appear so.'

SPRINGING THE TRAP

'Looking back, I realise that my first clue came on the morning after Peter disappeared. I hadn't slept well, and I recall stumbling into the kitchen in my dressing gown and noticing a smell of bleach. I didn't remember putting any in the sink, and then I worked out it was coming from the garage. I wondered if something had been knocked over during the previous evening's unpleasantness. I was going to investigate once I'd had a shower and some breakfast, but then the doorbell rang, and of course, it was the police.'

Jager spoke calmly, with a hint of self-reproach. It didn't sound like an impassioned plea to be believed, more a dispassionate laying out of the facts as though double-checking them for herself.

She was precise in what she was saying now, markedly less discursive than before. Parlabane was aware that liars tended to over-embellish; but equally that *good* liars knew the value of concision.

'Your first clue to what?'

'That I was being set up. I couldn't have realised it at the time, but I soon came to see where it fits in.'

'That's more than I can see.'

'Then allow me to fast-forward to when those two police officers returned to the house. You will remember Rodriguez asked me why the Liston knife was no longer on the mantelpiece. Peter did hate it: that part is true. He asked me not to have it on display, so I put it in the hall cupboard, on top of a stack of files full of notes from my research papers. When I went to retrieve it, it was gone.

'I stood in that cupboard for what felt like a long time, conscious that my absence was becoming conspicuous. I had to compose myself before I could face them again, because I felt so rattled. I suddenly realised the true reason the police had returned was that they were starting to suspect me, and now I wouldn't be able to produce this knife they were asking about. That was also when it struck me that the first time these two had turned up, to tell me about the accident, there was a smell of bleach wafting through the place. Cops are trained to notice things like that.'

Parlabane reckoned this was a lot to hang her story on.

'Is it possible you didn't put the display case where you thought?'

'The case was still there. It was the knife itself that was gone, and as I stood staring at where it should have been, it hit me like a train. Somebody had killed Peter that night and was trying to frame me for the murder.'

She ran two hands through her hair, re-threading the ponytail.

'As soon as the police had gone, I called Calum and told him not to come back. I didn't tell him why, but I knew that if the cops were starting to think I had done it, then having a lover in the picture was not going to look good.'

'But presumably he knew Peter had hit you.'

'Yes. I told him everything.'

'So were you worried what Calum might think?'

She shot him a look, the closest she had come to a show of temper. Calum was clearly a sensitive area.

'Calum would never think anything like that about me.'

'What, not even after he read my exclusive?'

He didn't get to register a second hit. She had identified an area of her own vulnerability and reined in her reactions, reading his intentions when he prodded it again.

'Agnes Delacroix smacked her head on a rock when our canoe capsized. I had already talked to Calum about how traumatic that was for me. That's why he understood how painful it was to have it cast up again by way of innuendo and accusation. Calum knows I'm innocent.'

'So why are you asking me to help you? What is there that you think I can do that he couldn't?'

'We'll come to that. First I have to make you understand

something crucial. In my paranoid state I went looking for planted evidence, afraid that if the police came back and searched the place, they would turn up the Liston knife somewhere, with traces of Peter's DNA on it.

'It was while I was rooting around that I began to find tiny drops of blood dotted about the floor and finely sprayed on walls and other surfaces. It was like someone had used an atomiser. That night, while your story was rolling off the presses, I was on my hands and knees, scrubbing the stone floor of the garage, the walls, the worktops. I'll never forget the sting of it in my eyes and the way it caught in my throat, but the hardest part was the fear that it might not be enough: I had no way of knowing where else Peter's blood might be found. I could wash the obvious places until my skin was raw, but I knew there was bound to be somewhere I missed.'

'Your car.'

'That's right. I was so fixated upon the garage being set up as the locus for the murder that I forgot that transporting the body would be part of the narrative too.'

'But they found bone fragments. I get that someone might be able to transfer a blood sample, but . . .'

'Powder: that's all they found. Just enough to be verified in a test and thus imply there must have been a lot more. You could obtain the quantity required for that from a deep cut to a finger.'

Jager remained silent for a few moments, the first hints of apprehension on her previously impassive face. Whatever she thought Parlabane could do to help, his involvement hinged upon him believing her, and perhaps she was beginning to think it had all sounded more convincing in her head. She had an explanation for everything, including all of the physical evidence against her, but nothing she had said could be independently verified. More problematic still, she had failed to answer the biggest question her story posed.

'Why? That's the alpha and the omega here, the key to whether anybody should believe you. Why would someone do this? Who else has a motive? Who would go to these extraordinary lengths to frame you? And why would they plant tiny quantities of evidence? Why not plant your husband's body somewhere in the grounds of your house for the police to find, with your Liston knife still sticking in his back?'

She stared back across the table, a blank expression of defiance quickly betraying itself as a façade. She looked lost and scared, but trying not to show it. Or perhaps that was what she wanted him to see.

'I don't know. But it has to be related to the project. Peter was under enormous pressure to the extent that he was stealing my money to buy himself time. He was so secretive about the whole thing that I've come to assume it can't have been all legal and above board. I think he was in business with some dangerous people, and I think they killed him and set me up to take the blame.'

She leaned forward again, her voice lower, as if she was concerned about being overheard.

'Peter kept his laptop on a permanent lockdown, as I've told you, but he spent all his days at Sunflight House. I need someone to go and have a look around inside the MTE office, because I'm sure there must be something in that place that will tell us what's been going on.'

'So why don't you put your lawyer on it, or your boyfriend? Give them the keys and let them crack the case. Why ask the reporter whose story helped put you in here?'

'Because I have no keys, and from what Austin told me, you're no ordinary reporter.'

Parlabane rocked back in his chair.

'Wait. You're asking me to break into a building – to commit a crime – on the off chance that it uncovers some evidence that supports this improbable cover story of yours. Why would I do that unless I already believed you?'

'Because if I'm lying, what would it cost you? Just a wasted trip, and you still got this interview out of it. But if I'm telling the truth, Mr Parlabane, that's one hell of a story.'

LOCKDOWN

Sunflight House was a two-storey office building on an industrial estate close to the dual carriageway that ran from the A9 to the centre of Inverness. According to Jager, it had been built as a single premises for a travel firm but was then converted into smaller units by a developer after the original owner went belly-up. She also said that it looked so dull and nondescript that its principal security measure was the fact that nobody would expect to find anything inside worth stealing.

Parlabane wasn't so sure about that. He noted that the welcome sign at the entrance to the estate, upon which all of the major resident companies were listed, also bore the logo for Cautela Security, warning that their personnel monitored and patrolled twenty-four seven. Whether this applied to all premises, including the care-worn office building, seemed unclear. Parlabane assumed it depended upon whether Peter's landlord had opted into a contract. Jager's scorn concerning how cheap the rent was suggested not, but he wasn't taking anything for granted.

He parked his car across the road in the lot outside a courier depot, hiding his vehicle from direct view of the Sunflight building behind an articulated lorry. If anything went wrong here, he didn't want his to be the only car in conspicuous vicinity at this time of night.

He still wasn't sure he was going through with this. He would just go and check it out, he had told himself as he drove north. Case the joint, then make a final judgement on the risk-benefit ratio.

He wished there was someone else he could talk to about this, though he took it as a sign of progress that this wasn't merely a symptom of missing Sarah. There would have been no need to

370

talk to her regarding this kind of quandary, as her answer was always the same: don't. Mairi had been more of a willing confederate when it came to his more dangerous methods, but his welfare hadn't been her highest priority at the time. She might see it differently now.

The woman he most wanted to talk to was the last person he could tell. In fact, the potential impact upon Lucy was one of the things keeping him wary of Jager's motives. She was a woman who had in the past gone to extraordinary lengths to avenge herself upon those she felt had wronged her, and there had been no love lost between her and her sister-in-law. She had let Evan Okonjo sweat the possibility of HIV infection after stabbing him with a potentially contaminated hypodermic, and that was just for hacking her password. If she knew she was going down, then it was possible that she was striking back at the people who had brought her low in the only ways that were still available to her, such as giving Lucy the impression her beloved brother had been a criminal.

How she might be planning to punish Parlabane remained unclear, as sending him on a wild goose chase wasn't the most wrathful vengeance he could imagine. He kept thinking of those carefully quoted words: *You alone will discover the secret of what happened to my husband.* Something about how precisely that had been phrased made him uneasy.

There were plenty of reasons to distrust her, plenty of reasons to stick instead of twist. In that respect she had been wrong about the stakes: he had the interview whether he followed it up or not. But there were also a few reasons to gamble on the bigger jackpot.

The first was that there *was* something in Jager's account that could be independently verified. He had researched Liz Miller and quickly found that her story checked out. She had been jailed for stabbing her partner in a case sufficiently controversial as to have received widespread media coverage and consequently featuring high up the list of search results against her name. He wasn't sure what light it shed upon Elphinstone's dodgy business dealings, but there was definitely something odd about the haste with which he had proposed to two different women.

Secondly there was the involvement of Sam Finnegan as an unlikely major investor in a computer software project. According to Catherine McLeod, Finnegan was as greedy and resourceful as he was ruthless and sly. He was a man who went to brutal lengths to ensure his effete reputation didn't make anyone think they could ever get away with screwing him over, and it seemed Peter Elphinstone was struggling to deliver whatever he had promised.

It would be, as Jager suggested, a hell of a story, which was where the biggest reason kicked in: this was what Parlabane lived for.

He walked across the road and through the Sunflight House car park at a leisurely pace, not wishing to appear hurried or furtive to any CCTV cameras that might be trained on the site. The main entrance had a glass double door, further panes flanking either side. There was more glass above, through which he could see a return staircase leading to the first floor. Sunflight must have blown the architectural budget on this central vestibule, as the rest of the place was drab and dowdy, a grim testament to eighties capitalist functionalism.

Everyone was long gone for the night, only darkness visible beyond the glass. Nonetheless, the sodium glow from the street-lamps was sufficient for Parlabane to decide that he wouldn't be going in the main entrance. There was a keypad entry system, which Jager had neglected to mention, and he didn't have the code. There was also a conventional lock to override the automated system should the electronics fail, but picking it in full view of the street was not a risk he felt like taking tonight. Sometimes he could pop these things in twenty seconds, other times it might take five minutes, but he could never be sure until he started working.

He walked around the building and found another door at the rear, most probably an emergency exit. From the absence of cigarette butts he deduced that it didn't see a lot of action, which was borne out by the extended time it took him to open it. It was stiff from lack of use: metal parts expanding and contracting together over decades until the mechanism inside would be hard to turn even with the key. It took patience and a couple of sprays from the miniature can of WD40 in his kit, but he could feel it gradually loosen up, and eventually the tumblers clicked and the bolt slid back.

The door opened with a grudging creak, into a narrow stairwell that was almost pitch black. Parlabane twisted on a penlight and made his way up to the first floor as directed by Jager. At the top landing was a fire door with a mesh-reinforced window at head height. He shone his penlight through it and watched the beam play along a corridor that ran the length of the building, from the emergency exit at the rear to the glass-walled vestibule at the front.

The hallway was a hazard of office furniture. There were filing cabinets, bookcases and old desks pushed against the walls, suggesting somebody was in the process of moving in or moving out.

He could see the name MTE on a door to his right. That was good, because it meant Elphinstone's office windows were on the side away from the main road, should he need to turn on a light.

He pushed the fire door open gently, stepping through it on tender feet even though he knew the place was empty.

That was when the alarm went off.

Parlabane played the torch along the top of the wall, looking for the source and hoping not to find a camera. His beam only picked out the infra-red sensor he had tripped, positioned to detect movement if anyone came through the fire door. A Cautela logo was legible on the base of the unit, which reminded him he had also seen it printed on the keypad outside the main entrance.

Shit. How could he have been so fucking gullible?

Keying in the entry code automatically deactivated the security. Jager hadn't told him about the keypad and she certainly hadn't told him about the alarm.

In a matter of seconds, the allure of a bigger story had vanished like a mirage and he could suddenly see that he'd been played. Sure, he had found reference to Liz Miller's story online, but it struck him too late that he hadn't bothered to verify the rest of it, such as whether she had ever been in a relationship with Peter

Elphinstone or even heard of Diana Jager. Jager could have simply remembered the case and thrown in Miller's name because it helped embellish her bullshit story.

He had tried phoning Miller earlier that evening, but when he got no reply he hadn't made establishing contact a priority. His reasoning was that Jager wouldn't have got her lawyer to supply Miller's number if she wasn't telling the truth, because one call would have blown it all apart. But how did he even know it was Miller's number? According to the cops, Jager had already used a disposable mobile as part of her previous deception.

He caught his breath, reined in his flight instinct, told himself not to panic. His first thought was to get out of the building and run for his car, but that might be the worst thing he could do. The sign at the estate entrance mentioned patrolling. That meant that the Cautela guards might be mobile, in which case they could be outside this place in two minutes: less if they happened to be around the corner when they got the call.

He ran to the front of the building and looked through the windows. The car park was still empty and there was no traffic on the road.

Okay.

He ran back to the fire door and made his way swiftly but carefully down the stairs. Pushing down on the bar to open the emergency exit door, he thought ruefully of how difficult it had been from the other side.

He had just walked through it when he heard the sound of an engine and glimpsed a vehicle pull into the car park, two figures inside.

Parlabane flattened himself against the wall, out of sight. He knew the first thing these guys would do was split up and perform a perimeter check. There was no way to sneak past them.

He was fucked.

He looked back towards the emergency exit, where the door was inches from swinging closed again. Parlabane lunged for the gap and jammed his lock-picking kit between the door and the frame before it could click shut. Wedging it open as much as he dared lest it squeak, he slipped inside again and pulled it closed. With any luck the guards would complete their circuit, see that the place was secure and then call HQ to get the alarm turned off remotely.

He climbed the stairs and made his way towards the front, crouching near to the floor. With the lights off it was easier to see out than to see in, so he would be able to watch for them making their exit. He only had to hold his position, keep his nerve and stay patient.

Then a pulse of fright shook him as he heard a sudden rumble from outside. He looked up in aghast disbelief to see the lorry he had parked behind switch on its headlights and then begin to slowly roll out of the courier depot parking lot, leaving his car guiltily isolated in view of Sunflight House.

As the lorry turned on to the dual carriageway he saw the two Cautela guards meet in front of the main entrance, and heard the squelch of a two-way radio.

All clear, he willed them to say, but he knew it wasn't going to be that kind of night.

'Control says the alarm was tripped inside the building,' one of them relayed to his partner. 'Need to do a full sweep.'

'You got the code?'

'Oh, aye, right enough. Control, you got the entry code? Five nine eight seven? Okay, cheers.'

Fuck.

Parlabane heard the buzz from directly below him as the entry system unlocked the door. The alarm ceased sounding, making his breathing and movement seem all the more audible.

Fool, he told himself. Vainglorious, incorrigible, weak, desperate fool.

This was what he lived for, he had just admitted that to himself, and Diana Jager knew it.

If I'm lying, what would it cost you?

She said Austin had warned her about him, and she must have done her research once she suspected that Parlabane was a threat. She must have known what had happened to him, where his career had once taken him, and how low he had fallen since. His exclusive on Diana Jager had got him back in the game at long last, but her revenge would be to make it the shortest journalistic comeback of all time. He would be back on the scrapheap, back in jail and professionally fucked for ever if he got busted for burglary again.

ILLUMINATION

Parlabane looked into the gloom of the corridor, probing the darkness with his penlight for somewhere he could hide. He saw four locked doors along either wall, noting with growing despair that they all boasted sturdy-looking strike plates indicative of five-lever mortise locks.

'Right, a quick once-over,' he heard one of the guards say from below, the clarity of his voice a warning about how close they were and how easily the sound would carry. 'We'll check everything's secure down here first, then up the emergency stairs and back along. Probably an electrical fault, but we'll stick together in case some bastard comes flying out from nowhere.'

Parlabane wouldn't have time to pick even the flimsiest of locks, and as an art rather than a science it wasn't something that was ever easy to do under pressure. As always when he was in trouble like this, trained instinct told him to look up, to think in three dimensions. This time, however, there was no window to climb out of, no outside wall to scale: only a low ceiling of crappy polystyrene tiles.

A low, suspended ceiling, he would bet, and it was the only bet he could make.

In a second he was on top of one of the filing cabinets that were littering the corridor, wincing at the hollow sound it made due to being empty. He gave one of the tiles a gentle push. It wouldn't lift. He pushed a little harder. Still nothing, and he noticed the frame move with it. It might be glued. It would be easy enough to punch through but he couldn't afford to leave a hole, or the resultant pile of crumbled polystyrene beneath, advertising his escape route.

He nudged the tiles either side. Neither moved.

He took a breath, cautioned himself not to panic. He gave one of them a harder push, driving the heel of his palm firmly against the corner. It popped up and almost tumbled through his startled grasp as it fell.

He slid it out of the way and hauled himself into the gap, his fingers finding a vertical suspension spar either side, supporting a lattice of aluminium. It took his weight, though there was a worrying creak as his midriff cleared the gap and his balance shifted forward.

He was sure he heard a door close below: most likely the fire door on the ground-floor access to the emergency stairs. They would be in this corridor in seconds.

He executed a limb-wrenching turn in the cramped and awkward space, manoeuvring himself one hundred and eighty degrees among the pipes and spars in order to be able to achieve a position from which he could replace the ceiling tile.

He slotted it into place just as the top fire door opened and a click of a switch later he found himself bathed in light.

He held his position, sinews straining, aware that the tiniest adjustment and resulting shift of balance might cause a tell-tale groan from the metal structure. It seemed impossible that they wouldn't see him anyway, a human shape silhouetted against the white tiles. The light was from beneath him, though, projecting downwards.

'All looks clear,' one of the guards said, in such a bored tone as to suggest he had long since passed the night when he last expected anything interesting to happen on his shift.

'Aye, probably an electrical fault right enough,' his partner agreed.

'Or maybe a moth. They can set off the sensors. Actually, I mind there was a bird one night over at Plumbcentre. Set off every sensor in the place fluttering aboot.'

'Must have been the first overnight excitement involving a bird you ever had anyway.'

'Fuck you.'

Despite his protesting limbs, Parlabane held his position until he was sure they had gone down the main stairs. As he waited, he looked around. This moth that had tripped the sensors was right up among the lights, and his position was giving him a very different perspective on the building's integrity.

Despite all those heavy-duty locks on the doors, the security was only two-dimensional. The developer had done a cheap and superficial conversion job in subdividing the units, the gypsum partition walls only going as high as the suspended ceiling. From where Parlabane hung, up above the tiles, he had a clear path to drop down into any office on this floor.

Given that he was going to have to wait a while after the guards buggered off before risking an exit, he reckoned he might as well have a snoop around MTE while he was here.

THE PLAYER

Parlabane landed in a crouch in the centre of a sparsely furnished unit. He had imagined that with eight on each floor these offices would be cramped cells, thoroughly claustrophobic places to work, but Elphinstone's was so under-utilised it looked like it could offer accommodation to half the homeless furniture out in the hallway.

There was an integrated worktop, a wall press with butterfly doors, and a small filing cabinet; this last item shorter than the mini-fridge that was buzzing next to it.

All of it looked like a collection of afterthoughts, or peripheral satellites in service of the centrepiece: a two-metre desk supporting a dual widescreen 4K monitor set-up, connected to a towering PC.

He saw three older machines tucked away side-by-side next to a surge-protector, cables trailing from their rears. Parlabane couldn't decide if they were functioning as an improvised server farm or they were waiting to be cannibalised for parts.

There was a Razer keyboard and programmable mouse in front of the dual monitors, a boom-mic headset resting on what Parlabane recognised as a force-feedback chair. This was Elphinstone's work-station, but to Parlabane's eyes, it looked principally like a high-end gaming rig.

He knew the guy's laptop was always password protected, and in keeping with the NDA stipulations referred to by both Jager and Lucy, there seemed little chance his office PC would be left unlocked. However, there might be a way to bypass that, which was why he had Buzzkill on standby.

Buzzkill was a hacker who had insinuated his way into Parlabane's activities with the same ease as he had penetrated the networks of corporations, media outlets and even political parties. Parlabane had decided early on that, despite the temptations the hacker's rarefied skillset offered, Buzzkill was not someone to whom he wanted to end up owing favours. Nonetheless, in the short time since he first made contact, Parlabane had found himself running up a bigger and bigger tab.

Buzzkill claimed not to see it that way, claiming they were kindred spirits and often reiterating the mantra that 'friends don't keep score'. Parlabane was never comfortably convinced of the sincerity of this sentiment, reckoning loan sharks probably said much the same thing. Friends' relationships tended to be more reciprocal. Buzzkill seemed to know everything about Parlabane, having introduced himself by way of hacking into his files. Parlabane, by contrast, knew almost nothing about Buzzkill, to the extent that he hadn't even heard his real voice, all their communication being text-based or electronically ventriloquised via a speech synthesiser.

He switched on the PC and had a poke around the office while he waited for the machine to boot up, the backlit keyboard glowing green as the system's fans hummed into life.. Behind the doors of the wall press he found six shelves, four of which were empty. Of the exceptions, one bore a rudimentary selection of stationery and office supplies, including a short stack of headed notepaper bearing the MTE logo and the Sunflight House address. The other was stocked entirely with bags of crisps.

He opened the fridge, which contained two six-packs of Pepsi, four cans of high-caffeine energy drink and two family-size slabs of chocolate.

The small filing cabinet provided the only further indication that a business was being run from here. It comprised two deep drawers, each housing an alphabetised divider system. Parlabane trained his penlight inside and saw that there were official-looking documents tucked away in several of the pockets. He pulled a few out at random: Articles of Incorporation from Companies House; a supplier invoice from a graphic designer; a VAT return showing no income but reclaiming the tax on the purchase of computer equipment.

Parlabane glanced towards the monitors, which were now fairly lighting up the room. To his astonishment, they were showing a normal desktop configuration, rather than the log-in screen he was expecting. The system appeared to have come out of hibernation mode, rather than a cold boot, which was perhaps why there was no password prompt.

It was as sparse as the room itself, a default wallpaper showing a swirl of blue in varying shades to provide a high-contrast background. There were icons for the browser, mail client, Skype and a freeware office suite, as well as a shortcut to the hard drive and two shortcuts to folders stored there: one named MTE and one marked Games.

He clicked on the MTE folder, expecting the password request to pop up now. It didn't. Instead it opened a window containing two further directories: MTE Project and MTE Admin. He opened the former and tried launching a file called Build_3.1.

A narrow vertical window opened on the left-hand monitor: indecipherable lines of code scrolling up the screen in white on black. He waited for a corresponding graphic user interface to appear on the right-hand screen, but it remained blank.

Parlabane hovered the mouse over another file, but held off launching it. He didn't know where to begin with any of this stuff, and he could end up hanging the system. A full restart would surely invoke a security prompt, and he would lose this unexpected access.

Instead he sent a copy of everything in the MTE Project folder to Buzzkill for his expert analysis. Meantime Parlabane would have a look around for the kind of thing he might better understand.

Waiting for the files to transfer, he looked again at all the state-of-the-art kit, little of which seemed justified by simple programming needs. He went back to the desktop and clicked on Games, then opened the first of several directories inside, one name SR4. It opened a busy window full of programs, text documents and multiple sub-folders with arcanely technical names, a messy contrast to the sparse neatness of the MTE Project directory.

An executable file bearing the icon of a sword-wielding warrior decoded the abbreviation as standing for Sacred Reign 4: The Exalted, an online role-playing game.

He heard a muted ping from the headset and was alerted to an instant message from Buzzkill. It had only been a couple of minutes since Parlabane had sent the files, which seemed no time to make even a cursory analysis, but the hacker was full of surprises, and on this occasion apparently full of wonder.

Buzzkill: This is revolutionary. Seriously leading-edge stuff.

Parlabane eagerly typed a reply.

Me: What does it do?

Buzzkill: It allows you to view remotely stored information such as text and video on your computer, rendered in the form of pages.

He was confused. It sounded like Buzzkill was describing a web browser.

Me: You mean like Chrome or Firefox? What's revolutionary about that?

Buzzkill: I was being sarcastic. And it's not *like* Firefox. It *is* Firefox. He's just copy-pasted the code so that it will run in a compiler window. I'm guessing it's so that if someone was looking over his shoulder, it would give the impression he was working on something. I don't know what this guy's been doing with his time, but he's definitely not been programming.

What indeed, Parlabane asked himself, navigating back to the Sacred Reign folder.

He launched the game. It wouldn't let him log in without a username and password, but it did allow him to browse the specs and stats of existing profiles. There was only one. Elphinstone's avatar was named Necronimous and it appeared he was ranked as a demi-god. Parlabane guessed that took some serious commitment.

A sub-menu offered a highly detailed breakdown of session logs and in-game statistics. He scrolled up and down, taking a few notes and doing calculations.

Parlabane was agog.

It appeared that Elphinstone was clocking up sometimes nine hours a day in the fictional realm of Calastria, five or six days a week for the past few months, starting from the moment MTE set up operations in this office.

Parlabane quit out and opened the other folders, each of which contained launch shortcuts to games: Starfire, Age of Attrition and Death or Glory. All of these were principally multiplayer games, and their in-game stat logs showed that Elphinstone had been putting in regular, sustained play time on all of them.

Was that really what had happened here? Had Peter Elphinstone seduced a career-driven and well-salaried woman such as Diana Jager into being his wife simply so that he could sponge off her? Spending his days playing videogames at a fake job, keeping an authentic-looking work program handy in case anybody had reason to pop their head around the door?

No. Because though Elphinstone might be faking his work, MTE wasn't a fake company. Parlabane had seen the documents, and he had met one of the investors, an individual you would not want to be taking money from under false pretences. He thought of what Alan Harper had told him regarding Elphinstone's desperate final phone call, sounding scared and talking about being in over his head. Was that it, then: that he had snared Sam Finnegan with a lucrative but bafflingly techy-sounding proposal, naively credulous of the gangster's 'legitimate businessman' front? Had he been disastrously mistaken in thinking he could string his mark along until Finnegan stopped throwing good money after bad and wrote it off as a bad investment?

In that case, what of the other investor: Courtney Jean Lang, the former girlfriend whom Jager was convinced wasn't so former? Jager claimed Finnegan had leaned on Elphinstone in a recent email by saying that what he knew about her could make things very awkward.

Parlabane opened the email client and began skimming through the contents. There were several emails from Finnegan, but not the one Jager had mentioned, and none of them engaged a tone that was anything other than businesslike. In fact all of the emails – sent and received – were dry and formal, nothing chatty or personal about any of them. Everything was project-related: sounding out availability, commissioning work, dealing with invoices.

Jager had described her husband getting agitated over missed deadlines by a developer who had been sub-contracted to design the user interface. There was nothing here to give that impression. Everything appeared to be running smoothly.

Parlabane assumed that Elphinstone's more private correspondence with Finnegan – and perhaps others – was managed from a different email account that he only accessed from his permanently secured laptop. Everything on this machine appeared to have been sterilised for public consumption, which was perhaps why it hadn't been password protected.

Parlabane clicked the MTE Admin folder, where he found a small trove of official company documents. There was presentational material, alluding to MTE's intended place in the market: polished photos of a smiling young couple, trendy but not too hip, standing at a supermarket queue, the bloke holding out his phone rather than a credit card. Clearly they were trying out different taglines. One read: 'Bringing e-currency into everyday commerce.' Another stated: 'Small change, big business.'

He found scans of the Companies House documents he had already seen, as well as a heads of terms agreement which he hadn't. He opened it, expecting more boilerplate and legalese. Instead it caused his jaw to hang.

Finnegan and Lang had each agreed to invest four million pounds in MTE over the next five years. There was a schedule for the staggered tranches of payment, contingent upon delivery milestones, satisfactory progress reports and the meeting of minimum targets for further fresh investment.

Eight million: that's what they had agreed to sink into Peter Elphinstone's one-man show.

In a sub-folder named Financial, Parlabane found Elphinstone's rudimentary book-keeping file. He hadn't felt the need for any fancy accountancy software, just a word-processing doc keeping track of all transactions by date. According to this, he was being paid a modest salary of two thousand per month, with office rent, utilities bills and equipment purchases also coming out of the company account. The biggest regular outgoing, by a substantial margin, was a monthly payment of ten thousand pounds for what was listed only as 'KEI'.

Parlabane launched the browser and searched the abbreviation. The first results were a Suzuki car and the Korean Economic Institute. Further down he found a listing for Knowledge Ecology International: 'an NGO dealing with issues related to the effects of intellectual property on public health, cyberlaw and e-commerce, and competition policy.'

Cyberlaw and e-commerce. This was promising, but why would a tiny outfit like MTE be shelling them ten grand a month?

With Firefox running, it occurred to Parlabane to check Elphinstone's browsing history.

It didn't take long. Like his emails, his surfing appeared to have been as innocuous as his usage was light. He had few bookmarks and didn't seem to have googled much either. Given the hours he was spending playing videogames, perhaps it didn't leave much time for anything else, but Parlabane suspected this was another front.

A quick scan of his hard drive revealed that he had a second browser installed: a copy of Chrome without a desktop shortcut to advertise its presence. This one had a shedload of bookmarks, mostly gaming and social media stuff. Parlabane checked its history, and found it blank. Blank meant deleted, but why would you delete your history on a secret browser?

On a hunch, Parlabane keyed in the address for Holobase and navigated to the support forum. As soon as the log-in screen appeared, the browser auto-completed the username. The password field remained blank, but that didn't matter. He had seen what he needed to.

The username was KwikSkopa.

Peter Elphinstone had posted the sex tape link himself, and Parlabane was certain that it had also been him who uploaded the file.

Why in the name of Christ would he do that? Was this a strategy for precipitating a divorce, and thus setting the stage to claim half of Diana's estate in the settlement? After all, he could point to having thrown himself headlong into his business in order to provide for her, working punishing hours and stretching his finances thin. Nobody knew the truth about how he was really spending his time, and the NDA meant nobody ever would. With the right lawyer, he could have made himself out to be the victim here. There was no shortage of evidence that Diana's behaviour had been unreasonable: he could have called upon Alan Harper as a witness; bring up her illegally accessing his medical records; and then, of course, there was the legacy of the blog.

All of which looked a lot like a motive for Diana to have gotten rid of him after all, if it turned out she'd caught wind of this.

Parlabane returned to the filing cabinet. None of this was quite adding up. He needed raw data. If there was ten grand going out every month to this KEI, whoever or whatever it was, there would have to be paperwork. He tugged the drawer fully open and trained his torch inside. There was nothing under K/L, but he knew from personal experience how easy it was to misfile on the wrong side of these dividers. He pulled open the pocket marked I/J, where he found a thick and glossy cardboard folder bearing the name Arrowflint Corporate Insurance, stating that it contained 'Your Policy Documents'.

Parlabane opened it, scanning the print with the penlight. He had to read it twice to be sure he wasn't confusing a comma with a decimal point when he saw the figures involved.

KEI was not an organisation: it stood for key employee insurance.

Parlabane almost dropped the thing, so stunned was he by the implications.

MTE was a sham, and Peter must have every day been congratulating himself on fooling not only his wife into believing he had prospects, but also his investors into committing such substantial funds. Clearly, however, he had never read the small print on *this* thing before shoving it carelessly into a drawer. The document in Parlabane's hand demonstrated that – to joint policyholders Courtney Jean Lang and Sam Finnegan, at least – Peter Elphinstone was worth considerably more dead than alive.

DEATH BENEFITS

Parlabane connected a portable solid-state drive to Elphinstone's main computer and set about copying as much as he could: not only the MTE folders and the email cache, but the program files and system folder too, so that he could sift through them under less straitened circumstances. Having left it to transfer, he began shooting photos of the hard-copy documents on his phone, methodically working his way through the contents of the filing cabinet.

He checked his watch, mindful of the fact that the sun would be coming up soon, and that on an industrial estate such as this, people might be showing up for work any time from seven onwards. He figured the security system would have been reset by the Cautela guards upon exit. Given how swiftly they appeared on site the first time, he knew they would be back there even quicker if there was a second alarm, and their investigation might be less cursory too,

He hauled himself up through the ceiling again and made his way slowly and carefully across the suspended lattice before dropping out into the emergency stairwell, out of range of the sensors.

Dawn was breaking as his car sped south, a dim glow silhouetting the hills beneath clear skies. Watery winter sunshine was starting to streak through gaps in the pine trees, and in Parlabane's head a lot of things were coming into focus.

The Arrowflint policy was the kind of insurance you'd be wise to take out if you were planning to sink eight million pounds into a project that essentially came down to one man executing his genius idea: an idea that, in the interests of intellectual property protection, nobody else could be told.

However, what Parlabane had worked out was that neither Finnegan nor Lang was really intending to invest four million

389

pounds: they merely had to demonstrate that they intended to. It was all to provide the façade of authenticity that would justify them taking out a twelve-million-pound KEI policy to protect a non-existent investment in what they had sussed to be a phantom project.

Parlabane had seen the documents. Elphinstone had undergone the medical: he was fit and healthy, a non-smoker and moderate drinker on no medication. He had a clean driving licence, didn't own or drive any high-performance vehicles and didn't take part in any high-risk leisure activities. On top of that, he had no debt or criminal convictions and was the scion of land-owning aristocrats who could trace their ancestry back five centuries. Arrowflint Corporate Insurance had approved the policy, MTE commenced paying the premiums, and suddenly Peter Elphinstone was a living and breathing cheque for twelve million quid, made out to Finnegan and Lang.

The tricky part was that in order for them to cash out, he couldn't be living and breathing any more.

Parlabane understood then that Elphinstone's remains would never be found. Whatever happened to him on that final night had been long in the planning. A few hours after he walked out of Jager's garage, his BMW had gone into the river in an apparently tragic accident. Arrowflint weren't going to pay out on that, though: not without a body, and it could take seven years for Peter to be declared legally dead. However, if his wife were to be convicted of his murder, that changed everything.

As Parlabane followed the A9 on its snaking course between the rolling hills of the Elphinstone family's native Perthshire, he was struck by a shattering new possibility for what Sir Hamish had been scornfully alluding to during the telephone conversation Jager had overheard.

It didn't work the last time and it won't work now.

Parlabane had initially assumed Hamish was talking about Liz Miller, perhaps aware of Peter's abortive attempt to become engaged to her. But now he realised it was something else entirely.

Peter had been married before: to Courtney Jean Lang.

Maybe she was one of those misapprehending gold-diggers, and had married Peter for money he didn't have; or maybe Peter had married her because he thought the idea of becoming a husband and prospective father would soften Sir Hamish's position on sharing out the family fortune; and maybe neither of these things was true. But at some point, finding her route to the Elphinstone fortune was barred, Lang had come up with a new way of making Peter her golden ticket.

THE SILENT PARTNER

Parlabane sat in the reception area inside New Register House, sipping a large coffee to fend off the fatigue that was starting to catch up with him after his overnight endeavours. He had stopped off briefly at the flat to freshen up, then headed straight out so that he'd be here as soon as the place opened.

He was thinking about Sarah. It was unavoidable. Like so many locations in this city, he knew this one would always bring her to mind, even if he merely saw the address written down. She had once told him that physicians got patients to say the words 'West Register Street' when they were checking for speech disorders.

He was waiting for one of the staff to come back with information: an old contact of his who had worked there for decades. Archie Cairnduff had proven both a useful and easy person to cultivate as an ally. He was a man who liked to talk, perhaps because he spent the rest of his time among the silence of records and documents. He liked a dram too, and Parlabane had bought him a few over the years next door at the Café Royal, back in the days when the *Saltire* newspaper offices were a short walk away on North Bridge.

New Register House hosted the national register of births, marriages and deaths. Parlabane had gone there in search of confirmation that Peter Elphinstone had once been married, however briefly, to Courtney Jean Lang. As he sat on a plastic chair, looking at the closed door beyond which Archie was searching, he thought of how his own marriage was recorded in this building somewhere, and wondered whether in here at least it still survived, waiting for the fatal update that would wipe it out.

He now understood that marriage itself could have its own birth and death. Dead marriages. Dead souls.

Parlabane allowed himself a wry smile. In the unfinished Gogol book of that name, the title referred to dead peasants. KEI, it turned out, was alternatively referred to as 'dead peasant insurance'.

It reminded him that what he had discovered overnight meant even though Sarah was always going to creep into his thoughts from time to time, right now he had reason to look forward with hope, rather than only back with regret.

Lucy.

He could make this work, he was sure. He wasn't going to tell her until he had harder proof, but it would surely change things between them were Parlabane to be the one who delivered some kind of justice for herself and her brother. Much as he hated the term, he realised that what Lucy was looking for from this horrible mess was closure: she came to him with the suspicion that Peter had been the victim of something callous and underhand, and Parlabane would finally be able to offer her vindication, as well as binding answers. What comfort she might take from that remained to be seen, though it had to be better than the hollow void of not knowing, the state she was in when he first encountered her.

As these thoughts passed through his mind, it suddenly struck Parlabane to wonder why Lucy never said that Peter had been married before. In all those concerned conversations about what a vulnerable person he was, and how problematic some of his relationships had been, she had never mentioned that Diana was not his first wife.

Had he got this wrong after all? Maybe there had been no marriage, and Peter's relationship with Lang had been a secret from everybody. But if that was the case, it would be a hell of a coincidence if his sister happened to recruit her as a silent partner in his ostensibly grand venture.

Lucy told Parlabane that she had procured the investors in MTE. That made sense with regard to Finnegan, whom she had previously worked with, but she admitted she knew almost nothing about Courtney Jean Lang. They had never met, in fact: Lucy had got in touch via a friend of a friend.

For some reason Cecily flashed into his mind, that out-of-focus possibility he couldn't quite comprehend. Their families were close since they were children: the three of them went back decades. He recalled Lucy suggesting there was something going on behind the scenes between Cecily and Peter.

Courtney Jean Lang had blog posts and a Facebook page but there were no pictures of this woman on her profiles.

Courtney. Cecily.

Could it be? Jager had mentioned she wore Blackberry and Bay, the scent he had smelled on his business card, the same scent Peter had given his wife as a Christmas present. But Cecily was marrying Sir Hamish. He still couldn't see how it fitted.

'Jack, this is mission control, come in.'

Parlabane snapped back to earth, wondering how many times Archie had already tried to get his attention. He climbed to his feet and approached the reception desk. From Archie's expression he could already tell he'd come up negative.

'It was definitely *Peter* Elphinstone you wanted to know about?'

'Yes. How come?'

'Because it was his sister who had a short-lived marriage. Petronella Lucille. Married six years ago and annulled shortly after by mutual consent.'

'Annulled? Why?'

Archie shook his head and gave him a strained look.

'I'm not permitted to say.'

'What if you accidentally left the document lying around while you were answering the phone and I just happened to catch a glimpse?'

'Seriously, Jack, no. You can't ask me this.'

Parlabane shrugged. He understood, and he wasn't going to ask Archie to cross a line for him, even if he thought there was a chance he'd say yes.

'Can you tell me who the guy was, at least?'

Archie smiled.

'That much I can do.'

EXILE

The Abbey View bar sat on the main road into Melrose, opposite the rugby ground. It was an unpretentious place, the kind of pub that had its own kind of elegance about the fittings and the furniture, but from which you'd probably get barred for describing any of it as 'an aesthetic'. Parlabane found it comfortingly old-fashioned, and he was in need of a bit of comfort right then.

It was lunchtime by the time he had driven down from Edinburgh. He didn't have much of an appetite but he knew he ought to eat. He hadn't slept in about thirty hours, and if he added hypoglycaemia to the mix he would be too cranky to engage anyone in fruitful conversation. He ordered a burger and a pint of a local brew called Dark Horse.

'Is Gordon Holman around?'

The barmaid was an attractive woman in her forties with a plummy accent that made Parlabane picture her in a riding helmet and jodhpurs.

She glanced at the clock.

'He's usually in about half past one.'

'How long has he had the place, do you know?'

She looked up, calculating, then seemed surprised at her own answer.

'Must be six years. I'd have thought less, but it's six years sure enough. Where does the time go?'

Six years. That was about right.

Parlabane took his pint across to a table by the window. From the pub's stereo, he heard the military cadence and tinkling piano that comprised the first bars of a song by Augustines, entitled 'Headlong Into the Abyss'.

No kidding.

He had been venturing deeper down the rabbit-hole with every step, and it kept getting darker and more labyrinthine. Since learning Peter definitely hadn't been married before, he was now convinced that it had been Cecily Greysham-Ellis who was in his flat that night, and that Sir Hamish had been alluding to Liz Miller after all when Diana overheard him on the phone. His scorn at an unsuitable fiancée might be about to prove ironic in a very costly way.

He recalled what Lucy said when they first talked about Cecily.

Just because you come from money doesn't mean you're not a gold-digger. In fact, wouldn't appearing to be uninterested in money be the perfect cover for a gold-digger?

If his fiancée turned out to have a double identity, Sir Hamish might be in for a nasty surprise: or worse, because if Cecily was also Courtney, then it was possible she was going to end up with not only the insurance payout, but the family inheritance too. For that to happen, Peter wouldn't be the only Elphinstone to meet with a tragic demise shortly after getting married.

To get to the bottom of this, and quite possibly to save the life of its ennobled head, Parlabane needed to find out more about this vastly wealthy but utterly dysfunctional family. Finding Lucy's ex-husband seemed the obvious place to start. He just couldn't bring himself to ask Lucy about this herself, because he'd have to tell her why, and he wasn't ready to do that yet.

Parlabane clocked Gordon Holman for the man he was searching for the second he came through the door, even before he made his way behind the bar. He looked about Parlabane's age, something of the veteran rock fan about him. He was wearing biker-style boots, black jeans and a Mogwai T-shirt. He guessed it was Holman's iPod feeding the hi-fi.

Parlabane approached the bar, bringing his empty plate as a helpful gesture.

'Gordon Holman?'

'Aye?'

An uncertain smile indicated curiosity rather than suspicion.

'My name is Jack Parlabane. I'm a journalist. I need to talk to you about Lucy Elphinstone.'

Holman took a slight step back from the bar, stiffening.

'That's not something I'm prepared to discuss.'

'It would be off the record, I only—'

'On or off the record, I'm not prepared to talk about that area of my life. Now, can I help you with anything else? A refill.'

He was keeping his tone polite, but the politeness itself sounded like a warning to back off. Parlabane had never been good at heeding such warnings.

'Did you see what happened to Peter Elphinstone?'

'Sure. Now they're saying his wife bumped him off.'

'I think she's being set up. I'm trying to stop an innocent woman from going to jail. If there's anything you know . . .'

'I've told you twice already. I won't tell you again.'

Parlabane did a quick calculation.

'You bought this place six years ago, right? You got hush money, didn't you?'

Holman's expression turned grim and he put down the glass he had been drying.

'I want you out of here right now. If you don't leave at once, I'm calling the police.'

That was as much of an answer as Parlabane was going to get: even admitting a confidentiality agreement existed would put the guy in violation of it. He raised his hands and backed out of the door.

Parlabane went for a slow walk around Melrose Abbey and then sought out the tranquillity of Harmony Garden across the road, finding a quiet spot to sit for a while despite the cold. He wanted space to think, and after downing a pint he had to kill some time before he could get behind the wheel again, especially running on so little sleep. Maybe all he needed was some proper kip, and after that he'd be able to see whatever he was missing.

Lucy's ex wasn't going to allow him an easy route into the murky depths of the Elphinstone family history; or rather, it was more likely Sir Hamish's deep pockets were barring the doors. But maybe he should be taking the more direct route. After all, it was Cecily who had blocked off Parlabane's access to her intended; and not, he suspected, in order to protect him.

He felt a vibration against his chest and pulled out his phone. It was a text from Buzzkill.

Necronimous just showed up in Calastria.

Parlabane spent a bleary moment reminding himself what Buzzkill was referring to, then endured a further, vertiginous few seconds as he came to realise what this meant. He was grateful he was sitting down.

'You have got to be kidding me,' he said aloud, staring incredulously at the handset.

Necronimous was Peter Elphinstone's in-game character, a unique online identity to whom only he had the login details.

The fucker was still alive.

GAME THEORY

With a single line of text on his phone it was as though Buzzkill had typed in a code and simply decrypted the chaos of which he had spent so long trying to make sense. It suddenly resolved itself into a clear picture, utterly unrecognisable from what he had been looking at moments before.

Elphinstone's BMW had ended up at the bottom of the river not to frame Diana Jager for a murder she didn't commit, but to frame her for a murder that never took place. The fly bastard was planning to cash in on his own life insurance policy.

This hadn't been cooked up between Lang and Finnegan: it had been cooked up between Lang and Elphinstone, with Finnegan merely a backer. As Peter wasn't among the named policy holders, he would need to have absolute trust in one of his partners in order to get his share of the money, and that was never going to be a Glasgow drug dealer. It made sense then that his collaborator would be someone with whom he had been secretly in a relationship going back years, possibly decades. They may never have been married, but these clandestine lovers had cooked up a way to get rich and give themselves the lifestyle they wanted.

Now Parlabane understood where Liz Miller fitted into the bigger picture: she had been earmarked as the original candidate to take the fall for a non-existent killing. These conspirators had clearly been working on this for a long time. A couple of years back, Elphinstone had set about wooing a woman who already had a conviction for the attempted murder of her partner. This would have made her the perfect mark, but Miller bailed when she thought things were moving too fast. Things had moved pretty fast the second time too, when Elphinstone embarked upon a whirlwind romance with someone else who had shadows of death and venge-ance looming ominously over her past.

Parlabane doubted chance had played any part in Jager crossing paths with the new IT tech who had recently transferred to a post at her hospital. In fact, he was sure that whatever was wrong with her computer that day had been Elphinstone's doing.

He had, as she claimed, seduced her, but for more brutally cynical purposes than Jager could have possibly imagined. And having secured a wedding ring on her finger, he had set about creating plausible reasons for her to kill him, culminating in his leaking of the sex tape and a single act of violence that was deliberately intended to leave a mark.

The theft of her money would have played in as a factor too, though Parlabane reckoned that was a secondary consideration. The primary motive was that Finnegan was demanding a bigger share of the final payout, presumably due to being the one who was fronting the insurance premiums, and Elphinstone was trying to offset that.

Finnegan wouldn't only have been providing money, though. Given what McLeod told him, Snobby Sam had connections that would have proven vital to the creation of a new legal identity for the recently departed, including official documents – forged or fraudulently acquired – such as a birth certificate, national insurance number and passport. Now Elphinstone was in the wind, lying low God knows where under a new name.

Years in the planning, years more in the execution, and it had been going perfectly for them until only a few moments ago.

When you put in the hours, when you make the long-term commitment, you've got to feel you're entitled to your rewards. Elphinstone had quested several months in the virtual realms of Sacred Reign, pretending to be at work while he waited for his marriage to reach a plausible point of crisis. The guy had spent arguably more waking hours in Calastria than he had in the real world, building up his character to demi-god status. There was no way he was going to simply abandon that and start again: not when he had several more months to kill while he awaited the murder conviction and consequent jackpot. And certainly not when there was nobody in the online universe who knew his real-world name anyway.

Parlabane texted Buzzkill, asking whether it was possible to trace an individual player's IP address. The response pinged back a few seconds later.

> The game servers log all IPs, but they have security measures in place to prevent unauthorised access to that information.

It took him a moment to detect that Buzzkill was being sarcastic. Unauthorised access was where Buzzkill lived.

His phone vibrated again a few moments later, the next message showing a string of digits and dots: an IP number.

Parlabane sent his reply, thanking the hacker for coming through once again and mentally adding another favour to the Faustian tab.

Then Buzzkill texted a fourth time.

> I can do better than that. Geolocation came up trumps. Would you like his current address?

He allowed himself a smile.

They must have known they were playing a long game: one that would take a few years to pay out, but for that magnitude of return, it would be worth it in the end. The big catch was that the scheme involved Peter becoming married to someone else. It had to be tough: being apart, grabbing those stolen weekends for secret liaisons; tougher still that part of the deal required Peter to be fucking another woman. That was why he had taken solace in the photographs and videos of his true love that he kept on his laptop. But very soon, they must have told themselves, they would be reunited: together at last, with a rich future to look forward to.

Parlabane intended to be there to share the moment.

A BETTER LIFE

The last of the dragon-riders had crashed to earth under a barrage of flame-damage unleashed by his fire-sword, hailed by cheers from the warriors manning the ramparts. This latest attempt to storm his citadel had ended in a rout, a fragile alliance of rival guilds no match for the small but powerful force he commanded. News of the failed sortie would travel far and fast. The same players who had attacked him would soon be queuing up to join his ranks. His name was one of the most-quoted in the realm of Calastria and on the Sacred Reign message boards. He was Necronimous, the wizard who had become a demi-god. But it was nothing compared to the miraculous transformation he had effected in the real world.

As the noise of battle faded, he could hear the sound of a car pulling up outside, slightly muffled by his headphones. He glanced out of the window and his heart soared as he saw her leaning into the front seat of a gold Mercedes, paying the cab driver. She was here. At last she was here.

'*Bon jeu, tous le monde,*' he said into the headset mic, signing off for a while. He had always logged on to a French Sacred Reign server since the creation of his character and had spoken only French in-game. The subscription and payment details were in his new name, a persona he had been building up online for years longer than Necronimous, one that had credentials in the real world too. This place was rented in that name, the utilities were billed to it and the new graphics card he had ordered this morning would bear it on the address label too.

He spoke French like a native. It had always been a big deal with his family: they had a private tutor, and when they came here on holiday, there was a no-English rule. His father often talked about how throughout Britain in centuries past, French was the language of the high-born, stressing that only the peasants spoke the local tongue.

Peter had enjoyed those holidays, the freedom of disappearing off to the village, away from the stultifying atmosphere of a house that always seemed oppressive despite its sprawl. That was because any building containing his parents was oppressive. They were bloodless, joyless wretches, trapped by inheritance and expectation, lacking the imagination or *joi de vivre* to live what could otherwise so easily have been remarkable lives. Bad enough that they contrived to be so miserable despite their privilege, but why were they so bloody determined that he should end up that way too?

The only thing he didn't enjoy about those French summers was the absence of his computer, insisted upon by his father. Every year he paid a driver to haul a van full of riding gear, bikes, fishing tackle and even two canoes, so it wasn't as if it was a logistical issue. The bastard just hated how much pleasure Peter derived from it.

Games had always been his refuge and his retreat in a home full of tension, conflict and obligation, a cold regime governed by the most immutable paradigms. Games were a place of freedom, of exploration, of imagination. That was still true today, but they were no longer the thing he cared about most.

It was at the age of fifteen that he had discovered a different source of comfort, a new realm full of pleasure and excitement: a refuge and retreat full of human warmth and companionship.

A real world of love.

And Jesus, what a pale shadow of it he had been forced to endure in order to pull this off: living a lie for the best part of a year. There was only one woman on this earth he would go through that for, and it was hell being away from her. She was here now, though, and his body was already tingling with the anticipation of her embrace.

As he made his way eagerly towards the front door, he briefly wondered where Diana was now. Held in a cell, no doubt, on remand, waiting for the trial.

As was he.

Did he feel bad about what he had done to her? About what would happen to her?

There were times when he had enjoyed Diana's company. They had shared some good times, no question. You couldn't go through all they had together without feeling something. But he had learned from the best when it came to compartmentalising. Throughout his life he had seen how his father could be charming and open with people, warm and close as old friends, and then treat them like objects as soon as circumstance required it.

When a family has had money for centuries, it is because it passes down the principles that ensure they keep hold of it. Didn't people notice how that other Diana, the 'queen of hearts' and our national patron saint, left precisely nothing to a single charity? You stay rich by keeping your money, and by understanding at all times that other people are quite simply worth less than you.

Other people are *worth less*.

His father had drummed that into him from an early age. Other people's value is to be measured in terms of what they can give you, what they can be used for. That doesn't mean you can't be civil to them, but you never lose sight of the difference in your social standing.

So yes, it was a pity for Diana. It was nothing personal: merely collateral damage. He didn't wish her any ill, but if he was asked to do it again to someone else, then he wouldn't hesitate. Peter and his future wife were building a life together: a life they had worked for, a life they deserved, and it was finally within their grasp.

He opened the door as she was making her way up the path. The moment she saw him she dropped her case and ran to his embrace.

'Oh God, Peter. I've missed you so much.'

He pressed against her, kissing her deeply.

'Courtney.'

UNDONE

As Parlabane pulled out of Orly and hit the hire car's accelerator, he tried not to think how long it had been since he lay down in a bed and slept properly. He had managed to doze briefly on the two flights it took him to reach Paris from Edinburgh, but cumulatively he must only have had his eyes closed for forty minutes. Sleep wasn't an option right now, but nor was it a necessity. He was running on caffeine and adrenaline; nothing kept him buzzing quite like the scent of an exclusive.

The sat-nav guided him towards his destination through gathering darkness and swirling rain. It took a couple of hours, following the GPS coordinates Buzzkill had supplied. They were a precise fix on the IP address from where Peter Elphinstone had been logging into his Sacred Reign account, most recently that same afternoon while Parlabane was booking flights and doing some last-minute shopping.

It was after eleven when he got there, having to place great faith in Buzzkill's numbers as the route led him down ever narrowing roads beyond the last village. The rain had let up at least, though there was a cold wind whipping past as he opened the car door and travelled the last forty or fifty yards on foot so as to keep the car out of sight.

It was an isolated cottage, set back from the single-track road. Parlabane approached cautiously, using the glow of his phone for light, though not engaging the full torch app. The grounds were unkempt and the exterior somewhat ramshackle: not quite where he pictured a tech geek holing up, though an icon on his phone reported that the house was rocking a strong Wi-Fi signal. This was definitely the place. Parlabane guessed it was either a fixer-upper or merely a temporary bolthole. Either way, Peter's accommodation

405

budget was intended to jack up dramatically in the near future.

Parlabane could see a glow from behind closed curtains through a window on the left towards the rear. He could hear music: the only time he was ever grateful to be listening to James Blunt, as it would cover the sound of his approach.

He proceeded on soft feet, walking over grass to avoid the gravel path. There was a Citroën C3 parked on a narrow driveway to the right of the house: uneven flagstones overgrown with grass and weeds. He crouched next to it and attached a GPS tracker out of sight inside the wheel arch. Stuff that was once the preserve of the security services, you could now pick up in Halfords.

It would be easy enough to get photographic proof in the morning, stay out of sight and take the shot from distance with a telephoto lens, but ideally Parlabane wanted face-to-face confirmation. He wanted to look the guy in the eye and witness the moment he realised his plan had crashed and burned. One of the potential consequences was that he might go on the run and try to disappear: hence the tracker.

Another potential consequence was that Peter might turn violent, as Lucy had specifically warned could happen when he felt cornered. That was why Parlabane hadn't yet ruled out the telephoto option. For now he was simply getting the lie of the land, and would decide on his play once he knew what he was dealing with.

As he got closer to the house he observed that there was a sheet of paper taped to the front door. He held up his phone and read it by the glow from its screen. His French wasn't great, but clearly they were expecting a delivery the next morning and didn't want woken up to answer the door. It stated that the back door was unlocked and to leave the parcel in the kitchen. Couriers needed a signature before they were allowed to follow such instructions, and the note was signed off: '*Merci, Courtney Jean Lang.*'

Merci indeed, thought Parlabane.

He ventured around to the rear of the building, circling right to stay away from the window where the light and music were coming from. The back door was a sturdy old thing, heavy and weathered and easily a hundred years old. Parlabane reckoned the lock mechanism would have taken him no time to pick, but either way the biggest challenge was opening it quietly and hoping it didn't squeak or shudder. He put a firm shoulder to it and twisted the handle, nudging it forward in a smooth and controlled movement.

He stepped inside, leaving it slightly ajar. The kitchen was in semi-darkness, light spilling through the partially open doorway to the hall. It was a large and airy room, dominated by a heavy wooden table in the centre. Parlabane noticed a couple of unopened letters lying on it, the envelopes bearing the automated print of utility bills. He held his phone close and read the addressee: Courtney Jean Lang.

The music still played from somewhere along the hall, but he could hear human sounds becoming louder beneath it: rhythmic male grunting and the moans and shrieks of a woman in the growing throes of orgasm. It ceased shortly thereafter, and was replaced by the quieter, muffled sounds of the afterglow: billing and cooing, giggling.

Then a male voice spoke up, loud and distinct, the accent 'middle-class Scottish', as Diana had described it.

'Yeah, stick a couple of slices on for me as well. I'll be through in a sec.'

He heard a door open down the hall, followed by footsteps. She was heading for the kitchen.

If he moved now, he could maybe get out before he was seen, though he wouldn't be able to close the door without it being heard. They had just had sex, though: they would never be more vulnerable or unsuspecting as this.

He held his ground. When she walked in here in about five seconds, he would get hard proof of Cecily Greysham-Ellis's secret alias, while down the hall lay incontrovertible evidence that Diana Jager was innocent.

Parlabane's phone was already recording everything, but for back-up he set his camera to video mode and placed it down on the table next to the letters.

That was when it struck him that he was in France, where Courtney and Jean were both men's names.

Parlabane felt a sudden lurching, like the floor was shifting beneath him.

Courtney Jean Lang wasn't his lover's alias: it was Peter's new identity, acquired no doubt with the help of Sam Finnegan. This meant Peter didn't need to trust the other beneficiary named on the insurance policy: he *was* the other beneficiary.

Parlabane's mind raced, trying to calculate the consequences. He couldn't see how this changed anything substantial, so why did he have the gut-wrenching sensation that he had missed something crucial, something that had been right in front of him the entire time?

Why did he have the horrible fear that he was about to be blindsided?

His heart began thumping and he involuntarily took a step back.

The door pushed open and she walked in wearing just a T-shirt, oblivious as she reached for the switch. The lights came on and she was revealed to him at last.

Peter's conspirator. Peter's lover. Peter's sister.

A FAMILY AFFAIR

He had been sent to spend the night in the unused maid's quarters, a cold and largely unused little room containing only a bed and a nightstand. No books, no music, no television and definitely no computer. This was punishment for when his father discovered the phone bill he had run up. It was back in the dial-up days, and what did the tight-fisted bastard expect when he wouldn't spring for a deal on a dedicated ISDN line for the internet? Even paying at that per-minute rate, it was a drop in the ocean for a man of his means, who thought nothing of spending twice that on a single bottle of wine.

He had been sitting there on the bed, still tearful after the ferocity of the dressing-down: his father's words about him 'never amounting to anything if he wasted his time on computers' seeping into his psyche like poison. Then there was a knock at the door, and Lucy came in. She put her arm around him. It started as a hug, really. But then it became something else, and in that moment how they saw each other changed for ever.

Yes, it was an aberration. Early on, they frequently forswore what they were doing and vowed it would never be repeated. Then a dam would break, and it never felt like it was only one of them who cracked first. It always felt mutual, almost telepathic, and it always went that bit further than the last time, until there were no barriers left to cross.

They started off being discreet to the point of paranoid, but gradually they came to realise what had developed between them was so out of the ordinary that no one ever thought to look for it. It seemed amazing to them: as though their relationship was invisible, a secret protected by an enchantment that meant nobody else could see what was right in front of them. But inevitably they took that for granted.

They got careless. They got caught.

Father acted as though they had done it specifically to hurt and offend him, like they had planned the whole thing as a personal affront. In his mind, of course, it was always about him.

That was when he told them they were getting nothing: that they were not only disinherited, but would be receiving no financial assistance once they left school. He dressed it up as something else when he was explaining it to other people – some bollocks about learning self-sufficiency – but it was his sulk, his vengeance.

He relented slightly with regard to their university careers, but only so that he could ensure the pair of them weren't staying in the same city, terrified of the shame if some rumour got out. Hence Lucy went to Edinburgh and Peter to St Andrews.

It wasn't a great distance, but the fact was that they could have gone to Aberdeen and Oxford and it would have made no difference.

They thought Father's rage would pass, that he would climb down if they gave the impression it had simply been a weird phase that was now over. And at that stage, for a while at least, they did try to convince *themselves* that it was over. Lucy even got married.

It had been painful for Peter, but they talked about how it might be for the best: that he would find someone too, and they would put all this behind them. Furthermore, they hoped that there would be fatted calf on the wedding menu for Sir Hamish's prodigal daughter, and both his heirs would be restored to his good graces; not to mention his will.

Unfortunately he remained immovable and unforgiving, though it didn't help that during Lucy's short-lived marriage, their attempts at abstinence ultimately proved as successful as their efforts at discretion. Lucy's husband Gordon discovered them. It cost Father money to cover up the mess, and they knew then that there was no way back.

Husband, wife. Brother, sister. These were only labels, definitions. You were defined by your actions and feelings, not by nomenclature. You might be married to someone, but that didn't mean you were in love with them. Not like the two of them were in love.

They didn't choose this: that was what nobody ever appreciated. Other people would be appalled by their breaking of this sacred taboo, but other people didn't have what they had: this kind of bond, this kind of unity. And that disapproval only forced them closer together. They understood quite implicitly that they didn't need anybody else, and that nobody else mattered.

Nor did other people know what it was like to be brought up so close to all of that wealth and never be allowed to enjoy the freedoms and pleasures it could unlock. They had been forced to endure all of the duty and responsibility that was drummed into them about their heritage, but now that they had come of age, they were being denied its privileges.

They had often talked about living abroad, starting a life together somewhere nobody knew them. Even then, they knew that one of them would need a new identity. That was when the idea of faking Peter's death first came up. That way, he could become somebody else, cutting off all ties to the past. They could even get married. He remembered discussing it one intoxicating night, Lucy telling him how this Finnegan bloke she once worked with had all kinds of dodgy contacts that might make this possible. As a joke, Peter said it was a shame he didn't have life insurance.

That was when their plan was born.

This time he was the one who would be getting married, living a lie and sleeping with someone else. It would take a lot of work and sacrifice, years in the planning and the execution, but they could both work all their lives and come nowhere close to earning this much money.

It took patience to find the right candidate. There were women who were perfect but to whom he couldn't get close, or who would never give him a second look; and there were women to whom he did get close, only to find their other credentials didn't seem as convincing as he had envisaged.

Liz Miller had been ideal, but he had blown it with his impatience. He had moved too fast at a sensitive stage and she had started to sense something was wrong.

Then his job with Cobalt had taken him to Inverness, where

411

he found out that this scary surgeon the IT guys detested was none other than the infamous Doctor Diana Jager. Having worked in hospital IT in the past, he knew all about Bladebitch, so when Lucy delved deeper into her background, discovering the accidental death of her student flatmate, they realised they had a winner.

THE VIOLENT KIND

They stared at each other, mutually uncomprehending, mutually horrified.

She let out a startled gasp but she did not scream, because although he was an intruder, he was not a stranger. It took her a moment to place him in this context, to work out why he shouldn't be here, and then to realise the enormity of the fact that he was.

Parlabane felt like he was falling. That lurching beneath his feet had opened a chasm that was swallowing him.

Headlong into the abyss.

He had thought he was venturing into the darkness on Lucy's behalf, ever wary of dragging her down with him. But all the time, she had been the one leading him there, and he hadn't seen it.

She had been in the same position as Peter: raised with the trappings of great wealth but denied the privileges and freedoms to which she must have thought she would be one day entitled. She was the one who came to Parlabane with her doubts over the accident, and if she had never done that, then certain apparently damning evidence against Diana would never have come to light.

Follow me down.

Jesus, it was so obvious now. She had given him a list of names: some of them unknowingly primed by Peter to pass on just the right information. Now he understood why Alan Harper was puzzled that Peter should be reaching out to him of all people, confiding in him about his married life and depicting his wife as a controlling obsessive. It was so that Harper would feel the need to unburden himself later, troubled by the fact that Peter had left a distraught message on the night he apparently died, worrying about being in too deep.

Follow me down.

413

When Parlabane had begun to think there was probably nothing more to the story than how it appeared, he had gone for a drink with Lucy, at her request. She left before him, and shortly afterwards he was abducted, drugged, driven around in a van and then dumped back at his flat. All he knew about his assailant was her distinctive scent, which Lucy knew to be Blackberry and Bay, because Peter had given it to Diana as a present.

Follow me down.

Peter had primed Harkness by mentioning Diana's student-years tragedy, and then Lucy had subtly nudged Parlabane in the right direction so that he would track down Emily Gayle. She said there was a friend Diana was still in touch with from her time at Oxford, but pretended she couldn't remember the name, so that he didn't twig he was being manipulated.

She had been part of the insurance con from the start. She had recruited the money and assistance of Sam Finnegan, and it had then been her crucial role to drip-feed the story to some mug of a journalist who would think he was discovering all of this for himself.

Somewhere amidst the maelstrom he found his voice. He surprised himself by how calm he sounded. He surprised himself that he didn't scream with hurt and anger.

'Hello, Lucy.'

He heard hurried footsteps, Peter having emerged from the bedroom to realise something was wrong. In a moment he was at his sister's side, his ashen face a mix of incomprehension, outrage and fear. Like Lucy he had pulled on a T-shirt, the kitchen being too cold for sitting around in the altogether. He had a bandage around his shin: a shallow place to cut to the bone.

'Who the hell are you? What are you doing in our house?'

It was Lucy who answered, her voice low and broken.

'Peter, this is Jack Parlabane.'

It was possible to see it in his eyes the moment he deduced what this meant: the flash of panic Diana had described.

'Sounds like you shag pretty well for a deid bloke. But if you thought you were well fucked five minutes ago, I've got some difficult news.'

Peter looked around, frantic, calculating, like he was searching for a way out. Parlabane couldn't see one.

He edged past Lucy and lunged towards a worktop, hauling open a drawer and brandishing a carving knife.

'Peter, what are you doing?' she asked, tremulous, afraid.

'He's the only one who knows. If we get rid of him . . . if we . . .'

He couldn't even bring himself to name it. That didn't augur well for his ability to do it, but the guy was desperate, and right then he believed Parlabane was the only thing standing between him and several million pounds.

'I'm not the only one, Peter. My associate knows where I am and knows everything else too. This phone has been uploading video of everything since I got here. It's being relayed straight to Detective Superintendent Catherine McLeod of Police Scotland. Believe me: this is over.'

Peter began advancing. His eyes were wild, his hands shaking. He *needed* to believe there was still a way out of this.

'Why did you come alone, then? You're lying.'

Parlabane held his ground. He knew the back door was still open, so flight remained an option, but he had a reason to believe it wouldn't come to that.

Peter stopped. His expression was aghast, haunted as he gripped the knife in front of his face. He wasn't coming any closer, but Parlabane knew he still needed to talk him down.

'The hardest part of this was when you had to hit her, wasn't it?'

Parlabane saw that flash in his eyes again: an awareness of his own vulnerability.

'It was crucial to the plan: on the night you disappeared, you had to provoke a final argument, and you had to hit her. Diana told me. She thought you were shaking because you were angry, but you were trembling because of what you knew you had to do. You had to hit her hard enough to leave a mark for the cops to see. Doing that took more guts than cutting yourself.'

Peter didn't have a brutal streak, cornered or otherwise: it was merely another of Lucy's lies, part of the narrative they had constructed.

415

'It was only one punch, but it was harder than all the other stuff, wasn't it? Ruining Diana's life, pretending to be in love with her, setting her up for a murder conviction: you could do all that. It was a game: a real-life role-playing game. That's second nature to you, but violence is not. When you bundled me into that van with a sack over my head, it wasn't just so that I couldn't see your faces. It was so that you couldn't see mine.'

Parlabane watched him crumble as he spoke. His eyes closed, wincing in remembrance of the punch, then tears fell as he let the knife slip from his grasp.

Lucy ran to him, putting her arms around his shoulders as he fell to a crouch. Down on the cold tiles they clung on to each other, helpless and broken. They flinched from Parlabane's gaze, as though in his eyes they saw how they would be regarded when the world found out. They were wretched, naked in their shame. In that moment, he understood that not everything they had told him and Diana about their upbringing was a lie. He could see that they didn't choose this, and for that he felt a brief moment of sympathy.

But they did choose what they had done to Diana, and what they had tried to do to Liz Miller. They did choose what they had done to him.

Eventually, Lucy looked up at Parlabane.

'What was the hardest part for you?' he asked her. 'Faking that you liked me?'

She looked away again, said nothing.

MORNING SICKNESS

Ali was coming out of the toilets when she saw Diana Jager making her way through the station, heading for the exit. Ali knew she was in the building: she had come in to give some more statements, this time helping shape the prosecution. They made eye contact before Ali had a chance to scope the passageway and pretend not to see her.

She wasn't feeling so great, and she had eight hours to get through. Kicking off the shift with a dollop of awkward mixed in with a ladle-full of guilt and regret was not going to make it pass any quicker.

Jager didn't scowl or indeed visibly emote in any way, but that wasn't going to stop Ali projecting.

The good (and innocent) doctor's attention was principally fixed on the reception area ahead, where Calum Weatherson was ready to take her home. He was the guy they had seen getting into his Porsche outside the cottage that time. Turned out she was having an affair with him before all this kicked off, so maybe that explained *some* of why Ali had thought she was acting suspicious.

Rodriguez was waiting for her, a newspaper tucked under his arm as he stood against a wall, all set to begin his shift. She was particularly pleased to see him on a day like this. He always had an energy and positivity about him that she could leech off of when she was running low.

The newspaper was folded but Ali could see Jager's eyes staring out at her from the front page, and couldn't help but feel a stab of accusation.

'You all right? You look a bit, well, like you'd be pale if you were, you know.'

'I'm okay. Just had a mutual eyeball with Diana Jager, that's all.'

'Bet you wish we'd kept quiet for two minutes and let somebody else take the call that night. I've heard CID are requesting we get banned from responding to an RTA ever again.'

He looked like he was only half joking. Ali knew that they'd be getting grief over this for about a decade, but that was polis for you. They never forgot.

'I felt awful, though: seeing her, knowing what I put her through. I feel like I ought to write to her and apologise.'

'Absolutely not. That's not how it works, and you know that. It wasn't you who put her through anything.'

'I played my part, though. I was suspicious of her from day one, and I was completely wrong.'

'No. You were suspicious from day one because something about the situation *felt* wrong, and it turned out you were right about that. You've got good instincts, Ali.'

'So I was wrong but for the right reasons. I'm afraid that doesn't feel reassuring.'

'Well, it should. It's better than being right for the wrong reasons, because that just means you were lucky. Being wrong for the right reasons will serve you better in the long run.'

Ali nodded. She knew he was right, but that didn't make her feel any better in the here and now.

They began walking out to their car. She thought back to their first shift together, which felt like months ago. It had been less than a fortnight.

'Hell of a way to christen your new post,' she said.

'Christ, you're not wrong. My days at the Met already seem like another lifetime. I'm starting to get a handle on this place. I feel like a different person up here.'

'Aye, you'll be fighting off the girls with a taser, soon enough. I mean, when you're ready for all that,' Ali added, realising it might have been inappropriate.

'No doubt,' he said.

Rodriguez smiled, that strange wee look on his face that he wore whenever she skirted this area.

'Except, they won't be girls.'

It took her a second, then a lot of things belatedly clicked into place. He'd even asked her about being religious, sounding her out in case she was going to have a problem with it if he told her. Bloody hell, how had she missed it?

'Some poliswoman I am. Can't see what's right under my nose.'

Ali burst out laughing. She couldn't help it. A whole host of different tensions gave way and she simply lost it. Rodriguez began laughing too, the pair of them ending up like a couple of hysterical kids.

Eventually she managed to compose herself enough to suggest they get in the car and actually get to work. Rodriguez asked if he could drive, eagerly skipping around to the other side of the car when she acquiesced.

Ali climbed into the passenger side a little gingerly, wincing at another twinge of discomfort as she slid into the seat.

Rodriguez noticed it. His tone was sincere and concerned.

'You sure you're all right? You're clutching your tummy there like John Hurt in *Alien*.'

'I'm fine. Just my time of the month.'

HER DAY IN COURT (II)

Nothing transpired the way we intended, and yet as the jury files out to consider its verdict, I can't escape the feeling that it worked out the way it should.

This was not meant to be my trial. Diana was supposed to be in the dock, and I was supposed to be the one watching from the gallery: looking on in anger and outrage at the crime that had been perpetrated against my brother, against me. But as Jack Parlabane once said to me, it is what it is.

I wanted to plead guilty, but I couldn't convince Peter to join me, so I knew that if I confessed everything, I was throwing him under the wheels. This was all largely my idea, after all. Pleading guilty would have spared us a trial and resulted in a smaller sentence, but Peter convinced himself we could cast enough confusion over everything as to get a not proven verdict at least.

We came up with this bullshit about Peter having some kind of breakdown over his business and his marriage, faking his death so that he could drop out of his life and run away. We told the court that when Jack found me in France, it was because Peter had suddenly got in touch and I had rushed over to help him get his head together, having been pledged to secrecy. We claimed that Courtney Jean Lang was a real person, who had promised investment and then absconded, resulting in the pressure Peter found himself under. Peter therefore knew Lang's place in France would be deserted, which was why he decided to lie low there.

It made just enough sense to cast doubt on the conspiracy theory, we hoped. But it all relied upon nobody believing the single worst truth about us.

That was the thing I was always most afraid of, and yet now that we can't hide it any more, I am relieved. It is amazing how a secret loses its power, how the burden sheds its weight once it is out there in the open. I might be going to jail, but in other ways I have been liberated. For the first time, I feel truly free.

I have come to realise the ways in which I was trapped. I felt trapped when I married Gordon: partly deluding myself that it was real, all the time aware that it was a charade to fool my father. Father paid him off, but I lived permanently under the shadow of him some day revealing what he had discovered when he came home one night after a cancelled business flight.

At the time, when I regarded what I did to Gordon Holman, what I was doing to Jack Parlabane and Diana Jager, they were like pieces on a board, and I prevented myself from seeing them as human beings. It reminded me of my father, and I hated myself for that. I knew it was wrong, but it was as though I refused to acknowledge any reality other than the one I was constructing.

When Jack asked me if the hardest thing was pretending I liked him, something inside me screamed. I wanted to tell him it was the easiest thing. The hardest thing was knowing that I had to use and discard him, pretend he was nothing.

Peter can do that. He's more like our father that way. I couldn't fake it: I had to live it.

At times when I was with Jack, like that night in the bar, it was as though I could simply step over a line into a world where our growing closer was real. I could choose to live in that world instead. But I loved Peter, and everything was already in train by the time I even approached Jack at his flat.

I still love Peter, but what happened has freed me, shown me that I have been in pursuit of a single notion for so long, I had stopped seeing the wider world around me. I was so full of anger, full of resentment at what I felt I couldn't have, that it blinded me to all that I could.

I actually liked Diana. I admired her. Now I can admit that. I couldn't before, because of what I was complicit in doing to her. I told myself she would only get a few years in prison: she ought to be able to argue self-defence, given that Peter had hit her. But these were merely lies I told myself so that I didn't have to think about what this was ultimately costing an innocent woman.

I look across the courtroom at her now and I see her take her partner's hand, excitedly placing it upon her swollen belly. I don't need to be a lip reader to know what she is saying to him:

'It's kicking.'

ABOUT THE AUTHOR

Since his award-winning debut novel *Quite Ugly One Morning*, Chris Brookmyre has established himself as one of Britain's leading crime novelists. His Jack Parlabane novels have sold more than one million copies in the UK alone.